The SERIAL KILLER Guide to SAN FRANCISCO

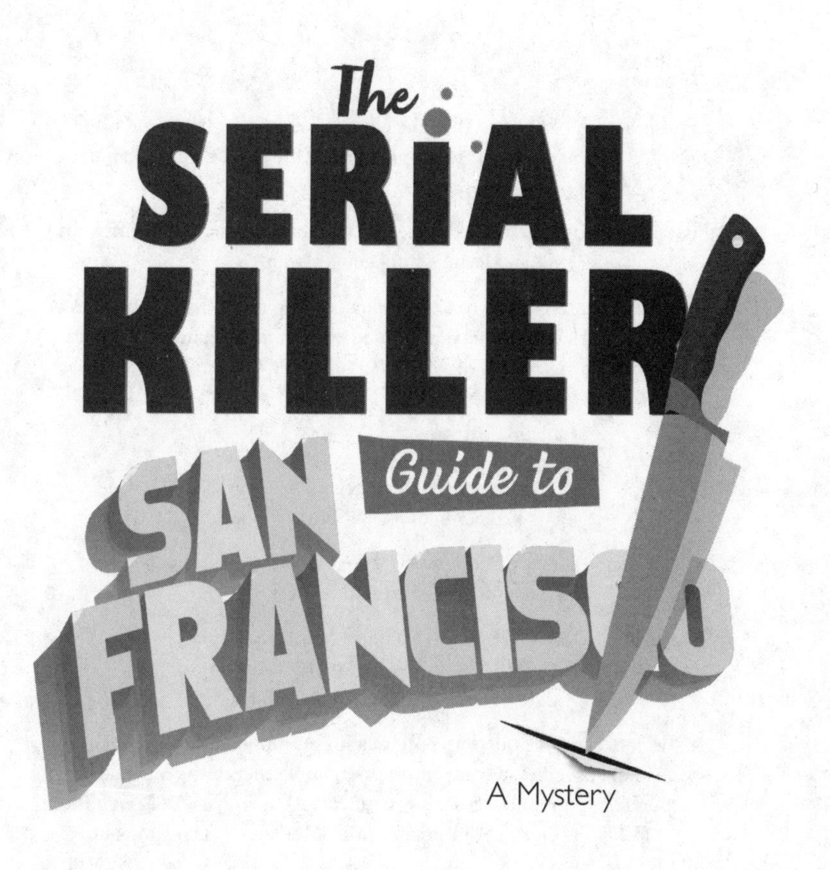

A Mystery

MICHELLE CHOUINARD

MINOTAUR BOOKS
NEW YORK

This is a work of fiction. All of the characters, organizations, and events portrayed in this novel are either products of the author's imagination or are used fictitiously.

First published in the United States by Minotaur Books, an imprint of St. Martin's Publishing Group

www.minotaurbooks.com

Designed by Meryl Sussman Levavi
Knife: pink.mousy/Shutterstock

The Library of Congress Cataloging-in-Publication Data
is available upon request.

ISBN 978-1-250-90999-2 (trade paperback)
ISBN 978-1-250-35930-8 (hardcover run-on)
ISBN 978-1-250-91000-4 (ebook)

First Edition: 2024

1 3 5 7 9 10 8 6 4 2

For Lyssa

The Serial Killer Guide to San Francisco

SF Killer Crime Tours

The Legion of Honor

Tucked near towering eucalyptus groves and ghostly cypress trees on the Pacific coast, the Legion of Honor museum is a stately beaux-arts palace built to commemorate the fallen Californian soldiers of World War I. A gift from San Francisco's "Sugar Daddy" (and alleged attempted murderer), sugar magnate Adolph B. Spreckels, this French Pavilion replica sits adjacent to Lands End National Park. Follow the fog-shrouded paths twisting through secluded woods to multiple points of interest, including shipwrecks creeping from their coastal graves, a memorial to those lost on the USS San Francisco, *and ethereal views of the Golden Gate Bridge.*

At least two of San Francisco's most notorious serial killers also strolled along these paths—and slayed their victims here. The Doodler, still at large, slashed Harald Gullberg's throat near the Legion in 1974, and brutally bludgeoned Warren Andrews with a rock and branch at Lands End in April 1975; the SFPD recently raised the reward for information leading to his capture to $200,000. The Trailside Killer, David Joseph Carpenter, stabbed Mary Frances Bennett twenty-five times on a Lands End trail in 1979; he's currently awaiting the closure of death row in San Quentin State Prison, a short, scenic drive just across the Golden Gate Bridge from Lands End.

Whichever sites you choose to take in, remember to dress in layers—the chill of a San Francisco summer can be deadly.

Prologue

Katherine Harper hurried out of the Legion of Honor as fast as the slippery pavement and limited visibility allowed. As a San Francisco native, she took pride in her ability to navigate whatever the fog threw at her, but tonight's was exceptionally heavy and she'd stayed far later than intended. She took in a deep breath of the damp, eucalyptus-laden air and tried to put her worries aside. The ins and outs of organizing charity events would take time to master—these other women, they'd been born to it, while she'd spent most of her life closer to eating in soup kitchens than donating to them. But she was smart, she was determined, and she took no prisoners. She'd make it happen.

Shifting the stacks of inventories and guest-list biographies in her arms, she glanced at the time. Almost midnight—Steve would be worried sick. And she still had to review the bios and tweak the seating chart before she went to bed—her attempt to integrate the new-money tech crowd with the old-money socialites had been met with raised eyebrows and the admonishment that *we do things a certain way for a reason*. She'd have to reorganize the groups away from each other, but ensure their respective placements were of equal prestige.

And then she had to be up at six in the morning to oversee the flowers and caterers before the luncheon.

She shivered, both because the temperature had dropped, and because everyone except the museum's night guards had gone home. The still, oppressive quiet seemed to be tracking her, and the fog wrapped around her like a snake swallowing a mouse.

Pulling the stacks of papers into her chest for warmth, she quickened her step. Given she couldn't see more than a few feet in front of herself and her hands were full, she considered following the road that wound down around the museum to the lower parking lot rather than struggling with the stairs—but that route would take twice as long to reach the safety of the car. So she shifted the stack again as she jostled down the steps, gripped the railing, and took each step one foot at a time until she reached the bottom.

Something cracked a few feet to her left.

She froze, eyes wide, trying to peer through the thick fog. "Hello?"

But the sound didn't repeat.

Most likely a squirrel or a raccoon, she tried to convince herself. Some creature as scared of her as she was of it. Ridiculous to be so jumpy—anybody hiding in the dark and fog couldn't see her any better than she could see them.

Still. Best not to linger.

She launched forward, following the edge of the pavement. She monitored the tip-tap of her low heels, screening for any additional sounds. She heard nothing.

Then, thankfully, her champagne Lexus materialized out of the fog in front of her.

She fumbled for the correct button on her keys. Deeply relieved to hear the *thunk-clunk* of the door unlocking, she pressed the button beneath to also release the trunk.

As she reached to lift it, something crashed into the base of her skull.

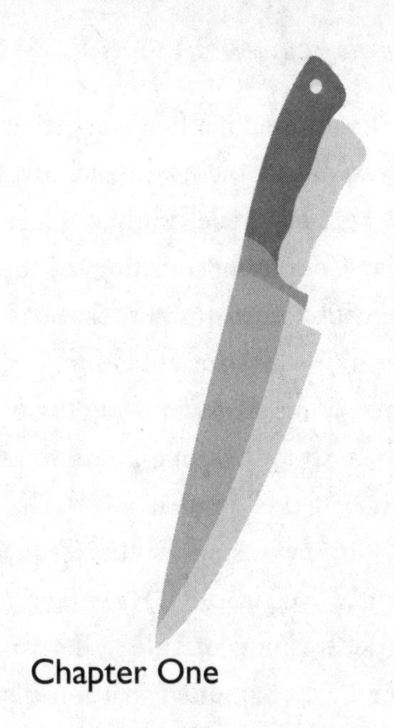

Chapter One

"Okay, everybody, we have to get a move on if we're gonna be on time for our next stop." I motioned toward the tour van, then positioned myself to monitor the guests' safety as they boarded.

A pasty, forty-something blond man who'd previously identified himself as Kevin sidled up to me, accompanied by Virginia, his blonde, skinny-jeaned wife whose pants were so tight they made *me* gasp for breath. "Hey. Is it true that you're the granddaughter of—"

My hand shot up to cut off the question, and I pinned on my most charming smile. When I led any of my serial killer tours, it was a matter of when, not if, the question came up, and I'd learned early on how to deal with it adeptly. I bent toward them and lowered my voice. "It *is* true, and it's actually part of the reason I started SF Killer Crime Tours. But let's hold questions about that till the end so we can keep on schedule. We finish up at Lenny's speakeasy and can chat over coffee or a cocktail if you'd like."

Kevin's pale blue eyes narrowed at me, judging if I were shining him on. Apparently he couldn't decide, because he shoved his hands into his worn chino pockets and glanced over to Virginia.

She clapped her hands together. "Ooo! That sounds like the best conversation topic *ever* to have over a drink in a speakeasy!"

I kept my smile firmly in place and my resigned sigh firmly internal. Constantly revisiting the topic was like walking a twenty-mile hike with a burr in my sock, but I'd learned to focus on the bright side—this way I got to tell *my grandfather's* side of it, and hopefully change a mind or two along the way. For now I needed to move on to the next tour talking point, so as soon as Kevin and his wife were safely belted in, I hurried to do so.

"Our next stop is the Tenderloin apartment where Richard Ramirez lived in 1984. He committed his first murder there—the first murder we know of, at least. I say that because the police didn't even know he'd committed that murder until twenty years after he'd already been sent to jail, when DNA found at the scene was matched to his." I glanced around to check everyone's expressions, then continued on autopilot.

If you'd told me when I was seven that I'd make my living giving serial killer tours of San Francisco someday, I'd have looked at you like you were crazy and galloped off on my invisible zebra. But the eventual course of my life was set irrevocably into motion when, one day when I was an eight-year-old standing in line for my turn at tetherball, a girl named Stacey informed me my grandfather was a serial killer. Not in those exact words—hers were more along the lines of "Your grandpa was a psycho who murdered people"—but she got her meaning across just fine without the advanced terminology.

I didn't believe her, of course. She was mean, the sort of girl who smiled biggest when other kids were crying, and I knew well enough to steer clear of her. So I turned my back and kept talking to my friends. But I mentally flinched when, rather than get louder and more in-my-face, Stacey just laughed. "Ask your parents. They'll tell you," she said, then walked away. Even back then I had enough emotional intelligence to realize her willingness to temporarily drop the issue did not bode well.

For the rest of the day, her words rang through my head and flopped in my stomach. Despite telling myself repeatedly I shouldn't even waste breath bringing her nasty gossip to my parents, I didn't last a full five minutes after my mother got home from work before blurting the whole thing out to her and breaking down into tears. I watched her face, waiting for anger at such a vicious lie to wrinkle her brow, or shock at such audacity to drop her jaw. Instead, her eyes studied my face the same way she looked at my knees when I scraped them, and I knew beyond a shadow of a doubt Stacey'd been telling the truth.

My mother sat me down and pulled out her tin of amaretti cookies, and if I hadn't already realized the situation was dire, that would have clued me right in. Amaretti cookies were reserved for special occasions—birthdays, visits from relatives, dinner parties, holidays—and the only other time I'd ever been given one was when I fell off my bicycle so hard I broke my arm. So I wasn't surprised when, as I nibbled on the crunchy almond mound, she patted my hand and told me that my father's father, William Sanzio, was in jail for killing several women.

I picked up on her phrasing—even at eight I was good with words. "He *is* in jail. I thought Grampa Sanzio was dead?"

She sighed and shifted in her wooden kitchen chair. "No, honey, he's not. Your father was planning to tell you the truth when you were older."

I pushed away the rest of my cookie; that was an awful lot of reality for an eight-year-old to process, and my stomach twisted and churned as I slid all the pieces into place.

She reached for my hand. "How are you feeling?"

My mother had always been big on feelings. Exploring them,

validating them, putting them under the microscope, until the only thing you were feeling was fed up with feelings.

I ignored her question. "Grampa killed people?"

She grabbed one of the cookies for herself and unwrapped it. "He says he didn't. But the jury believed there was enough evidence to convict him."

I latched on to the faint hope with every bit of my soul. "What evidence?"

She cleared her throat. "I don't know exactly. It happened before I met your father."

I glanced up at the oversized clock hanging above our refrigerator. "That's okay, Dad'll be home soon. I'll ask him—"

She tensed, and gripped my hand. "Honey, the thing is—well—your father doesn't like to talk about any of this. It upsets him."

I blinked at her, because what else was new? *Everything* upset my father. If my mother excelled at laid-back and peace-loving, my father's expertise was in high-strung and intense. When the Giants struck out, he got upset. When we ran out of salami, he got upset. If his remote wasn't on the arm of his chair when he got home, he got upset. And his *upset* generally involved yelling at something or someone: the television, the refrigerator, my brother or me. But I *couldn't* just leave it like this, not knowing the truth, with everything I ever thought I knew about my family destroyed and with no idea what that made *me*—

She must have read the stubborn on my face because her jaw clenched—a rare, certain sign I was bordering on trouble. "It's better if you don't ask him about it. He wasn't much older than you are now when his father was arrested, and he's had to live in the shadow of it ever since. He's been beaten up over it, he's lost jobs because of it, he almost changed his name to get away from it. That's how bad it is."

"But if you don't know and I can't ask him, how am I going to find out?" A thought occurred to me. "Wait, if Grampa's still alive, can I go visit him?"

All the blood drained from her face. "Don't even *think* such a thing around your father."

The blood that left her face rushed into mine, and my voice turned petulant. "But he's my *grandfather*. I want to *meet* him. And if he says he didn't do it, maybe there's something we can do to help—"

The sound of my father's car pulling into the driveway interrupted me. I jumped up and ran out the door, ignoring my mother's voice ringing out behind me. When I reached him, I blurted out what Stacey had told me—and that I wanted to go visit my grandfather.

I really should have listened to my mother.

My father didn't yell. He calmly—far too calmly—told me to go to my room and stay there. An hour later, he came and told me that as long as I was living under his roof, I was never to mention William Sanzio's name again. That he was a bad man who had lost the privilege of knowing me or anyone else in the family when he destroyed our good name.

I fought back my tears. "But Mom said he said he didn't do it!"

His jaw clenched and unclenched. "Jails are filled with men who won't take responsibility for their actions, and the world is filled with gullible people who want to believe them."

"But Stacey—"

His hand flew up. "I'd hoped after all these years people would forget, but I was kidding myself. Stacey may be the first person to ask you about your grandfather, but she won't be the last. So you might as well learn sooner than later to ignore people like her." He stood and crossed to the door before sending a parting shot back over his shoulder. "And that's an end to it."

But of course it wasn't. All his stricture accomplished was making sure I was obsessed with the notion that my grandfather had been wrongly convicted. I couldn't do much about it at age eight other than cry myself to sleep, and back in a time before the internet's all-seeing eye roved over the world, gathering information of that nature was next to impossible. I learned a little, but not much: only that William Sanzio had been known as Overkill Bill because he bashed his three victims on the head, stabbed them to death, then sliced their throats after the fact. To make up for that dearth of information, I read everything I could find about *other* serial killers, hoping to glean some sort of insight into what my grandfather had done, or hadn't done, and why. My desperation to learn more ultimately led me to a bachelor's degree in journalism—but it didn't lead to any closure about whether my grandfather was guilty.

"Um, Capri?"

The voice startled me back into the here and now. Ryan Navarro, driver of vans, master of IT, and unlikely friend given he was twenty years younger than my forty-nine, widened his green eyes and flicked them back toward the passengers. I'd finished my orienting information about Richard Ramirez's Tenderloin apartment, but hadn't transitioned into my background on Mei Leung, his first victim, a nine-year-old girl found murdered in the basement of her apartment building. I chastised myself mentally and jumped in, refocusing my energy on her. Because I might not be able to find out the truth about my grandfather, but I could damn well make sure as many murder victims as possible weren't forgotten.

• • •

An hour and a half later, Kevin stretched over his O'Doul's near-beer and peered closely at my face. "I knew it was true. You look just like him."

I leaned in conspiratorially and lowered my voice. Lenny's speakeasy always made me feel like a character in a 1940s noir film, which is exactly what it was designed to do—it was done up as a fictional detective agency, from the metal-grated faux window with Lenny's name stenciled backward to the file cabinets and war-era desks that functioned as tables. The menu came in a manila case-file folder and the lighting came from period lamps, which lent the space an odd mix of anonymity and danger that managed to be both welcoming and exhilarating. "A lot of people tell me that," I replied.

To this day it wryly amuses me when people comment on my resemblance to Overkill Bill. Not because they're wrong—we have the same jet-black hair (although mine is longer), the same deep blue eyes, and the same high cheekbones above the same slightly pointed chin—but because after the ten thousandth time people scour your face trying to find a serial killer, it takes work not to develop a complex about it. So I remind myself they mean no harm and wait, because usually it only takes a few seconds for the person to realize the implication of what they've said to me and—

Right on schedule, Virginia's face plummeted and she whispered something to Kevin.

Kevin turned red and stammered. "Oh, I'm so sorry, I didn't mean to say you look like a killer—"

I waved off his objection and picked up my dirty martini. "Don't worry, it doesn't bother me because I don't believe he *was* a killer. I believe he was innocent."

Kevin's face twitched as it shifted away from embarrassed, and I waited to see which emotion he'd land on. He'd either be intrigued by my claim and ask about my alternate theory with a true-crime twinkle in his eye, or he'd feel sorry for the middle-aged woman deluding herself about her family's lurid history and sit back with a wary cast to his expression.

"Oh, really?" Now *he* dropped his voice and leaned conspiratorially toward *me*. "Why do you say that?"

"Partly because his alibis were incredibly detailed. Not the sort of thing you make up and stick by with any sort of consistency."

Kevin's brow creased. "Oh, yeah. Something about being out

with prostitutes, right?" He turned as Virginia tugged his sleeve. "What?"

I smiled at her. "No, don't worry, it's okay. He was very open about the fact that he wasn't faithful to my grandmother. Being unfaithful doesn't make you a serial killer. But unfortunately for him, the women he claimed to be with during the first two murders were themselves subsequent murder victims, and the one who was alive and able to testify was vilified by the defense attorney. The jury decided she wasn't a reliable witness."

Virginia didn't like the sound of that. "They wouldn't believe her just because she was a prostitute?"

The anger tinging her voice resonated with me, but I took a sip of my drink to keep my reaction measured. "Women, especially women of color, are routinely ignored and discredited even today, especially if they do drugs or have any sort of a record. The Cleveland Strangler had victims literally escape his rape-murder den and report him directly to the police, but the cops believed his story over theirs—even though he'd previously served *fifteen years* for rape and attempted murder."

Virginia's eyes grew wide, and her mouth formed a gentle O.

Kevin shifted in his chair. "But wasn't there something about Overkill B—William Sanzio paying her to provide an alibi?"

"That's what the DA claimed, without any proof. Both William and the witness denied it, but the suggestion was enough for the jury."

He nodded, but the twinkle in his eye diminished, another reaction I'd seen a thousand times. *She just wants to believe the best of her grandfather*, it said. *It's not exactly a stretch that someone willing to sell her body would sell her testimony*, it said. And I'm sure that's exactly what the members of my grandfather's jury thought, too.

I shook it off, despite the indignant little girl screaming in the back of my brain. If the situation were reversed and Kevin was trying to convince me of his cheating grandfather's innocence, would I be skeptical? You betcha. And I wasn't so egotistical as to believe I knew the truth for certain. "At the end of the day, there's no way to know for sure. Forensics back then weren't what they are today."

He sipped his near-beer, watching my face. My cell phone chimed, and I checked the notification. No matter what it was, it would be an excellent segue to end the conversation. I clicked to find a missed call from my daughter, Morgan. My pulse sped, and I cursed the underground-basement bunker's spotty cell reception. My twenty-four-year-old daughter, die-hard Gen-Z-er that she was, never made actual phone calls when texts would do.

I smiled up at Kevin and Victoria. "Looks like an urgent matter needs my attention. I'm so sorry to cut this short. It's been great talking to you."

I stood and gestured to Ryan. We called to the tour-group members now scattered over several tables and I gave my standard spiel officially ending the tour and thanking them for spending the afternoon and early evening with us. We gathered our tips, said our goodbyes, and headed out.

Ryan's expression changed as soon as we pushed through the upstairs exit and into the chilly evening air. "Short after-party. You okay?"

I flashed him Morgan's missed call.

His brows shot up. "Not good."

"No," I agreed as I called her back. "Not good at all."

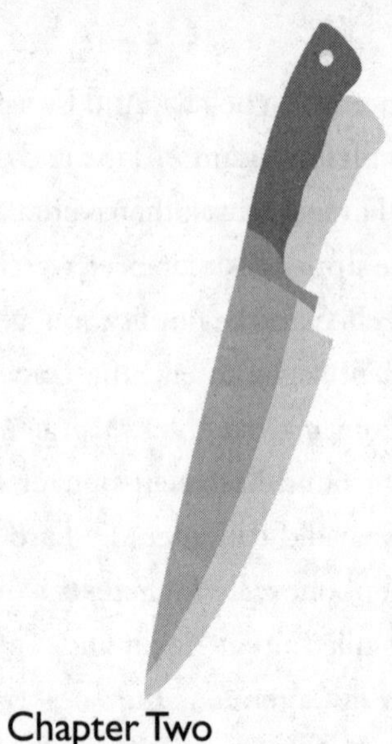

Chapter Two

Morgan didn't pick up the phone. But each ring ended with the annoying beep that indicates the person you're calling is talking to someone else, so relief replaced my fear—if she was on the phone, she was physically okay. I left a message, then sent her a text letting her know I was trying to reach her.

We rounded the corner and headed the block and a half to The Hub, our loving nickname for the physical location of SF Killer Crime Tours, passing a pizza parlor, a women's clothing boutique, and a botanicals skin-care spa all housed in the ground floors of subdivided Victorians. San Francisco is a city of neighborhoods; depending on when and who you ask, there are between thirty-five and sixty different enclaves in the 46.9-square-mile area, which averages out to about a mile each. They all have their own distinct feel and say a lot about the people who live in them. Hayes Valley, the neighborhood where I live and work, has gone through some of the most dramatic shifts in San Francisco history, from a working-class neighborhood that housed nineteenth-century construction workers who built nearby mansions, to a twentieth-century drug-and-prostitution-infested den, to a now-hip, diverse twenty-first-century zone featuring jazz music, boutiques, and excellent food.

Still worried about Morgan, I pushed into the ground-floor office I shared with Ryan and Heather Chen, my lifelong friend and recent business partner. The space reminded me of an IKEA showroom in that we'd each decorated our sections according to our tastes. My section favored earthy tones and classic furniture that gave the overall vibe of a Victorian library, while Heather favored sleek, modern design and bright oranges and pinks that vibrated with energy. Ryan's section was what I'd generously call "functional"—electronics covered the gray bare-bones modular furniture he'd selected for efficient use of surface area rather than aesthetics.

Heather sat rifling through a filing cabinet. My internal worry must have translated to an external black cloud on my face because as soon as she looked up at us, her posture stiffened.

Heather and I have been ride-or-die since the first day of kindergarten. I was instantly drawn to her ability to fly over monkey bars like she had wings rather than hands, and she loved that I made her laugh so hard milk shot out of her nose. Heather is a disconcerting blend of Grace Kelly and Kathy Griffin—she's tall, lean, and elegant with a pixie-cut hairstyle and huge brown eyes, but you can never be certain what's going to fly out of her mouth. When the animation company she worked for relocated two years ago and she realized she didn't like her job enough to look for another incarnation of it, I asked her to become my partner in the tour business. Thanks to four generations of family raised in San Francisco's Chinatown, she knows secrets about the area that have gotten people killed, and her flair for uncensored drama leaves tour groups breathless.

Heather's lips pressed tight as she searched my face. "You already heard."

My mind flew to Morgan, and my heart rocketed back into my

throat. "No, I haven't been able to reach her yet. Are you who she was talking to?"

Confusion crossed her face. "Talking to? How would that even be possible?"

"I just called her, and she was on the phone with someone—"

When Heather's jaw dropped, Ryan flapped a hand between us. "You guys are talking about different things."

Heather's eyes flicked from him to me. "What are *you* talking about?"

"Morgan. She actually *called* me, but I missed the call in Lenny's. What are *you* talking about?"

Discomfort replaced her surprise. "I really don't want to be the one to tell you."

I dropped my bag onto my table, then crossed my arms over my chest. "Out with it."

"Drina quit today. We're going to have to find another receptionist-assistant."

I winced. The current hiring market made it easier to find one of Willy Wonka's golden tickets than someone willing to work for just above minimum wage. But forty-odd years of friendship doesn't miss much, and I detected a flash of relief on her face that told me Drina's departure was a smoke screen. "That's not what you were going to say."

Heather's face turned somber and she reached for her phone. She tapped and scrolled and tapped again, then thrust it out to me.

I glanced at the headline: SOCIALITE FOUND DEAD AT LEGION OF HONOR.

Why was she showing me this? "Did you know her?"

She shook her head. "Keep reading."

Katherine Harper, wife of software genius Steve Harper, was found dead early Friday morning outside the Legion of Honor. She'd been bashed in the head, stabbed several times in the chest, and had her throat cut postmortem.

The room wobbled as the implication hit me, and I dropped into my office chair before my knees gave out. "It's the Overkill Bill signature."

Heather nodded. "The *Chronicle* is calling it a copycat."

My mind struggled with the shock. "Or maybe it's the same guy. My grandfather said all along he didn't do it."

Ryan looked up from unpacking his messenger bag. "Didn't those murders happen back in the mid-sixties? Wouldn't that make the guy, like, a hundred? What did he do, bash her in the head with his walker?"

I turned my best mocking grimace on him. "I know at your age it's impossible to imagine anyone over forty having a reason to exist." He was right, though, and my brain had oriented enough to recognize it.

But before I could say so, my phone rang. "Sorry, guys. It's Morgan. I have to take this."

• • •

As soon as I hit the button, sobs poured over the line. A vision of Morgan filled my head, her brown eyes red from crying, long brown hair shoved behind her ears like she did whenever she was upset. "Honey, are you okay?" I asked.

"No, I'm not okay," she said, voice flirting with hysterical. "Grandma Sylvia called to tell me she's cutting me off."

"Take a deep breath for me." I waited as she inhaled slowly, then exhaled. "Now start again. I thought Sylvia was taking a long weekend in Hawaii paddleboarding with her friends?"

"She got back today."

"Ah. But what do you mean she's cutting you off? You mean your tuition?"

"Since that's the only thing she pays for, yeah, obviously I mean my tuition," she sniped.

I took my own deep breath and reminded myself to be patient. My daughter, a graduate student in forensic psychology at Palo Alto University, was a kind young woman who treated me like a human being—except when stressed. "Whatever's happening, we'll fix it. Now tell me exactly what she said."

"It's all a jumble. But I remember her saying she's been coddling us since you divorced Dad, and we need to stand on our own two feet. She said since she already paid for this quarter's tuition, I have time to make alternate arrangements. That means I'm going to have to come up with eighteen thousand dollars in the next couple of months before winter quarter starts, and I'm already at the max for student loans. I can save a few thousand if I drop the health-care plan, but that's not nearly enough."

Anger simmered just below my surface, threatening to boil over. *Stand on our own two feet? Coddle us?* The only thing my cheating ex-husband's mother had ever coddled was her resentment toward me—as the daughter of working-class parents and the granddaughter of a killer, I'd never been good enough to marry her son. Sylvia Clement, née Renard, was descended from *the* Jacques Renard, a dry goods importer who had the tremendous good sense (meaning, luck) to open up shop in San Francisco a year before the gold rush hit. When it did, he became one of the wealthiest men on the planet. While the burgeoning numbers of his children and grandchildren divided up that fortune into increasingly small portions, it was still impressive by the time it reached Sylvia. And her lineage meant the money was "old." For reasons I'd never been able to fathom, that meant it was better, and it qualified her to sip cocktails in the "right" country clubs and lunch with the "right" people, most notably some fancy organization called the Ligue Louis Quatorze, for rich people of French ancestry in San Francisco. Having a déclassée daughter-in-law was a chip in the upper-echelon walls that divided her from the less-than, and she'd never missed an opportunity in twenty-five years to let me know it.

Still, she'd never before let her bias against me bleed over onto her granddaughter; she loved Morgan more than anything in the world. "And you're sure she didn't say anything else? There has to be some reason this is coming out of the blue."

"She didn't. That's what's so confusing."

I wracked my brain—and a potential reason didn't take long to hit me.

My ex-husband, Todd Clement, had recently signed the deed of "our" house, the house we'd lived in when we were married and that Morgan and I had remained in after the divorce, fully over to me. We'd signed the paperwork about a year ago, before he headed off to South Africa with a new business partner to research a series of safari retreats. He's a luxury travel agent, which only sounds made-up. He curates one-of-a-kind "experiences" for ridiculously wealthy people, the kind so rich they live off the interest made by their money's interest and refer to vacations on their yachts as "boating weekends." He'd transferred the house over to me, to protect it in case his new business venture went south—something that had happened all too frequently in the past—and because he felt the need to "get his affairs in order" before he left. Few things frightened my ex-husband, but wild animals with sharp claws and hefty fangs were apparently prominent on that short list.

Despite having given the house to both of us as our wedding gift, Sylvia had never been okay with me living in it after the divorce. It had been in the Renard family for generations, and she saw it as part of her birthright. He must have finally told her he'd signed it over to me, and her head must have exploded.

I squeezed my eyes shut against the possibility. "Don't worry, honey, I think I know what the problem is. Between your father and I, we'll figure this out."

"How?" The hysteria crept back into her voice. "Dad won't make money off the safaris until next year, and you're already struggling as it is."

Despite their truth, I bristled against the words. "I'm not as pathetic as all that. If I do a few extra online tours each week, I'll have a few thousand before you know it—"

"But that won't be enough, and you already work so hard as it is."

"—and Drina quit today. You can take over for her if it comes to that. You know the job inside and out, and you can do it from home like she did. Let me make a few phone calls and see what I can arrange. Now, I want you to go grab some of the Ben and Jerry's I know you have hidden in your freezer, spend the evening watching *Real Housewives of Whatever,* and get your mind off of this. Your grades are what's important, so you need to relax and get some sleep."

Morgan snuffled, then blew her nose. "Okay, Mom. I'm so sorry to dump this on you. I can take over for Drina as soon as you need me to, just let me know."

I murmured a few more soothing things before ending the call, then immediately tapped on Sylvia's contact.

Much to my surprise, she answered almost immediately. "Capri. I don't have time for this, I'm expecting a very important call."

I gritted my teeth. "I won't keep you long. I just heard from Morgan, and she's very upset. I think she misunderstood something you said, and—"

"She didn't misunderstand. There comes a time for all of us to stand on our own two feet."

"I agree. But that time came in the middle of her graduate education?"

Her tone rose. "I paid for Morgan's private high school and for her undergraduate degree at Stanford. That allowed her to focus on her grades and get herself into a good graduate program. But she has a strong foundation now, and it's not unreasonable to expect her to make her own way through graduate school. Grades don't matter at this point, and it will behoove her to find an additional internship or some such so she'll be ahead of the curve when she has to navigate the job market."

I paused to choose the right words. "I'm just not clear on why you decided this a year and a quarter into her graduate program."

She felt no need to pause and choose hers. "You've lived off my son for twenty-five years now, Capri, and I should have put my foot down long ago. It's one thing to marry up in the world, it's another to hang on to the side of that family after a divorce like a barnacle that can't be scraped off."

With that, she hung up on me.

Chapter Three

I've always thought the expression "I saw red" was metaphorical, but in that moment, I realized it was very, very literal. The world in front of me took on a red tinge as my blood pressure skyrocketed and the capillaries in my eyeballs swelled at the vicious unfairness of her accusations.

I started my tour company ten years ago, after Todd and I divorced. He paid fair child support and agreed I should stay in the house, since it was the only home Morgan had ever known and he spent all his time traveling. But even though the house had been a gift from his mother, we had to borrow against the equity to make needed repairs, so we had a mortgage payment. A relatively small one by the hugely expensive standards of San Francisco, but big enough that the child-support payments left me far short of what I needed to provide even a frugal life for myself and Morgan.

But I'd been about as employable as a pet rock. I'd done a brief stint as a freelance-writer-slash-journalist right out of college, but gave that up to raise Morgan. That meant my last stab at freelancing was back in the days before AOL was even a thing and most people didn't know the difference between "the internet" and "Interpol." But by 2011, the vast majority of people had only vague memories of reading their news anywhere other than online, and nobody wanted to hire a nearly forty-year-old journalist who barely knew what a meme was and who still believed in the old-school journalistic style of *put your information up front* rather than *maximize the number of ads people have to scroll past.*

Heather had helped me find my new path as we drowned my sorrows at Lenny's. "The trick," she said as she gestured at me with her espresso martini, "is to find a way to monetize your passion."

I'd sighed. "Mommy blogs are overdone and passé."

She downed half of her martini while looking like a sixties screen siren. "That's not your real jam."

I took a far-less-elegant gulp of my far-less-elegant dirty martini. "Okay, I'll bite. What's my *real* jam?"

"Serial killers. True-crime mysteries." She'd leaned back triumphantly and draped the arm still holding her martini glass over her chair. "You could sell articles to all sorts of online publications. And there's always blogging. Or a podcast."

I rolled my eyes and laughed. "I don't get podcasts. There's a reason TV replaced radio, you know."

I'm not too proud to admit blowing off the podcast wasn't my brightest moment. But that major flub aside, the more I thought about true crime as content, the more excited I became. I started a true-crime blog and turned the posts that got attention into larger stories I sold to a variety of media, both online and off. But things really blew up when I posted about sites around San Francisco associated with famous crimes. I received a deluge of mail from people planning trips asking for more recommendations, and to this day Heather claims she saw the light bulb go off over my head. I put together several tours, some self-guided, some guided by me, and was astounded when almost overnight I couldn't keep up with the demand. For the last nine years I'd busted my hump night and day and made a good living for myself and Morgan. The picture Sylvia wanted to paint of me sitting at home watching *Oprah* and shoving bonbons down my gullet was beyond insulting.

My thoughts must have been parading over my face, because Heather rolled her chair over to me and squeezed my hand. "There's a special corner in hell for mothers-in-law."

I rolled my eyes. "Says the woman whose mother-in-law worships her."

"Oh, couldn't agree more. Rose got the awful mother-in-law in our relationship. Point is, Sylvia may have paid for Morgan's tuition, but who put food in her belly and clothes on her back? Who paid for her softball trips and her summer camp and a thousand other things? That was you, girlfriend."

I smiled, and squeezed her hand back.

"But that doesn't solve the current problem, which is why you need mondo revenue ASAP." She pushed her rolling chair back over to the filing cabinet.

I shrugged nonchalantly, trying to at least convince myself I had things under control. "Like I told Morgan, I'll add a few more tours to my schedule. The demand for online tours is still high despite the pandemic restrictions easing. I can run a few more no problem, and we've all been wanting to branch out with a Hitchcock tour and a Dashiell Hammett tour anyway. I can start researching those later this week."

She wagged a finger at me. "Work smarter, not harder. Especially since Morgan has, what, two and a half more years of graduate school?" She raised her eyebrows. "You know what I'm about to say."

I winced. "Podcast?"

She tilted her head at me. "Long overdue, but that won't be enough. You need to get serious about writing your Overkill Bill book."

I rubbed my face with my hands. Once, amid the hubris of youth and the pony-keg lubrication of a frat party, I'd declared to Heather, loudly and with much slurring of speech, that I wanted to write a book exonerating my grandfather. Much to my drunken delight, Heather leaped onto my bandwagon with both feet and we'd danced the night away in celebration of my illustrious future as a warrior of truth, justice, and the American Way. When I woke the next morning, the part of my brain that had birthed the announcement did its requisite walk of shame through the glaring daylight of reality: I'd barely taken a single journalism class at that point, I didn't even know if my grandfather was truly innocent, and my father would disown me if I even thought of such a thing. So I patted the idea on its metaphorical head and let it settle back into the dark recesses of my mind.

"She's right, you know," Ryan chimed in from his desk as he organized the paperwork from the evening's tour.

I turned and stared at him. "I need money *now*. Even if I worked at the speed of light, I'd need at least a year to put a book together. And just because I write the book doesn't mean anyone's going to want to publish it."

Heather crossed her arms over her chest and set her jaw in a way I was all too familiar with. "That's why you don't do it *in addition* to a separate podcast, you make *the journey of writing the book itself* the podcast. You can start making revenue right away with sponsors and a Patreon."

I flipped back to glare at her. "A Patreon for who? It takes time to build up a following, let alone a paying one!"

"Sure does." She popped her brows at me. "Thank goodness you've been doing that part for the last ten years. I know for a fact you've got thousands of followers on your blog, and we have an extensive mailing list for Killer Crimes."

"The mailing list is for tour guests, and not all of our tours are even about serial killers—"

Ryan cut me off. "How many times a week does someone ask if you're Overkill Bill's granddaughter?"

I whirled around and gave him my best *et tu, Brute* look.

"At least two or three a week," Heather said as she pulled open a drawer. "And those are the ones who have the guts to ask you to your face. People are clearly interested in the insider perspective of Overkill Bill's granddaughter. So you'll do the podcast, and if that's all that ever comes out of it, that'll be good enough. But you'll find a publisher in weeks, because nonfiction books are usually sold from proposals, before the book is written. And authors get *advances*. Money *before* the book is finished. Or you'll self-publish. If only ten percent of your platform bought a copy, that would see you through the lion's share of Morgan's tuition."

My stomach flipped. "You're forgetting the most important issue. It's riding a line dangerously close to exploitation for me to profit off the death of people my grandfather may have killed, with either a book or a podcast."

"By that logic, nobody should ever produce true-crime books or podcasts," Ryan said.

I shook my head vigorously. "It's different when it's written by a detective who worked the case or a journalist who's investigating. Someone who's related to the killer has a conflict of interest."

Heather's head jutted toward me. "If you found conclusive evidence that your grandfather committed the crime, would you lie about it?"

"Of course not. I just want to know the truth. But who's going to believe that?" I said.

"That's why you report *what you're finding in real time on a podcast*," Heather sing-songed.

"Besides," Ryan said. "Didn't you say the victims had no families? So it's not like you're going to be digging up painful memories for them."

"Even if they did, I'd damned well want to know the truth about who killed *my* loved one." Heather stabbed a finger into her chest.

"And you always say the true-crime genre is important because it keeps focus alive on unsolved cases and raises awareness about safety and the psychology of criminals," Ryan said.

Whipping back and forth between the two of them was making the room spin. I grabbed my phone and my bag and stood up. "Guys, I know you're just trying to help, but please stop with the double-teaming. I'm off tomorrow, so unless there's some sort of emergency, I'll see you Tuesday, okay?"

Heather and Ryan exchanged glances.

"Right, no, totally get it," Heather said, and swung back around to her filing cabinet.

"I'll close out the paperwork for tonight's tour," Ryan said.

"Thank you, I appreciate it." I made my way to the door. "Have a good night."

"One last thing, though," Heather called, not making eye contact. "With that copycat murder hitting the papers, interest in the Overkill Bill case is gonna blow up. If you don't get onto digging into your grandfather's case soon, somebody else will."

I winced, clenched my jaw, and let the door slam into place behind me.

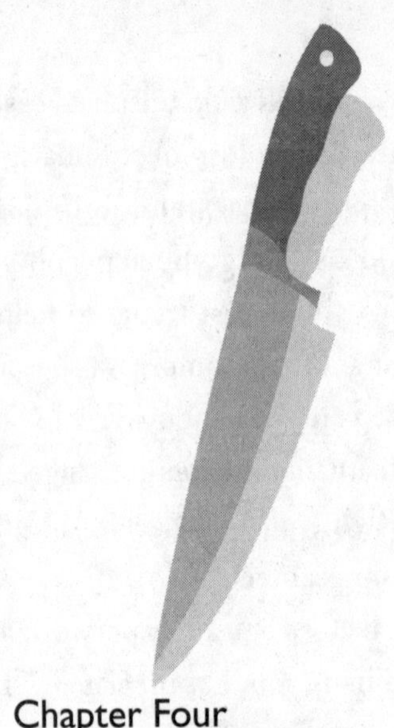

Chapter Four

Trying to ignore Heather's voice in my head, I briskly marched the two blocks uphill to my house, hoping the sight of my elegant sage Victorian poking out from her row of sisters would raise my spirits. I'm not too proud to admit I was grateful when Todd agreed I should stay in the house, not just for Morgan's sake, but for my own. I'd spent two decades slowly tinkering it into being the perfect reflection of my personality, filled with warm colors and vintage pieces, and I love it second only to my daughter.

That night, however, all I could see was the reason Morgan's future was in peril. As I turned onto my street, I gazed up and cursed the solar panels now obscured by darkness. Maybe if we'd left them off the list of repairs we'd borrowed for, I'd have enough equity left to refinance for Morgan's tuition. As things stood, the current payment was all I could afford.

After dumping my messenger bag into my study, I nuked myself a burrito for dinner and glanced around my quiet kitchen. Since divorcing Todd ten years before, I'd been on my own—for the most part, happily so. Raising a daughter and hustling to start and maintain a business are both time-consuming propositions, and that filled my days just fine. But every once in a while, especially when things got a little too stressful, I missed the feeling of having a partner to come home to who'd curl up on the couch with me and listen to my worries over a glass of wine.

I sighed, gobbled down my food, then settled into my art-deco-inspired black-white-and-gold bathroom for a long bubble bath with an Agatha Christie novel. But as I'm sure Heather knew would happen, our conversation circled around my brain like a hamster on a wheel, destroying any semblance of peace. I figured the only way to get the podcast-slash-book out of my head was to come up with a better plan, but despite tossing and turning all night trying to devise something, I came up short.

At the crack of dawn, I padded back into my study to check my email. Lovingly decorated with winged leather armchairs, a massive mahogany desk, and floor-to-ceiling bookshelves on one wall, the study makes me feel like I'm hanging out in a cozy eighteenth-century library even despite my laptop and cell phone anachronisms. I opened the computer to discover a deluge of messages from people wanting to be put on the waitlist for one of Killer Crimes' in-person tours. Any of the tours—they didn't care which one. I glanced over to the delightfully archaic landline phone sitting on the far corner of my kitchen counter; that was the number I'd used back in the day when setting up my business, and which was easily available in the public domain. Sure enough, the red light that signaled voicemail was blinking furiously.

Coincidence? Not likely. The newspapers weren't the only ones making a connection between the current murders and the Overkill Bill murders. And rightfully so—there was a reason this killer chose to copycat my grandfather's case, and that meant the Overkill Bill murders would be key to understanding the current murders and finding the killer.

So as the coffee maker in my sleek white-black-and-brass kitchen gurgled and spat, I googled *Overkill Bill copycat*. Five entries I hadn't seen the night before popped up. Heather was absolutely right—time was running out on the mental gymnastics I'd been doing since the age of eight. And if I was honest with myself, Heather and Ryan were right about all the rest of it, too. There was really only one reason, the biggest reason, left not to investigate my grandfather's case: my father.

I dug my palms into my eyes and moaned. Was I really willing to upset my father over this? With a failed marriage, a mother-in-law who hated me, and a brother who'd moved halfway across country, my mother and father were all the family I had.

Except that wasn't true—I also had Morgan. My baby girl, my pride and joy, the only thing on the planet that could have convinced me to leave my career in journalism behind the moment I knew I was pregnant. And like it or not, I could only see one viable way to get the rest of her tuition money. I literally couldn't afford to let my father's ridiculous inability to face a painful chapter in our family history stop me from doing what needed to be done.

I had to do the podcast and write the book.

Decision made, I poured myself another cup of coffee—this was going to take every bit of gumption I could pour down my throat.

• • •

Once my system was vibrating with caffeine-induced courage, I strode purposefully into my office, grabbed a fresh Moleskine notebook, and spread out across my desk to begin my attack.

Under normal circumstances, the smartest place to start any investigation was with primary sources, the actual people involved, because written reports or records were always subject to error and open to interpretation. But in this case, were any of those sources still alive?

My grandfather, the most important source of all and the logical starting place, had passed before the turn of the millennium. Luckily, I'd thwarted my dad's wishes and visited him once before he died. Not as a child—then I'd had no choice but to respect my father's wishes. It wasn't like I could just roll up to San Quentin on some random Sunday and take a stroll down death row to see good ol' grandpappy—I know because in a fit of adolescent angst, I tried. But my teenage rebellion was squashed like a cantaloupe under a tank when I discovered that not only do minors have to be accompanied by an adult to visit a jail, that adult has to be on an approved visitors list. Disappointing, to be sure. But the minute I turned eighteen I made the necessary arrangements.

The visit was emotional. I subconsciously expected my grandfather to match our family pictures, so when a wrinkled, stooped man with a shock of white hair appeared, all the years stolen from us hit me hard. But his eyes were still bright and his warm smile tugged at my soul, and he cried and I cried, and after asking me about my own life, he answered all my questions about his. I'd taken myself very seriously as an aspiring journalist and had carefully documented the conversation; the notes I'd jotted down immediately after were up in the attic, along with the other information I'd researched about the case.

I'm a relatively organized person, so it only took me a few minutes to dig out the old storage box I'd marked OVERKILL BILL. I slid the box onto my office desk and popped off the lid to examine the contents. I rolled my eyes at the two steno pads perched on the top—for some reason back then I'd thought steno pads reeked of investigative reporter—and shifted them to access the groups of manila envelopes I'd labeled by date. I set aside the interview notes to review, then pulled out the articles I'd previously researched about the killings; I scoured the bylines for the names of the journalists who'd covered the story, hoping one of them had been a young newbie who was still going strong. Unfortunately, all five of the men I identified turned out to be now reporting for the great newspaper in the sky.

Next I gathered the names of the homicide inspectors who'd worked the case, because what the police knew and what they told the press were two different things. But a few short minutes' research found all three had passed away; there would be no earnest, nostalgic conversations picking their brains. But since the case was officially closed, I should be able to get my hot little hands on their files with some sort of FOIA request. Or, given Katherine Harper's murder, it might be smarter to talk to whatever homicide inspectors had been assigned to her case, since they'd be interested in William Sanzio, too. I refilled my coffee and pulled up the articles on Katherine again. The first quoted Homicide Inspector Dan Petito, so I stuck his name into Google.

A slew of articles, several accompanied by an official portrait, popped up. I leaned in to peer closely at them; hovering around his mid-fifties, Petito had short, gray-sprayed black hair with a hint of curl and crystal-blue eyes that grabbed me and tugged me into the computer screen. Their deep intensity was balanced by a warm, appealing smile and crinkle of crow's feet; together they gave the impression of a kind, compassionate man who could be trusted, but the steel in his jaw made clear he shouldn't be underestimated. After reading about several of his commendations, I decided he was a very promising starting point, so looked up the number for SFPD's homicide detail and asked for him by name.

A brusque officer whose name I didn't catch because he didn't give it informed me Petito wasn't on the premises. After a brief interrogation about why I was calling, the officer rattled off a number he said was for the Harper case. Knowing it was likely some sort of tip line that would consign my call to a limitless limbo unlikely to reach Petito before I hit menopause, I spewed out that I was the granddaughter of Overkill Bill before he could hang up. He rewarded me with a momentary stunned silence, then gave me Petito's direct number. I got his voicemail and left a message with my name, my number, and the reason I was calling.

After hanging up, I tapped my Pilot Precise against my oak desk as I considered my other possible sources. I didn't foresee having much better luck with the few witnesses involved in the case, but I compiled a list to track down anyway. They turned out to be a bit trickier, because a quick Google search didn't pull any of them up; unfortunately, a death-records search did, and one by one I crossed them off my list. Since the victims hadn't had families, that left only one last possible set of primary sources: William Sanzio's family and friends. William was the youngest of his siblings, who were now all also gone. His friends had distanced themselves after the murders, but they, too, were no longer with us. He'd only had two children, my father and my uncle Vincent; Uncle Vinnie had been killed in Vietnam before I was born. My grandmother, Philomena Sanzio, passed away not long after—my father always said between what my grandfather had done and my uncle's death, she died of a twice-broken heart.

When I turned back to my Moleskine, the lack of potential paths glared up at me with stark intensity. There was only one possible source left: my father.

Just the sight of Fred Sanzio's name circled on the page made my lizard brain screech bloody murder and beg me to wait for the case files. That idea was seductive, but I had no idea how long it would take to get them, and the clock was ticking on Morgan's tuition bill.

The inner-child portion of my brain, the part that knows exactly which parent is most likely to give the answer I seek in any given situation, suggested I recruit my mother—maybe she could convince him to help me for Morgan's sake. Except the adult portion knew doing that would put my mother in a really ugly position, asking her to do something she knew one hundred percent her husband wouldn't want her to do. It wasn't right for me to put her in the middle like that just because I was too chicken-scat to face my father.

I trudged back into the kitchen to refill my coffee. As I sipped, staring across my kitchen searching for answers, I caught a reflection of my stressed face in the oven glass.

I stiffened at the sight. This wasn't like me, at all—I'd never let difficult situations intimidate me before. I'd raised my daughter single-handedly for most of her life, even before my divorce, since Todd had always been away researching his trips; I'd built my own successful business from scratch, overcoming complications like pandemics and near-financial ruin along the way. How in the world could a woman who routinely neutered aggressively handsy clients turn into a quivering child at the thought of upsetting her father? No way would a real journalist allow herself to be frightened off because an interview would be uncomfortable.

I'd never backed down from a fight before. I damned well wasn't going to start now.

Chapter Five

As I pulled up in front of my parents' house twenty minutes later, I crossed myself (have I mentioned I was raised an atheist?) and asked God to have mercy on my soul.

I could have sworn I saw a patch of buzz-cut black hair disappear behind twitching curtains as I approached. But my mother answered the door, a huge grin spreading over her face as she stepped back to let me in. "*Cap*ri! What a lovely surprise! Come in."

As always, I winced at my mother's pronunciation of my nickname. Everyone else in my life pronounced it like the island: Kuh-*pree*, emphasis on the *pree*, and I preferred it that way. But despite my pleas, my mother put the emphasis on the *cap*, as in "Capricorn." Why? Because Capricorn is my well-hidden actual first name. While the Summer of Love had long since come and gone in the rest of the country, San Francisco in the early seventies was still hippie-heavy, and my mother clung to the flower-power culture like a premenstrual woman clings to chocolate. It lives in her heart to this day—and unfortunately on my birth certificate as well.

"Hi, Mom," I said. "I need to talk to Dad. Is he here?"

Her smile dimmed but hung on. "I think I just heard him head out to the garage. He mentioned he was going to change the oil in the Corvair today. What do you need?"

Working on the Corvair was my father's happy place, but also where he went when he wanted to lay low. My fledgling courage flickered, and I tried to puff it back up. "Actually, I'd like to talk to you both."

The rest of her smile faded, and she looked down at the dish towel in her hand. "Okay. Let me just set this down."

I followed the vague swishing sounds of her boho skirt as she crossed into the kitchen, tossed the towel onto the counter, then continued on into the garage.

She called tentatively as she pushed in. "Fred. Capri wants to talk to us."

After a brief pause, he rolled out from under the car. He stood slowly, pulled off his blue nitrile gloves and dropped them in his small trash can, then took a long gulp from the can of Coke on his workbench before responding. "You want to talk to us together?"

Their mutual uncomfortable apprehension tugged at me. They'd always made an odd couple; my mother was flowy garments and long, untrimmed brown-and-gray hair while my father was crisp trousers and military haircuts. To this day, he wore an undershirt beneath his button-downs and she refused to wear a bra.

I tried to infuse my voice with positivity. "I do. How are you, Dad?"

"What's wrong?" he asked.

So much for small talk. I cleared my throat. "Morgan and I are perfectly fine, but we've had a problem come up. There are two things I need to tell you." I gave them an overview of Sylvia's decision to stop paying for Morgan's tuition.

"Why am I not surprised?" my father muttered. "That woman has always been a—"

My mother reshoved the already-tucked hair behind her ears and hurried to cut him off. "We'll help as best we can, but we don't have much. Maybe we can—"

I raised a hand and hurried to cut *her* off. "No, Ma, that's not why I'm here." My parents were both retired and lived on a comfortable, but fixed, income. "There are a few ways I can expand my work to bring in the extra money, and I wanted to talk to you about them."

My father crumpled the empty Coke can. "I don't like where this is going."

I planted my mental feet, reminded myself it was only a matter of time before he found out anyway, then stared directly into my father's eyes. "Did you hear about the woman killed at the Legion of Honor two nights ago?"

My mother answered, eyes wide. "No. Was it someone you know?"

I shook my head, but continued watching my father. "She was bashed on the head, then stabbed, then her throat was slashed postmortem."

My mother gave a strange gasp-grunt. My father's jaw tightened.

"The news outlets are already talking about a copycat killer," I continued. "They're resurrecting the Overkill Bill case. We're all going to have to deal with it one way or the other."

"What do you mean?" My mother's voice shook.

I forced myself not to fidget. "The press, Ma. They've already been calling *me*, and Dad's the only person left alive connected to the case. They'll want interviews, and they'll track down your number and address any time now."

"I know how not to answer my phone and my door." My father's voice was icy.

"It won't just be journalists, Dad. It'll be the police, too."

He barked a laugh. "Let 'em come. I was *twelve* when he was arrested. Whoever this new psycho is, it's got nothing to do with us."

"That won't stop them from plastering our family's name everywhere. The news, blogs, podcasts." I took a deep breath, and said another little prayer. "This is our reputation, and if someone's going to write about it, it should be me. I can do it in a way that will be respectful."

His eyes narrowed dangerously. "And there it is. You've been wanting to wallow around in the family mud your entire life. How many times do I have to tell you? *He's not innocent.*" He took a step closer to me, his finger raised. "So I'll put it plain. If you have any respect for me or the family, stop this now or I wash my hands of you."

Something about the steely, controlling threat stripped open some deep-seated truths I hadn't been willing to confront until that moment. "You know what? You're right, Dad. I do want to believe he's innocent, and I find it impossible to understand how *his son* won't even consider the possibility. You're not the only person who's been hurt by all this. Leo and I have also been taunted and teased our entire lives, and so has Morgan. Do you think it's a coincidence she's studying forensic psychology? We've both had countless nightmares about the blood of a psychopathic murderer running through our veins. The only way for *everyone* to heal from this is to face it head-on."

We stared at each other. I braced myself for the yelling.

He turned on his heel and walked out of the garage.

Unprepared for this new strategy, I stood frozen for a moment before turning to my mother. "Do you think he actually heard any of that?"

My mother's voice came out in a quivering whisper. "I wouldn't count on it."

"You know I'm right." I kept my voice strong.

"Tereza," my father called from the kitchen. "Where did you put that salami you bought this weekend?"

He knew very well where the salami was—in the same refrigerator deli drawer it'd been in my entire life.

"Go, Ma. I don't want him angry with you." I pointed to the external garage door. "I'll see myself out."

She enveloped me in a quick hug, then hurried into the house.

I closed the door behind me and strode out to my car. Once safely inside, I stared out the windshield.

"Well," I said aloud. "That went better than expected."

• • •

Although my brain wanted to sit dumbly and ponder the unpleasant mysteries of family, I knew my dad was watching me from some window or door crack or peephole. So I plastered an *I'm just fine* expression on my face, pulled out of the driveway, and made my way around the corner while gripping the steering wheel so hard I got a charley horse.

It was what it was. But I had to move forward, and I just couldn't believe there was no family information to be had. So how could I get it?

I chewed my lip as I considered. When my grandmother passed away, my father inherited all of her belongings, along with what was left of William's and Vincent's. In fact, the very house I'd grown up in, and that he and my mother lived in to that day, had been Philomena and William's. Surely there was something tucked away somewhere that could help me? Because, paradoxically, my father was a sentimental man—he'd clung religiously to several items my grandmother and uncle had owned, like my grandmother's armoire and my uncle's classic Chevy Corvair. Would he really have tossed the rest of it? My grandfather's stuff, sure—he'd probably danced naked around a bonfire of everything *William Sanzio* had owned. But surely my grandmother had pictures, scrapbooks, souvenirs that meant too much for him to destroy?

Surely. But I had about as much chance as a three-legged mouse at a cat convention of convincing my father to let me anywhere near it.

I again briefly considered asking my mother for her help, and again rejected the possibility. For reasons I'd never understood, despite being a strong woman who'd raised me on a generous diet of female empowerment, the importance of standing up for what you believe in, and the need to control my own destiny, she disappeared into the shrubbery whenever it came to my father and this topic. She'd never cross him on this.

As I slammed on my brakes at a red light, I tried to remind myself that pain was at the core of my father's reluctance. But my whole life, when my brother or I failed at something or had something go wrong, my father's response was always the same: "Face your problems and do what needs to be done." Why was that true for us, but not him? Why did he get to lick his psychological wounds for his whole life, and why was my mother willing to let him inflict that psychological wound onto us? It was BS, and we all knew it.

As the light turned green and I jammed my foot onto the gas pedal, my phone rang, startling me out of my mental rant. Careful to keep my eyes on the road, I reflexively hit the answer button on my steering wheel without checking the dash to see who was calling.

"Capri?"

I grimaced—it was my ex-father-in-law, Philip Clement. I got along with him far better than with Sylvia, but given my conversation with her the night before, I couldn't imagine what he had to say was gonna be pleasant. And after the scene with my father, I needed another confrontation like I needed ten million holes in my head.

"Hi, Philip," I said cautiously. "How are you?"

"Oh, thank God." His words tumbled out, voice abnormally high-pitched, and he sounded like he couldn't catch his breath. "With Todd out of the country, I didn't know who else to call."

A cold dread filled my chest and pricked the nape of my neck. "Call about what?"

He choked out the words. "Sylvia's missing."

SF Killer Crime Tours

Pacific Heights

Overlooking expansive views of the bay, Pacific Heights is the Beverly Hills of San Francisco. Studded with houses that sell for forty-five million on a bad day, the neighborhood boasts famous actors, business magnates, rock stars, and tech moguls, all nestled into majestic examples of every architectural style known to man. While the stodgy crowd is copiously represented, the neighborhood isn't without a sense of humor; keep an eye out for the anatomically too-correct robot statue gracing one of the mansions.

If you're old enough to qualify as vintage, you'll remember the 1990 Michael Keaton thriller named after the area, based on an allegedly true story about a psychopathic conman. That's only the beginning of the neighborhood's history of bad behavior, which includes a corpse delivered to his own house in a rum barrel, a voodoo queen who allegedly blackmailed rich San Franciscans and pushed her lover off a second-story window, and at least one wealthy wife who shot a cheating husband. It was also the home of sugar magnate Adolph B. Spreckels, who allegedly attempted to murder the editor-in-chief of the San Francisco Chronicle*—and allegedly tampered with the jury to get an acquittal.*

Money may buy a lot of things, but an escape from the dark side of human nature ain't one of them.

Chapter Six

After an abrupt U-turn, I pulled up into one of the spare parking spots in my in-laws' garage fifteen minutes later. The fact that they have "spare" parking spots in a city where space is at a premium second only to Manhattan should tell you all you need to know about their house—basically a *tell me you're rich without telling me you're rich* situation. Built in 1894 by one of Sylvia's ancestors, "The Chateau" had never been owned by anyone outside the Renard clan and was Sylvia's pride and joy. A single-family dwelling with six bedrooms and six baths over four floors (something no normal human can afford within the confines of San Francisco proper), the house flirts with being a mansion. It looks like it was imported directly from the streets of Paris, with a mansard roof, tall windows that open to small, ornately decorated balconies, and a patch of garden in front so meticulously landscaped it could have been flown in from the Palace of Versailles. Only the off-white exterior differentiates it from the traditional rich cream of Parisian architecture.

As I made my way up from the hidden garage, the familiar-yet-not-mine vibe made me feel like a servant arriving late for my day's work.

Thank heavens that wasn't true, because I'd light myself on fire within a day if I were responsible for keeping it clean—the inside was just as off-white as the exterior, and by that I mean *every* wall, *every* ceiling, and *every* floor in *every single room*. To be fair, each room had an accent color associated with it, but barely; if you stayed in the "green" room, that meant you were in the bedroom whose off-white throw pillows contained the gentlest hint of sage green known to mankind.

I found Philip in the dining room, his hand shaking as he attempted to pour a tot of brandy into a snifter. Not surprising considering I'd barely been able to get anything coherent out of him over the phone, but still disconcerting considering his usually laid-back demeanor. His short white hair was slightly mussed, another discordant note for a man who took pride in an impeccable appearance and an impressive pompadour flip. I lifted the decanter out of his hand and poured the drink for him, then watched him toss it back.

My relationship with Philip has always been complicated. We had an odd bond from the start, because despite the fact that the depth of his personality plunged only as far as his morning-gym-afternoon-golf-evening-cigars routine, neither of us was *to the manor born*. His family was also firmly working-class, and he knew the pain of marrying into a family who saw him as less-than, even if he'd done a much better job of molding himself to the ways of his new world. I'd always had the sense he and I were secret allies against the wall of Renard that defined every aspect of Sylvia's life.

Once his glass hit the table, I jumped in. "Okay, start at the beginning. What do you mean, Sylvia's missing?"

"I mean just that. She's nowhere to be found. I've looked everywhere."

"She's probably just out at some charity meeting or something." I wasn't quite sure what Sylvia did with her spare time (she always said discussing business affairs was "gauche") but I knew that, in addition to the self-sustaining fortune she'd inherited, she always had "several irons in the fire" that brought in income.

He shook his head vigorously. "Her bed wasn't slept in last night, and her shower wasn't used."

Although Philip and Sylvia often slept in the same room, they each had their own suites for times they didn't want to disturb each other. "Maybe the maid cleaned up after her?"

"The housekeepers come Tuesdays, Thursdays, and on Saturdays when we have events."

Today was Monday. I thought back to my phone call with Sylvia the night before. "But she got back from her trip yesterday, right?"

"Yes, just before six. I'd waited dinner for her because we'd planned to go out together once she got home, but she said she had some vital calls to make and told me to order myself something. Then she disappeared into her office, obviously irritated. By the time I went to bed, she still hadn't come out."

My face flushed at the thought of one of the "vital calls" I knew she'd made. "And you're sure she was still in the office when you went to bed?"

His face fell. "The light was on, so I assumed."

When I talked to Sylvia, she'd mentioned waiting for another call. "What was the vital business she had to deal with?"

"She was very vague about it all. You know how she is."

I did indeed: private and untrusting to a fault, and not just with me. It had been a sore spot with Todd, but he'd never been willing to confront her when she waved him off her business matters. "So if something important was going on, maybe she went somewhere without telling you?"

"Her car is in the garage, and her purse is on the entryway table where she always leaves it. She'd never go out without it." He rose and strode from the room.

I hurried after him. "She has dozens of purses. Maybe she took a different one? Did you try calling her?"

"I did. Her phone's inside." He reached into the bag and extracted several objects. "Along with her wallet, and lipstick, and sunglasses—"

I grimaced and nodded agreement. "Even if she'd gone out without her purse, she never would have left her phone."

"But her keys are missing." He pointed into the bag.

I stepped over to peer inside the now-empty bag, then ran my hand along the inside to check for hidden pockets. There were none. "We should check the house again, just to be sure."

He nodded vacantly. "Two sets of eyes are better than one."

We systematically made our way through the house. For once I was grateful for the immaculate surroundings—the few items that were out of place were easy to detect.

"Her suitcases are out," I said as we entered Sylvia's walk-in closet. "Should we go through them and see—" But the look on Philip's face stopped me. "What?"

He crossed quickly to the suitcases and tugged on the zippers. "She always unpacks before she goes to bed. She can't sleep until she knows everything she'll need in the morning is in place."

A wave of nausea rolled over me. "Maybe something in her office will tell us what's going on." I hurried out to the office, but the invisible hand of classical conditioning stayed me as I reached for the knob. This room was her sanctuary—I could count the number of times I'd been inside with only single digits, and opening the door felt like breaking into Fort Knox. I steeled myself against the piercing admonitions in my head, then pushed my way in.

The lavender notes of Sylvia's signature scent tugged accusingly at me, as though she were watching from behind one of the off-white Louis XIV bergère fauteuils on either side of the room. Everything was pristine. The oak desk, accoutered with an off-white desk set, phone, and laptop, was otherwise empty. No papers left out, no

Post-it notes stuck to the edge of the computer, not even an empty tea cup left after her evening's work. The off-white bookshelves were immaculately organized, with every book and tchotchke in perfect, symmetrical order. If even a paper clip had been knocked to the floor, it would've blared out from the off-white carpet like a siren.

"Dammit. Nothing." I reached to pull open the top drawer of the desk, but it didn't budge; my arm yanked against the unexpected resistance, breaking one of my nails.

Philip waved angrily. "She always locks it, ever since she walked in on one of our maids rifling through it. Fired the woman on the spot, but still decided she couldn't risk anyone trespassing again."

I nodded—whether you considered Sylvia to be vigilant or paranoid depended very much on your own personal level of neurosis. "Well, that's a good sign, right? At least we know nobody broke in and—" Philip's face dropped, and I hurried to change tacks. "Does she keep important papers anywhere else? Safety deposit box, anything like that?"

"She doesn't trust safety deposit boxes, nobody in her family ever has. They believe firmly in having everything close at hand. Her walk-in has a built-in safe we use for her jewelry, but I've never seen papers in there. She always keeps her papers locked in here." He waved at the wooden behemoth.

"We should take a look, and check the rest of the house."

We searched from the attic down to the garage, but found no evidence of her anywhere.

A thought occurred to me. "You have security cameras, right? They'll show when she left, or if anyone came in."

He shook his head. "I already looked. We have two cameras, one on the front porch, and one at the back. Neither one of them show any activity."

"And they're working correctly?"

"As far as I can tell."

I rubbed my temples. "How is that possible? She didn't disappear into thin air . . ."

"The only way is the garage," Philip said. "She uses the shortcut when she goes for her walks."

A small path ran between the neighboring property lots, from near the garage to the street behind, creating a faster way to reach the two nearby parks. "You don't have a camera on the garage entrance?"

Frustrated tears pooled in Philip's eyes. "Why would we bother? You'd need an industrial forklift to force up the garage door, even without the security gate in front of it."

"Right, of course." The garage was only accessible to those of us who had remotes. "Does she go for walks at night?"

"Sometimes, but usually in the morning."

I wracked my brain for options. "We should call her friends. Maybe she's with one of them."

"I've called the ones I have numbers for. Nobody's heard from her since they parted at the airport yesterday."

"Let me check with Morgan." Maybe Sylvia had a fit of conscience about the tuition and took her out to lunch to make up for it. I composed the text carefully to avoid alarming Morgan, especially in case she was in the middle of a class.

Have you heard from Grandma Sylvia today?

Her response came back almost immediately: Not a word.

Yeah, it had been a long shot. Sylvia wasn't much for second-guessing her choices.

I passed the message on to Philip. "What about her schedule? She must have a day planner?"

He rubbed his forehead. "She does it on her phone, and I don't have the password."

"If it's her calendar app, we can probably access it through her computer, too."

"I don't have the password for that, either."

I made a mental note to make sure Morgan had a complete list of all my passwords in case something happened to me, then braced myself and cleared my throat. "I think we need to call the police."

Chapter Seven

I'm an excellent person to have around in an emergency—I'm a quick thinker and my reactions kick in without pause. Once, when Morgan gashed open her inner thigh so bad while climbing a chain-link fence that rivulets of fat poured out, I applied a tourniquet without batting an eye and drove her to the ER, all while we sang Lady Gaga songs at the top of our lungs to keep her mind off what was happening. Not until she was sound asleep later that night curled up around her favorite American Girl doll did I break down into near-hysterical tears.

But if people I love are hurting and there's no action I can take? I'll go completely insane. Sylvia and I may not have gotten along well, but she and Philip were family and the last thing I wanted was for anything bad to happen to them.

After Philip and I called the SFPD and filed a missing persons report, I sank down into a dining room chair and considered taking my own healthy gulp of the brandy. But I needed to stay clearheaded, even if I had no idea what else to do. I stuck my thumb on Sylvia's phone just in case biometrics were really all a big con, but no dice—the phone wasn't fooled. I considered physically searching the neighborhood for her, but since she wasn't a toddler or puppy who'd strayed out of the yard, I couldn't see how it would help. And with Philip wandering around the room like a homesick ghost, I wasn't sure it was a good idea to leave him alone.

My years as a mother, and as a tour guide dealing with hard-to-please guests, had taught me the multifaceted value of distraction. I grabbed a pad and pen out of my purse and shoved them across the table to Philip. "You should write down everything you can remember since Sylvia got home last night so you can keep the details clear in your head." I'd read a lot about eyewitness testimony thanks to my obsession with true crime, and the sooner you made a record of everything, the less likely the memories were to degrade or become confused. But even if that didn't work, it would give him something to focus on until we heard back from the police.

As soon as he started writing furiously, I excused myself to check the house again, the best method I could come up with to distract *myself*. This time I left no off-white accouterment unturned: I checked behind every chair, in every closet, and under every bed in the house, terrified of what I might find, swerving from room to room like I was trapped in a nightmare I couldn't rouse myself out of.

As I made my way back down to the first floor, the leaden chimes of The Chateau's doorbell echoed through the house. Philip shot out of the dining room, and we hurried together to answer the door.

Three individuals with the dense, hyper-aware presence of law enforcement stood on the portico giving us a detached, experienced once-over. A thirty-something Latino man, tall and lean with short, dark hair, hovered in the back. An Indian woman, black hair pulled into a tight chignon, surveyed us from the side, her face alert and professional but with an underlying kindness emphasized by deepening smile lines. And a tall, vaguely familiar-looking older white man stood authoritatively in front of the other two while staring down at his phone. When his blue eyes raised and pierced through me, I recognized him—Inspector

Petito, the homicide detective I'd googled earlier. The energy he put off was somewhat different from his picture; there was still a kindness to him, but it was overlaid with an odd combination of wariness and strength to his face, like he was too familiar with what bad the world had to offer, but had chosen to harden himself *against* it rather than *because* of it. Whatever it was, the upshot was both intimidating and reassuring—this was a man you wanted on your side, and I breathed easier having him there.

As soon as that reaction registered in my brain, I mentally rolled my eyes. Morgan had once told me about a psychology study where students secretly given large doses of caffeine interpreted the physical stimulation as attraction to the other person in the room. I'd scoffed at the time, but apparently all it took was a missing mother-in-law to turn me into a damsel in distress.

He shifted his jacket to flash us the badge on his hip. "I'm Homicide Inspector Dan Petito, and these are Sergeants Alice Kumar and Hector Garcia. You filed a missing persons report for a Mrs. Sylvia Clement?"

My chest tightened as the significance of their titles hit me. I could have sworn I remembered reading somewhere that the *special victims* unit worked missing persons cases, not the *homicide* unit. Regardless, the SFPD were extremely busy, even on a Monday afternoon, and for them to show up at the door so soon after we filed the report didn't seem like a precursor to happy news disseminated over tea.

Philip must have been thinking the same thing, because he lost the power of speech. When all he managed was a mute nod, I took over. "Yes, we did. This is Philip Clement, Sylvia's husband. I'm her daughter-in-law, Capri Sanzio."

All three detectives had lasered in on Philip the moment the door opened, but upon hearing my name, Petito's eyes snapped to me like paper clips to a magnet.

"Capri *Sanzio*?" he asked.

My name was throwing him for a loop when a woman was missing? "Yes, sorry, her *ex*-daughter-in-law, actually. I changed back to my maiden name after I divorced my husband."

His expression didn't change. "You called and left me a message earlier."

I mentally smacked myself—of course that's why he was reacting to my name. "Right, yes, that was me."

"You're Overkill Bill's granddaughter?" His voice turned clipped and efficient.

I glanced over at Philip, whose emotions were cycling between confused, terrified, and desperate. Was this really the right time to discuss my personal provenance? "I am, yes. But I can talk to you about that another time. Sylvia's what's important right now."

Petito followed my gaze to Philip, then bounced right back to me. He started to say something, stopped, and then started again. "Is there somewhere we can sit?"

"Sure, sorry, of course." I stepped away from the door, and Philip dropped back to follow me.

I led them to the kitchen, then gestured to the whitewashed country farmhouse chairs around the table. "Would any of you like a cup of coffee?"

Kumar and Garcia shook their heads. Petito said, "No, thank you. We have a few questions we need to ask you. Please sit."

Philip and I chose chairs across from them, next to each other.

Petito cleared his throat. "A few hours ago, a woman matching Sylvia's description, without any identifying information, was found dead in the Presidio by an early-morning jogger. Because of the description and the proximity to your home, we'd like to eliminate the possibility that she's Sylvia. We need to show you a picture of the woman we found."

My stomach churned at the thought. Despite the hundreds of crime-scene photos I'd studied in my forty-odd years of reading true-crime cases, the prospect of coming face-to-face with a dead person I knew was more than I could bear. I stood up and placed my hand on Philip's shoulder. "I'll be in the dining room if you need me."

Petito's eyes sharpened. "I'd like you to take a look, too."

I clutched my abdomen. "I—um—Philip knows Sylvia better than anyone. And I'd really, *really* rather not."

Philip started to speak, but Petito cut him off. "I'm afraid I have to insist."

On top of the churning, knives now stabbed into my stomach. Why on earth would he need me to identify Sylvia when he had her husband to do it? Did they routinely need two identifications to be certain, like journalists need sources? I swallowed hard and sat back down.

He pulled out his smart phone, then tapped and scrolled. When he found what he wanted, he slid the phone toward us. All three detectives watched us intently.

I forced myself to look down.

At the edge of a soft berm, Sylvia lay on a mossy carpet of eucalyptus leaves, blouse untucked from her pants, zipper undone. Supine, arms and legs akimbo, eyes closed. Face slack, as though she were in a deep sleep.

I stared, transfixed and horrified. Primarily from the shock of seeing my mother-in-law dead. But also because the bloody, hair-matted dent in her skull indicated she'd been bashed on the head, the red stains on her shirt indicated she'd been repeatedly stabbed in the chest, and the absence of blood around the gash across her throat indicated it had been slashed postmortem.

Suddenly Petito's heightened interest in my last name made alarming sense.

I jumped up, ran across the kitchen, and vomited into the sink.

—

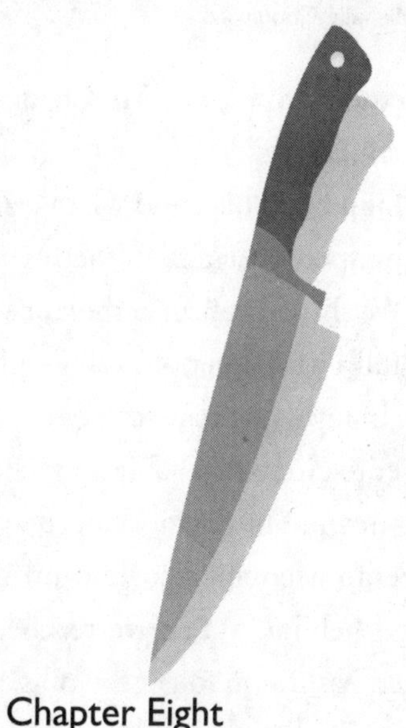

Chapter Eight

After I finished throwing up, I ripped a paper towel off the holder and swiped at my face as I turned to Philip. He'd gone completely still and his face was blank, as though he were staring at something none of us could see. If he'd been in the shallows of shock before, this plunged him fully into the deep end.

Then he crumbled. He gasped suddenly, then dropped his head into his hands. "Oh, God. My Sylvia? She *can't* be gone." Sobs ripped through him, muffled by the hands covering his face, and his body shook.

I dropped into the chair next to him and wrapped my arm around his shoulder. Tears pricked the back of my eyes, but didn't overflow onto my cheeks. It's a strange quirk of my makeup that I've never understood—when other people are crying, my own tears dry up, no matter how much pain I'm in. It's like some twisted reverse-empath thing that focuses me so much on their emotions my own get put on hold.

After several minutes his sobs turned to stuttering gasps, and he lifted his head. "I can't—I can't—"

Petito's brow knit. "Mr. Clement, are you all right? Should we call an ambulance?"

Philip lifted his hand. "Panic attack. I need—my Xanax."

I jumped up again. "Where's your Xanax?"

"We should call an ambulance to be sure," Kumar said.

Philip waved her off, still gasping. "No point. That's why—I have pills. In my—medicine cabinet."

Petito circled the table and held out a hand for him. "Let's get you lying down. Ms. Sanzio, can you get the Xanax?"

Petito accompanied him up the stairs while Kumar and Garcia stayed behind. When we reached the bedroom, I shot into the attached bathroom to get the pills and a glass of water. Once I handed both to Philip, now settled on his bed, Petito guided me back out of the room.

"He won't be able to tell us much until he's calmer. For now we have some questions we need to ask you."

I was quite sure he did, and I was equally sure I wasn't going to like them—several avenues of horrible had just slammed together, and I was the nexus of each and every one. From his perspective, Overkill Bill's granddaughter had called him with lightning speed after a local murder copycatting her grandfather's MO; then, before he even got a chance to return the call, she popped up like a bad penny as he was following up on a second murder using the same method. It didn't take a genius to realize how it all looked, and if I were him, I'd've already read me my rights.

When we reached the kitchen, I slipped back into my chair, wishing I'd palmed Philip's bottle of pills.

Kumar took the lead, her voice gentle. "When exactly did you and Mr. Clement notice Sylvia was missing?"

I recounted what Philip told me about the last twenty-four hours, trying to remember as much detail as I could. Both Petito and Kumar watched me carefully, and each asked a smattering of follow-up questions. Their interest intensified when I mentioned Sylvia's self-sequestration in her office to deal with business.

"He said she seemed agitated?" Kumar asked.

"Very."

"Was that something that happened often, her being so worried about business that she'd cancel a dinner date with her husband after not seeing him for a week?" Petito asked.

I frowned. "I—I'm not really sure, you'll have to ask him. But he seemed to feel it was noteworthy when he told me."

"And you have no idea what she was doing in the park?" Petito asked.

"None. She likes to take walks, I know that."

Kumar nodded. "What type of work does she do?"

I took a deep breath and tried to explain Sylvia's situation and her penchant for secrecy. "She never even told Todd very much, at least not back before we divorced. Her son," I clarified.

"How long ago did you divorce?" Kumar asked.

"Ten years."

Petito's eyebrows popped up. "Ten years, but you're the one opening the door when your mother-in-law is murdered."

My face flushed indignantly—when you put it like *that*, of course it sounded weird. "Todd is their only child, and our daughter Morgan is their only grandchild. Todd travels almost constantly for his job, so I'm the connective tissue between them and Morgan."

He nodded, and Kumar moved on. "So, the last time anybody had contact with Mrs. Clement was yesterday at"—she glanced down at her notes—"about six in the evening?"

My stomach sank into my knees. "Um, no, actually. The last contact with her was when I, uh—called her around seven last night."

All three detectives stared at me, unblinking. "You talked to her?" Kumar asked.

"Yes. Not for long, but yes."

"Did she sound upset or worried? Anything out of the ordinary?" Kumar asked.

I winced mentally. "Not worried, but upset, yes. Or more like irritated."

"Did she say about what?" Petito asked.

"She was annoyed at me, and at my daughter." I wrapped my arms around my abdomen, gathered my courage, and blurted out the story of my argument with Sylvia.

Petito's blue eyes, now far more menacing than appealing, pierced mine. "So in the last known conversation anyone had with Mrs. Clement, she cut off your daughter's tuition, called you a gold digger, and left both you and your daughter in dire financial straits."

Yep, that about summed it up—and threw up a great big neon sign flashing MOTIVE! over my head. Where, since Sylvia was killed using my grandfather's MO, a second sign flashing MEANS! was already smugly waiting for it.

I squeezed my eyes shut and nodded.

"That must have made you angry," Kumar said.

There wasn't any point denying it, so I lifted my chin. "Yes, it did. Morgan doesn't deserve that. If Sylvia was annoyed with *me*, she should have taken it out on *me*."

Petito's brows twitched. "Why was Sylvia annoyed at you?"

Dammit, dammit, dammit. A pit opened up in my stomach and my internal organs hopped into it. How was it every time I opened my mouth, I managed to look even more guilty? "I—um—I wasn't her favorite person. And my ex-husband recently signed our house over to me."

"Why would he do that?" Kumar asked.

"He's in a volatile business. He's had different partners over the years, and had some of the incarnations fail. I guess he had to personally invest more into whatever the current one is, because he didn't want anyone coming after the house if there was some sort of problem." I shrugged. "I'm paying the mortgage anyway so it made sense. He knows either way it'll end up going to Morgan."

"Isn't that what your mother-in-law wanted?" Petito asked.

"She was probably worried I'd instantly sell it and fly off to Las Vegas or something. It's very important to her that it stays in the family."

He nodded, still watching my face. "Where were you last night and this morning?"

"I was home, alone. I took a bath, tried to read, then went to bed. This morning I visited my parents. Then Philip called me." And the trifecta was complete: OPPORTUNITY! now flashed alongside MOTIVE and MEANS.

"And you called and left a message for me *before* you knew that Mrs. Clement was missing," he said.

My answer came out in a squeaky whisper. "About the *Katherine Harper* murder. Everyone's calling it a copycat, and I'm writing a book about my grandfather and . . ." I stopped talking, because there really wasn't any point in saying more. It was only a matter of seconds before Petito whipped out the cuffs and hauled me away to jail. There was no way this could get worse.

Except it could.

"We'll need to speak to your daughter," Petito said.

A deep cold settled over me. "Morgan? She doesn't have anything to do with this."

"Her grandmother disappeared less than twenty-four hours after cutting off her tuition, and you and she were the last people to speak with Mrs. Clement. We need to talk to her." He held my eyes. "As soon as possible."

My stomach tried its best to expel something, but thankfully there was nothing left. It was one thing for them to suspect *me*, but Morgan? My inner mama bear reared on her hind legs, and my hand itched for my phone so I could warn her.

Instead, I recited Morgan's number and address to Petito.

"We also need to know where you were Thursday night and early Friday morning," Kumar asked.

The night Katherine Harper was killed. "Same. After my evening tour I went home, watched some TV, and went to bed. But I've never met Katherine Harper in my life."

Kumar nodded. "Had Sylvia?"

I scoffed. "I highly doubt it."

"They were both socialites," Petito said.

I shook my head. "Not the same kind. The Harpers are Silicon-Valley-start-up wealthy. Sylvia was openly disdainful of 'new money.'"

Petito sent a smirk to Garcia and Kumar before answering me. "Old or new, it pays the bills just the same."

I studied his face. Was he testing me, or being flip? Sure, I'd never known about the dysfunctional snobbery before I married into it, but there was no way a wizened detective wasn't aware of the schism between established money and tech money that rent San Francisco's elite like an earthquake fault line. Beginning in the 1990s, the tech boom hit Silicon Valley, just south of San Francisco, like a wrecking ball wrapped in hydraulic hammers. The entire Bay Area underwent metaphorical seismic shifts, and the tech pioneers ended up with more money than God. By the 2010s, San Francisco's status and tax incentives started attracting the mega-millionaires and billionaires to the wealthy neighborhoods, much to the horror of the established owners. This influx was seen by the old-money elite not just as *déclassé*, but as destructive—the interlopers had no connection to San Francisco's history, nor, supposedly, any desire to protect its future. According to the noblesse-oblige old guard, the tech barons didn't give to local causes, didn't support the arts, and didn't involve themselves in the local political issues that were their responsibility.

Something buzzed through to all three detectives' phones, and

Garcia looked down to check whatever it was. "ME's ready for us," he said.

Petito stood, and the others followed. "As soon as Mr. Clement is awake, we'll need to talk to him, and we'll likely have more questions for you. Are you able to stay here with him and call us when he wakes?"

I also stood, arms again wrapped around my abdomen, and nodded. "Today's my day off. I have prep work I have to do later, but no tours."

Petito held out a card. "Just in case you don't still have my number."

Ha, ha.

The second they were out the door I called Morgan. She didn't answer, most likely because she was in class. Since "Your grandmother was killed in the Presidio by someone pretending to be your great-grandfather" wasn't news anyone should ever receive via voicemail, I left an awkward, halting message trying to convey urgency without leaving specifics, but probably only managed to sound like I was in the midst of a stroke. Then I called Todd, hoping to get his voicemail so I could put off delivering the bad news at least a short while longer. So of course he picked up immediately, and I again found myself struggling for words.

My ex-husband has never been good at dealing with any type of unpleasantness, so I braced myself for his response. But he didn't melt down; he listened in intense silence, then asked how his father was doing. When I told him Philip was currently sleeping off Xanax and brandy, he said he'd arrange to drive home as soon as possible—turned out he was already back in the States, just a few hours away in Los Angeles dealing with business there. Which said it all, really, because normally no force under heaven or earth could pull Todd away from his work.

Once he hung up, I called Heather, and swore fiercely when she didn't pick up. I checked the clock—she was out on a tour. I left her a message with a quick version of what had happened, then did the same with my mother's voicemail.

I set the phone down on the table and glanced around the empty house, waiting for the tears to come, thinking about all the arrangements that had to be made. But my emotions camped out under my ribs, swelling and swirling, unable to come to a consensus on how to express themselves. Heartache for Philip and Morgan and Todd, and guilt because my own relationship with Sylvia had been so strained. Sadness and horror that she'd been murdered so brutally. Terror that my worst nightmare was coming true: the police suspected that Morgan or I (or both) was the psychopathic reincarnation of my grandfather. And fierce anger at the unknown stranger who'd caused it all.

But a sliver of logical hope breached the pea soup of my emotional fog. Because once you scratched the surface of it, the case against Morgan and me didn't hold up: If one of us had murdered Sylvia because she'd cut off Morgan's tuition, how could Katherine Harper's murder, which had occurred three days before, possibly be related?

Easy, the true-crime part of my brain pointed out to me with withering scorn. *Maybe you knew about the copycat murder, and when you needed a way to deal with your annoying mother-in-law, you copied the copycat to make Sylvia's death look like a random serial killing.*

The back-and-forth reverse-psychology zigzagging gave me mental whiplash, and I angrily told that part of my brain to shut up. Because, I argued back, who would be stupid enough to put themselves on the police's radar by calling the cops after killing someone?

Lots of people, that true-crime lobe shot back immediately. Criminals often tried to insert themselves into investigations. Killers showed up to crime scenes, returned to where they'd buried their victims, helped during searches and emergency neighborhood meetings, even contacted the police via letters or calls. Some wanted attention. Some wanted to relive the thrill of their kill. Some wanted insight into how much the police knew in an attempt to cover their tracks.

I rubbed my temples—if my own brain was on the verge of convicting Morgan and me, there was no way I was going to talk the police out of it without proof that someone else was responsible. If I didn't want to spend, or have my daughter spend, the rest of our respective lives in jail, I needed to figure out who had really done this.

And fast.

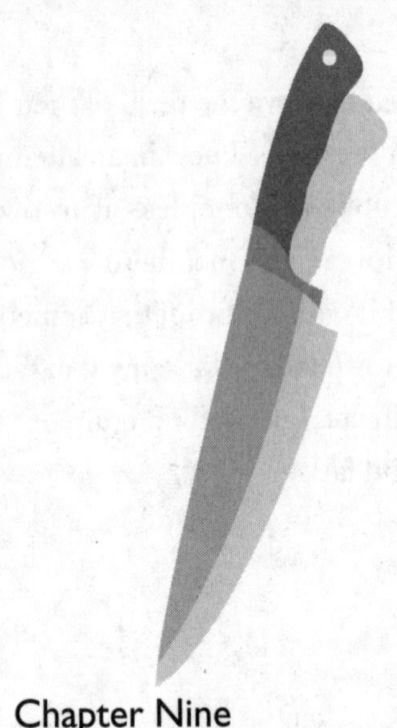

Chapter Nine

I bypassed Sylvia's Keurig and rummaged through her cabinets for the moka pot I'd given her years ago—the environmental consciousness my mother instilled in me couldn't get past the reports I'd seen on single-pod coffee systems' impact on the environment. Once I'd made myself a strong cup of coffee, I settled in to figure out where to start.

There were two possibilities I could see. One was that the two killings were random, coincidentally both caused by a serial killer hunting down women in San Francisco's major parks and copying my grandfather's signature. To catch someone like that, who chose their victims by chance availability, you needed resources. Officers to canvass the area, databases of suspicious people, tech labs to analyze any evidence they found. I didn't have any of that. But I did have a personal connection to Overkill Bill that would give me a leg up, psychologically speaking, since his methodology was somehow connected to the killer's choices. And creaking back in the rusty section of my brain were solid journalism skills that just needed, like the Tin Man in *The Wizard of Oz*, a few squirts of oil to get them all limbered up again. Because my father was right about one thing: when I set my mind to something, I was like a terrier digging up a gopher who'd stolen one of my bones.

The second possibility was that the two women weren't chosen at random. Of course, even so, the killer had still purposefully used the Overkill Bill methodology, and that meant that an important key lay in understanding the relationship between the two sets of murders. But I had to admit it was creepily improbable that someone who chose to copycat *my* grandfather's methods also stumbled on *my* mother-in-law as a random victim. Given the differences in Sylvia's and Katherine's social circles, it was unlikely they knew each other, but sometimes tech money and old money did come in contact; it was possible that somebody who knew both Sylvia and Katherine wanted each of them dead for some reason. So I needed to find out who or what they had in common. And the other phone call Sylvia had mentioned to me throbbed in my memory like a severed artery—was *that* related to whatever was behind her death?

I sipped my coffee and followed the logic through. Sylvia had holed herself up as soon as she returned from the airport, so most likely either something happened when she was on the trip or she received some troubling communication when she got back. The trip had been, according to Morgan, a girls' getaway, but business and pleasure intersected heavily in Sylvia's social circle; it was very possible something happened in Hawaii that required immediate action on her return. Even if it hadn't, I was well acquainted with how a phone could blow up once switched off airplane mode.

I slammed the rest of my coffee and glanced up toward Sylvia's office. I needed facts, not speculation. Whatever the issue was, there had to be some evidence of it locked up in that desk, or on her computer or phone.

I took a five-second dip into the ethics of violating Sylvia's personal privacy and quickly decided there was no expectation of privacy in the afterlife. Besides, Sylvia was just the sort of person who'd spend eternity haunting me if I let her granddaughter—keeper of her family legacy—be carted off to jail, and I just didn't have space in my house or time in my schedule to deal with a poltergeist.

Decision made, I glanced at the time. The detectives had been gone for half an hour, and Philip had been asleep for twice that. He could wake and they could return at any moment.

I had to act quickly.

• • •

On my way up to the office, I glanced down at Sylvia's phone in my hand. The police would want to examine it when they returned. But I'd already stuffed my thumb onto the phone's screen once hoping to get inside it; if someone else's print had been there, I'd already destroyed the evidence. So before I could talk myself out of it, I clutched the phone to my chest and continued on to the office.

Once inside, I shoved the office chair back and dropped down onto the carpet in front of her desk. I tapped the phone on and swiped to enter a PIN, then stared down, trying to figure out what hers might be. Birthdays seemed like the best bet, so I tried hers, Philip's, Todd's, and Morgan's, and then her and Philip's wedding anniversary. None of them worked. Possibly she used some strange mash-up of those important dates, but if so, the permutations and combinations could go on forever. She and Philip had no pets, since animals and off-white houses were not simpatico, and try as I might, I couldn't remember much about her childhood.

I grimaced down at the phone. Trying to nail down the dark enigma that was Sylvia's mind was getting me nowhere fast, and the laptop would likely be just as futile. The locked desk was a far better bet since I could physically rather than mentally break in. I had a crowbar in my car, but something told me that when Petito asked to see her office, having to explain why her desk was splintered into pieces was a conversation I didn't want to have. What I really needed was some way to pick the lock.

Fortunately, I had zero problem finding a disturbingly large number of videos on YouTube more than willing to show me how to pick locks with a variety of household implements. Since I had a pot of paper clips in front of me, I selected a corresponding video and (after a solid minute of hysteria-edged laughter triggered by the disclaimer "This is for home use only") followed the instructions on how to turn one paper clip into a "tension wrench," and another into a "rake." Then, inspired and assured by the twenty seconds it took the man in the video to open a locked door, I spent a good thirty minutes swearing like a sailor at Sylvia's desk before the lock clicked open.

Some sort of metal bar engaged all three drawers, so I thankfully only had to go through the madness once. I pulled open the narrow center drawer first to find a smattering of office supplies—and two memory cards tucked in their midst. Since I'd need a computer to look at them, I slid them into the pocket of my pants to examine later. Buried under them was an odd rectangle of patinaed wood, about the size of a business card and about an inch thick, with the Renard crest carved into the top of it. When I picked it up to examine it, my hand tugged—it was far heavier than I'd expected. Despite a seam on either end, I couldn't get any part of it to move. Maybe it was some sort of small puzzle box? I shook it, but couldn't detect any movement. A paperweight? Normally you kept those on *top* of the desk, but maybe despite being a family heirloom it hadn't suited Sylvia's sensibilities? Whatever it was, it wasn't any help to me, so I threw it back in and moved on.

The second drawer contained stationery, mostly monogrammed, all off-white, all with visible linen thread counts. The third drawer opened to reveal—ding, ding, ding—a set of hanging folders meticulously labeled and filled with papers.

I worked from the inside out. The first file contained medical records, mostly insurance forms and a few records of copayments. The next few files, with a variety of contracts that seemed fairly cut-and-dried, were equally unenlightening. I paused at one marked PRENUPTIAL AGREEMENTS and opened it. My mouth dropped open when I found a copy of *my* prenuptial agreement with Todd on top—we'd been divorced for ten years and she *still* had a copy of our prenuptial agreement? And she had the nerve to accuse *me* of not being able to move on? The irony ran still deeper, because while the prenuptial agreement specified that if *I* cheated, I got nothing, Todd was the one who'd done the cheating.

I expelled a derisive puff of air through my nose, slammed my prenuptial agreement back on top of Sylvia's below it, then continued on. But the next file, labeled MORTGAGE AND LOAN RECORDS, knocked me back hard onto my butt. I'd heard at least a million times about how the house had been in the family since the day it was built in 1894, and as far as I knew, the house hadn't been mortgaged in generations. Maybe not ever, because the Renards who built it most likely paid cash. So what was going on?

I stopped and chastised myself for making assumptions. My own house had a substantial mortgage despite being a family heirloom due to needed repairs and upgrades, and The Chateau was even older than our house. It shouldn't be surprising that it would need a little reconstructive surgery, too.

But, my mind answered me back, *why would someone with Sylvia's money need to* borrow *for any sort of renovation?*

I pushed back against the objection. During the course of my marriage I'd learned that rich people did all sorts of strange things when it came to money, like pay their property taxes well after the due date because the late penalty came to less than the interest their accounts generated by leaving the money in. Maybe this was more of the same, and the interest they paid on a mortgage was less than what they made in whatever 401-hedge-fund-tax-shelter their money was stashed in? Most likely that's what was going on.

Except that wasn't what was going on.

The topmost document was a recent property assessment, and when my eyes slipped down to the assessed value, my mouth fell open again: twenty million dollars. I mean, I knew this wasn't just any old house, even amid the most expensive neighborhood in San Francisco, itself one of the most expensive cities in the world. And I joked all the time about how it was a mansion rather than a house, so I don't know what I'd expected. Maybe twice the value of my own house, worth a paltry-by-comparison three million dollars because of its four bedrooms, three baths, enclosed garden, and rooftop patio. Maybe triple, since The Chateau's floor plan was almost double in square footage, as was her outdoor space. But nearly seven times the value?

And yet, as difficult as *that* was for me to process, what I saw next completely blew my logic circuits.

Beyond the property assessment I found paperwork for several loans. Four in fact: two mortgages and two business loans, together totaling over nineteen million dollars.

Again my jaw and I sat in stunned silence. How was it even possible to borrow that much against equity? I cast my mind back to the mortgage we took out on our own home nearly fifteen years ago, but I couldn't remember what percentage was allowed. I grabbed my phone and quickly clarified. Generally speaking, Google informed me, I could borrow up to eighty percent of my equity. That was more than I'd anticipated, but still not enough to account for the numbers in front of me.

Then again, people with money and connections often made things happen that mere mortals couldn't begin to understand. Maybe the Renard name alone was enough to get people to throw money at Sylvia hand over fist.

The bigger, more important question was why? Renovation wouldn't account for a quarter of the money borrowed here. I dove back into the drawer, looking for any folders relevant to bank accounts or stock portfolios. I found one, with a checking and two savings accounts, one long-term and one short. Between the three of them they contained less than two hundred thousand dollars—an amount that would have impressed me in any other context, but felt breathtakingly inadequate as things stood. From what I could decipher, their stock portfolio was also anemic. There was a recent investment in the consumer goods giant The Beautiful Life Home Products that seemed to be doing well and another for Steve Harper's software company—and thus a connection to Katherine Harper—but as I paged back through the records, the bulk of their holdings had been liquidated. I searched for any additional properties they owned; when I was married to Todd, they'd had what they'd ironically referred to as a "cabin" in Lake Tahoe. They still owned it, but it, too, was mortgaged to the five-million-dollar hilt. There might be something I was missing somewhere, but I couldn't come up with any scenario that made sense out of borrowing over twenty million dollars, no matter what sort of financial reindeer games rich people played.

The longer I sifted through the papers, the clearer it became: Sylvia and Philip were, for all intents and purposes, broke. Even if Sylvia sold the house for full price, she wouldn't have enough equity left to cover the Realtor commission, fees, closing costs, and taxes.

I scraped my teeth along my bottom lip as the connections snapped together in my head. This was the real reason Sylvia had cut off Morgan's tuition. Between the loan payments and property taxes coming due, the money in their bank accounts wouldn't last more than another couple of months at best. Pointing the finger at me was her way of deflecting uncomfortable explanations away from herself.

A voice boomed out behind me, and I nearly jumped out of my skin.

"What in the *hell* do you think you're doing?"

Chapter Ten

I whirled around to find Philip striding toward me. He snatched the papers out of my hands and up from the floor next to me. His eyes raked over them, and his face turned puce.

My own face and neck burned with the fire of a thousand suns. "I'm so sorry, Philip, it's not what it seems. I'm just trying to figure out what Sylvia was so upset about yesterday—"

He threw up a hand to cut me off, then turned away from me toward the window.

Not sure what to say or do, I sat in stunned silence. When he didn't respond after what felt like hours, I tried again. "I didn't mean to invade your privacy, I didn't think I'd find anything that was . . ." I stumbled and stopped, unsure how to finish the sentence, finally understanding there wasn't really anything more I could say.

He turned back toward me and nodded stiffly. "You don't have anything to be sorry about, you're just trying to help. My head's still disoriented from the Xanax, and when I saw you going through Sylvia's desk, all I could think was you had something to do with her death or—" His eyes squeezed shut and his hand rubbed his forehead.

I pulled Sylvia's office chair over to him so he could sit down. "No, of course. I'm so sorry to give you another shock. And I'm sorry that I saw—um—"

He slid into the chair, looking infinitely tired, and tossed the papers on the desk. "Don't be sorry. It was only a matter of time before it came out anyway."

I tapped my index fingernail against my thigh. "How did this happen? How can the money all be gone?"

He rubbed his face, and spoke through his fingers. "How do things like this ever happen?"

I understood his need to avoid eye contact—the only thing that could possibly make me more uncomfortable than asking about what I'd seen on those papers was asking about their sex life—and that might still be preferable. "A couple of those loans are recent. Do you think they have something to do with the business she was upset about yesterday?"

One hand flicked toward the stack of papers. "It's very possible. I knew some of the business ventures weren't going well, but setbacks are part and parcel. She always says you have to play the long game, and that money can smell fear." His voice choked. "Said."

"And because you trusted her, you just signed the papers," I said.

He looked confused. "I didn't have to sign anything. She didn't need *me* to get loans. My financial acumen and backing was about as useful as a rooster for laying eggs."

Right, of course. I'd learned all about this when I got my loans for Killer Crimes, before my divorce was legally in progress. Unless a loan was secured by co-owned marital collateral, your spouse didn't have to sign off on it; because my small business loan very purposefully hadn't been secured by my house, Todd didn't have to be involved.

I finished my thoughts aloud. "I'm guessing only Sylvia's name is on the house?"

He nodded. "Her parents left it to her, not to us. But I would have signed them if she needed me to, because yes, I trusted her decisions completely."

My hat was off to Philip—no way would I ever hand off that sort of control to my spouse. But then, I guess when you marry the sort of money that gifts your wife a twenty-million-dollar house, you probably figure there's plenty of safety net to keep you afloat. "Does Todd know about it all? I can see her not wanting to tell *me*, but . . ."

"Oh, God—Todd! And Morgan!" He jumped up and pulled his phone out of his pocket. "They need to be told. They—"

I hurried to reassure him. "I called them earlier. Todd's driving home from LA as we speak. Morgan must be in class because she hasn't called me back yet, but I'll tell her as soon as I can."

"Thank God he's on his way." He looked back to me. "You asked me a question. What was it?"

"Did Todd know about all the debt?"

"I doubt it. She couldn't bear letting him think she didn't have everything under control." He dropped back into the chair. "But I still don't understand. How can this be related to someone randomly attacking her in the park?"

My throat tightened. "She came home upset about business, then went off for a walk without telling you. That feels like a pretty big coincidence. I think we need to know exactly what she was dealing with, and why."

He nodded, his eyes darting back and forth across the floor. "I suppose we have to at least consider the possibility. I'll tell the police."

My teeth raked across my bottom lip. "Right, we need to tell them. But I think we need to know for ourselves what was happening, too. I'd like to finish going through her papers."

His brow furrowed. "Isn't that interfering with a police investigation?"

"Only if you alter or destroy any of it, which I'm not going to do. I'll take pictures of it all, keep it exactly as it is, then we can examine it more closely later."

He shook his head and stood. "I don't think that's a good idea. They're the professionals."

"Right, but here's the thing." I met his eyes and held them. "Because of Sylvia's call about Morgan's tuition, and because of our relationship to Overkill Bill, they think either Morgan or I had something to do with this. We need to know what's really happening."

His face went slack. "They think Morgan did this?"

I nodded fiercely. "They took her contact information and told me we're both persons of interest."

He glanced from my desperate face to the desk, and resignation settled over his face. "As long as we make sure not one page is out of order when they get here. And I'll help."

I'd like to believe he wanted to help for time's sake, but more likely he just wanted to make sure I didn't pull any shenanigans. Which I had no intention of doing, so that was fine by me. "Let's get to it."

Then the doorbell rang, nearly giving us both a heart attack.

• • •

We hurried to the front door. When Philip opened it, a tall white woman who struck a vague chord in the back of my memory waited on the portico. As I struggled to place her, she tilted her asymmetrical curtain of silver hair at me and raked me head to toe with her nearly black eyes. She was a member of their social circle to be certain—if the perfectly laid look of everything from her gold-rimmed sunglasses to the belted, oversized blue tunic dress hadn't clued me in, the large Birkin bag hanging from her elbow would have clinched it.

"Nancy." Philip's voice and face were both confused. "I'm—not sure—"

My brain mentally face-palmed itself. Nancy was one of Sylvia's two closest friends. She'd given me a set of engraved lobster crackers for a wedding present I'd stowed lovingly in the back corner of my attic.

She breezed past Philip. "Is Sylvia in her office?"

My heart contracted as Philip struggled to keep his face from crumpling. There wasn't any way to avoid it, so I stepped toward her and cleared my throat. "Sylvia passed away this morning."

Nancy's hand flew to her throat as she turned back toward us. "She—what? What happened?"

"We're not fully sure yet." I reached one hand gently toward her and the other back to the door.

She glanced at my hand. "But we had an appointment. I canceled another meeting for it last minute."

I gaped at her. While it certainly tracked that one of Sylvia's friends would be that self-involved, more likely the implications of Sylvia's passing were having a hard time penetrating her shock. And once I worked that out, the significance of what *she'd* said penetrated *my* shock.

"You had a last-minute meeting with her?" I asked. "Why?"

"She didn't say." She gave me another up-and-down. "You're her *ex*-daughter-in-law, isn't that right? Elba or Ischia?"

"Capri."

"One of those islands." She waved her hand at me.

Like I hadn't long since become inured to every "Capri" jab known to mankind, be it island-, pants-, or Ford-related. "You canceled plans without knowing why?"

She lifted her chin at me. "I'm not sure what business it is of yours?"

Philip interjected, his voice tight with emotion. "Someone killed

Sylvia, and we're trying to figure out what happened. Her plans for today may be important."

Her expression softened. "I see. Of course. I only know she called me last night and said she urgently needed my help with something, but wouldn't say what."

"What time did she call you?" I asked.

With a glance that suggested I belonged in a mental facility, she pulled out her phone and scrolled through her call log. "Five fifty-five."

So just before Sylvia got home and canceled dinner with Philip. She must have made the call on the way home from the airport.

"And you have no idea why?" Philip asked.

"She said she didn't want to talk about it over the phone." She held up one hand. "But you know Sylvia, she has a penchant for drama."

The clang of pots calling kettles black was nearly deafening, but didn't drown out a note of something that didn't sit right. I watched her closely and said, "You're a good friend to drop everything for her like that without even knowing why."

Her eyes flashed ever so quickly away and back. "Well. Of course we do what we can for our friends." She turned toward Philip and drew her brows together. "But Philip, you must be distraught. What can I do? Just say the word."

Philip's brow knit. "Did the two of you have some sort of joint business venture, anything like that?"

She shook her head like she was in pain. "No, nothing. I've been wracking my brain since she called. I haven't seen her much lately, I've been so busy with the board of Luminous Face."

Several pieces of information coalesced in my brain. Luminous Face was a fancy cosmetics corporation, and if I wasn't mistaken, it was owned by The Beautiful Life Home Products, the company I'd just seen in Sylvia's portfolio. Also, at Morgan's family birthday dinner a few months back, Sylvia had mentioned a friend who'd become part of the board. She'd said more, but I'd tuned her out since I had no frame of reference for the Lifestyles of the Rich and Board-Appointed. Even so, I could've sworn I remembered tinges of envy in her voice. "Could she have wanted to talk with you about that?"

Her expression turned vacant. "I can't see why. She's not on the board."

My jaw snapped shut as I tried to figure out how to explain it to her, but before I could, Nancy stepped toward Philip and put a hand on his arm. "I'm just so sorry. Are you sure there's nothing I can do?"

His voice came out choked. "No. Thank you."

She dropped her hand and nodded. "Well, in that case, I'll get out of your hair. Don't hesitate to call if you need anything." She crossed toward the door and hurried down the front stairs without waiting for a response.

Philip swung the door closed and looked at me. "That seemed strange. Did that seem strange?"

I wasn't sure what aspect of the strange he was referring to—the clandestine meeting Nancy dropped everything for without explanation, or the speed at which Nancy escaped the house once we started asking her about it all. But it really didn't matter. "Yes. That seemed strange."

He dug his palms into his eyes and shook his head. "I can't—I need to do something. We need answers. You said we need to photograph those documents before we turn them over to the police?"

I nodded and started back toward the stairs. Of all the ways to deal with this shock, a call to action was probably the best for him—it would keep him busy and focused. "And they'll be here any minute. They said to call when you were awake again, so if they don't hear from me soon they'll just show back up. They can't do much until they talk to you." That popped a memory back in my head. "Oh, they asked me if Sylvia knew Katherine Harper. I told them I couldn't imagine her canoodling with tech money."

He strode beside me. "Katherine Harper? Why?"

I winced and swore silently at myself—he didn't know that part yet. "Right, sorry." I tried to keep my voice gentle. "They found Katherine Harper dead at the Legion three nights ago, killed the same way Sylvia was."

He stopped abruptly and grasped my arm. "But Sylvia *did* know Katherine Harper."

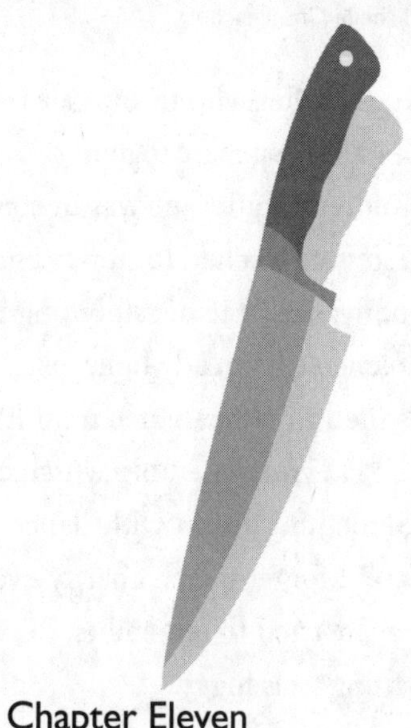

Chapter Eleven

My head jerked around at Philip's unexpected revelation. "Sylvia and Katherine Harper were friends?"

His brow knit. "I wouldn't call them *friends*. She's never been a guest in our house. But Katherine Harper was doing some charity work for one of the organizations Sylvia supports. She was killed the same way?"

"Yes." I nodded as I tried to reorient myself. "So they knew each other but didn't get along?"

"Oh, I don't mean *that*. Just that the Harpers are still finding their way in society." He reached for his phone.

I almost laughed at the euphemism—such a lovely way of putting something so ugly. "Finding their way in society" meant climbing an insurmountable wall of presuppositions and prejudices to change minds more rigid than a frozen woolly mammoth.

"But Katherine made it onto the edges of Sylvia's society radar." I glanced at his face for confirmation I'd read the situation correctly.

"Yes. She's working hard to break in via charity circles. You know the kind of thing." He tapped and scrolled.

I did. Ladies who throw galas over lunch. "So they were working on something specific together?"

"God, no. Katherine was in charge of it but didn't know what she was doing. Sylvia had to step in and clean up several messes, much to her annoyance." He began typing into the phone. "I have to send my condolences. It already looks like I've been neglectful."

I stifled my impatience until he finished and set the phone back down. "Do you remember which charity?"

"Something to do with dance scholarships, I think? Or abused women? I forget which charity event is which." He rubbed his forehead as he tried to remember. "I can't seem to get my mind to work, everything feels foggy."

Brandy and Xanax will do that to a person. I gently reached for his arm. "You should probably lie back down."

He shook his head, and tears pooled in his eyes again. "No, I need to keep myself busy or I'll think too much. We need to photograph the—" His phone dinged a notification. "An out-of-office reply from Steve Harper. It says he'll be slow to respond to email while he attends to the death of his wife, and it gives a list of services. Rosary, funeral, celebration of life."

An idea pricked at my brain. "Can you forward that to me?"

His brow creased, but he tapped at the phone. "There. Why?"

I grabbed my own phone and pulled up the email. "The celebration of life is later tonight." I glanced at Philip's pale face. "If you like, I can go and represent the family. Express our condolences."

He reached over to squeeze my hand. "That would be a great help. Would you mind? I'm not sure I can face it."

"Not at all. It's the right thing to do. And we should talk to him, since the same thing that happened to Sylvia happened to Katherine." I glanced up toward Sylvia's office. "But we need to take pics of those docs so we can call the police as soon as possible."

He followed me up and we began the mind-numbing task. We quickly slipped into a pattern—I snapped, he flipped to the back, I snapped again, he moved to the next page. As the automation threatened to drive me insane, I consoled myself with the hope that Steve Harper could tell me something more about how Katherine and Sylvia knew each other and that something in these documents would clue me in to why that acquaintance had been a threat to Overkill Bill's copycatter.

My phone rang, startling me out of my thoughts. I saw Morgan's name and picked up immediately.

"Oh, God, Mom, is it true?" she asked. "Is Grandma dead?"

I stammered, taken aback by her response. "What—how do you know about that?"

"Dad left a message while I was in class. Is it true?"

I gritted my teeth—sometimes my ex-husband's sensitivity could evade an electron microscope. "What exactly did he say?"

Her voice quivered, and I could picture the tears puffing up her eyes. "Just that he was on his way home to take care of Grandma Sylvia's funeral arrangements."

My annoyance at him faded. He must have assumed she already knew, and just wanted to comfort her. "I'm so sorry, honey. Yes, it's true."

"Oh, God." I heard a choking sound, and a sob. "What happened?"

I closed my eyes and gathered my courage—there was no point in sugarcoating what would be splashed over the news by day's end. "We don't know yet. She was attacked in the Presidio last night." I summarized the facts as concisely and gently as I could.

She was silent for a long moment. "Poor Grandma," she finally said. "And Grandpa, he must be devastated. Is he—"

I glanced up to find his eyes squeezed shut as he listened to my side of the conversation. I cleared my throat and chose my words carefully. "About how you'd expect."

"I'm on my way over." Her voice steadied with resolve. "I'll stay with Grandpa tonight. He shouldn't be alone."

I hurried to object. "I was planning on doing that. You're not going to be in any fit state yourself. And don't you have classes tomorrow?"

"I'm upset, yes, but I'd honestly rather be with him than anyplace else right now. And I only have Monday-Wednesday-Friday classes this semester so I can work on my research. But I know for a fact *you* have work tomorrow."

I grimaced—I hadn't thought that far ahead. Because Mondays were my day off, Tuesdays tended to be my busiest. I had a morning in-person tour, a virtual tour in the afternoon, and another in-person in the evening. I could cancel them, but we desperately needed the money. "You're right, I do. But are you sure?"

"I am. Please just let me be there for Grandpa."

I stared up at a picture of her on Sylvia's wall. Decked out in her black college graduation cap and gown, long brown waves set off by her red honor stole, hugging Sylvia on one side and Philip on the other. "Of course, honey. I'll see you when you get here. I'm so, so sorry this happened."

I heard her stifle a sob. "I know you are, Mom. I love you."

I swiped at my tears as I ended the call. Philip was openly relieved to hear she was coming, which reassured me. We hurried through the remaining documents, then I called Detective Petito to let him know Philip was available to talk with them.

As I hung up the call, I checked the time. "Katherine Harper's celebration of life started a few minutes ago. Will you be okay if I run over there?"

He waved me off. "Go reach out to Steve Harper. He has to be as devastated by this as we are, and hopefully he can shed some light."

• • •

As I made my way to Simms Brothers Mortuary, I tried to convince myself that using a memorial service—even one referred to as a "celebration of life"—to interrogate Katherine's husband didn't make me an irretrievably garbage person. He was just as invested in finding out who'd killed Katherine as I was, I told myself, and what I was trying to do was of benefit to us both. And it wasn't my fault if he was such a VIP that this was the only way I'd ever get anywhere close to him.

Overlying my guilt was my struggle with the concept of a "celebration of life." Everyone grieved differently, I got that. And it made complete sense why you'd want to focus on the positive rather than the negative. But I personally had never been able to find a space in my brain where "death" and "celebrate" could coexist, at least not in the short term. Months after losing someone, maybe. But within days? My own emotional system wasn't wired to make that shift quite so quickly.

As my GPS guided me, a large, domed, neo-neoclassical structure loomed up in front of me. I recognized the structure—I'd always assumed it was some sort of government building, fully private due to the ornate wrought-iron fence and gate that surrounded the large parcel of land. There were no signs suggesting what it contained, but when I pulled up to the gate, I found a discreet speaker mounted on a post. A male voice came over the line, clear and static-free as if the man were standing next to me.

"How may I assist you?" the disembodied voice asked.

Clinging to the hope I was in the right place I replied, "I'm here for Katherine Harper's service."

"Your name?"

"Capri Sanzio. Daughter-in-law of Sylvia and Philip Clement."

There was a brief pause as he checked whatever list or Magic 8 Ball he used to establish who got in and who didn't. Then, with a gentle click and whir, the gate opened. "My condolences for your loss, Ms. Clement."

I didn't bother to correct him, just pulled in and scanned the large circular drive for a parking spot, then wedged myself between a pair of black Lincoln MKTs. Then, staring up at the gilded dome as I approached, I braced myself, preparing to pretend I belonged—a skill I'd never quite perfected during my years of marriage to Todd.

With my nonchalance pinned firmly to my face, I took in the interior. It resembled pictures I'd seen of ornate ancient Roman villas, complete with mosaic floors, columns lining walls, medallion-shaped moldings, and scrollwork. Chairs intermittently dotted the circumference of the space, although few people were sitting. About two hundred people stood chatting in groups as waitpeople passed around champagne and canapés.

"Madam?"

I jumped—I hadn't noticed the waiter glide up next to me. I grabbed the flute closest to me; no way I was going to drink and drive, but walking around empty-handed would only call attention to myself. I thanked him, then returned to surveying my surroundings. I recognized Steve Harper from his omnipresent media coverage, standing next to a tasteful printed canvas of a woman, hopefully Katherine, set on a sleek easel. I'd always found his appearance to be strangely contradictory. His graying brown hair and the deep lines across his forehead signaled someone in his fifties, but his crumpled clothes, unflattering glasses, and semi-hunched posture made him look like a high-school AV team member who didn't realize he'd aged out. As I made my way toward him, I spotted Nancy standing off against one curved wall with her husband Robert. Another couple stood chatting with them; I knew the other woman, a petite blonde with large blue eyes—Beth something, another of Sylvia's close friends. As I searched my memory for Beth's last name, Nancy spotted me back. She said something to Beth, who turned to stare at me. I nodded my acknowledgment and quickly continued on.

Why hadn't Nancy mentioned Katherine Harper's death during her visit earlier? Surely the coincidence, even though she didn't know how Sylvia died, would have been too much not to mention?

As I waited for the person currently talking to Steve Harper to finish, I signed the oversized journal next to the easel, then flipped through the other messages of sympathy penned within. I recognized many of the names but, despite my long-shot hopes, didn't find any incriminating admissions.

When Harper's conversation ended, I sidled up and extended my hand. "Hello, I'm Sylvia and Philip Clement's daughter-in-law. We're so sorry for your loss."

His eyes zeroed in on mine, and after shaking my hand, his own shot up to scratch his beard. "And I'm sorry for yours. I'm touched you were able to come, given the situation."

News sure traveled fast—I resisted the urge to glance back over my shoulder at Nancy. Then again, maybe Petito's team had already contacted him about it all. Either way, it made things easier.

"I was actually hoping to talk to you about the situation," I said.

His brow creased. "What situation?"

Not the police, then.

I lowered my voice to what I hoped was a diplomatically gentle tone. "The detective who brought us the news told us Sylvia and Katherine died the same way."

His face went blank; he gently took my arm and guided me several feet away from Canvas Katherine and the nearest guests. With a glance around, he stepped closer to me. "Tell me."

His eyes continued to monitor the guests as I quickly explained. "I'm trying to piece together how something so strange could have happened to two friends."

His eyes snapped back to mine. "Sylvia considered Katherine a friend?"

Well, that confirmed what Philip said, at least. "I don't really know, I never spoke to Sylvia specifically about her. I just assumed."

His face went blank again. "Ah. I see. Of course."

I hurried to clarify and, if I'm honest, to ease my discomfort. "That doesn't mean anything, though. She didn't talk to me much about any of her friends. I'm her ex-daughter-in-law, actually."

"*Ex*-daughter-in-law." He gestured to a waiter, and as he downed half a glass of champagne, appraised me again with something new in his eyes. "So you understand, then. It's never easy being the new kid on the playground."

"It really isn't." I peered around. "But you seem to be managing well. Definite crossover here from the jungle gym."

He followed my gaze to Nancy and Beth, then gave a tight smile. "Ah. Well. People who need my software or expertise have reason to be *cordial*. But that's entirely different from being *welcoming*." He turned back to me. "Why haven't the police told me about this, if they think the same person killed them both?"

"I don't think they've had time. They only found Sylvia a few hours ago." I cleared my throat and forced myself to continue on. "I know Katherine was working on a charity luncheon, but Philip says Sylvia was only incidentally involved. Were they connected in some other way? Something else they were working on, anything like that?"

His brows pursed. "The police made it all sound like a random attack, maybe the work of some copycat serial killer. So why would it matter if she and Sylvia knew each other?"

Shit, shit, shit.

Under the best of circumstances there'd be no diplomatic way to mention my grandfather was the purported originator of the method that took Katherine's and Sylvia's lives. Under the current circumstances, it would open up a can of worms I really didn't need tying knots around my ankles.

I cleared my throat. "It's just that it seems strange the only two victims knew each other in a city this size."

He gave a slow head shake. "I'm not aware of any connection. In fact, Katherine hoped they'd become friends during her time organizing this luncheon, because she'd been trying to establish a connection. I can have my assistant double-check her calendar if that will help." He pulled out his phone and tapped on it. "I'll have her contact you. What's your information?"

"I'd appreciate that." I pulled one of my business cards out of my purse, along with a pen, and jotted my personal email address and cell number on the back. "She can reach me here."

He tapped my number into his phone, slipped the card into his pocket, then retrieved me one of his own. "Thank you." I cleared my throat again. "I—I know this is hard to think about right now, but—do you know of anybody who would have wanted to hurt Katherine?"

His eyes darted back and forth as he considered. "Nobody. When you achieve any level of success you make enemies, but those would be directed at me, not her."

"Maybe someone who was jealous over her being put in charge of the luncheon? Anything like that, even if it seemed silly at the time?"

His eyes flashed, suddenly replacing the awkward AV nerd with the powerful mogul. "She was put in charge of the luncheon by default. It wasn't *prestigious* enough for anybody else's time. But she wanted to prove herself, so she didn't care if it was the bottom of the barrel." His eyes narrowed slightly. "You said you were Sylvia's *ex*-daughter-in-law. Didn't you divorce some time ago?"

"Ten years ago," I said.

"Yet you're the one here representing the family?"

Someone moved behind me, and Steve's head popped up to see

who it was. A gray-haired Indian man reached his hand past me and laid it on Steve's shoulder. "How are you holding up?"

Figuring now was an excellent opportunity to stop monopolizing Steve's time, I stepped back out of the man's way. "Thank you for talking with me," I said. "I'm so sorry for your loss."

He opened his mouth to stop me, but the newcomer launched into a string of questions. I turned and hurried away, hoping to ask Nancy and Beth a few questions about Sylvia and Katherine on my way out. They were no longer standing where they had been, so I glanced around to see if I could find them. I couldn't.

But when I looked back, I *did* see Steve watching me over the shoulder of his new conversation partner, with eyes hardened to steel.

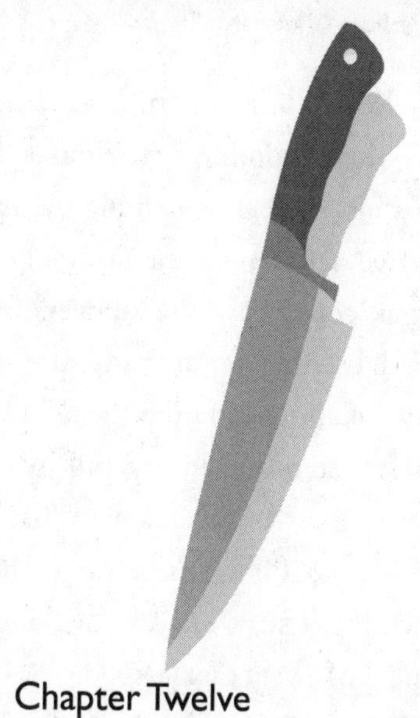

Chapter Twelve

I drove back from the memorial service more confused than ever. Katherine Harper had known Sylvia only in the most tangential of ways, and Katherine's own husband didn't think it was plausible that someone who'd known her and Sylvia had killed them. Was I wrong thinking the murderer had known them personally? Was their selection as victims really just coincidence? After all, there couldn't be all that many women walking around San Francisco parks after dark, especially if this serial killer was looking for older, affluent women. Maybe this truly was just a case of being in the wrong place at the wrong time.

The true-crime portion of my brain was skeptical, but the rest of my brain reminded me that whether *I* believed it or not, I couldn't count on *Petito* believing it. It was up to me to keep Morgan and myself safe, and to do that I had to assume something else was at play here. At the very least I needed to look carefully through Sylvia's documents for anything that obviously overlapped with the Harpers.

By the time I got back to The Chateau, the police had come and gone. With Philip's permission, they'd emptied the contents of her desk—thank goodness we'd taken pictures of everything. I encouraged Philip to eat something by making him a dinner of salad, basmati rice, and lemon-dill salmon; he barely touched it, but I figured Morgan could have the leftovers if she had any appetite. When she arrived, I settled her in, made sure she was okay, then headed back out to my own house to prep the following day's tours.

Heather returned my call just as I was unlocking my internal garage door. "Are you okay? What happened?"

"I'm fine. Philip and Morgan, not so much." As I updated her on everything, I strode across the kitchen to the refrigerator and pulled out a jar of sweet pickles.

"Nancy McQuaid, I remember her." Heather drew out the vowels. "She cornered me at your in-laws' Christmas Eve party back in the day and wanted me to get her son an animation job. When I told her we weren't hiring, she gave me a look like I was simple and said she was 'sure I could find something.'"

"I'm not at all surprised." I popped the seal on the jar. "In her world, opportunities appear as if by magic."

"Please tell me you aren't doing that disgusting pickle deal you do when you're stressed."

I stuffed a gherkin in my mouth and crunched purposefully—we'd had this conversation at least once a year since our college days. "What's wrong with eating pickles?"

"Blech. Those are *garnish* pickles, they aren't *eating* pickles. At best, they're *put-inside-potato-salad* pickles. Just imagining all that sugar gives me the heebie jeebies." She gave a fake verbal shudder.

Grateful to her for making me smile, I pushed the jar away for the moment and finished catching her up. "If any brilliant ideas or insights come to you, please let me know."

"I will. Keep me updated. I'm going to call Morgan and let her know I'm here if she needs me. I'll check in on you later."

• • •

I grabbed my jar of pickles and headed into my office to get to work on the next day's tours. Not surprisingly, I found it hard to focus, even with the extra sugar flooding my system—my mind kept wanting to return to Sylvia's documents. I forced myself to keep my head down, do the necessary paperwork, then review my itineraries. But the instant I finished, I switched greedily to the cloud folder where all my pictures automatically backed up.

You'd think going through someone's private papers would be compelling reading, a deliciously forbidden glimpse into their deep, dark secrets. But the reality alternated between distressingly embarrassing, like Sylvia's and Philip's medical records, and tragically mind-numbing, like the paperwork for Sylvia's business concerns. Philip wasn't kidding when he said he couldn't keep up with her investments—there were dozens over the years, from spas to restaurants to office-supply companies. Some of them had performed well, but she'd sold her interest in almost all of those to cover the losses from other investments. For years everything seemed to balance out, but over the last decade, the tide had turned against her. She invested more, lost more, borrowed money, and invested still more. The pattern reminded me of a gambler who blows the month's mortgage payment and desperately tries to win it back, only to lose the whole house. Which, I realized, was the literal truth here—investments were a gamble, and Sylvia had swirled down that hole to hit rock bottom.

As I reached current day, I found three companies she was currently invested in. The first was a dance company, Prima Pointe Dance Conservatory, that had branches throughout California and the rest of the Pacific Northwest. The next, My Kind of People, was some sort of online dating app. The final, Rithmology, was a start-up that had something to do with algorithms that made other apps more effective.

I took a moment to reflect on the bizarre trilogy. The dance company seemed right up Sylvia's alley—posh, sophisticated, cultured—and she'd been funding it for nearly twenty years, so I mentally set that one aside. The other two were newer acquisitions she'd made within the last two years. I wasn't sure exactly what Rithmology did, but online dating? That completely floored me. Sylvia had been actively horrified by the concept. And, honestly, it was odd to me that she would have invested in anything tech-related at all. Maybe that was just a sign of the times, but it still struck me as deeply discordant with what I knew about her priorities.

I shook my head and switched gears—maybe it was just a question of context. Hopefully when I googled Katherine Harper some connection to a mobbed-up online-dating-czar-cum-app-designer would leap out at me like a meth-addled frog.

Armed with a woefully caffeine-free mug of chamomile tea, I dug in. Katherine Harper, née Laurent, came from a working-class family and met Steve when she hired on as an administrative assistant for his company back before it shot to stratospheric success. For the first twenty-odd years of her married life, I couldn't find much that mentioned her specifically, but the last few years indicated a plunge into charitable works. The events were on the smaller side, at least based on the charity work I'd seen people like Sylvia and Nancy do, and had no central unifying theme. That fit with what both Philip and Steve had told me—Katherine was trying to pry her way into a new social circle, and was doing whatever she needed to in order to make that happen.

I flipped back and forth between my notes on Katherine and the ones I'd taken while going through Sylvia's papers. If I was looking for a crossover between the two of them, the elephant in the room was that two of Sylvia's current investments had to do with tech, specifically apps, and Steve Harper was a software king. Weren't apps just software? My understanding was Steve designed big, corporate-type software, like operating systems that ran devices. Maybe those operating systems played an important role in the development of Sylvia's app companies? Maybe Sylvia's investment companies were even under Steve Harper's umbrella—that would mean Sylvia and Steve shared a business concern he hadn't seen fit to mention to me, and that would be a definite link between her and Katherine.

I did some googling, but couldn't find any easy answers about whether My Kind of People and Rithmology were related to HarperWare. I jotted a note to myself—I was going to have to do a deep dive into California business records to see if I could find anything more. Probably lots and lots of records.

I moved on, throwing Nancy's name into the search engine. Nancy McQuaid, née Malger, came from an old San Francisco family. She'd been one of San Francisco's few debutantes in 1975, an impressive feat to people who cared about those things. Sylvia had wanted to put Morgan up for deb consideration when she was a senior in high school; while I was personally horrified that debutante balls were still a thing, I told Morgan it was up to her. Much to my bursting pride, she railed against the notion of dangling women as marriage prospects based on their family's money, their "respectability," and a smattering of other criteria that made me weep for humanity.

I confirmed that Nancy had recently ascended to the board for Luminous Face, and found she consulted on the boards of several charities. I took a moment to verify that yes, the parent company that owned Luminous Face was The Beautiful Life Home Products, the same one I'd seen in Sylvia's portfolio. That made the second connection between Sylvia's investments and her circle. And Nancy's husband, Robert McQuaid, was a high-powered financial-genius financier who advised a slew of companies' investments. Since their circle was so incestuous, it was highly likely Sylvia had consulted Robert about her investments.

I stopped for a moment to connect the dots. Sylvia and Nancy shared common business concerns due to the The Beautiful Life Home Products connection. Sylvia had invested in tech companies, and Steve Harper was the king of tech. Steve had also indicated to me when we spoke at the memorial service that the McQuaids needed his expertise for some reason. Add to that the fact that Robert McQuaid's expertise was in financial investing, an area currently causing Sylvia significant problems, and the sides of a cryptic triangle began to creep together.

I needed to know who exactly owned all the companies involved. But the records offices wouldn't be open until morning, so I wouldn't be able to pull any documents until then.

Something about that thought tugged at the back of my mind. What?

I squeezed my eyes shut and tried to figure out what was bothering me, but I couldn't put my finger on it. Something about Sylvia's documents? The tugging intensified, indicating I was on the right track, but the answer still wouldn't come. After a long moment I gave up, shaking my head in frustration. When my brain screeched to a halt, trying to force it to engage was like wrestling a greased pig. My only option was to set it aside for a while and think about something else. The best thing to do was sleep on it, except the events of the day still had me wired.

My eyes slipped to the Overkill Bill files I'd dug out earlier that day. I kept coming back to the only thing that was completely clear—Katherine and Sylvia's killer had used Overkill Bill's methodology. Whether Katherine and Sylvia had been chosen by the killer for personal reasons or were coincidental random victims, there was a reason why the killer was copycatting Overkill Bill. And that meant there was a clue in the past that would help me understand what was happening in the present.

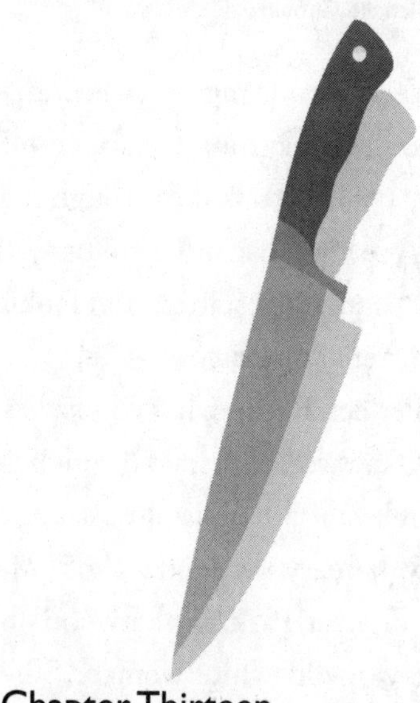

Chapter Thirteen

After refreshing my chamomile tea, I decided the best approach would be to go through my files as if I'd never heard of the case before, organizing facts as I went. I cleared off the whiteboard that hung above my mahogany chest of filing cabinets and set up a time line and space for all the victims' details. Then I grabbed the first envelope and slid out the stack of yellowed printouts, notes, and copies of articles I'd pulled from microfiche—a method of research that felt strangely archaic now—and jotted notes as I read from the stacks covering the desk.

A text buzzed through on my phone from Heather: You up?

Isn't that how the kids these days text for booty calls? I texted back. Are you trying to make Rose jealous?

The phone rang; I connected and put it on speakerphone.

"Rose is out of town this week, remember? So I'm lying here worried about you because I know you're not asleep with everything going on."

"You know me too well. I just started going through all my notes about Overkill Bill."

"Yeeesssss. Hang on a second." I heard taps and shifts, then the TV in the background snapped off. "Right. I have my wine and my comfy blanket. Talk me through it."

It wasn't a bad idea, actually; having a sounding board would help. "I only just started. I'm looking for some clue that's relevant to the current copycats."

"Perfect. Recap what you have so far and we'll go from there."

"Okay, well." I rustled through the sheets I'd examined so far. "The first relevant article is almost a throwaway. On the morning of Saturday, January sixteenth, 1965, Marielle DeShayne was found dead near Pioneer Park, in the woods by Coit Tower. She was a twenty-three-year-old white woman. Sometime between the late hours of Friday and the early hours of Saturday, she'd been first smashed over the head, then stabbed in the chest, then had her throat sliced post-mortem. The murder weapons were never discovered, a detail that's always bothered me."

"Maybe he took them away because they could help identify him?"

"Maybe, but without DNA testing back then, you wouldn't think so. Anyway, the rest of Marielle's coverage is sparse, too. I think that's because the police decided since she was a prostitute, she was most likely killed by a pimp or a john, especially because it happened in Pioneer Park." Pioneer Park was close to North Beach, San Francisco's unofficial red-light district.

"And that's okay?" Her voice rose with righteous indignation.

"Hey, I'm just the messenger." I held up both hands even though she couldn't see them. "That's how things were. And it may be why they didn't hold back how she was murdered. They wouldn't have thought it was a serial killer at that point."

"Did they even use the term 'serial killer' back then?"

"Not until the seventies."

"See how much I've learned from you?" she crooned.

I rolled my eyes and flipped through my notes. "The next relevant coverage came on May fifteenth, 1965. Denise Jefferson, also a twenty-three-year-old prostitute but this time Black and average height. Found dead in Golden Gate Park, in a wooded area near Hippie Hill. At first nobody connected her death to Marielle DeShayne's, but the next day some eagle-eyed reporter or inspector noticed the similarities, and speculation exploded from there. Lots of interest in why the killer desecrated the victims and whether it meant a madman was on the loose."

"Safe assumption." Heather's leather couch squeaked in the background as she shifted position.

"Agreed. Within days someone adopted the moniker 'the Overkiller.' But just about the only useful thing they report is that Marielle and Denise both worked in the same section of North Beach. No reliable leads were found, at least according to the press."

"And that was just that?" Heather asked.

"More or less, until the final murder, which took place late on Friday, August twentieth." I paused to jot the information on the whiteboard for easy visual parsing. "At nine twenty that evening, Sally Reyes, a petite, thirty-year-old Latina, was found dead at the far end of Golden Gate Park, in a copse of trees bordering Spreckels Lake. This time they got lucky with determining time of death. A young couple had been making out near the lake and left just after nine. They realized the woman left her scarf behind and went back to retrieve it. Instead they found Sally Reyes, who most definitely hadn't been there half an hour earlier."

"Let me guess. Sally was also a North Beach prostitute, and was bashed, stabbed, and slashed."

"You're on fire." I skimmed as quickly as I could without losing detail. "And the more precise time of death helped the police find a witness. Vera Schmidt, also a prostitute, saw Sally with a man around eight thirty, less than an hour before she was found dead. It was dark, but she got a good look at the man because they turned toward a streetlight. About six foot and lean, with black hair and blue eyes. The police put out a composite sketch. Here, I'll send it to you." I snapped a shot of the composite and texted it to her, then did the same with the picture they ran of my grandfather.

"I hate to break this to you, but . . ." she said once she received it.

"It looks an awful lot like him? Yeah, I know. Except for one thing. The large diamond-shaped birthmark on my grandfather's forehead isn't in the composite."

"Did she maybe not see that side of his face?" Heather asked.

"If she didn't see that side of his face, she only saw his profile, and that's not a very good basis for a front-view composite," I said.

"That's for darn sure. I can't count how many times I've seen someone I thought was a hottie from the side, then wanted to run when they turned to face me." Heather let out a low whistle.

I rubbed the bridge of my nose, but didn't allow myself to get pulled in. "So, you get it. Regardless, they arrested my grandfather that Sunday morning, August twenty-second, on the basis of eyewitness testimony. That's when they shifted from 'the Overkiller' to 'Overkill Bill.'"

"And you're sure she didn't see or say something else that pinpointed your grandfather?" she asked.

I slouched back into my padded red leather office chair. "No, I'm not. That's why I need the police files."

"Gotcha."

"So the relevant question becomes, can any of this shed light on the current copycat kills? How much do you know about copycats?"

"Not much. Enlighten me."

I took a fortifying gulp of my tea. "Okay, well. Very few copycats imitate the original killings exactly, usually only one or two aspects of the murders, whatever is personally meaningful to them in some way. So the aspects this killer copied should give us insight."

"With you."

I stared down at my notes, but my brain balked as it tried to fit the two sets of murders together, like it was trying to parallel park into a too-tight spot. "I can't get a good handle on it. First off, Katherine Harper was a fifty-year-old socialite, a far cry from twenty-something prostitutes, and seventy-year-old Sylvia is even worse."

"And, the original victims were picked up in North Beach then taken somewhere else, right? But Katherine and Sylvia were already at their respective parks?"

"Good catch. The current killer waited for them. So what do those differences tell us?"

We thought in mutual silence for a minute, until I spoke. "The psychology of the original murders suggests Overkill Bill has some sort of hatred for prostitutes. So if we translate that to the current kills, it would suggest our copycat has some sort of issue with socialites."

"I bet a lot of people do," Heather said. "And that would make sense why he had to wait for them. It's easy to pick up prostitutes, that's sort of their deal. But middle-aged socialites aren't just going to hop in a car with you."

"Very true," I said. "The other similarity is the method, using three types of attack rather than just one. It definitely counts as overkill—"

"Hence the nickname," Heather interjected.

"—and overkill usually indicates some sort of deep emotion, usually rage. So that indicates someone has deep anger at socialites, or at Katherine and Sylvia in particular."

"That makes sense if this is about business or money shenanigans," Heather said.

I pushed aside my notes in frustration. "Speculation is all well and good, but I need the police files. Who knows what information is in there that wasn't released to the press? Without it, I'm shooting in the dark."

Heather sighed. "I hear you. But we've made a really good start. Since what you need to focus on now is putting your daughter through graduate school, I say pause, put what you have into an Overkill Bill podcast episode, and go to bed."

We hung up, and I followed her advice. After jotting down an outline, I pulled out the audio setup I used for my online tours, took a deep breath, and hit record. The four-decade-long-repressed need to talk about my grandfather must have been weightier than I'd realized, because everything came pouring out effortlessly, and before I knew it, I had a half-hour episode. I sent it off to Ryan with a plea for his help with the editing, then took myself to bed, hoping that my subconscious would coalesce everything as I slept.

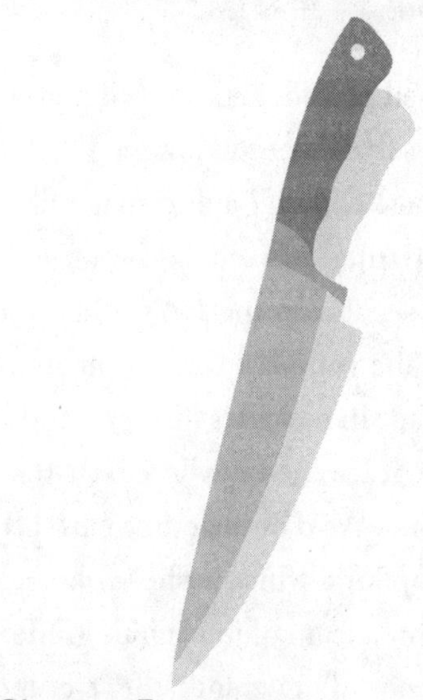

Chapter Fourteen

My subconscious most definitely did some coalescing as I slept, deluging me with dreams that sliced and diced the two sets of murders into frightening Frankensteins. In one of them, Sylvia decided to run a bordello hidden deep in the Presidio to keep from losing The Chateau. In the other, two of the Overkill Bill victims, Sally Reyes and Denise Jefferson, had to plan a charity gala, but couldn't move forward with the plans without Sylvia's approval. I woke dazed and confused an hour before my alarm and considered trying to fall back asleep, but couldn't face the prospect of another dream connecting Sylvia even tangentially to prostitution. So I jumped in the shower and spent the time trying to untangle the investigations along with my hair.

When I got out, I found a message from Inspector Petito asking me to come give an official statement and leave a DNA sample. As I listened, my throat went Mojave Desert dry and my lizard brain screamed at me to look up one-way fares to Mexico. Petito must have anticipated that reaction, because he ended with a honey-trap promise to have a copy of the Overkill Bill case files for me when I came.

Well played, Petito—well played. I needed those files like California reservoirs needed water.

But I couldn't afford to act like I'd just fallen off a Central Valley turnip truck. My second-best friend in the world, Jacinda Rogers, was a prosecutor in the DA's office—such an effective prosecutor she'd been the youngest Black woman promoted to chief assistant district attorney in the city's history—and she'd kick the ever-loving crap out of me if I went anywhere near the Hall of Justice without talking to her first. We'd been getting each other out of scrapes ever since I took the rap for a window she broke in seventh grade, and she helped me take on a team of four ninth-graders intent on giving me a beatdown in honor of my grandfather's crimes. I was pretty sure it would be a conflict of interest for her to represent me as a potential suspect in a homicide investigation, but she could at least give me some quick advice and recommend a skilled defense attorney.

After leaving a message for her, I sent a quick text to Morgan checking on her and Philip, then two more to Heather and Ryan to coordinate our day. Now officially late, I ran out the door, forcing my mind to focus on the history of crime, corruption, and scandal in San Francisco's Barbary Coast.

• • •

The tour went off without a hitch. In fact, I was grateful for the distraction of gold-rush-era crime and punishment, which somehow managed to look quaint against what I'd seen the day before. An interesting discussion cropped up as we strolled along Pacific Avenue—once home to a short, dense stretch of rollicking dens of iniquity—about the historic tango between street gangs and corrupt politicians. And, thankfully, probably because the group had all booked before the copycat news broke, the guests were more interested in history than true crime, which meant nobody asked about my grandfather.

The tour ended where it began, at Pacific and Montgomery, the edge of San Francisco's original waterfront before landfill extended the city into the bay. That put me closer to the Hall of Justice than I'd be for the remainder of the day. My brain did a little tango with itself, wanting to avoid Petito on the one hand—just the thought of being in the same room with him again made my pulse race—and wanting access to the Overkill Bill files on the other. When I couldn't get the music to stop, I told myself I'd let whether Jacinda answered my call determine whether or not I went.

This time she picked right up, and launched in without preamble. She'd put in a few calls to quality criminal attorneys for me, and hoped to have one I could talk to by the next day. "My advice," she concluded, "is to wait to talk to him until you have an attorney with you, and don't give them any samples of any sort before then, DNA or otherwise."

I paused before answering. Because some stubborn part of my brain, now faced with the prospect of *not* getting its hot little hands on the files for several days, had decided having them was *absolutely essential*. "Won't it look bad if I delay helping the police?"

"Of course it won't reflect well on you. But trust and believe, your innocence won't protect you from needing a lawyer. Innocent people go to jail every day."

My mind flew to my grandfather—and thus again to the file waiting for me. "What if I'm just really careful what I say?"

Jacinda paused, and I could practically hear her dark eyes narrow at me. "What's the real issue, Capri?"

I hurried through a brief explanation of why I wanted to get my hands on the files. "I don't know how long they'll delay giving them to me if I don't cooperate, or even if they'll refuse to give them to me at all. He has no obligation to hurry them for me."

She sighed, and now I could practically hear her pinching the bridge of her nose. "We both know you're going to do exactly what you want no matter what I say. So if you're determined to go, tell the truth succinctly—don't volunteer a single syllable they don't ask for. And no samples until you have representation."

I told her I understood, hung up, then drove to Bryant Street. I found a parking lot with a slightly less larcenous flat rate than average, then hurried toward the massive gray concrete-block building. I pushed through the glass-and-metallic doors, navigated my way through the antiseptic-scented brown-marbled halls, and waited my turn to ask for Homicide Inspector Petito, all the while praying he was out so I could pick up the files without having to see or talk to him.

No such luck. As soon as they called to let him know I was there, he showed up, cerulean-blue eyes raking my face, and escorted me back to a worn room with gray desks and dilapidated office chairs. As I watched him write my name and the date on a little dry-erase board for the benefit of the camera, the stubborn portion of my brain switched allegiances with alarming speed, now utterly convinced I should have listened to Jacinda.

The beginning of the conversation went well. He sat back, relaxed, and actually smiled—a kind, crooked smile that popped a dimple on the left side of his face and made me wish I'd left my coat in the car.

I mentally shook my finger at myself. This was a strategy, a good-cop-after-bad-cop sort of deal designed to put me at ease and make me talk. I had no doubt he knew how handsome he was, and regularly used that half-dimpled smile to elicit certain reactions from the ladies. No way was I going to be one of them. And I could play the game as well as he could—I mirrored his posture and his smile, because I also knew all about how to manipulate body language to elicit trust.

He asked the same series of questions he'd asked the day before. I gave him the same answers—succinctly.

Then he leaned forward. "What sort of relationship did your in-laws have?"

I blinked at him and considered my answer. "They had a typical relationship."

"What's a typical relationship?" he asked.

I narrowed my eyes at him. "They loved and respected one another. They raised a son together, they played tennis together, they went to parties and criticized the catering together."

"Did they fight?"

"Everybody fights. But more than most people? No. No abused spouses, no screaming matches, no hurled insults."

"Do you think Philip Clement loved his wife?"

"They've never been the demonstrative sort, but they're devoted to each other." I cocked my head at him. "Yesterday you were treating me and my daughter like suspects, now you're asking about Philip. Are you just going after everybody?"

He cocked his head back at me. "Going after everybody is what I'm paid to do. And there's strong reason to consider all three of you as persons of interest."

"But Philip has never even met Katherine Harper," I said. "He doesn't have a motive for killing either of them."

"Are you sure?" His tone was casual, but he was watching me carefully. "Have you seen Sylvia's will?"

I burst out laughing. "Unless she's changed it, Todd inherits the bulk, and Morgan gets the rest. Philip gets a small trust and gets to live in the house, but both revert back to Todd when Philip dies. That ensures Philip can stay in the house that's become his home, but the assets stay with the Renard line. It leaves him significantly worse off than having Sylvia alive." I leaned back in my chair. "But none of that matters. Because *you* clearly haven't seen her equity line."

His eyes widened for a brief moment, and I reveled in knowing something he didn't. "Tell me about it."

I summarized for him, careful to leave out how I'd discovered their financial status. "So," I ended, "if you want to follow the money, find out what her urgent business problem was. And find out why Sylvia called a last-minute meeting with Nancy McQuaid. And look into Sylvia's investments."

To his credit, Petito jotted down what I was saying before he changed the subject. "We haven't heard from your daughter yet. Have you?"

That was strange, and not at all like her. "I did. She's taking care of her grandfather until her father gets in from Los Angeles today. She hasn't contacted you?"

His eyes held mine. "Nope."

The mama bear inside me growled. "Give her some grace. She just lost her grandmother and dropped everything to come take care of her grandfather. I doubt it's the first thing on her mind."

"And you said your husband was in Los Angeles? I thought you initially mentioned something about him being out of the country?" he asked.

I flipped up my hand to show how little I knew. "It was a surprise to me."

He nodded, then stood up. "I think that's all for now. We'll have a statement printed out for you to sign."

I stood as well. "You mentioned you'd expedite me a copy of the Overkill Bill investigation files?"

"I did, yes. Come with me." I followed him past a series of rooms to a generic desk with generic accouterments.

He reached over to a waiting stack of folders, pulled out three thick ones, and handed them to me. "This is what we have."

"Thank you." I glanced back down the hall. "I'm a little turned around. Can you point me in the right direction?"

"I'll walk you out."

He did so in silence, until we reached the final door. "Please let your daughter know it's vital I talk to her *today*. We have some important questions we need answered, now even more than before. We'll bring her in if we have to."

Now even more than before? What did that mean?

I glanced back at him, and the deep blue eyes now sent a chill into my bones. Too late, Jacinda's warning blared through my head with flashing lights and sirens.

He'd played me like a Stradivarius.

In my smug hurry to inform him that Philip didn't inherit anything of value from Sylvia, I'd confirmed for him that *Morgan* very much did. Because while the relatively paltry amount left in Sylvia's account wouldn't sustain even a week of Philip's lifestyle, it would make *all* the difference to Morgan's.

SF Killer Crime Tours

The Presidio

The Presidio was an active military base from 1776 until 1994, when it was turned into a national park. Filled with beautiful hikes and stunning views, the Presidio also gives a unique glimpse into military life; most of the official buildings still stand, and rows of identical military housing line the thoroughfares, some now rented by civilians, others occupied only by the ghosts of the past.

Because despite being a military base, the Presidio wasn't safe from murderous behavior; in fact, it was the location of what some believe is San Francisco's first documented murder case. In 1828, when "Alta California" was still a Mexican territory, Ignacio Olivas and his wife returned from a dance to find their two young children strangled in their beds. Francisco Rubio, a soldier with a nefarious past, was found guilty and was executed—although some believe the testimony that condemned him was fabricated. In 1969, the Zodiac Killer murdered Paul Lee Stine just outside the Presidio's boundary; witnesses reported that the suspect fled toward the Presidio and may have escaped into it. Since Zodiac's identity is still unknown, he may be walking its trails to this very day.

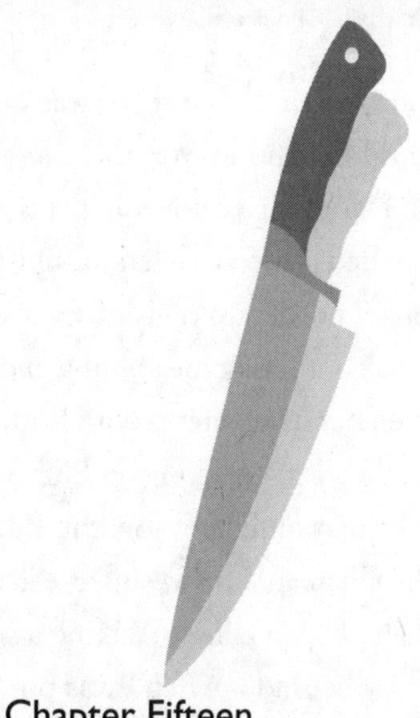

Chapter Fifteen

The sick, breathless sensation stayed with me as I left the Hall of Justice and made my way back to my car, still berating myself for running at the mouth. Petito didn't know me or Morgan and had no reason to put a generous spin on the facts building up against us.

And what was all that about Philip? My protective indignation screamed that Petito couldn't really be serious, he must just be ticking boxes. But then the true-crime portion of my brain reminded me that the significant other is *always* the first suspect. So I sat in the car, wiped my mental slate clean, and considered the possibility from that angle. Maybe Philip had been having an affair with Katherine? But that didn't make any sense—the police would have already obtained a warrant for both Katherine's and his phone records by now, and if he'd had any contact with Katherine whatsoever, they'd have him in custody. *Or*, the true-crime portion of my brain whispered, *maybe he'd heard about Katherine's death and decided to copycat the copycatter in order to get rid of Sylvia*. Except Philip only had motive to keep Sylvia *alive*. There was no money to kill her for; she might have been able to borrow against her reputation and get them out of the financial hole they were in, but there was no way in hell Philip could do that without her. And even if there *had* been money, all but a very small amount would have gone to Todd and Morgan, not Philip.

I sighed. I needed action, not just thought, so I considered my options. I needed to revisit Sylvia's paperwork, see if I could identify what was bothering me about it and dig into any possible intersection between her investments with Katherine's and Nancy's business concerns. Between checking on Philip and my next tour, I wouldn't have time for that until later tonight. But since the Presidio was right next to The Chateau, I *could* squeeze in a quick trip to see the scene where Sylvia had been killed. Walking a site always helped me to synthesize the story behind it when I was putting together my tours; maybe that would help me here.

The detectives hadn't told us exactly where inside the Presidio Sylvia had been found, but the crime-scene photo contained enough information to activate the tour-guide portion of my brain. The eucalyptus trees in the background had been divided by a languorous swirl of horizontal tree trunk that existed in only one location: Andy Goldsworthy's *Wood Line*, a living art exhibition made with fallen eucalyptus trees placed in a sine-wave walking path undulating through the greenery.

I parked on the street next to The Chateau and pulled my jacket close against the chill that signaled fall's rapid approach. As I hiked the steep block to the Presidio entrance, I scanned the area for security cameras on the three houses I passed. In one case, the entrance was set far enough back into the lot there was no chance it captured the sidewalk, especially at night. In the other, the entrance was completely obscured. In the last, the entrance and camera were pointed toward the cross street. No help there.

Once I crossed into the Presidio, I followed the sweetly named Lovers' Lane path northwest; luxurious brick houses that once served as officers' quarters lined one side of the path, dotted with intermittent lampposts. Even in the dark of night, this part of the walk would be relatively open and well lit, perhaps lulling Sylvia into a false sense of security.

As I moved off the path toward the *Wood Line*, the sharp, medicinal scent of eucalyptus intensified. Back in the 1800s, army planners planted rows of cypress and eucalyptus trees here; the cypress died out, leaving a eucalyptus grove with an odd hollow running through it, the site Andy Goldsworthy used for his installation. Accordingly, the trees were denser in some places than others, and clumps of natural detritus—sheared-off bark and fallen branches—accumulated from the remaining trees. Immediately I could see the art piece in the distance, sandwiched between the cars driving down Presidio Boulevard on its other side. In daylight, it would be impossible to kill someone without being seen.

Night, however, would be a different story. The lampposts were now few and far between, and the light they shed wouldn't penetrate far into the grove. I googled the moon phase for the night Sylvia was killed; new moon, which would have provided no light. But maybe she brought a big Maglite with her, or used the flashlight app from her phone. Not her phone, I reminded myself. She'd left her phone at home.

Which brought up an interesting question—why would she leave her phone at home? I could understand why she might not want to carry a purse, but the phone would have fit in a jacket pocket. Had she just forgotten it? Or maybe she didn't want the location tracker or tower pings to show she'd gone out? But why would she want to hide that information?

Either way, I'd need to check to see if the police had found a flashlight with her.

I headed toward the telltale squiggle of felled tree. Here, even with a strong flashlight beam, the trees and clumps of undergrowth would have thrown strange shadows—someone had even made makeshift lean-to structures around some of the trees with branches and bark, spaces that could have concealed someone in the dark. A killer could easily have waited there, then crept out behind Sylvia once she'd passed.

I started to evaluate the landscape, looking for the berm I'd seen in the picture; a scrap of crime-scene tape caught my eye with a yellow flash. Sure enough, this area featured a denser-than-elsewhere copse of trees, angled slightly away from the open walking area. The berm would have partially obscured her body even in the light of day. But Sylvia wouldn't have stepped away from the main path—she'd have to be tricked—or dragged—away from it.

The farther I walked, the less sense it made. Sylvia wasn't stupid or reckless, no matter how upset she was. The only way this made sense was if she had arranged to meet someone outside the park, on the well-lit streets, then walked inside with them.

But who? A business associate? Why wouldn't she just have them come to the house? The only reason I could see was if she didn't want Philip to know. If a friend or associate like Nancy had something they didn't want Philip to hear, they might have asked Sylvia to meet outside the house. Nancy's little drop-by yesterday hadn't felt right to me from the start—maybe she'd made up that supposed meeting to cover for the actual meeting she'd had with Sylvia the night before?

The path name "Lovers' Lane" flashed through my mind. Could Sylvia have been having some sort of illicit affair? That would certainly explain why she slipped out without telling Philip. Maybe she'd been upset about a paramour rather than business? But that possibility didn't sit right with me; the one and only time I'd ever seen Sylvia get truly angry with Todd was when she'd found out he was cheating on me. Then again, lots of people condemned infidelity until they found themselves smack-dab in the middle of it.

Still, if that was what had happened, where did Katherine Harper fit? I gasped—maybe Sylvia had been cheating with Steve Harper? Or with Nancy McQuaid's husband Robert, and maybe Katherine found out? Or maybe Robert McQuaid had been sleeping with both Sylvia and Katherine, and Nancy killed them both? Or—maybe *Sylvia and Katherine* were the lovers, and Steve Harper had killed them both?

I sent a last grim glance around, then turned to head back. The trip had convinced me of one thing, at least. Between the phone left at home and the undeniable risk of walking through an unlit portion of the park at night, random violence made far less sense than a murderer known to Sylvia. And that made it more vital than ever that I figure out what had upset Sylvia the night she died.

Chapter Sixteen

On my walk back to the house, I left Petito a message asking if his team had found a flashlight at the crime scene and telling him about my theory that Sylvia must have been meeting someone. Then I pulled my car into The Chateau and ran inside to check on everyone. Morgan told me Philip had taken another Xanax and was sleeping up in his room; her father hadn't arrived yet, and she was taking advantage of the quiet to study. She was shaken, but insisted I go tend to my own work. I gave her a hug and a kiss, reminded her to call Petito, and told her I'd be back after my early-evening tour.

Then I remembered I'd never heard from Steve Harper's assistant about Katherine's schedule. Maybe I'd misunderstood and I was supposed to call her? I pulled over and put through a call to his office.

"Steve Harper's office, this is Saskia." The twenty-something voice screamed efficiency.

"Hi, Saskia, this is Capri Sanzio. Steve Harper said you could look into Katherine Harper's schedule for me, for any connection with Sylvia Clement. Any meetings, anything like that?"

"He never said anything to me." Her tone shifted to accusatory—

she was busy and important and didn't have time for my shenanigans.

"That's strange. But is there any chance you can check for me?"

She huffed an angry burst of air. "I need to confirm with him. Hold, please."

The 1970s standard "Afternoon Delight" blared out from the phone, several hundred decibels louder than Saskia's voice had been. I hurried to turn the volume down, just in time for Saskia to pick up and say something now too low for me to hear.

"Sorry, could you repeat that?" I stabbed at the up-volume button.

"I *said*, I can't find any mention of Sylvia Clement in her calendar."

"What about Philip Clement?"

This time she didn't put me on hold. With another huff, she typed something. "No mention of Philip Clement."

"Did she keep separate calendars for personal appointments?" I asked.

"All her appointments are in this calendar, and every minute of her day is accounted for so we can coordinate as needed with Mr. Harper's. Now—"

"Just one more question." I only paused for a split second, throwing out another fishing line. "I'm pretty sure Sylvia Clement and Mr. Harper were with her Thursday night. Do her records show that?"

Her voice went cold. "Mrs. Harper was at the Legion of Honor on Thursday night. It's where she was—where she died." She cleared her throat. "She was organizing a charity luncheon. There's no indication anyone other than the museum staff was with her. Now—"

"One more thing. Can you please have Steve call me as soon as he has a chance?"

That stalled her for a second. "Regarding what?"

"Regarding Katherine's death."

An awkward pause ensued, and for reasons I couldn't put my finger on, I got the sense someone was directing her as we spoke. "I'll pass on the message." She hung up, not giving me a chance for another one-more-thing.

Unless she was lying, that closed the door on the possibility that Katherine had any sort of relationship with either Sylvia or Philip. Which left me confused and drained and in need of a few moments to sit, sip coffee, and think.

I was just blocks from the psychological refuge of home when Petito returned my call.

"Ms. Sanzio. I gather from your message you hunted down the crime scene?"

My hackles rose, and my color flushed at the displeasure in his tone. "Yes, I did."

"Why?" His tone was sharp.

I sat up straighter and gripped my steering wheel—I wasn't a child to be scolded. "I'm a big believer in situational context. I am a tour guide for a living, after all."

He made a sound that was dangerously close to a frustrated harrumph. "You're determined to insert yourself into the investigation. Why?"

I laughed a *you must be kidding* laugh. "I'm not *inserting* myself into the investigation, I've been *shoved* smack-dab in the middle of it because of my relationship to Overkill Bill! I'm not going to twiddle my thumbs while you put together a case to lock up me and/or my daughter. There's no law against me looking around a public park."

He paused, and I swore I could hear his nostrils flare. "Interfering in a police investigation is a crime, Ms. Sanzio."

"You're already investigating me for a crime, Detective, so how exactly would that change my day?"

He started to speak but stopped. Then his tone shifted, softening but intensifying. "It's also dangerous, Capri. Someone's killing women, one of whom was about your age. I'd rather see you locked up than find your cold body slashed in a park."

His concern for my well-being stopped me for a moment—maybe I'd misjudged his motives. *Except,* I realized, *that's exactly what he wanted me to think.* He was probing for the tack that would get me out of his hair. I'd already experienced firsthand how good he was at mental sleight of hand, and I wasn't going to fall for it again. "Arrest me if you have to. But I know more about Sylvia Clement's habits and moods than you do, so my insight might be helpful."

He sighed, and mumbled something under his breath I couldn't make out. I waited for him to say more, but he didn't. "Did you find a flashlight with her?"

He paused, and I thought he wasn't going to answer me. "We didn't," he finally said.

I nodded as I swerved to avoid a jerk driver who suddenly stopped in front of me to grab a rare parking space. "It was dark that night. If she didn't have one, that tells us something."

His response was measured, like he was discussing brunch options. "Maybe she never intended to go off the lit path."

"Or maybe she was meeting someone she thought she'd be safe with. Or maybe she had one and that's what the murderer used to bash her on the head. Did you find any sort of murder weapon?"

"I'm not at liberty to say."

"Okay then. Good talk. Let's do it again soon." I didn't try to keep the sarcasm out of my voice.

"I'm not your enemy, Capri," he said, his voice softening again. "I promise we're on the same side. I need to protect the evidence so I can get justice for your mother-in-law."

"Got it," I said.

He sighed. "One more thing before you go. I hurried your access to William Sanzio's files for a reason. I don't believe it's a coincidence that these two women were killed the same way your grandfather's victims were. I'd like to hear your thoughts about that once you have time to look at the file."

A string of reactions raced through my head—surprise and pride that he wanted my opinion, suspicion this was just another tactic, annoyance that the cooperation went only one way. Snarkiness won by a nose. "I thought you didn't want me *inserting* myself in the case?"

"Reading a file from the safety of your home isn't inserting yourself. You're the closest thing to an expert witness on your grandfather's murders I can find."

I narrowed my eyes at my windshield. After dealing with my husband's family for nearly thirty years, I was as fluent in veiled threats as veiled insults—if I didn't help, I'd end up even higher on his suspect list. But he wasn't the only one who knew how to play a situation to his advantage. "If you want my take, I need you to be up-front with me. No murder weapons were found in the original Overkill Bill murders. I need to know if that's the case here."

He paused for a long moment, and I enjoyed a mental image of him furiously pantomiming a conversation with Kumar and Garcia on the topic. Finally he answered. "We didn't find any murder weapons at the scene."

I internally reveled in his capitulation. "Thank you. I'll take a look at the file as soon as possible." A thought occurred to me. "Since this is a copycat, whoever's doing it may have also requested the file. Do you have a list of such people?"

"I do." He hung up.

I gritted my teeth and let loose a string of profanity through them as I pulled into my garage. I took a series of deep breaths and tried to remind myself that he was just doing his job—and that, as a San Francisco citizen, I'd be outraged if he ignored such an obvious suspect as myself or gave out too much information about the case. It all made perfect sense and was perfectly appropriate.

But somehow that didn't make it feel any better. Not just that I was a suspect, but that he was manipulating my emotions so he could use me.

• • •

Once inside the house, I did a quick time check. I had mere minutes to put something into my body that would keep me going for the rest of the afternoon, and so had to make a fast choice between substantive food and caffeine. Caffeine will always win that particular battle, so while my coffeepot gurgled and spat, I grabbed a protein bar from the cabinet and scuttled into my office to adjust my equipment setup back from podcast to online tour.

If I'm honest, I never expected the online tours to be successful. Our first batch were freebies offered as an apology for the in-person tours we had to cancel when quarantine hit; by the time we realized the pandemic wouldn't end quickly and our income screeched to a drastic halt, we'd worked out the technological kinks and were able to monetize. We were stunned when demand for our tours actually *increased*—by the time people ran out of Netflix shows to binge and were itching for any illusion of freedom, word about the online versions had spread. We were deluged with clients from all around the globe, including people who hadn't been able to travel to San Francisco even before the pandemic due to health or financial restrictions. And while logistics and voice strain forced me to limit my in-person tours to between ten to twenty, I could be far more lax with the numbers in my webinars. Demand stayed high once the world opened back up—turns out, a fair few people love being transported from their corner of the globe to mine, and I love transporting them.

Once Ryan let everyone in, we took off running. Our first tour of the day was an expanded version of the Richard Ramirez tour; the format allowed me to go all over the north bay and even down to LA in our hour and a half. When I opened the mics, the questions were lively, and I hated having to cut the discussion off so I could get to the second tour, which delved into Alcatraz's most notorious criminals.

Four hours later I finished, energized by my guests' excitement and enthusiasm, raring to dive into hours of dredging through Sylvia's files. This time I already had a general sense of their content, so I was able to refocus my attention to a bird's-eye view of the documents as a whole, and I dropped into the rhythm of Sylvia's highly regimented organizational method. Before long I could anticipate what I'd see next—market research, business plan, financials, etc.—as I went along.

That's why, as I scrolled through her My Kind of People dossier, it was like a staircase fell out from under me when several of her standard documents were missing. And it felt like falling over a cliff when almost everything was missing from Rithmology's, including even a basic market research report, business plan, or financial history.

That's what had been tugging at me—not something I'd seen, but something I *hadn't* seen. Things that should have been there, but weren't, like the dog that didn't bark in the night. Because if I knew one thing about Sylvia, it was that she'd never invest in a company without doing her due diligence first.

Something tingled at the base of my spine. Documents didn't just go missing without a reason. There was something important about them—and I was damned well going to find out what.

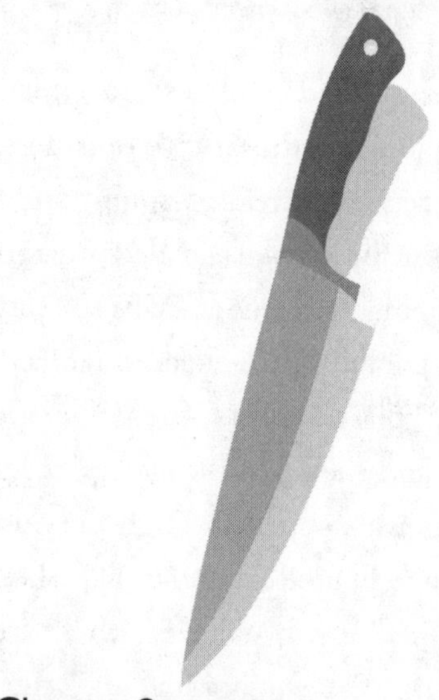

Chapter Seventeen

My phone's alarm startled me out of my mental fist-shaking, alerting me that I had to leave for my last tour of the day. While my Dark Side of San Francisco tours, which take guests to spooky spots after dark, are walking tours, Ryan still attends with me as a safety measure, and if I didn't leave immediately, he'd be stuck vamping for the guests. I'd again failed to leave myself enough time to eat anything healthy, so I grabbed another protein bar and scarfed it down as I dashed to the Haight, where this incarnation of the tour was taking place.

The tour flew by, probably because my mind was only half-present. I knew the tour by heart, so while giving my spiel, my mind kept boomeranging to Sylvia's missing paperwork and the strange paucity of information I'd been able to find regarding her current investments.

Once we'd finished the tour and sent the group on their way, Ryan turned to me. "I am staaaarving. You wanna grab some pizza?"

My stomach rumbled at the thought of an ooey, gooey combination slathered in stress-battling cheeses and meats, the only thing that could keep me away from those documents for a moment longer. "Oh, God, yes *please*. I'll call Heather and see if she wants to join."

We strolled across several streets to Salerno's, one of my favorite pizza joints in the city. To outsiders, the neon sign and embattled façade reeked of food poisoning and regret, but to neighborhood residents in the know, it signaled pizza good enough to make native Italians weep. Inside, it was a 1950s stereotype of Italian restaurants come to life: red-and-white-checked tablecloths, a trellised ceiling with clusters of plastic grapes, Chianti unapologetically served in wicker baskets, and chefs hand-tossing pizza crusts in an open kitchen.

As we stepped through the door, the scents of basil, garlic, and oregano swirled around us like a heavenly olfactory hot tub. Ryan and I slipped into the table Heather had already commandeered.

"How are you holding up?" she asked.

I shrugged my fatigue. "As well as can be expected. Morgan is watching over Philip, and her father should be there by now. I managed to wrangle the Overkill Bill case file from the SFPD, but I haven't had time to look at it since I've been going through Sylvia's paperwork."

"I noticed you were distracted tonight," Ryan said. "Just let me know if you need me to take over for you."

A thought occurred to me. "Actually, do you mind if I run something by you? You know a fair amount about software and things."

"I've been known to dabble in a little software engineering." He attempted, and failed, to look modest. Heather rolled her eyes.

My reply was interrupted by a smooth-but-strong vocal purr. "Buona sera. Extra-large special?"

Gianna Marco, Salerno's owner, fit the restaurant in exactly the same way the King of England fits a swap meet. While the restaurant's atmosphere cried out for a tight-bunned nonna dressed in black telling everyone to *mangia*, Gianna looked like an outtake from *La Dolce Vita*. Fashion-house sharp, silver hair perfectly bobbed, lipstick smear-free and perfect no matter how busy the restaurant was. She spoke both flawless English and Italian, but we could never get her to tell us if she'd been raised in Italy or the US—or how she'd come to oversee a restaurant so different from her personal vibe.

"You want to split, or you guys want your own?" Ryan asked us.

"Split," I answered. "Otherwise I'll be up shoving leftover pizza down my throat at one in the morning, and my self-esteem can't risk seeing that reflected back from my kitchen window."

Once Gianna glided away to the next table, I caught them up on what I'd found in Sylvia's oddly techy portfolio. "Since I have to investigate anything wrong or suspicious, the missing documents bother me. I have to assume they, and her dire financial situation, have something to do with all this. That makes me think there's something suspicious about these businesses, and I need a better understanding of what they do."

"Let me take a look." Ryan grabbed my phone and scrolled through the paperwork I'd pulled up for him, then did a few searches on his own phone while Heather watched over his shoulder. "My Kind of People is easy. They run an app that matches people with similar interests."

I pursed my lips. "Yeah, that's what I thought. But my mind reels at the thought of Sylvia investing in a dating app."

Ryan's face scrunched. "It's not just a dating app, though, it has multiple purposes. Business, networking, friendship. So, if you're new to town and looking to make friends who are into the music scene, it can hook you up. Or it can connect someone with a bakery to restaurants that need baked goods, or to wholesale baking supply."

Light broke through the clouds of my brain. "Ah, okay. That makes far more sense—Sylvia was big on networking."

"This second one, Rithmology, is trickier." He grimaced down at my screen. "You're right, there's next to no information in her files."

"There's really only this." I scrolled to a page of information about the business. "I guess you could call it a business plan?"

"If that's what it is, it's beyond incompetent. Both product and mission are underspecified." He grimaced down at his own screen. "The website is cryptic, only buzzwords. My guess is they specialize in developing algorithms for other apps. Like direct-marketing platforms, that sort of thing."

"English would be a tremendous help," I said.

He rubbed his chin. "You know how when you search the internet for, say, Rollerblades, every website you visit for the next month shows you ads for Rollerblades?"

"Ah yes," Heather said. "Makes me feel like Big Brother's watching."

He half smiled. "Everybody's watching when it comes to your data. In that example, you made it easy: you told the artificial intelligence what you wanted to see, and it relayed that to other sites, so they can target ads to you. Where it gets trickier is designing an artificial intelligence algorithm that can predict what *else* you want before you ask for it. People will pay serious bank for programs that take information about your internet behaviors and use it to make effective predictions about you."

"*Behaviors.* Like the websites I visit?" I asked.

He nodded. "Yep, paired with whatever demographic information the system has about you. But not just that, even what you *don't* do. Every time you click or don't click on something, some form of AI uses the info to make better predictions about you. Even how long you spend looking at a certain thing. So, like, with Instagram. You pause on some things and scroll past others. Some you even hit 'like.' Their algorithm takes all that and uses it to fill your feed with other content and ads it thinks you'll like. There's a really cool documentary about it you should check out, called *The Social Dilemma*."

"So, the better the algorithm is at reading your mind, the more money it can make for advertisers." I grabbed the Diet Coke that magically appeared as Gianna floated past our table.

Ryan took a gulp of his newly appeared beer. "Much more valuable to get your ads in front of people with a high probability of being interested rather than people who'll ignore them."

Heather's arm froze in a perfect arc, holding her espresso-tini. "And they're accurate?"

"To a degree. That's why they're always working to improve them."

"But apps like Instagram have their own algorithms. So where does a company like Rithmology come in?" I asked.

He pointed toward my messenger bag. "Some do, some don't. Our laptops are HPs, right? But they have Intel processors, not HP processors. You know that whole slogan, 'Intel inside'?"

"Ah, okay." My brain fog cleared again, and out popped a theory. "So Rithmology sells technology to other apps that help predict users' behavior. Apps like, potentially, My Kind of People."

His brows popped. "Now that's an interesting possibility. Because a company like Rithmology doesn't just sell the program. They'll oversee it to continually make it better, but they may also use it to synthesize what they learn about clients of one system with clients from another." He saw the confusion on my face. "So when you hire a company like Rithmology, you aren't just paying for the program, you're paying for the information about people that Rithmology's program collects. So, several apps may work together, combining information for a more complete picture. And an app like My Kind of People, where people fill out questionnaires to be matched with other people and businesses? That would gather a metric crap-ton of information. Pairing that with information about people's online behaviors would yield extremely powerful results."

My alarm bells went off. "Isn't it illegal to sell specific information about individual people that use an app?"

"Not if you agree to have your data collected. And in order to use most apps, you have to agree to have your data collected."

"Like website cookies," Heather said, eyes wide.

"Not *like* cookies, *including* cookies. And then the app or whoever can do whatever they want with your info, including sell it. And believe me, lots and lots of people want to buy it."

Pieces started clicking into place. "So if I'm looking for something that might have gotten Sylvia killed, especially since Sylvia has an aversion to tech and would never invest in companies with next to no information, this is a possibility I need to take seriously." I gestured toward my phone. "Because what you're describing sounds ripe for abuse."

"Absolutely. That's why there's been so much focus on privacy laws recently. But plenty of people break them."

I nodded silently, my mind racing with possibilities of what could happen with that data in the wrong hands—and if being involved with companies like that could end you up dead.

Chapter Eighteen

I spent the rest of the meal processing the possibilities. If Sylvia's two tech investments weren't on the up-and-up, someone might well kill to keep that quiet, and copycatting the MO of a local serial killer who happened to be related to the victim would be a smart way to misdirect suspicion. But I was making about a hundred assumptions in the course of all that logic, based only on some missing papers and my gut. I needed more.

After dinner, I let myself into The Chateau. As I rounded the corner into the living room, I spotted my too-handsome, six-foot-one ex-husband slouched forward on the couch, elbows on his knees, head in his hands. He looked up, then stood to greet me, and my heart did the dip-and-swerve thing it always does whenever I see him after a long period of time. Morgan thinks I'm harboring a secret desire to get back with him, but that's the wishful thinking and oversimplification of youth. I've worked hard to keep a good relationship with him so we can co-parent Morgan, but I'll never be able to look at his face without the familiar stabs of betrayal that put the kibosh on anything more.

He tried to smile as he came to hug me, but it came out watery and tugged at my heart. "How are you?" I asked, feeling like it was the stupidest question anyone'd ever asked.

"I don't think it's real yet. Mom was such a force of nature it's hard to believe anyone or anything could take her out." He stepped back from the embrace.

"I'm sure that long drive didn't help, either." The late hour registered with me. "Nothing went wrong on the drive, did it? I thought you'd get here much earlier."

He looked away and shook his head. "I should have just taken a red-eye out Monday night, but I didn't want to leave my car in the long-term parking there. As it was I had to take a sleeping pill to fall asleep, and then I overslept and was too groggy to drive until about noon. Anyway. Thank you so much for taking care of Dad."

I glanced up toward Philip's room. "How is he?"

"Sleeping. But Morgan says—"

Morgan appeared through the doorway and crossed over to Todd, and I was struck by what a perfect mix of him and me she'd turned out to be. Her hair is a longer version of her father's medium brown, shiny and thick and straight, and she had his deep brown eyes. But her five-foot-seven stature, her curvy silhouette, and the shape of her features are all me—my almond eyes, my button nose, the point to my chin.

She wrapped her arms around her waist. "I say what?"

"You were just telling me that Grandpa has been in and out of sleep all day," Todd said.

Her face clouded over. "I keep trying to feed him when he wakes up, but I can't get him to eat very much."

Behind her, Philip appeared, then beelined for Todd. They embraced for a long moment. "Thank you for coming back so quickly."

"Of course, Dad."

Morgan's eyes filled with tears, and I suddenly felt like a second-string intruder on a first-string family moment. I excused myself, mumbling something about beverages.

By the time I returned with the tray, they were settled on the couches discussing funeral arrangements. As I doled out tea and coffee, I asked Morgan if she'd called Petito.

She tucked her legs up under her chest. "We're playing phone tag. I don't understand why he wants to talk to *me*?"

My child-rearing philosophy, probably born from my father's refusal to discuss Overkill Bill, had always been one of transparency. I didn't believe in hiding truths from my daughter, or skirting around difficult situations. "He needs to talk to everyone who had contact with Sylvia on Sunday. He'll want to hear about what Sylvia had to say, and how you reacted."

She nodded, her brow furrowed.

I turned to Philip. "I've been looking through Sylvia's documents. She currently has investments in three companies, a dance company and two tech-related companies. It seems strange to me she'd invest in tech, and there's not much information about those companies in her files. I don't suppose you know anything about them?"

He cradled his mug of chamomile tea with both hands and sipped cautiously. "She's been involved with the dance company for years. She always wanted to be a ballerina, did you know? But she didn't have the body type for it." He turned to stare out the window.

"I didn't know." My heart panged. "What about the other two?"

"No idea. She's been skeptical of anything to do with the internet ever since she invested in that one company way back when." He turned to Todd. "What was it called? The one with the sock-puppet dog?"

"Pet dot com." Todd shook his head. "What a crash and burn that was."

Philip took another sip of his tea, wincing at the heat. "I'm surprised she went anywhere near that sort of thing again."

"So you don't remember her saying anything about algorithms or dating apps?"

Philip looked at me like I was insane. "She thought dating apps were leading to the downfall of society."

I hurried to clarify. "Not just dating. It deals with other things, like clubs and businesses, too."

He shook his head. "I can't imagine it."

"I don't know," Todd said. "She's always thought private clubs were 'the cornerstones of success.' Like that French one she was always on me to join. The Ligue Louis something or other?"

"The Ligue Louis Quatorze," I said. For the longest time I'd thought it was a society for the preservation of French baroque furniture. Turned out it was a headquarters for people of French ancestry to hobnob. "Did your mother tell *you* anything about the investments?"

A flush tinged his ears, and he flicked a hand at me. "Said it was bad manners to ask about business you weren't involved in. And that was before I pissed her off by refusing to work for her father's brokerage and 'scarpered' off into luxury travel."

I pondered the irony of a stockbroker's daughter ending up in dire investment straits. "So why didn't your mother follow in those family footsteps if it was so important to her?"

Todd shifted in his seat. "Grand-Père was traditional when it came to gender roles."

As was Todd, but this didn't seem like the right time to stir that particular pot.

"I'm surprised he didn't ask *you*," Morgan said to Philip.

Philip's face clouded over. "He did. I turned him down. Sylvia would never have forgiven me."

"I don't understand," Morgan said. "Why would that be a problem?"

Philip met her eyes, firmly but calmly. "If you were told you couldn't get your PhD, but your husband, who knows nothing about forensic psychology, was going to be given one along with a plum job in the profession, would that make you feel personally fulfilled?"

Morgan winced. "I see what you mean. It wasn't about having representation in the business, it was about feeling valued and capable."

Philip stared back down into his mug, nodding.

I cleared my throat, eager to change the subject. "Did Sylvia have any associates you know of who worked with her on her investments?"

Philip gave a defeated shrug. "Any of them. All of them? That's the insularity of the circle. Advice whispered over cocktails, doors opened over dinner. Connections are vital in our world. But specifically in these instances? Your guess is as good as mine."

I sighed. "Hopefully Steve Harper will call me back soon. Maybe he can give me some insight into the companies."

Philip's brows rose. "You've been trying to reach him? He called me earlier."

My jaw clenched in annoyance. "He called *you*? Why?"

"To express his condolences and thank me for your visit to Katherine's memorial. You must have made an impression." Something occurred to him, and his brows knit. "What did you say to him?"

My stomach dropped. "Other than expressing my condolences, I only asked him how exactly Sylvia and Katherine knew each other. Why?"

He rubbed his chin. "Oh, nothing. I got the sense he wanted to be sure I was aware you'd been there. Maybe he was annoyed I didn't come myself."

That made sense—he must have wanted to be sure I really was who I said I was. "If you talk to him again, will you ask him to call me?"

Philip shrugged. "I doubt I will, but if I do, I'll ask him."

• • •

I headed back home restless and frustrated. Was I grasping at straws thinking Sylvia's business concerns might be shady? And if they were, how did Katherine Harper fit into it all? Steve Harper claimed not to know, but he could very well be lying. I could go through Sylvia's considerable personal contacts one by one, asking questions and hoping somebody pointed me in the right direction, but that would take weeks, maybe months—and I wasn't even sure what to ask.

I took a mental step back for perspective. I had two strong leads at the moment. One was the Overkill Bill police files. I needed to get my head around the connection between the two cases; that was the genesis of everything, and without understanding it, I was flailing in the wind. If I could figure out who the real Overkill Bill was, that would help point me in the right direction here. Plus, having something useful to say to Petito about it all was crucial if I was going to keep him willing to talk to me.

My other possible lead was a deeper dive into Sylvia's circle and how they might intersect with My Kind of People and Rithmology. My Spidey senses were screaming that the Harpers' software empire was too much of a coincidence, but no way was Petito going to divert resources based on my Spidey senses. Either way, I needed something solid to bring to him.

I glanced at the clock—seven thirty. The Overkill Bill case files would be available to me long into the night, but if I wanted any chance of talking to a real person at either of the companies before tomorrow, I needed to dive in right away.

I settled in as quickly as I could with a cup of coffee and my laptop and started my deep dive with My Kind of People. Their website was predictably trite, featuring scads of happy people happily enjoying the outcomes of their happy My Kind of People hookups. I found two trade reviews of the app online, both of which championed the novel one-stop shopping model for all your social and business relationship needs. Surface level only, and I couldn't find much else.

So I downloaded the app and made myself a profile.

With Ryan's comments about data-sharing policies in mind, I was careful about which permissions I agreed to, and then lied my tush off as I answered the setup questions. Ryan's prediction was right—the application requested an astounding range of information on all aspects of my life: preferences, history, interests, skills, life goals. A fair amount of it was optional, but anyone legitimately using the app would be motivated to include as much information as possible to get the best matchups. Even knowing my answers were lies, I felt exposed and vulnerable.

I switched over to Rithmology, starting with their website. Ryan was again right about the buzzwords; without the scant paragraph of description I'd found in Sylvia's paperwork, I'd have no clue what they did. The dearth of information struck me as shady, so I switched into a broader search to see what the tech sites and blogs had to say.

The internet promptly slammed shut.

No reviews. No insider-business write-ups. No bloggers spilling tea on behind-the-curtains drama or trumpeting that the company was/wasn't the next best thing. I'd never had that happen for any business I'd searched, ever. How was it possible for *any* business to have no footprint on the internet, let alone one with an internet-based product?

With my Spidey senses now full-on radioactive, I pulled both companies' websites back up and searched for any phone numbers that would put me in touch with a human. I found one easily on the My Kind of People site; I listened carefully to their menu options, which the computer-generated voice advised me had recently changed. After tip-tapping my way through the options several times, I managed to find a publicity liaison whose voicemail cheerfully promised she'd call me back during regular business hours. I left a message identifying myself as a journalist interested in doing a story about their app—not exactly fully true, but not really a lie, either.

I turned to Rithmology. In the footer of the "About" page, I found a single phone number in teensy-weensy type—the kind a company includes to fulfill a legal obligation, hoping nobody will ever really find it. I dialed it, resigned to swing through an even bigger jungle gym of menu options.

So of course a human immediately picked up.

"Rithmology," a middle-aged male voice said.

While fighting an overwhelming urge to hang up and throw my phone across the room, I flailed for an approach to take, kicking myself for not having a cover story ready.

"Hello?" he said.

I forced my mouth open and prayed something useful came out. "Yes, I'm here, hello. To whom am I speaking?" I winced, wondering where this nineteenth-century Miss Manners dwelled undetected in my brain.

He paused before answering. "I'm Ted. How can I help you?"

If Rithmology was hiding something, they were probably well versed in parrying thrusts from journalists and law enforcement, so the truth wasn't going to be my friend here. "Um, a friend of mine told me that I need a better way of finding the right customers to build my business. Is that the kind of thing you do?"

His wariness eased, but didn't fully drop. "That depends. Tell me about your business."

If I knew one thing about lying effectively, it was that the best lies stick close to the truth. "I do tours of San Francisco."

"Very interesting," he said, but the large dent in his tone suggested the exact opposite. "A colleague of mine might be better for handling that. I'll have him call you back when he gets in tomorrow. What's your name and number?"

I wasn't keen on giving them, but since he most likely had my number on his caller ID, there wasn't much point in being cagey. I rattled them off.

"Great, I'll make sure he gets back to you ASAP." His tone shifted to an over-strained nonchalance. "Who was the friend who referred you?"

Damn—I hadn't expected that. "Oh, no, it wasn't a specific referral. They just told me there were companies that could place my ads more effectively and I just started searching."

"You found us through an online search." His voice froze over like the arctic circle.

Double damn—clearly that had been the wrong thing to say. Blood pulsed through my ears and my throat went dry as my brain desperately triaged. "Okay, so, that's not exactly right. My ex-mother-in-law is an investor in the company, but the thing is, she and I don't get along very well so I didn't want to mention her name." I turned on a false indignance—I was warming up now. "Because why should I hold my business back just because of her, you know?"

"Ah, I see." But his voice hadn't fully thawed. "Who's your ex-mother-in-law?"

"Sylvia Clement."

A fusillade of key clacks burst over the line at a pace that made me suspect I didn't want to be around for whatever they produced. "Anyway. Thanks so much for your help. I'll look forward to that call," I said, then quickly hung up.

I pushed the phone away from me, terrified Ted would immediately call me back. When he didn't, I crossed the kitchen, poured myself a glass of water, and forced myself to drink it. As my pulse slowly calmed, I caught a glimpse of my reflection in the oven door.

"I might just be a natural at this," I told it.

Neither my reflection nor my self-esteem were impressed by my plucky wit.

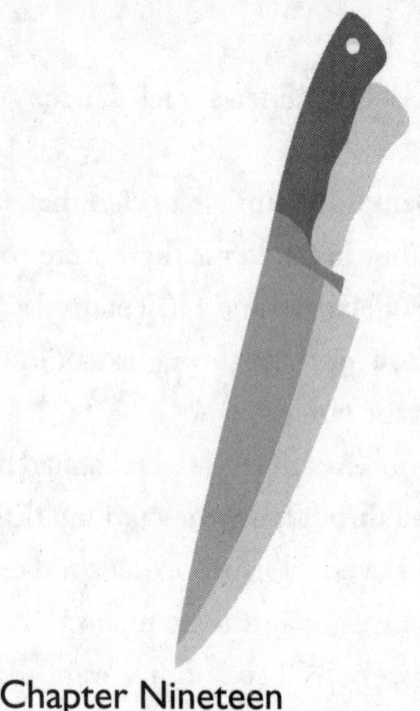

Chapter Nineteen

Once my pulse was roughly back to normal, I made a note on my to-do list—if I was going to be a serious investigative journalist, I needed some sort of app to mask my phone number before I made any more potentially dangerous calls, or maybe even a burner phone. Then, drumming my fingers on my phone, I mentally dissected the call with Rithmology.

Ted hadn't been overjoyed about the prospect of my business from the start. But once I implied I'd found the company via internet search, I became the enemy. That alone proved I was on the right track—businesses paid big money to optimize their search engine visibility, and if a business didn't want to be found, it was because they had something to hide. And if they wanted to hide that badly, I wanted to find them that much more. Every business left a paper trail: business licenses, permits, all that went through the government. I was fairly certain my starting point for that type of information was the Secretary of State's office, but they wouldn't be open in the evening. So I added another note onto my list; come morning I'd pull whatever I could find on both My Kind of People and Rithmology.

In the meantime, I could dive into the Overkill Bill files. My eyes turned to the fat folders Petito had given me earlier in the day, and I mentally rubbed my hands together—something in there had to be the key, and finding it would send me down the right track.

As I brewed myself a cup of chamomile tea, Heather called.

"Hey, I wanted to check in on you. How're you holding up?" she asked.

I gave her a quick recap of my day. "I'm just about to dive into the police's Overkill Bill files."

"Gimme five minutes, I'm on my way." She hung up before I could object.

• • •

"It took you *fifteen* minutes," I said, glancing at my nonexistent watch when Heather appeared at my door. "So I started reading. I figured you can start with what I just read, and I'll hand off to you as I go."

"Sounds good." She enveloped me in a huge hug. "I hope you don't mind me crashing your evening, because even if you do mind, I'm crashing anyway. You don't need to be alone through this."

"Of course I don't mind." And I really didn't, despite how late it was. With everything that had happened, the last forty-eight hours felt like a month, and while I didn't mind taking care of my daughter and my in-laws, it was nice to have someone take care of me a little, too. "I have tea ready. Let's jump on in."

We crossed through the house into my office, and I pulled a red armchair up kitty-corner to the desk so she could sit next to me. Once she settled in with a notebook in hand and a pen tucked behind her ear, I pointed amid the stacks of files to what I'd just read. "Okay, so. Right off the bat I found a strange detail the police never released to the press. All three of the original Overkill Bill victims had been found with their clothing completely undisturbed."

"Why does that matter?" She peered down at the page I'd indicated.

"Two reasons. First, in the picture Petito showed Philip and me, Sylvia's shirt had been untucked and her pants unzipped."

"So the copycat killer hasn't seen the police files," she said.

"Correct. And it's also weird because it's exactly backward from how it should be. If Sylvia and Katherine were killed due to some corporate malfeasance or socialite shenanigans, there would be no reason to mess with their clothes. On the other hand, Overkill Bill supposedly killed his victims because they were prostitutes, and every serial killer I've ever heard of that killed prostitutes stripped them nearly naked. The salacious nature of the women's profession is reflected in the killer's psychology, and in what he did to them, including their clothing. Charles Albright, the Eyeball Killer, left his victims naked or partly undressed; Gary Ridgway, the Green River Killer, left most of his completely nude. In fact, I can't come up with a single example that goes against that rule—except Overkill Bill."

She tilted her head. "The exception that proves the rule?"

I flipped my hands up. "Maybe. But if we're looking for insight, we have to assume anything odd signals something important. Maybe Overkill Bill didn't choose his victims because they were prostitutes, maybe that was just the easiest way for him to access women."

She glanced back down at the file. "But didn't you say last night that the overkill itself suggested some sort of deep-seated emotion? If he wasn't angry with them because they were prostitutes, why was he angry at them?"

"Excellent question." I chewed at my lip. "And right from the start it's been bugging me that the current killer is choosing women who *aren't* prostitutes. So this is strong evidence there's a different core motivation at play. Every killer's choices tell us something about them. So what does this detail tell us?"

She considered. "Maybe that his real problem was with his mother or something."

"Maybe. What else?" I squeezed my eyes shut in an attempt to step on my brain's gas, but apparently I'd flooded its engine. "I'm stuck. Let's keep going."

We made steady progress through the files until I reached Vera Schmidt's statement, the witness who claimed she saw Sally Reyes leave North Beach with a man fitting my grandfather's description. What I read there screeched me to a halt.

"Hey, listen to this." My pulse sped as I read. "Vera says the man she saw with Sally was in his early twenties, but my grandfather was nearly forty at that time. And she said he was wearing slacks and a 'short, open Harrington-style coat with a polo-type shirt underneath.' But my grandfather never dressed like that. It's part of our family lore that he always dressed in suits, because of the pride he took in his appearance. If he needed a coat, he wore a trench."

She leaned over toward the page in front of me. "People say a lot of things once someone has passed," Heather said.

I shook my head furiously as the ghosts of pictures past flashed through my head. "No. Every picture I've ever seen of him lines up with that."

"Maybe he put on a disguise to go pick out his 'dates,'" Heather said.

"In that case he'd've worn a hat to hide his face. And the coup de grâce is, even though she claims she got a full view of his face, nowhere in here does she mention the birthmark. It even says she told the police no scars, tattoos, or other identifying features, so it's not just that the police held back that information for some reason."

Heather pulled her legs up under her in a crisscross position. "Yeah, that's weird. How did nobody ask about that once they brought your grandfather in?"

"Hang on." I skimmed as fast as I could. "Turns out, someone did. His defense team asked both about that omission, and the discrepancy in age. That caused the inspectors to interview her again, and at that point she said he might be older than she thought, and she must have just assumed the birthmark was a shadow."

"Wait, hold up." She threw up a mocking hand. "A diamond-shaped *shadow*? That's total BS. And that's also witness tampering."

I answered almost by rote. "They wouldn't have thought so then. This was years before research on how questioning, especially repeat questioning, could influence a witness's memory."

"Lemme see all that." She reached toward me.

I passed her the pages, and watched red splotches creep up her neck as she skimmed it. "Total BS," she repeated.

"Maybe." I pointed to a passage. "But the description led several other area prostitutes to recall a semi-regular john they'd seen with Marielle and Denise. One of them provided William Sanzio's name. She also told them William had a reputation with the area girls for being kind, paying well, and wanting what we'd call today 'the girlfriend experience': he took them on literal dates, like to the movies or dinner." I looked up at Heather. "Maybe that's why the clothes weren't removed, if he saw them more as girlfriends than prostitutes?"

Heather frowned. "But if he didn't think of them as prostitutes, why kill them?"

I rubbed my temples, trying to keep the logic straight in my head. "Maybe he became too attached to them, and they rejected him?"

Heather's face scrunched. "Wouldn't you expect to see messed-up clothes in that case, too?"

"Maybe he fought with them for some other reason—but what kind of fight could he have with three different women in such close succession?" Still rubbing my temples, I pushed away from the table, mumbling as I marched out of the room. "Damn my father, and damn his embargo on anything to do with my grandfather. If I could talk to him about who my grandfather was, maybe I'd have a little more insight into all of this. And if I can't have caffeine, I need pickles."

• • •

After calming my frustration with half a jar of gherkins, I poured us fresh mugs of tea and headed back in.

Heather cocked a brow at me as she took her mug. "Feel better now?"

"I do, actually."

"Good. I kept going, to keep my mind off the thought of you and those pickles. And I gotta tell you, I do *not* care for the tone of this detective's notes from the interview he conducted with your grandfather."

"Inspector," I mumbled.

"Talk about condescending." She screwed up her face as she quoted. "*While his wife was home caring for their two young sons, he was out entertaining other women.* Glad to see there was no bias there or anything."

I nodded, and reached out my hand for the relevant sheets; she listened as I skimmed and verbally recapped. "Okay, so. On the night of Marielle DeShayne's murder, my grandfather claimed to have been out dancing with Denise Jefferson, who would end up being the second murder victim. And on the night of Denise Jefferson's murder, he claimed he'd taken Sally Reyes to see the movie *Goldfinger*, then to dinner before going to a hotel. No proof, because he never kept stubs or receipts so my grandmother wouldn't find them. And both businesses had been busy that night, so nobody could say definitively that he was there or not."

Heather leaned back in her chair and sipped her tea. "Weird that each girl he was out with was the next to die."

"Yeah, that's what the prosecutors argued, that it was too much of a coincidence and showed he must be the murderer. The jury agreed, but the circularity of the logic has always itched at me like a never-ending case of poison oak."

"How do you mean?"

"You remember the beginning of *The Shawshank Redemption*? When Andy Dufresne is accused of murdering his wife, and claims he threw his gun into the river earlier that night?"

"Yep."

"The prosecutor scoffs, and says it's 'very convenient' that the gun was never found and couldn't be compared to the bullets used to murder her. And Dufresne answers back that since that comparison would prove his innocence, he finds it 'decidedly *inconvenient*.' This has always felt the same to me, because if those women were my grandfather's alibi, it was decidedly inconvenient for him that they were dead. And if they weren't really his alibi, if he was lying, why would he willingly link himself to the victims in that way? Wouldn't it be smarter to claim to have been far, far away from all of them?"

She reached up and absently tugged at a hank of her hair as she weighed that. "You're right. That's just stupid."

"I've always figured it was flat-out coincidence, since the killer would have drawn from the same pool of prostitutes."

She suddenly leaned forward, pointing at me. "Unless it isn't coincidence at all. What if there *was* a relationship between your grandfather and the killings, but just not where he's the killer. Like—" She waved her hand, casting around for an example.

The pieces started to shift as I followed her logic. "Like, say someone was looking to kill prostitutes, but also wanted to find a way to throw suspicion off himself. Say he watched until someone came around that matched his general description. Then he could wait until his look-alike went off with a prostitute, and kill the same girl later, hoping the other prostitutes would misidentify his look-alike."

"Yes!" Heather kicked her legs back out from under her, and stood to pace in front of my bookshelves. "And let's say the other prostitutes didn't identify your grandfather. The creeper could have made sure the police looked at him by sending an anonymous tip or something. It's brilliant."

The back of my neck tingled, and I glanced excitedly at the notes I'd been taking. "That would explain the discrepancies in age, dress, and birthmark."

She stopped in front of the desk and pointed down to the files. "Were there ever any other suspects? Maybe one of them was our guy, but got dropped when the hookers pulled out William's name?"

I scoured the file for a list of other suspects. "Nothing. William Sanzio was named right away, and it was open and shut for them from there."

"Doesn't matter." She tapped my laptop. "We have a theory now, and a theory can be investigated."

But her words kicked my excitement squarely in the gut. "Sure. I just need a list of every twenty-something black-haired blue-eyed man in San Francisco at that time. Sadly, my time machine's in the shop and since I haven't been bitten by any radioactive spiders recently, my psychic powers are on the blink."

She narrowed her eyes at me for a long moment. "I see your point," she finally capitulated, then slumped back in her chair. "I may have jumped the gun."

"No, you're right, a theory is a starting point," I said to make up for my snark. "We just have to flesh it out and find something we can investigate."

"You know, this could connect to the current murders, regardless." Her eyes flipped up to the notes I'd taken on the whiteboard. "Maybe the current killer is doing the same thing, picking victims who are connected to someone else in order to keep the heat off themselves. In this case, you and Morgan, since you're connected to the original case."

The thought put my chest into deep freeze. "Oh, God. Up until now I just figured people in Sylvia's circle knew she had a connection to the case. You think they're looking specifically to frame me or Morgan?"

She gave me an apologetic look. "It would be a smart way to go. Especially since they knew you and Sylvia didn't have the warmest relationship."

"If I let myself think about that right now, I'll curl into the fetal position and never get back up. So let's put a pin in it and move forward." I gripped the files. "William did have corroboration for one of his alibis, the night of Sally Reyes's murder." I ran my finger over the page. "He claimed he'd taken Delilah Tyrell to the opening of a new restaurant in North Beach called Damiano's. Delilah verified his story in detail—she described the food they'd eaten and the decor of the place."

"Isn't she the one the prosecutors said your grandfather paid to testify?"

"Yep. And while they did manage to find a waiter who recognized my grandfather, he couldn't say for sure what night he'd been at the restaurant."

Heather nodded, pursing her lips and pushing them up toward her nose.

"And the clincher that erased any reasonable doubt from the jury's mind came in the courtroom. When Vera, the woman who'd supposedly seen William, came to testify, she made a big show of gasping and pointing at the onyx signet ring he was wearing. It had the initials WS engraved into it, and she claimed she'd seen it on him that night, but had forgotten about it until seeing it again."

"How convenient." Heather grimaced.

"Isn't it just? And even if she did really remember seeing a ring like that, it meant nothing. At least fifty percent of the Italian men from that generation wore similar rings. But the jury bought it."

"Huh. I remember you saying something about witnesses sometimes having charges dropped if they agree to testify about something. I wonder if Vera had some outstanding prostitution charges that suddenly went away after she testified?"

I pointed my pen at her. "Excellent catch. I'll ask Petito if he can check."

She grinned in shared pride, but the grin turned into a yawn.

I glanced down at my phone. "Holy crap, it's past midnight and we both need to get up early tomorrow. You want to crash in my guest room?"

She stood and stretched. "Nah, I'll head back to my place."

I walked her out, thanking her profusely for the help, then hurried through my bedtime routine with my mind racing. We'd made progress; the psychology of the Overkill Bill murders, especially the undisturbed clothing, actually fit the *current* murders better than the originals, and that told me something. Along with the indication that someone may have been watching from the sidelines—so I needed to keep that possibility in mind for the current murders, too. No matter what, I had theories and important discrepancies between the two murders I could report back to Petito—all in all, an excellent night's work.

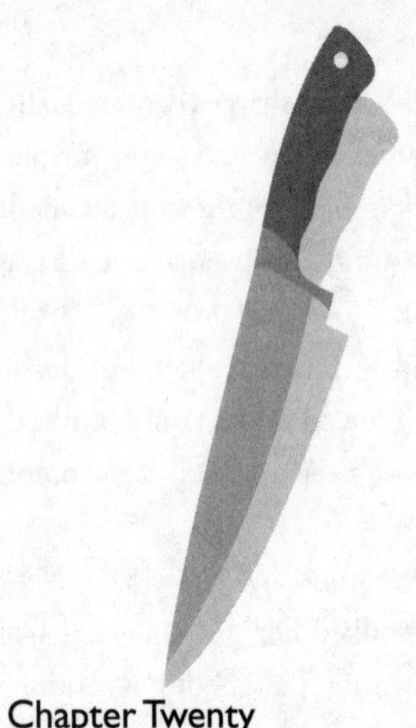

Chapter Twenty

My Wednesday morning tours were filled with inquisitive guests, some with questions about the tour, but more with questions about Overkill Bill. Going in, I was worried it would put me on edge to have to field questions about him, but as it turned out, talking the facts out with them helped me go over it all in my mind. Still, the extra questions made it tricky to keep on time, and trickier still to find a chance to check in with Todd and Morgan. It wasn't until lunchtime I was able to call and find out if they needed anything.

"Yeah, actually," Todd answered. "I can't find Mom's hallowed Rolodex."

"Rolodex?" I laughed. "Get with the times. She must have converted that over to her phone by now. Why do you need it, anyway?"

"We need to book caterers for her memorial service. Dad says she kept the Rolodex in addition because people still give cards and it organizes them all. He says he saw her flipping through it the night she got home from Hawaii."

That was strange—I was fully certain I hadn't seen a Rolodex. "Did the police take it?"

"Nope. Dad watched everything they took, and they left a list. No Rolodex."

The tingles in my spine returned. "I noticed some documents missing in the files I photographed, too. Philip said she kept everything in her desk, but is he sure there's nowhere else they could be?"

"I asked him that, too. He's adamant there's not."

"If he's sure the police didn't take the Rolodex, there must be. A Rolodex would have been too bulky for Sylvia to carry with her on her walk to the park, and nobody else was in the house or they'd have shown up on security footage. Maybe we should search the house again just to be sure."

"It's not a big deal and I've got a thousand things to do. I was just calling on the off chance you'd seen it," he said.

But I recognized the subtle wheedle in his voice. Seriously—a glorified travel agent didn't know how to google caterers in the area? But I caught and chastised myself—of course he knew how, but his mother had just died, and that hung a lead weight on top of everything, making the simplest tasks feel like climbing Everest. "I'll stop by as soon as I can and take a look. In the meantime, Killer Crimes has had a few catered events. I'll get you some numbers."

"Thanks a mil, Capri."

We said our goodbyes and I checked the time. I had about an hour before I had to haul tush to my next tour, plenty of time to figure out how to pull public information on businesses registered in California. Within a few minutes I'd confirmed those records were handled by the Secretary of State's office—and discovered they were available twenty-four hours, for free, online. I berated myself heartily for not checking that the night before, then did my searches and printed out my free PDFs.

The information on the documents was limited: addresses, basic information about the owners, statements of purpose about the businesses. I searched Prima Pointe as well for comparison, and again the contrast was stark. In the case of Prima Pointe, the company had directors and board members in addition to a human owner. For both My Kind of People and Rithmology, the space for board members was marked "not applicable," and the owner was listed as a corporation—the type of answers you put when trying to hide who owned something.

That got my attention, but what really sent my pulse jetting down the racetrack was that the same corporation owned both companies: something called Anchor & Shields, Inc. So My Kind of People and Rithmology were definitely in cahoots—the only question left was who owned Anchor & Shields, Inc.

I scanned for the individual agent required under "service of process." Again, the same man was listed for both companies: Brighton Keyes, whose title was listed as "CEO." But "CEO" didn't necessarily mean "owner." I jumped back to my computer and entered the parent corporation, Anchor & Shields, Inc., into the search bar.

The company didn't exist.

I drummed my fingers on my desk as I thought. The Secretary of State only gave access to California businesses—so if Anchor & Shields, Inc., wasn't present, it must have been owned elsewhere. I did a general Google search for the company, but nothing came up. I did several more searches combining names, but still got nothing.

So, I had two businesses owned by another business, none of which had any real internet presence. This was the dictionary definition of an umbrella corporation formed for criminal purposes. As in money laundering, pyramid schemes, organized crime, and other types of fraud. My pulse now rocketed into the stratosphere. But if Petito was going to take me seriously, I needed specifics. What *exactly* had Sylvia gotten herself into?

I started throwing the basics Ryan had schooled me on into Google, adding in the word "fraud." It didn't take long to find a surging ravine of malfeasance running through the areas of direct marketing and telemarketing—bad actors selling information they'd gathered about people through apps and websites, either legally or illegally, with the intent of defrauding those people. But I still wasn't sure how that actually worked, so I clicked a link to a recent prosecution of such fraud, *United States v. Maitlin*. I skimmed down a long list of defendant-appellants before realizing there were really only three people amid the thirty aliases. The charges were also multifaceted, including conspiracy to commit fraud, conspiracy to commit wire fraud, conspiracy to commit money laundering, and telemarketing fraud. I still struggled to figure out what exactly had been involved in the scams, although a quick search clarified that "wire fraud" and "money laundering" were catchall charges for any fraud committed over the internet. Helpful to know, but not specific enough for my current needs.

What *was* specific—stunningly specific—was the millions of dollars in restitution the defendants had been ordered to pay back to the people they'd defrauded. I'd been envisioning thousands of dollars stolen—maybe even a few hundred thousand—but not *millions*. And if the players involved were required to pay restitution, that meant Sylvia could be on the line to pay back millions of dollars to victims. If my suspicions were true, Sylvia wasn't just broke—she was potentially millions of dollars in debt.

My finger drumming turned into frantic pounding. I needed to understand *exactly* what this type of fraud involved to be sure it mapped onto Sylvia's companies—examples, with real-life details I could wrap my mind around. So I clicked on a victim-coalition link that kept popping up, for an organization designed to prevent others from becoming victims of this burgeoning area of fraud, headed by someone called Margie Francis. I hunted down Margie's contact information and slipped into her DMs, identifying myself and why I wanted to speak with her.

I'd barely returned to my search when my phone rang. I took a deep breath and tapped to accept the call.

"Capri Sanzio? This is Margie Francis," said a gravelly, scrappy older woman's voice. "I got your message saying you're investigating direct-marketing and telemarketing fraud?"

"Yes. I'd love to talk to you about your experience, if you have time."

"I got nothing *but* time. So buckle up, buttercup, 'cause you got an earful coming your way."

I scrambled to put the call on speakerphone and pull over my notebook. "You're the first source I've talked to, so I'd love to know what exactly happened to you."

Margie sucked in a breath accompanied by the subtle crackling of a cigarette, then exhaled with equal vigor. "I'm retired, on a fixed income. A little too fixed, if you know what I mean. Two years ago my daughter had twins. I made her these little holders to attach the babies' binkies to their onesies so she didn't spend forever looking for the binkies every time they got spit out. She loved 'em, and long story short, she encouraged me to start an Etsy shop to make some extra money."

Her pause indicated something was expected of me. "Sounds like something I would have loved when my daughter was young," I said truthfully.

"I didn't know anything about anything online, so she helped me set it all up. But she didn't know much more than me, and nobody knew the shop existed, so I had to figure out how to spread the word. I joined a couple of Facebook marketing groups where people share resources and started trying things out."

"That sounds like a smart approach," I said.

"You'd think. But anybody can add anything to a Facebook group, so it's up to you to figure out what's legit. I signed up for an online marketing tutorial, designed to help people learn how to use social media. Long story short, they sold my information to a bunch of other people, identifying me as 'vulnerable'—because older people who aren't informed about the internet are ripe for fleecing. They actually call it a 'sucker list,' if you can believe that."

I could believe it—empathy and remorse weren't hallmarks of most criminals. "How did they fleece you?"

"They knew I was trying to figure out how to promote my product, right? So I started seeing ads and getting contacted about other classes and 'social-media packages.' The classes seemed reasonably priced, and I figured learning what I was doing was an investment in my business. And everything preached the value of using social media effectively, so when someone called about a ninety-nine dollar social-media package that would send out tweets and Instagram posts on accounts followed by new mothers, I tried it. I figured I could check to be sure they did what they promised."

"And they didn't post like they said they would?"

"Oh, they did. But I know now that the majority of 'followers' on those accounts weren't real."

I winced. "Ah. Got it."

"I didn't get any new customers, so when the company contacted me again, I told them I was disappointed. They said I needed their more targeted package, this one two-ninety-nine. When that didn't work, I got a call telling me I needed dedicated branding and a website. That was more expensive—five thousand dollars."

My mind flew back to what I'd originally paid to have my own website designed, and I adjusted for intervening inflation. "Sounds about right for website and branding," I said.

"Oh, I did my research. They priced it just perfect, competitive, not on the cheap end or the expensive end, and they had links to other sites they'd designed. I even contacted the site owners asking them if they were satisfied. But of course the 'owners' were in on it."

"Oh, no."

"Oh, yes. And I couldn't afford five thousand dollars, but I was desperate to get a return on the money I'd already put in. They kept it so it always seemed just right out of reach, you know? So I took out an equity line against my house."

I winced again. "Let me guess—they disappeared with the money."

"Not before charging an additional ten thousand dollars to my credit card."

My jaw dropped. "How did they manage that?"

"They charged fifteen rather than five, and when I fought it, I couldn't prove that wasn't what I'd agreed to, because I'd authorized the charge."

"Holy sh—I mean, holy crap," I said.

"No, you were right the first time," she said. "And it's not like I could sue, because I didn't have money for lawyers. And believe it or not, I got off easy. All total, between the classes and everything, they got me for close to twenty thousand dollars. Lots of people got took for much more."

"Let me make sure I understand. Someone gathered data about you, your interests, your goals, and your demographics, then sold that information to people who used it in a targeted way to exploit your vulnerabilities."

"Couldn't have said it better myself." She inhaled and exhaled another turbo-puff from her cigarette.

"So you went to the police, and they went after the perpetrators?" I prompted.

"And then I met Prince Charming and rode off into the sunset." She snorted. "The police couldn't help."

Righteous indignation flooded me. "What do you mean they couldn't help?"

"A bunch of reasons, mostly not their fault. These criminals aren't stupid. They keep the amounts small enough that they're hard to prosecute."

"Fifteen thousand isn't small," I said.

"To people like you and me it's not. But there's so much fraud going on out there that in order for it to be worth prosecuting, it has to meet certain minimums or you're spitting in the wind. And the criminals keep things spread out over networks of slimeballs, purposefully. Think of it like a web, or a chain-link fence. Bunches of them sharing sucker lists and working from what they call 'sales floors' in different cities and states. When you try to point a finger at it, it's like trying to draw in water."

"So federal agencies have to get involved to pull it all together," I said.

"They call it 'aggregating the damages.' Grouping a whole bunch of victims together so the total of their losses reaches a number worth prosecuting. I was lucky enough to be included in one of the groups, but still haven't gotten my money back. I had to start working again to keep from losing my house." Her voice thickened like she was fighting back tears. "So much for my retirement. I'm seventy and have to stock shelves at Walmart with my arthritis while jerks like this are out there taking private jets to spa weekends on my money. So now I spend every free minute spreading the word so nobody else gets fleeced."

I glanced at the clock on my computer—if I didn't leave now, I was going to be late for my Alcatraz tour. "I really appreciate your time. Can I contact you again if I have more questions?"

"Anything I can do to help, any time."

I thanked her and hung up, then grabbed my cross-body bag and hustled out to my car, brain whirring and spinning. The combination of My Kind of People, who had people literally signing up to volunteer exactly the information fraudsters needed, and Rithmology, who knew the best ways to exploit those 'sucker lists,' was frightening. I was convinced something shady was going on—but had Sylvia known about it? And how was Katherine connected?

As I drove, I left a voicemail for Petito telling him what I'd learned, all while knowing he likely wouldn't take it seriously.

I needed evidence that all this was happening, and I needed it fast.

SF Killer Crime Tours

Alcatraz

Alcatraz is a small island in the San Francisco Bay that has functioned over the years as a lighthouse, various military bases, a protest site for Native American rights, and, of course, a federal penitentiary from 1934 to 1963.

The most hardened, incorrigible prisoners were sent to Alcatraz because the dangerous, shark-filled waters surrounding it were believed to make it escape-proof. While there may have been one successful escape—Frank Morris and brothers Clarence and John Anglin managed to flee the island and most likely drowned—the penitentiary did its job well. Psychologically as well as physically, because the San Francisco wharfs were clearly visible from the prison yard and windows, and on calm nights, sound carried tantalizing melodies of merrymaking to the prisoners.

Alcatraz was the home of some of America's greatest criminals, including Al Capone, George "Machine Gun" Kelly, and Robert "The Birdman of Alcatraz" Stroud. But even in a prison, if you pack an island full of murderers, someone's gonna end up dead. The most famous instance of an inmate murdering an inmate was dramatized (or, rather, nearly completely fictionalized) in the movie Murder in the First; *it tells the story of Henri Young, who, after trying unsuccessfully to escape with several other prisoners, later shanked one of his confederates, Rufus McCain, with a sharpened spoon. Henri never explained why he did it—and Rufus may very well be one of the ghosts supposedly roaming the prison grounds to this day.*

Chapter Twenty-one

The Infamous Criminals of Alcatraz tour is a pain in my rump to get to—I take the same ferry out to the island as anybody else—but it's totally worth it. A skilled tour guide doesn't just disseminate information, they create an experience for their guests; every choice and every emphasis is designed to build a mood that transports to a particular time and place. With Alcatraz, the setting takes care of most of that for me. As you board the ferry, the island looks deceptively close—*surely it wouldn't be that hard to swim the distance and escape*, you think. But as San Francisco retreats behind you, you're left with a disconcerting sense of separating from civilization, and the length of time the boat takes to cross the expanse allows you to feel how truly impossible escape would be. Then, as you step onto the island, an overwhelmingly institutional gray-beige four-story building looms over you, its lack of color a symbolic reflection of the prisoners' baleful existence. You must then march up a steep hill, gravity tugging at your psyche as well as your legs, until you finally make your way into the gray-beige cell block. Then as you stare down the vast, multilevel corridors at the seemingly endless gray-beige bars, the ghosts of the men who lived and died there whisper in the creaks and clangs and echoes snaking along each hall, and I only have to sprinkle in a few choice details to telegraph the desperation of the men imprisoned there.

Steely-gray clouds gathered over the site as I called my tour together, adding even more atmosphere to the tales I was about to tell. I led them through room by room, discussing inmates, prison escape attempts, and myths, walking slowly enough to allow the damp cold to seep under their coats and into their imaginations.

On the ferry ride back, I mulled over the potential fraud being wrought by My Kind of People and Rithmology. If Sylvia had returned from Hawaii to find evidence of the fraud waiting for her, that would certainly explain why she'd been upset. Katherine could have been involved in it all, maybe by exploiting connections she had from her husband's mega software business to create her own side hustle; maybe some third party—like Nancy or her husband Robert—blackmailed both her and Sylvia. But then why kill them? Or maybe Katherine had learned about the fraud through her husband's grapevine of connections and, hoping to gain favor with Sylvia, left her a phone message. Sylvia might not have checked in until she got back; she'd been annoyed about having to bail out Katherine's charity luncheon mistakes and might have assumed the call was about that. In the meantime, maybe the wrong person realized Katherine was poking her nose in where it didn't belong and killed her, then once Sylvia started asking around, they did the same to her. Tapping into the methodology of a notorious serial killer known for killing women would have been the perfect cover.

Sure, all well and good. But I still needed evidence.

So once back on dry land, I headed over to The Chateau. I'd promised I'd look for the missing Rolodex anyway; wherever it was, it was likely Sylvia's other missing documents would be there, too.

Morgan had returned after her classes and planned to stay over until the following evening, so she offered to help me search. Todd was out tending to details, but Philip was up, so he joined in, too. We started from the bottom of the house and worked our way up, checking under every picture frame or other wall covering, and under every area rug. Two hours later, the only thing I'd come up with was a complete lack of dust and dirt—Sylvia must have inspired complete terror in her house cleaners for them to be that thorough. So, in a last-ditch dash of desperation, we trooped up to the attic and went through the trunks and boxes that lined the space.

When we headed up, I was afraid the memories we'd stir up would be too much for Philip. As it turned out, I was both right and wrong. Since much of what we found was connected to events that happened either before Morgan was born or when she was too young to remember, she had tons of questions about it all, and the answers wove us gently in and out of Sylvia's life. She listened with quiet reverence at times and interjected her own memories at others. It felt almost religious, I reflected as I drove home; like we were engaging in some healing ritual ingrained deep in the human psyche, passing on a torch of respect and connection from the older generation to the younger. The way Morgan would someday pass memories of her father and me on to her own children.

By the time I made it home, it was nearly midnight and I was so tired I could barely walk. Having found nothing to help at The Chateau, I was at a loss for what next steps to take, and my brain refused to even pretend to come up with any options. I barely managed to throw on a nightgown before crashing onto my bed, without even brushing my teeth.

I woke the next morning rested but not refreshed, as though my body had slept but my mind hadn't. Thankfully I didn't have an early walking tour on Thursdays, because I couldn't bear to look around my neglected house any longer—I may not keep the meticulous house

Sylvia did, but even I had my limits. I told myself a vigorous round of housecleaning would keep my hands busy but leave my mind free to think, and jumped on in. I ran a load of dishes through the washer, once-overed the stack of snail mail, and gave my hardwood floors a quick Swiffering. Then I dragged my overflowing hamper into the laundry room and began to separate the contents.

As I tossed the pair of jeans I'd been wearing Monday into the washing machine, two memory cards fell onto the floor.

"Oh, crap." I snatched them up, wincing at my own stupidity. I'd completely forgotten about the memory cards I'd found in Sylvia's desk drawer. Never in a million years would Petito believe I hadn't withheld them on purpose—I needed to get them to him as soon as possible.

But . . .

There really wasn't any reason for me not to peek at them before I turned them over . . . because, really, what could it hurt . . .

Before my brain had a chance to pick apart that fragile logic, I pulled out my laptop, fired it up, and stuck the first card in.

It was password protected.

For the next half hour I found myself back in a déjà-vu hell of trying to guess what Sylvia would have used for a password. My imagination failed, and finally, frustrated, I yanked it back out and tossed it on my desk. I stuck the second one in, already resigned to the fact that it would leave me befuddled, too.

The card's folder opened right up.

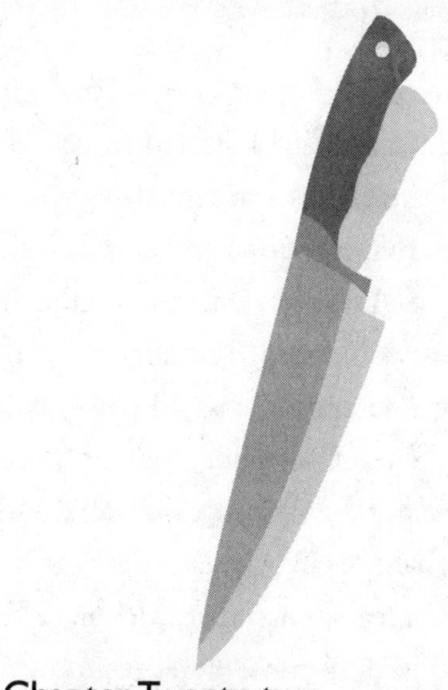

Chapter Twenty-two

I was so stunned that the contents of the card opened up I stared dumbly at it for a moment wondering what to do. Then I clicked, and inside found several setup and config files along with another folder, this one labeled DCIM. *That* I recognized—it meant some sort of pictures or video taken on some sort of device. I clicked through and found a single file titled "Nancy."

Blood whooshed through my ears as I launched the video, and my brain launched into a rousing game of generate-the-worst-possible-scenario regarding what I was about to see. As I fought back visions of a septuagenarian sex tape, the video opened—to reveal a view of Sylvia working at her desk in her office. On July twentieth at two ten in the afternoon, according to the date and time stamp in the corner. The angle was odd—not fully bird's-eye, but from behind and higher than where she sat, showing a full view of the desk in front of her and the chairs opposite.

I laughed out loud. Because *of course* Sylvia had a nanny cam.

Sylvia typed away at her computer, and I upped the speed on the video player, hoping to move forward more quickly but not wanting to miss anything important. After zipping through nearly an hour's worth of footage, I started to get antsy. Maybe that's why this card wasn't password protected—maybe it only contained junk footage. When Sylvia got up and left the room and didn't return for nearly ten minutes, I was ready to give up the ghost.

Just as I reached to click the video closed, Sylvia returned, carrying a tea tray, followed by two women: Nancy McQuaid and Beth Last-Name-Unremembered. I set the player back to normal speed as Sylvia put the tray on a side table and the two women settled into the armchairs facing Sylvia's desk. Sylvia poured and distributed three cups of tea, then sat back down.

"I've done most of the groundwork already, so I simply need your eyes on the final details." She clicked the mouse pad on her laptop several times, then reached to retrieve a stack of papers from her printer. She handed sheets to each of the other women and kept several for herself.

For the next hour, the three ladies went over details of a casino-night fundraiser. While the event sounded like fun, the minutiae they discussed ad nauseum were not, and by the time they finished, just the thought of a roulette wheel or a blackjack table made me nauseous. But in the process I remembered Beth's last name was Marcusson, and that counted for something.

Finally they agreed everything was in order. "You really have a knack for these details, Sylvie," Nancy said. "With your acumen and attention to detail, you'd make a great board member for Luminous Face."

I couldn't see most of Sylvia's face, but Beth's widened eyes and surreptitious glance at Sylvia clued me in that the comment wasn't as complimentary as it seemed.

"Is that an invitation to join Luminous Face's board?" Sylvia asked, with a laugh that was the tiniest titch too high-pitched.

"I wish I could," Nancy replied with an upper-echelon eye roll.

"It wouldn't be appropriate for me to make an overture like that. The board members are *so* top-tier, but the work we've been doing really shows me how valuable these skills are."

My eyebrows shot up. Was Nancy rubbing her appointment to Luminous Face's board in Sylvia's face? Was Sylvia jealous of that appointment? Beth's wince confirmed it for me—Little Miss Nancy was the sort of "friend" who moonlighted as a raging bitch.

Family's a funny thing. Sylvia had been downright cruel to me on multiple occasions, and I'd be lying if I said I'd never hoped she'd get a comeuppance. But to see an outsider give it to her raised my hackles, and I found myself wanting to slap Nancy's smugly *luminous face*.

After another glance at Sylvia, Beth's expression tightened. "Hats off to you, Nancy—I hear that was quite a little coup you pulled off there."

Nancy's head swiveled luxuriously toward Beth. "Oh? What did you hear?"

Beth's hand flittered up and away, dismissing her own comment. "You know me, I don't understand these nuances. But Gary said something about Robert making it happen for you."

Gary was Beth's husband, and of course Robert was Nancy's finance-expert husband. I rewound slightly to focus on the reactions to Beth's statement: Sylvia's head bent slightly forward, and a sly grin crept over Nancy's face.

"Well," Nancy said, "what's the use of having a husband who owns such an important company if they can't use who and what they know to your advantage now and then?"

Sylvia's posture shifted, mirroring the tension in my own—that sounded dangerously like insider trading to me.

"Ah, nepotism—it makes the world go around," Sylvia said. "I wondered how you managed it. Most companies don't like the optics of having major shareholders on their boards these days."

I leaned in. Beth's comment hadn't sounded like nepotism at all—what was I missing?

Nancy's artificial tinkle of a laugh cut off my thoughts. "Oh, he's not related to anyone at Luminous Face. If he had been, I'd have been on the board *ages* ago. Luckily, it turns out that while blood may be thicker than water, information is thicker than both. Opens *so* many doors." She gave a smug wink, and my desire to slap her rose up again full force.

Beth and Sylvia tinkled their own laughs, and a vision of the Stygian Witches flashed through my mind. I wasn't naive enough to think business wasn't conducted that way, but to have the evidence trotted out so casually took my breath away. And watching Sylvia masterfully prod Nancy into the admission was chilling.

Nancy stood up. "Well. I have to dash. So lovely to be able to chat with you two today! I'm so busy these days I don't get to spend nearly enough time with friends."

Beth and Sylvia also stood, and together they exited the room. I stared at the empty office, imagining the double-kiss rituals happening at the front door.

Then I heard the door click closed and Sylvia reappeared in front of the camera. As she reached to turn it off, I got a clear shot of her face: a mix of shock, excitement—and cunning.

• • •

I don't know how long I sat staring at my laptop's screen processing what I'd just seen.

Not the insider-trading part, that much seemed pretty clear-cut. What worried me was why Sylvia had kept the recording. Normally you'd want to get rid of information that could send good friends to jail as soon as possible. She'd made a specific decision to keep an admission that incriminated her friend, and there was only one reason to do that.

She intended to use it.

But how? Was it a coincidence that she'd demanded Nancy come over Monday afternoon for a reason she didn't explain? The most likely explanation was that, due to her newly dire circumstances, Sylvia had decided the day to pressure Nancy had come. Had Sylvia wanted some sort of entrée into Luminous Face? But if that were so, she would have used the recording long before. More likely what she wanted was help from Nancy's husband, the finance king. If he'd been willing to leverage inside information to help his wife out, maybe he'd trade a little more to help Sylvia, if it kept him and his wife out of jail.

And blackmail was an extremely compelling motive for murder. Nancy or Robert might have decided they'd rather get rid of Sylvia than be at her beck and call in perpetuity.

Thoughts whizzed and buzzed around my head like a cloud of meth-infested bees. The scenario would explain why Sylvia had gone out alone that night; she wouldn't have wanted Philip to know she was trying her hand at blackmail, and a quick stroll around the corner to the Presidio to meet Robert and/or Nancy wouldn't have seemed dangerous. It also explained why she left her phone behind—if she was doing something illegal, she wouldn't have wanted location data to track her.

I only had Nancy's word that Sylvia had asked her to meet Monday afternoon and not Sunday night. But why not pretend there was never any meeting to start with? Because she had to account for her *phone call* to Sylvia. The first thing the police would do is check Sylvia's phone records, and they'd see she'd called Nancy the night she died. Or maybe Nancy really had thought she was coming to deal with Sylvia on Monday, but without telling her, Robert had dealt with the problem the night before.

It was a strong theory, and for the first time I had some solid evidence in the recording.

My eyes fell on the first memory card again. If Sylvia hadn't bothered to password protect an incriminating video about her friend, what the hell was on the memory card she *had* felt the need to password protect? I needed to see for myself, but I couldn't get into the card.

Luckily, I knew someone who could.

• • •

Ryan glanced up in surprise as I pushed through the door to The Hub ten minutes later.

"What's up, boss? We don't have a tour for hours."

He knew me too well—I guarded my free mornings like a Gringotts vault. "I have a favor to ask you about Sylvia's murder." I produced the memory card. "I found this in her desk and wanted to check what's on it before I turn it over to the police. But it's password protected, so I was wondering if you could hack it."

Ryan's eyes lit up, and he took the card. "You want me to *crack* it, not *hack* it."

"What's the difference?" I asked.

He shrugged. "Historically, hackers were people who tested out holes in systems for the purpose of making them stronger, with good intent rather than malicious. Most people don't know the difference, but if you're talking to a pro, you might as well use the right term. If you're trying to break into something, especially for shady reasons, that's referred to as 'cracking.'"

I drew my mouth down in a *huh* smirk. "Learn something new every day. Can you crack it, then?"

He shot me a withering glare. "*Of course.* It's just a question of how long it'll take. Start with the basics about Sylvia so I don't have to go in full brute-force. Important dates, all that." He pulled over a pad and pen.

"I already tried the stuff I could think of," I said.

He flicked the pen back and forth over his knuckles and grinned at me. "Sure, but I'll put it into a program that will prioritize significant strings of letters and numbers. It's called a 'mask attack.' So, like, maybe she doesn't just use her husband's name and birth date, maybe she mixes them together, or puts a string of letters or numbers before or after it. Super common in people who know a little bit about avoiding stupid password mistakes."

"Impressive." I rattled off names and dates.

"Great," he said when I finished. "I'll get started."

"Any idea how long it'll take?" I asked.

"Not really. I could get lucky and get it within minutes, or it could take days. I don't have the best tools."

"No worries. Whatever time it takes, it takes. It's just that I need to turn it in to the police as soon as possible."

He cracked his knuckles and stared down at the card like a child staring at a Christmas tree. "Gotcha. I'll text you the second I get anything."

"Great." I gathered up my things. "I have an errand to run in the meantime."

Because, if Sylvia had a continually running nanny cam, that cam would have been recording the night she died and could identify her killer—onto a memory card that hadn't yet been removed.

Chapter Twenty-three

I spent the next twenty minutes trying to keep calm as I navigated traffic—the last thing I wanted when dodging double-parkers, random lane-changers, and kamikaze bicycle messengers was to be in an overreactive, jumpy state.

Morgan met me halfway up the stairs from the garage and wrapped me in a hug. "Mom, I didn't realize you were coming over. I was just about to start lunch for Grandpa. Are you hungry?"

I should have been, but adrenaline had dulled my appetite. "No, thank you. How's he doing?"

Her brow creased. "I think he's entering some strange version of the bargaining phase of grief. He's finally coming out of his room and has stopped taking Xanax, but now he's restless, like he thinks if he can figure out who killed Grandma, everything will be okay. I can't get him to settle down."

I gazed up toward the next floor as we climbed. "Not the worst thing in the world, if it keeps you and me out of jail—"

Her head whipped toward me. "You?"

The surprise in her tone surprised me, until I realized she didn't know I'd contacted Sylvia the night she died. "After I hung up with you Sunday, I called her. Our conversation wasn't pleasant. And on top of that, I'd just contacted the police about the Overkill Bill copycat killer."

Her eyes widened. "Copycat killer?"

Had I not told her about this? In the blur of everything, I must have forgotten. I caught her up as we climbed to Sylvia's office. "So where things stand now is, there's a nanny cam in Grandma's office and we need to find it."

"A nanny cam?" Morgan's hand flew to her neck. "I knew she wasn't the most trusting person, but, just—wow."

By that point we'd made it up to the third floor, and as we turned onto the landing, Philip appeared out of his room. "Who wasn't the most trusting person?"

"Sylvia." I took a deep breath. "I found two memory cards in her desk, and they turned out to have a video on them of a meeting she had with Nancy and Beth in her office. She must have a nanny cam in there, but I'm guessing if you knew where, you'd have mentioned it."

Philip's cheeks reddened, and his mouth opened and closed slightly like a stunned fish. "I—no. She mentioned something once about getting a camera when the incident happened with that maid. But she never mentioned it again, so I assumed she decided against it." His brows suddenly shot up. "Maybe it recorded what happened the night she was killed?"

"That's what I'm hoping." I turned and headed toward the office. Once inside, I pointed to the large bookcase behind Sylvia's desk, one of four that lined that side of the room. "From the angle of the video, my guess is it's here."

I ran my eyes over the contents but didn't notice anything that looked like a webcam. "It must be disguised as something else so the cleaners wouldn't realize. We'll need to check every item. Let's each take a shelf."

Philip and Morgan nodded, and we began to carefully pull off books and tchotchkes. I opened each book and riffled through, checking to see if anything odd was stuck anywhere. With the other items I searched every inch for any opening or crevice that could potentially house a camera.

Toward the end of the shelf, I found it. In a frame with a picture of Sylvia and Philip in front of an Alaskan glacier—a tiny circle in the bottom, disguised by swirls of gold filigree. I turned the frame over; even the back looked perfectly normal, but on the bottom, right where it sat against the shelf, was the telltale elongated oval of a micro SD card slot.

"Eureka!" I said, caring not one whit that I sounded like some prospector in a fifties B-movie. "I need a paperclip."

Philip handed me one from the top of Sylvia's desk, then leaned in with Morgan to watch me, both taut as stretched springs.

After a moment of fiddling the slot popped open to reveal the card. I reached into my pocket for the other memory card and swapped out the micro SD card from the adapter. "Can we use your laptop?" I asked Morgan.

"Hang on." She raced out of the room, and in less than a minute was back with it.

I slipped the card in and clicked on the icon to open. A few clicks later, a video of Sylvia's empty office started. The image shook slightly as the frame was slipped back into place on the shelf, followed by the sound of the office door closing. I glanced down at the date and time stamp in the corner. "Nine o'clock Sunday night. Whatever happened to her must have happened right around then."

I sped up the video, hoping to get more quickly to whenever Sylvia returned to the office. In the meantime I maximized the window and scoured for any details I could. The desk was pristine—if she'd been working in the office, she'd put everything cleanly away.

"Is there anything out of place you can see?" I asked Philip.

He frowned at the monitor. "Not that I can tell. But I'm not the best at those details."

An hour of recording time passed, and Sylvia didn't reappear. I clicked the speed up another notch. Morgan shifted in Sylvia's chair, Philip twisted his wedding ring, and I bounced my weight from one foot to the other.

No Sylvia.

I pointed to the time stamp. "Nearly midnight. I think that door closing must have been Sylvia going out for her walk. She must have changed out the memory card right before she left."

"You said you found two other cards, right?" Philip asked, perking up. "And one was password protected?"

I nodded. "Whatever sent her out on the walk must be on that card. She must have wanted to save it like she did the conversation with Nancy."

His brow knit. "You said your friend is trying to get into it? Can we be sure he won't damage it in any way? It may be the only chance we have to know what happened. I think we should take it directly to the police."

Morgan shook her head. "There's no way he can hurt it, Grandpa."

"Are you sure? What if he erases it accidentally, or if she had it set to self-erase after enough wrong password attempts?" His eyes flipped between Morgan and me.

I turned to Morgan. "Is that possible?"

Her face scrunched skeptically. "I know that you can set some devices to auto-wipe after wrong password attempts, but I don't think you can do it with a memory card. Even so, Grandma wouldn't have known how to set it up."

If I'd learned anything over the past few days, it was that Sylvia had far more layers than any of us realized. "She was investing in tech companies. Someone there could've taught her. Maybe we *should* get it to the police ASAP, just in case."

Philip nodded. "I'd really prefer we did. No offense to your friend."

"No, I completely understand." Despite my brain screaming out against never knowing what was on the card, I slid out my phone and tapped Ryan's contact number. The line rang several times, then went to voicemail. "Dammit," I said, then left a quick voicemail asking him to stop cracking the card.

I checked the time. "He's in the middle of Heather's afternoon Zoom tour. If I go now, I can get there in about twenty minutes."

I dove into the car and out of the garage as quickly as the slow-moving automatic gate allowed me, berating myself for not considering Sylvia might have booby-trapped the memory card. I was considering running the red light at the end of the street when my phone rang.

"Hey, Capri," Ryan's voice rang out. "I—"

I dove in. "Ryan, thank God! Stop with the memory card. Turns out it may be the last card she had in the camera before she died, and we're thinking we should get it to the police ASAP. We're worried there might be some sort of auto-wipe feature on it."

"There isn't."

"Right, but leave it just in case. I'm on my way to pick it up and take it to the police."

"Too late. I cracked it. I was just calling to tell you."

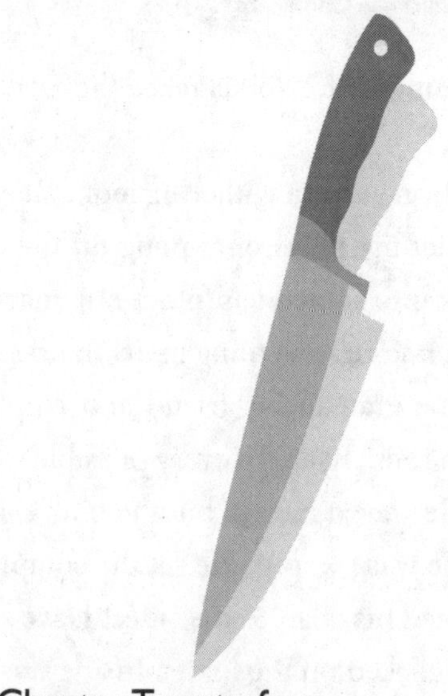

Chapter Twenty-four

I couldn't even remember driving from The Chateau to The Hub that day, I was so focused on what might be on that card. The first thing I remember is pushing through the door to find Ryan sitting at his desk, a smile that outshined the Cheshire Cat's winding purposefully across his face, and Heather sitting across from him, one long leg swinging with nervous energy.

"Thank God you're here, I don't think I coulda waited another minute." Heather jumped up and raced me to Ryan's desk.

"Waited? Ha!" Ryan said. "You tried to physically wrench the laptop out of my hands!"

"No idea what you're talking about," she said, making a dive for the laptop.

Ryan deftly swept it out of her grasp with a glare.

"What's on it?" I asked.

"I don't know, I haven't looked yet. That's why she's losing it." Hands full of laptop, he jutted his chin at Heather. "She threatened a very personal part of my anatomy. That's harassment, you know."

I couldn't condone her approach, but found it hard to argue with her sentiment. "You cracked the card, but didn't look to see what was on it?"

He gave me a withering look. "It's not my property."

I let my brain ping-pong off the logic of finding it acceptable to break into someone's folder but unacceptable to look at the contents, then, before something in my mind short-circuited, decided I should just be grateful my friend and employee had loyalty and integrity. "You rock, Ryan. In every possible way."

He waved me off, but the pink tinge that crawled up his ears told me he was pleased. He set the computer back down on the desk and scooted his chair to the side. "Have at it."

I clicked on the folder. Inside was another folder marked "Private Investigator" and a movie file titled "Philip_Pr." Given Sylvia's apparent willingness to engage in blackmail, I clicked the private investigator folder first, revealing several documents. I opened each in turn and skimmed through. Both Ryan and Heather watched over my shoulder, Ryan with the focused stillness of an apex predator and Heather with the uncontrolled emotion of a golden retriever.

"What *is* all that?" she blurted when she couldn't contain herself any longer.

I pointed to a name on one of the documents. "See this guy?"

Heather peered past my finger. "Yeah."

"He owns a cosmetics corporation called Luminous Face. Sylvia's friend Nancy McQuaid very much wanted to be on its board. Nancy's husband Robert is a finance mogul who knows all the dirt about all the people. Or, more relevantly, their companies." I pointed to another section of the relevant document. "This is evidence that the Luminous Face guy purchased a large amount of HarperWare, the company Steve Harper owns, right before it announced a new microchip manufacturing technology that would basically quadruple existing processing speeds and storage space."

"Steve Harper," Heather gasped. "As in the husband of the woman killed out at the Legion of Honor?"

"That'd be the one." I nodded, and clicked on another document. "This one contains documentation of the timing of HarperWare's announcement. And this next one shows that the day of that announcement, the company's stock value skyrocketed."

I checked both Ryan's and Heather's faces—they were paying rapt attention.

"This next document shows how dramatically the Luminous Face guy's investment increased in value because of that announcement." I paused to let that number sink in. "And this final document shows that two weeks after HarperWare's announcement, Nancy McQuaid became the newest Luminous Face board member."

Ryan's mouth dropped open. "Insider trading."

I nodded. "The other memory card, the one that wasn't password protected, had a recording of Nancy basically admitting her husband had traded information for her spot on the board. And I know that Steve and Katherine Harper have been trying to build relationships in the social circle—he must have mentioned something to Robert about the microchip, which Robert then turned around and used."

"Holy shit," Heather said. "And wait—didn't you say you think something strange is going on with the companies Sylvia invested in? Do you think Robert or Steve has something to do with that?"

"It's possible. It's also possible that Sylvia was blackmailing one or all of them with this tape. And since recording another person without their knowledge is illegal in California, these documents sure look like she hired someone to get proof she could actually use."

Ryan tensed. "You're saying she blackmailed Nancy?"

"I'm not sure." I told him about Nancy's visit. "It's possible Sylvia was *planning* to blackmail Nancy but didn't get a chance to follow through."

"Or she may have already contacted Nancy, and Nancy or Robert killed her," Heather said.

"That's what I thought, too. So I'm really hoping this other video will tell me what exactly happened just before Sylvia was killed, and whether it had to do with Nancy or someone else." I clicked the documents shut and made my way back to the video.

Their faces tensed, and we all leaned back in, as if the extra few inches would somehow reveal a deeper analysis of the recording.

As expected, the video was another piece of footage captured by Sylvia's nanny cam—from six thirty the evening she died.

"Hell yes!" I cried, and held out a fist for each friend to bump.

Sylvia was again alone in her office, and as we watched, she put through a call on her phone.

A voice came over the speakerphone, brisk and efficient with a side of used-car salesman. "Sylvia. How was Hawaii?"

"Let's cut to the chase, Brighton."

I paused the video. "Brighton Keyes," I said. "CEO of Rithmology and My Kind of People."

Ryan and Heather nodded acknowledgment, and I restarted the recording.

"Before I left," Sylvia continued, "you said several fires had cropped up, but you had a way to put them out. Now I get off the plane to find out we have to shut down operations completely? That sounds like the building is going up in flames."

He cleared his throat and the slick-talk edge disappeared. "Don't be dramatic. We'll be fine, but there's only so much risk I'm willing to allow with the current setup. We have to dissolve everything and start over, and that takes time."

"The entire reason I was willing to engage with this was your assurance there were too many levels of involvement to ever track the activity back to us. I told you last week I didn't feel safe, and you told me I was overreacting."

Brighton's sigh was deep and condescending. "I *now* know it's only a matter of time before this particular house of cards comes crashing down. So we're going to collapse it ourselves, that way we can control the fallout."

Sylvia clenched the pen in her hand so hard her knuckles popped up like squeeze toys. "And in the meantime, we have no money coming in. I made clear from the start I need money coming in. You promised me when I came on board that I'd be safe."

Brighton's tone took on an odd mix of annoyed and amused. "Stop with the innocent ingenue crap, Sylvia. You knew there was risk involved."

Sylvia's jaw tightened in profile. "Look, Brighton, I'm not going to sit here and—"

"No, *you* look, Sylvia. I don't know what threat you were about to throw out, but I'm not a manager down at the local Walmart you can go all Karen on. And I want to make sure you understand—I'm not in this alone. So think carefully about what you do, because whatever happens to us happens to you and your husband right along with us."

Sylvia's posture became oddly still, and her voice took on a precise, careful tone. "You know full well my husband doesn't know anything about this."

"You think anyone's gonna believe that for one minute? They certainly won't after I *tell them* he's involved."

Her fist clenched around the pen again. "You're threatening to lie and say he's a part of this when you know full well he knows nothing about any of it? I don't appreciate you threatening people I love."

My stomach clenched—her tone was deceptively dangerous, a phenomenon I'd been exposed to on several unfortunate occasions.

Brighton didn't pick up on it. "I'm well aware of how careful you've been to exclude him, *that's* how I know he's one of your few vulnerabilities. And I've done my research—there are only three things you value in this life: your husband, your son, and your reputation. I promise you, if you say or do anything stupid, I'll make sure I take down all three."

I expected the pen in Sylvia's hand to snap in two, or for her to physically throttle the phone. Instead, she visibly relaxed, letting her normally perfect posture sag against her chair. "You don't have to worry, Brighton. I need this all to work out as much as you do. I just need to know all my ducks are in a row."

"Good to hear. I'll call you back when I know more." He hung up.

Sylvia immediately stood and turned toward the camera. The recording abruptly stopped—but not before I got a clear look at her face, this time drawn tight with fatigued resignation.

Chapter Twenty-five

"Oh, damn," Heather said, still staring at the now-ended video. "That escalated quickly."

"Did it, though?" My mind raced as I considered Sylvia's odd reactions to the conversation. "Something's not right. Why would you keep a recording that clearly implicates you in something illegal?"

"Maybe she pulled the memory card out to destroy it but didn't get the chance," Heather said.

Ryan shook his head. "That's not the original card. The file is edited around the phone conversation, and there's the other folder of documents on it. She was intentionally keeping it."

"Exactly, and we already know she has a penchant for blackmail," Heather said.

"But look at the name of the file—'Philip_Pr' can't be a coincidence. I think the 'PR' stands for protection. She wanted to make sure he was in the clear." I started the video playing again, then moved to the middle of the phone call. "She goes out of her way to get Brighton to say Philip knew nothing about what was going on, then watch how she relaxes."

I watched them watch the replay. "She was poking Brighton to get him to say what she wanted," I said when it finished.

"Aw, that's kinda sweet." Heather tilted her head to the side and made puppy dog eyes. "She doesn't want him to go to jail."

"Or be liable for the millions of dollars of restitution I saw the fraudsters ordered to pay back to victims in *United States vs. Maitlin*," I said.

Heather's face shifted into a frown. "But then we're back to square one, because if she didn't use it for blackmail, I don't see how it could have gotten her killed."

Her words were a tub of ice water on my brain's logic circuits. "Dammit. It might not be related at all."

We all stared at each other for a long minute.

"Preemptive blackmail," I blurted out. "Brighton clearly admits to doing illegal things. Maybe she was worried he'd sell *her* down the river and wanted to let him know if he dropped dime on *her*, she'd take him out."

"First, I'm going to need you to stop watching 1930s gangster movies immediately," Heather said. "And second, wouldn't anything that implicated Sylvia necessarily implicate Brighton, too?"

My brain clicked and whirred. "No, right. So this isn't for blackmail, it's for *leverage*. It gives her something valuable she can use for a *lighter sentence*, or to keep Brighton on his toes. Maybe she wanted him to know he wasn't holding all the cards, and wanted to protect Philip in the process."

"Or maybe she took it to whoever owns that Anchor and Shields umbrella company. That could easily be Steve Harper or Robert McQuaid," Heather said. "More likely Steve Harper, because that would explain how Katherine got caught in the middle of it all."

"It's possible, I guess," Ryan said, frowning. "But do we even know for sure that Rithmology and My Kind of People are doing something illegal?"

I gestured wildly toward the laptop. "You just saw it yourself!"

Ryan rubbed his chin. "I'm not sure this recording proves anything illegal was going on. As we were listening, I was struck by how carefully Keyes was choosing his words, and how ambiguous it all was."

I started to scoff incredulously, but noticed Heather's stricken expression.

Ryan reached over and backed up the video. "Listen," he said.

As I did, my stomach sank to the soles of my feet, because Ryan was right. "He could just be talking about a supply problem or failed quotas they'll have to report to their parent company and investors."

"Or even the other companies Rithmology works with," Ryan said. "Any good defense attorney will dance circles around this clip. And that's *if* the police even think it's worth following up on."

I jumped up out of the chair and paced, chewing my lip. Morgan and me fighting with Sylvia over money was a much more clear-cut argument to put to a jury, so why should he bother to look elsewhere? I couldn't risk Petito putting this in the circular file. "I need those missing papers. Or even if I could get a look at her calendar, or her email, or her laptop or tablet, maybe something there would help. But the police have it all."

Ryan dropped into the chair I'd vacated and pulled the laptop closer. "You know her email address, right?"

"One of them. I'm sure she has several for business purposes," I answered.

"Sure. But most likely they're linked on a single client, like yours are on Gmail. If I can get into one I can probably find the others from there."

"You sure you want to risk trouble with the police?" I asked.

A smile pulled up the corner of his mouth. "No deleting, no altering, no jail time."

"If you're sure." I pulled up my own email account and located Sylvia's email address. "Here you go."

"I'll try the easy route first—hopefully she's the sort of person who uses the same password for everything." He opened a browser and pulled up her Gmail account, then plugged something in. "Nope. But no problemo—I'll do just like I did with the memory card."

"Great, thank you." I pointed to the memory card in the slot. "In the meantime, can you put a copy of everything into our Google Drive files? Then I'll get this over to the police. I don't want to be accused of interfering with a police investigation."

As he clicked and transferred, Heather crossed over to her desk and dropped into her chair. "I'll tell you what, my mind is blown. Like, *I need a drink* kind of blown. Here I thought Sylvia's circle were insipid stuffed shirts who throw luncheons and drink fancy tea, when every single one of them are puff adders slithering around insider trading and committing fraud and blackmailing each other. And they're all richer than God to start with, so it's not like they even need the money. It's all for social position, to determine who gets to sit next to whom at whatever cotillion's the end-all-be-all this year. Absolutely insane."

My face must have dropped while she was talking, because her eyes widened at me. "What?"

"I'm not sure." Something about what she'd said tugged at me, like she'd awoken something hibernating in the depth of my mind that was now struggling to breach a winter's accumulation of snow. "Say more about that."

"Nothing else to say." She waved me off and swiveled a perfect arc to face her laptop. "Except if that sort of handshake-backstab combo is what life's like when you have money, I'll stick to my non-felonious, paycheck-to-paycheck, friends-I-can-trust existence, thank you very much."

• • •

As I walked back home to get my car, I called Morgan and had her put Todd and Philip on a Duo call so we could all see each other.

"Ryan already made his way into the memory card." I reported what was on it and watched their jaws drop.

"Blackmail? And telemarketing fraud?" Morgan gaped at Philip.

He looked sick. "I can't believe it. I did know she was jealous of Nancy's position on the board. But blackmail?" He shook his head.

"How jealous was she?" I asked.

He ran a hand through his hair with a sheepish tug. "Very jealous. But then, she and Nancy have always been—I'm not sure what the right word is."

"Frenemies?" Morgan said.

He nodded.

Morgan shook her head incredulously. "Why be friends with someone you don't like or trust?"

Todd looked at Morgan as if seeing her for the first time. "I forget sometimes how much your mother protected you from this world. When you have money, it's nearly impossible to know whether people want to know you for you, or because of what your money can do for them. Especially because there are expectations about what 'friends' do for one another. Donations, introductions to people and clubs, all that."

A strange expression came over Morgan's face, and she nodded.

"Philip," I asked gently. "You seemed shocked at the idea she'd blackmail Nancy, but not at the possibility of illegal business activities."

He was silent for a moment. "I can't say that I am. I didn't know anything specific, but I've seen a lot of our circle play fast and loose with details. Large 'donations' to push through permits. Information and favors exchanged."

I nodded—I couldn't claim I'd never heard those whisperings myself. "Got it. I'm going to go get these cards to the police now."

"Thank you, Capri, that's a load off my mind," Philip said with a watery smile.

"Anything I can do to help. You know that." Which reminded me. "Morgan, have you talked to Petito yet?"

Her face scrunched, and she looked away. "I totally forgot. I'll call him now."

I belted myself into my Chevy Volt, fully intending to go straight to Petito with the memory cards. I swear.

But the specter of downtown afternoon traffic whispered into my brain's ear that it would be so much easier to slip back over to Pacific Heights and pay Nancy McQuaid a little visit . . . because unlike the police, I didn't have unlimited resources, and seeing the expression on her face when I showed her Sylvia's blackmail video might be the only shot I had at figuring out the truth.

So I backed out of the garage and quickly turned north rather than south before I could talk myself out of it.

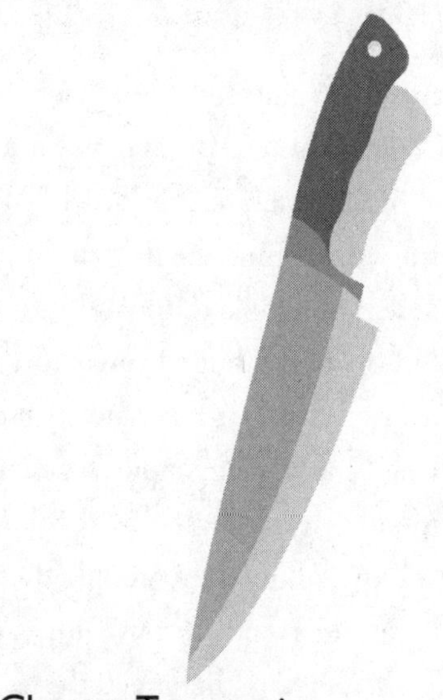

Chapter Twenty-six

According to the address Philip texted me, Nancy lived in Cow Hollow, a neighborhood adjacent to Pacific Heights both geographically and prestigiously. So named because it was once a center for dairy farming, you're now far more likely to find Wagyu entrées than grazing Guernseys, so the name has a quirky irony that sits perfectly on the San Francisco psyche. I followed the GPS's instructions to a faux-Tudor mini-mansion, peach with cream-accented "beams." Lavish by most standards, it was smaller than The Chateau, and I wondered how that would have played into the dynamics between Sylvia and Nancy.

A housekeeper in a pink uniform and cream apron informed me Mrs. Harper wasn't at home, but said I could find her at a committee meeting for a Sisters of Mercy charity gala at the Polk-Presidio Club.

I thanked her and trotted back to where I'd parked, my brain in overdrive. Because the Polk-Presidio club was one of the oldest, most exclusive clubs on the West Coast, with security that rivaled the White House's. I'd been there several times while married to Todd, and they always recognized the Clements instantly—but that was over a decade ago, and the chance of anyone remembering me was slim to none. So I had a ten-minute drive to figure out how to work around the system.

My brain generated all sorts of Abbott and Costello scenarios, like shouting "Did someone drop a diamond bracelet?" and bolting past when everyone looked down, but nothing actually feasible. So when I pulled up to the huge brownstone that used to house one of California's richest silver magnates, I found myself staring blankly at the towering facade while panic froze me in place.

I mentally took myself by the lapels. I could do this, I told myself firmly. I knew how these people thought and what mattered to them, and I was smart and resourceful. The trick was to be confident, assured, and act like I belonged there.

And resurrect my married name.

I put on my most regal posture and swept up to the uniformed guard at a very-important-date pace, not waiting for him to speak to me. "I'm here for the Sisters of Mercy luncheon meeting, guest of Nancy McQuaid, and I'm afraid I'm terribly late. Can you tell me where to find them?"

His expression shifted from one of suspicion to one of tentative sycophantism. He stepped back to check a monitor at his podium. "What did you say your name was?"

"Capri Clement." I put a not-so-slight emphasis on the "Clement."

His hesitation shifted to confusion when, despite my having dropped the proper event and hostess name, I wasn't on the list. "*Capri* Clement?" he asked. "I don't have that name."

I picked up the emphasis he put down and ran with it, waving my hand with a half-annoyed, half-apologetic air. "The list probably says *Sylvia* Clement. I'm her daughter-in-law. She passed suddenly on Monday, and I'm here in her place."

His expression instantly fell. "Of course. I do apologize. We did hear of the tragic accident. Our sincere condolences to your family."

"Thank you." Brushing aside the likelihood that I was going

instantly to hell for invoking Sylvia's passing, I threw an impatient glance toward what I thought I remembered was the dining area. "That's why I'm late—there's so much to attend to. So if you don't mind . . ."

"Of course, of course. I'll have a staff member escort you." He picked up a phone from next to the monitor on the podium and asked for an attendant to be sent out.

Almost immediately, a middle-aged brunette man in a white jacket appeared. "Bradley," the guard said, "Mrs. Clement is the guest of Mrs. McQuaid. Please escort her to the proper table."

Bradley smiled at me. "This way, madam."

I carefully kept the anxiety off my face. I'd been hoping the Clement name would give me a full pass to go in on my own. But with Bradley present, all it would take was a headshake from Nancy to have him toss me out on my butt.

Thankfully, she didn't notice me until we were on top of her and didn't have time to think.

"Mrs. McQuaid, your guest has arrived," Bradley announced.

A cavalcade of emotions paraded across Nancy's face while I stood hoping the omnipresent rich-person distaste for dramatic scenes would win the day.

"Thank you, Robert." She stood to dole out air kisses. "Capri, how lovely to see you," she simpered before turning back to address the table. "Ladies, you all remember Sylvia Clement's daughter-in-law, Capri?"

A chorus of condolences twittered at me, accompanied by shrewd eyes raking me for any clue as to why I was there.

"Please excuse me, we have an urgent matter we need to tend to." With a hand on my side, Nancy guided me firmly out of the dining room.

As soon as we rounded the corner into a vast hallway, she pulled me to the side and hissed a whisper. "What are you doing here?"

"I need to speak to you about Sylvia."

She glanced back toward the dining room. "I don't have time for this, Capri. We can meet later—"

I leaned in on her eagerness to be rid of me. "I'm more than happy to discuss it in front of your friends if need be."

She drew herself up to her full height. "I'll have you thrown out."

"I'm not sure the staff will risk angering Philip, given he's a member of this club, too—and recently bereaved," I said. "And you'd still have to explain to your friends why you threw me out, and they'll call me for the gossip before I'm off the premises."

She glared a fierce combination of hatred and fear at me. "You have two minutes."

"Great." Fast was good; it gave her less time to think up a lie. I pulled up my phone and tapped into Google Drive. I started the video footage playing at the relevant section.

Nancy's face reddened, and she grabbed at my phone while glancing around. "Shut it off."

I dodged to keep it out of her grasp, then tapped to pause it. "Talk to me."

She hissed another whispered response. "There's nothing to talk about except disgusting, unfounded accusations—"

I threw up a hand to stop her, then clicked open the folder of documents, holding the phone where she could see it but still out of reach. "Not unfounded. Sylvia had evidence. The only question left is whether you killed her to keep it from getting out."

The angry flush on her face paled to a sickly gray. "I—I—" She grabbed my arm and pulled me into the nearest room. A janitorial closet, I deduced when a container sent a splash of water onto my leg and a mop handle smacked my head. Luckily, an automatic light clicked on, saving me from serious injury.

"I would never harm Sylvia," she said, still hiss-pering. "I have no idea what she intended to do."

I waved the phone at her. "You really expect me to believe you dropped everything for a last-minute meeting with Sylvia without knowing why? Come on, Nancy. You may be able to lie to me, but you won't be able to lie to the police."

She crossed her arms over her chest and a Grinch-stealing-Christmas smile crept over her face. "Take it to the police, then. Go, now. I'll be home in an hour if they have questions."

That stopped me short. As I scrambled to make sense of her response, something Margie Francis said about the police not having the resources to prosecute instances of fraud came rushing back to me—was the same true for insider-trading-type crimes? But if that were so, Sylvia would have known that, too—yet she still blackmailed Nancy. Why?

Because Sylvia would have known the *police* weren't where Nancy's real Achilles' heel lay. Her *pride* at being a valued member of the board was.

"Fine." I raised my voice back up to a normal volume. "And on my way out, I'll stop by your social-totem-pole table and let everyone know that your appointment to the board was bought and paid for by insider information."

Her face paled all over again, and her hand shot out to stop me. "Wait—"

I wrenched my wrist away from her. "Then tell me what happened, *now*."

She took a long moment, but finally responded. "Yes, she called me about it. But she said she didn't have any problem keeping my secret because friends *help* each other." She put air quotes around the word. "And she said she was certain that as her friend, I'd want to help *her* as a thank-you for *her* helping *me*."

The wording sent a chill down my torso—I couldn't think of a more Sylvia-esque way to frame blackmail. "What sort of help did she want?"

"Information, of course. Like Robert gave Luminous Face. But Robert can't just produce information that will turn into investment gold overnight like a magician with a top hat. I had to wait *months*, more than a year, actually, for the timing of HarperWare's announcement to be right. I talked to Robert, and he said he'd take care of it, but Sylvia would have to bide her time. When I told her that, she said she was in dire need. I asked her why she didn't just ask Todd to help if she needed money. She just grunted at me and told me he couldn't help. Robert said I should give her some cash, so I told her I'd pull together what I could from our home safe and safety deposit boxes and bring it by the next day."

My mind flew to the ostentatious Birkin bag Nancy'd been clutching Monday.

"And that's all I have to say." Nancy pushed past me. "I'm sure you can see yourself out."

The timer on the automatic light went out, leaving me in the darkness to decide whether I believed she was telling the truth.

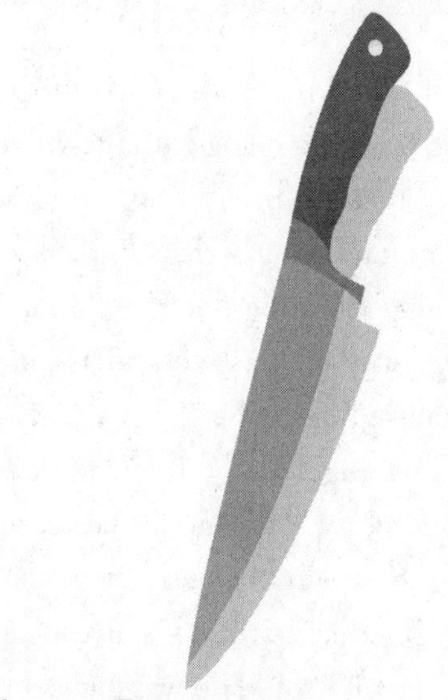

Chapter Twenty-seven

After leaving the Polk-Presidio Club, I drove to deliver the memory cards to Petito in a sort of stunned suspension while a panel of voices in my head shouted over each other, filling me with a soaking dread and sense of impending doom. Heather was right—Sylvia's social circle wasn't just dysfunctional, it was downright dangerous, with accusations and blackmail flying around with the greatest of ease.

Nancy could be lying—just because she said she'd satisfied Sylvia with a promise of cash didn't make it true. She could have killed Sylvia to protect her husband, then played off the phone call that she knew the police would find by showing up at Sylvia's the next day. Or, since Sylvia had been gathering evidence against Nancy and Brighton Keyes, what was to say she wasn't blackmailing someone else, too? Or maybe blackmail had nothing to do with it, and it was all to do with the sketchy companies and the direct-marketing fraud. Or maybe there was some sort of affair happening.

Except, that same mental panel screamed at me, the discrepancies and parallels I'd noticed between these murders and the Overkill Bill murders were only consistent with one of those possibilities.

Specifically, I was bothered by the psychology of why my grandfather would admit to being with the victims—it only matched up with the theory that an invisible someone had been lurking in the shadows of my grandfather's visits to prostitutes. Something about someone watching from the outskirts, watching other people's comings and goings lined up perfectly with the idea of a blackmailer. As the parallel crystallized in my head, my nerves crackled and buzzed—blackmail fit everything the best. It had to be at the center of all of this.

But for the moment, the far more pressing concern was how I was going to explain the memory cards, and my visit to Nancy, to Petito. More interference into his investigation wasn't going to endear me to him. But all I could do was focus on the evidence I'd found and hope it was enough to distract him from me and Morgan.

To drown out the remaining voices, I flipped my playlist on and sang with Taylor Swift at the top of my lungs about shaking everything off. But my sympathetic nervous system was not fooled, and little nervous pangs tingled through my tummy as I thought of facing Petito. Maybe my mother was right, maybe I really did need to take up meditation. Or some of Philip's Xanaxes.

I parked and trudged into the building, praying Petito would be busy so I could just drop off the cards and not have to face his blue truth-piercing ocular missiles. To force one foot in front of the other, I chanted to myself that he was most likely out following up on some lead or other. He was a busy man, after all.

That would almost certainly be the case.

• • •

Spoiler alert: that was not the case.

Petito appeared immediately after the front-desk guy called him. He beamed at me as he approached, his eye crinkles and welcoming smile warming me. I almost smiled back—until the memory of how he'd shifted tactics to get me thinking he was concerned about me bounced a ball of annoyance up into my throat. That was the thing about good looks and charm—they could be used for evil just as easily as they could be used for good. Morgan had told me all about it, something called the halo effect, how we believe good-looking people are smarter, more competent, and more trustworthy on sight.

Forewarned was forearmed.

"Capri," he said when he reached me, the charming smile spreading into a single dimple on the left side of his face.

Thank goodness I'd prepped myself for it, and was able to keep my resolve in place and my face stoic. "I'm here because I found some memory cards that belonged to Sylvia, and I wanted to get them to you as soon as possible." I thrust them out toward him.

He took them from my hand. "I appreciate that. Where did you find these?"

I opened my mouth to explain with breezy, non-suspicious confidence, but the words tumbled out at a suspiciously non-breezy pace. "I, um, found two of them in her desk, before we knew she was dead. I put them into my pants pocket to check later and then, well, in the shock of it all I forgot about them and they fell out of my pants when I went to do my laundry."

His charming smile faded. "You put them in your pants, then forgot them until you did your laundry."

I gave myself a mental shake and a fierce directive to curtail the verbal diarrhea. "Yes. I know it sounds weird, but there was so much happening that day between trying to help Philip and processing those pictures you showed us, and I guess my mind just had too much going on. Anyway, the point is, I wanted to get them to you ASAP."

Nailed it. That didn't sound nervous or guilty *at all.*

His gaze didn't waver. "I appreciate that. What's on them?"

Dammit—I was really hoping he wouldn't ask. My lizard brain screamed at me to claim ignorance despite the resolutions I'd made on the way over, and I was sorely tempted. But I swallowed hard and stuck to the carefully phrased truth.

"One of them is password protected. The second has a recording of Sylvia and two of her friends in her office. Beth Marcusson and Nancy McQuaid, who pretty much admits to insider trading."

His attention sharpened. "Insider trading?"

"Yes." I hurried on, hoping to deflect any inconvenient questions. "And Nancy showed up to the house right after you left the other day, claiming she had an appointment with Sylvia."

"Did she say what the appointment was about?"

I chose my words hoping to cover that I'd recently accosted her. "She claims Sylvia asked for a loan and Nancy was bringing her money."

His eyes narrowed at me. "So Sylvia was blackmailing her?"

"Nancy says she framed it in terms of two friends doing one another mutual favors."

He didn't blink. "And she just volunteered this information?"

I didn't blink back. "I guess I have one of those faces people trust."

"Ah." He poked at the cards in his palm. "So you were only able to see what was on one of the cards?"

I gritted my teeth. It was one thing to leave information out, but the police weren't forgiving when they caught you in a lie, and I was seventy-five percent certain those eyes could see directly into my soul. "I, uh, well, actually, after a few guesses the password on the second card turned out to be a combination of Philip's name and birthday."

His fist clenched around the cards. "And?"

"There were a bunch of documents related to Nancy's husband's insider trading, and another video with one of her business partners that seems to insinuate something unsavory was going on."

All traces of charm were gone, and his voice turned to stone. "And the third card?"

I stiffened my spine—there was no way to tap dance around this one. "The videos on the first two cards made it clear Sylvia had a nanny cam in her office, so I thought I should check if it was still there. I found it in a picture frame. That's the card from inside."

"And, not wanting to delay a second, you raced it over to me without even looking at it." Sarcasm dripped from his voice, along with something else I couldn't define.

I lifted my chin. "I wanted to see if it showed what happened in her office the night she died. It doesn't."

As Petito's mouth opened to spew something I knew I wasn't going to like, Kumar appeared around the corner.

"Dan. We need to get over to that deposition," she said.

Petito's eyes flicked to her and back to me, and he swore under his breath. "This conversation isn't over. Will you be at home later?"

"It depends when. I have a lot going on right now." My phone rang, and I glanced down at my purse. "I have an afternoon tour and one in the evening, so things are pretty tight."

"Then I'll stop by tomorrow. In the meantime, if you see or hear from your ex-husband, please have him call me. I haven't been able to reach him. And we still haven't heard from your daughter. Must run in the family."

That stopped me in my mental tracks. "She still hasn't called you?"

"No, she has not." He pointed back the way we'd come in. "Can you find your way out?"

I nodded, and took off as fast as I could without running.

Back in my car, I dropped my head into my hands—I didn't know what super-suspicious behavior sounded like, but was pretty sure I'd punched right through the bull's-eye. And why the hell hadn't Morgan called the police yet? And Todd—he'd never been good at returning calls, but in these circumstances I'd've thought he'd prioritize this. But, I tried to reassure myself, as shady as we all surely seemed, Petito had all the evidence now. Once he looked at it and put the pieces together, he'd get off our case and none of this would matter.

I pulled out my phone to check the call I'd missed, expecting it to be from Morgan or Todd—but it was from my mother.

I dialed her back and she picked up right away. "Ma?"

"Capri. You sound strange. Where are you?"

"Just leaving the Hall of Justice." I gave her a quick explanation.

"How are Philip and Todd? Do they need anything?"

"Not right now. I'll keep you posted. Is that why you called, to check in on everyone?" Typical of my mother to worry about others.

"No, it wasn't, but . . ." Her voice trailed off the way it did when she was thinking about something important. "When do you think you'll be home?"

Tiny alarm bells rang in the back of my mind. "I'm on my way right now, so about twenty minutes? Why?"

"I thought I'd drop by, and I'm at your house right now."

My spleen plummeted into my small intestine. Despite her anti-establishment, peace-love-and-flower-power past, my mother believed harmony came from consideration, and had reared me with a firm grasp of etiquette. She'd never, ever, *ever* drop by without calling first—unless there was some sort of emergency. "What's wrong?"

"Nothing," she said, her voice half an octave higher than usual. "I just thought it would be nice to have a chat over coffee."

Yeah, right. And she'd given all her Stevie Nicks skirts to Goodwill on the way over, too. "Let yourself in with your key. I'll be there as soon as I can."

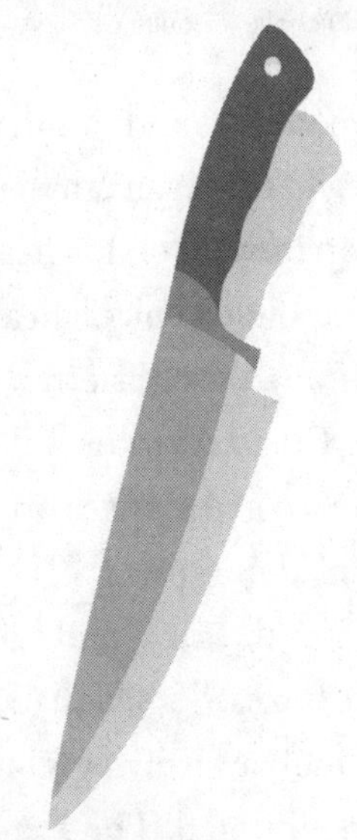

Chapter Twenty-eight

I pulled up into my house twenty minutes later to find my mother perched on the porch, staring up into the dark clouds drifting and morphing their way across the sky. I parked in the garage, then scuttled up the stairs to open the front door from the inside. "Ma. I told you to let yourself in."

She waved me off. "I don't feel comfortable just walking into someone's house when they aren't at home."

"You lived on a commune for a year before you met Dad."

She gathered me into a hug. "Where do you think I learned the importance of boundaries?"

A laugh burst out of me—it never occurred to me she hadn't enjoyed her time there, I'd just assumed she'd given it up for my dad. "I can see how that would be."

"Can you give me a hand with these?" She pointed down at three moving boxes on the side of the porch.

I jumped over to them. "Oh, sorry, I didn't see them. What are they?"

"Let's talk inside."

Another round of tiny daggers stabbed at my internal organs—at this rate, I'd be an adrenaline addict by the end of the week. I lifted the top box. "Oof. It's heavier than I thought it would be."

She smiled enigmatically and picked up the second.

After we'd transferred the boxes to my dining room table, I threw some Chips Ahoy on a plate and brewed some coffee, torn between desire to rip the boxes open and dread that I wasn't going to like what was inside.

Once the carbs and caffeine were in front of us, she pointed to one of the boxes. "Open that one first."

I took a fortifying glug of my coffee, then flipped open the box she'd indicated. The scent of nostalgia wafted up at me, a lovely combination of aging paper, dust, and mothballs. An oversized brown leather album, tooled in a worn filigreed grapevine pattern with gold accents, perched on the top. As I removed it carefully and set it on the table, a different kind of tingle radiated up my spine. Was this—

My mother cleared her throat. "Grandma Sanzio kept diaries and scrapbooks."

My voice came out in a hoarse whisper. "Does Dad know?"

"That she kept them? Yes. That I brought them to you? No." She sipped her coffee and said nothing more.

A torrent of emotions flooded me. Reverence for the precious items in front of me. Gratitude for my mother's courage. Shame that I'd underestimated her. For once in my life I struggled to find words. "Thank you," I whispered.

"You're welcome," she said.

"You have no idea how much this means." I hadn't told her everything going on because I hadn't wanted to worry her, but now it all came gushing out. "They think Morgan or I killed Sylvia, and I've been struggling to figure out who actually did kill her, and everywhere I look there's another horrible thing I can't make sense of. But one thing I know for sure, *something* about the Overkill Bill murders is relevant, more than just its relationship to me. And this"—I gestured to the boxes—"may make all the difference. But I didn't want to ask and make you go against Dad."

She took another sip of coffee, then set her cup down resignedly. "Your father isn't always the easiest person to understand, or to love. I've respected his wishes regarding his father because William isn't my father and it's not my story to tell. But he *is your* grandfather, and that means it *is* part of *your* story. What William Sanzio did or didn't do has an impact on your life and Morgan's life just as much as your father's. More so, if the police think you're involved in Sylvia's death because of your relationship to William. Your father's power to choose ends when your freedom is at stake."

I nodded silently, afraid to derail whatever she had to say.

"Your father loved his mother very dearly, and these boxes contain everything he couldn't bear to part with. Scrapbooks and photos, mostly. She also kept a diary, from the time she was a teen. I can also tell you what little your father has told me, if that helps."

"Yes, please. Anything might help."

"Well"—she took a deep breath—"to start, you should know that your father's pain comes from how much he loved William. Worshiped, really. And it's painful enough for any child when they realize their parents aren't perfect, so you can imagine how hard it was for that bubble to be burst over accusations of murder."

I picked my words carefully. "I guess that's the part I don't understand. If I had that level of admiration for someone and they told me they were innocent, I'd go to the ends of the earth to find a way to believe them."

"But you're forgetting—your grandfather *admitted* to cheating on your grandmother. Multiple times, with prostitutes. And your dad adored his mother as much as his father." She gestured toward the boxes.

I drew in a slow, deep breath as I worked through the implications of that. "Loyalty against loyalty. He had to make a choice, and since his father had already admitted doing something wrong . . ."

"How much further is it to believe he'd commit the other sins he's accused of?" she finished for me.

A vision of my father as a boy filled my head, small and trusting, huddled into his mother's abdomen. "Got it."

She rotated her mug between her palms. "I want you to understand the context because when it comes to this, he's never going to be the clearheaded one. I'd hoped someday he would be, but after your last visit, I see that won't happen on its own."

"I understand." She was telling me that if there was a way to build a bridge, I'd have to be the one to do it. And that, whatever I found out, she was trusting me to deliver it the kindest way possible.

"So. Your father never discussed the details of the accusations or the alibis with me. The only thing he'd talk about was the legacy of pain your grandfather caused, about how he—and I'm quoting—'destroyed the whole family because he couldn't keep it in his pants.'"

"That's why I didn't tell Morgan about what Todd had done until she was an adult, one of the few things I ever held back from her. And even then I was careful how I approached it."

"You didn't want her taking sides. That was the right thing to do."

Her expression darkened. "Your grandmother chose a different path."

"She turned Dad against his father?"

She wagged her head. "I wouldn't go that far. But she didn't hide her pain, and while she was a loving woman, she could also be sharp-tongued. Even years after it all happened, she never held back in front of your father or me. She explained to me more than once that he'd betrayed her and failed to take care of his family. And she always waited for my response, wanting to be sure where I stood. If I felt her pressure to condemn William, your father did, too."

"I always thought his silence was designed to protect *her* from the pain of hearing about it."

"No." She took a long sip from her mug. "And she said something once that has always seemed odd to me. About how William hadn't been 'man enough' to tell the police he'd committed the murders."

I nodded. "I've heard Dad say things like that. About how William caused the family more pain by going through a public trial rather than pleading guilty."

Her eyes scanned the wall behind me. "For your father it was about the embarrassment, yes. But that didn't seem to fit his mother's perspective. For her the big betrayal was his failure to take care of his family, and how hard she had to struggle to do it on her own. From that I would have thought the outcome she'd have hoped for was for him to be found not guilty, since he couldn't support them from behind bars." She shook her head, clearing the cloud on her face. "But maybe I just didn't understand her."

I seriously doubted that—my mother's instincts about people were usually sound. She's the one who taught me to always listen to the little whispers in the back of my head.

She looked down at the silver filigreed watch that had belonged to her mother. "Well. I should get going. I told your father I was going to Costco, so I'll need to stop off there to pick some things up before I go home, and it's already been suspiciously long."

I walked her to the door and gave her a hug before she stepped out on the porch. "Thank you again."

She smiled sadly. "If you come up with any specific questions, ask—it may bring back a memory of some sort. And let me know if there's anything I can do to help regarding Sylvia. I'll call Morgan when I get home."

I watched to be sure she drove away safely. Then I flew back to the dining room, just barely managing not to break my neck in my hurry to get my grabby paws all over the contents of those boxes.

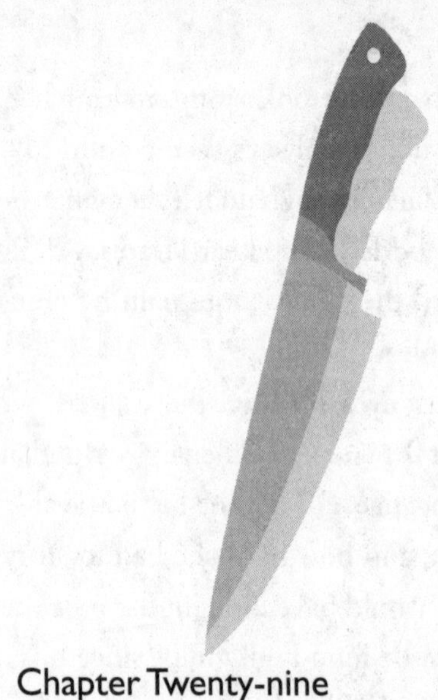

Chapter Twenty-nine

The next several hours flew by as the scrapbook and diaries transported me back through time and into my grandmother's mind. The Italian-dotted entries started with her teen years, plopping me directly into World War II. I knew a fair amount about San Francisco during that war thanks to my tour-guide research, but her voice and memories brought it to life in a vivid and personal way, like I was channeling her soul directly into mine. I was excited to discover my grandmother had been a USO hostess, tickled by her admission she'd lied about her age in order to do it, and downright delighted when she speculated that her "generous bosom" was the reason they believed her. She twittered and gushed in typical teenager fashion about her growing cabal of admirers, and I followed along as flirtations grew into dates, then became pen pals when the men shipped out, and my grandmother enjoyed her carefree existence.

Until the first was killed in action.

The boy's mother had sent her a letter thanking her for her kindness in writing to him, a letter she'd slipped between the pages of the diary. The words were streaked with tears; I wasn't sure if they were the mother's or her own.

The following month her own older brother was shot down somewhere over Europe, and her best friend's cousin died in France. Over several short but intense entries she grappled with how such vibrant men could be alive one day, then dead the next.

The carefree teen disappeared, replaced by a survival pragmatist. She still did teen-girl things, but the dances and dates now had an undercurrent, as though any fluff had been sanded down to a sharp edge. She approached her "friendships" with fewer promises, even after the war ended.

She met my grandfather in 1947; he'd seen battle as a soldier, and it seemed they understood what loss had done to one another. I followed their courtship through movie house tickets, napkins, restaurant matchbooks, and finally a wedding invitation.

Her first child came almost nine months to the day after their wedding, and the tone shifted again, away from romance and onto family. Pictures from the era were posed on family occasions like birthdays, first with the three of them, then joined by my father as a baby. Every single one, whether from a wedding or next to the family Cadillac, verified my grandfather's pride in his appearance: hair always perfectly combed, ties even when his suit coat wasn't present, shirts crisp and button-down.

Philomena's love of being a mother leaped from the diary pages, filled with pride in her boys' milestones and laughter at their hijinks, and seeing them through her eyes gave me a new perspective on the uncle I never knew and the father I thought I did. She referred to Vincent as the "old soul," serious and responsible, who did his homework unbidden and got up before dawn to deliver papers—eventually with the used car he purchased from his own earnings. My father, on the other hand, was *"il buffone,"* the one who made everyone laugh, never thought ahead, and got himself into all sorts of scrapes. My mind reeled and my eyes filled with tears as I read about him chasing a raccoon under a porch after dark, only to get stuck there while the raccoon ran off safe and happy—this was so far from the father I'd experienced, my brain refused to process it. The disconnect joined forces with my mother's earlier disclaimer about him, and tears slid down my cheeks as I, for the first time, viscerally understood how life-altering the Overkill Bill murders had been for my father. To take such a fun-loving boy and turn him into a closed-off, surly man—that wasn't the result of awakening to the world's realities, it was the result of having your spirit crushed.

As the entries moved closer to the date of the murders, I found glimpses of the storm to come. Whatever my grandmother was, she wasn't stupid or oblivious. Whispers of suspicion crept into the entries, and then, just under a year before the first murder, she stated them outright:

Tonight William came home reeking of perfume. He claimed it was his secretary's, because they hang their coats on the same tree. I nodded and made sure to look relieved. But tomorrow we'll see.

I tensed. Whatever was about to happen, I knew it wouldn't end well. And sure enough, the next entry was devastating:

I made a lovely batch of amaretti cookies and paid William a surprise visit at work. As I handed them around, I took great care to check every lady's perfume. The one I had smelled on his coat was not there.

When he came home, I confronted him. He tried to pull himself from the muck by saying I was mistaken, then insane, then finally that his secretary must have worn a different perfume that day. I told him to have it his way, and left it at that. But I'm not mistaken, or insane, and this will not be the end of the matter.

As good as her word, she hatched another plan and executed it a month later:

He "worked late" tonight. He does it on my bridge nights because he thinks he'll be safe that way. Furbo come una volpe, *but I can be sly, too. I called everyone and told them I wasn't feeling well, then went down to his office. The building was dark, including his window. I pounded on the door, but the night guard said nobody was there. When he came home, I handed him a suitcase and told him to get out. But he refused to go. He said what he does is none of my business, since we no longer have relations. He says he will not stop, but if I want a divorce, that's my right and he won't fight it.*

I shuddered, then stared up at the wall. Having also suffered a cheating husband, it was tempting to side completely with my grandmother. But unlike my grandfather, Todd had never been fully honest with me, swearing up and down that it had been a drunken mistake, he'd learned his lesson, he'd never do it again. I'd fully believed he and I were still in love—our sex life had been robust, while Philomena's wording made clear theirs wasn't. Did that make a difference? I wasn't sure. But what I did know was my grandmother's solid Catholic faith abounded on every page of the diaries and scrapbooks, and back then the Church wouldn't have seen infidelity as an acceptable reason for a divorce. Had she chosen to leave, she would have been a pariah, and unable to support herself. She was caught in a cage she couldn't escape from.

Sylvia sprung unbidden to my mind. Something about the pressures she and my grandmother suffered tugged at me, sounding a similar chord of women trying to protect their families. Sylvia had also found herself caught in a cage she couldn't escape from—but hers was of her own construction, and she'd ultimately committed criminal acts.

I shook off the line of thought and returned to the pages, watching as my grandmother struggled for agency by enlisting the pressure of their extended family to get my grandfather to change his ways. When I reached her entry for the day before my grandfather was arrested, I hesitated, holding my breath, as though refusing to turn the page would prevent it all from unfolding. I had to force myself to flip to the next page.

It was blank. As was the one after it, and the one after that.

• • •

The weight of those blank diary pages flattened me.

Why would a woman who'd documented her life from the time she was a teenager suddenly stop? I'd have assumed she shifted to a new diary, but if there was one thing I knew about my grandmother, it was that her Depression-era waste-not-want-not ethos had been her defining characteristic, the same way my grandfather's dapper nature had defined him. She wouldn't have left perfectly good pages blank—this was a shift in psychology. The only explanation was that she'd stopped writing because she didn't want any record of her thoughts; she didn't want evidence of her state of mind or what she was doing. And if she didn't want to leave evidence behind, that could only be because—

My pulse rocketed so out of control I could hear the blood whooshing in my ears. I'd just seconds before told myself my grandmother was different from Sylvia because she hadn't committed a crime to get out of her situation—but what if she had? My theory so far had been that the real killer noticed William with the prostitutes and, because William looked like him, decided to throw suspicion on William by targeting his "dates" as victims. But what if the person watching William *wasn't* a stranger, and had been watching for a very different reason? What if my grandmother had been watching and waiting for an opportunity to make the problem permanently go away?

She'd said it herself—she was a smart woman, smart enough to catch him in his lies about working late. Maybe she'd sneaked out other nights, too, spotted who he was out with, then targeted those women. It was a story as old as time, one I'd never understood, of the injured party taking out their rage on their partner's *lover* rather than the actual partner who betrayed them. Still, if you desperately needed your husband to keep providing for the family, you wouldn't kill *him*—but killing his lovers might seem like an excellent way to scare him straight.

I stared down at my shaking hands—they didn't seem to belong to me. I jumped up and strode around the dining room, forcing myself to take some deep breaths. Reminding myself I had to keep perspective, not jump to conclusions or get attached to theories. I had to be systematic.

Once the breaths returned enough oxygen to my brain, I pulled my notes over and stared back down at the evidence against William. Philomena also had black hair and blue eyes. And if she were the killer, that would explain the strange combination of the passionate overkill and the undisturbed clothes—Philomena's rage would have been very real, but wouldn't have come from twisted sexual desire. Perhaps most of all, it would explain why each of the women William chose subsequently ended up dead.

I flipped the diary back to the night of the first murder. William supposedly had to work that night, his usual cover story, and Philomena had her twice-monthly bridge club. In her recap of the evening she mentioned gossiping with her sisters as the kids played Monopoly and watched TV in the other room. I double-checked the night of the other two murders; one was another bridge night, and the final evening she'd gone to her mother's house to help nurse her through a bout of flu that had veered dangerously close to pneumonia.

I riffled the pages across my thumbnail. Philomena could easily have written whatever alibi she wanted in the diary. But the police would have checked with the other people supposedly present, right? Except—I literally laughed out loud—her sisters would certainly cover for her. And with the kids occupied in the other room, they'd never have noticed her slip away for part of the night.

In a desperate bid for something approaching evidence, I flipped through the photos back to the time of the murders. But as I pulled them closer, the possibility flickered out. My grandmother was short, a full head shorter than my grandfather, *while* wearing heels. And she had gorgeous, thick black hair that fell to her shoulders—but the witness had described a man with short hair, who wasn't wearing a hat. No disguise could have accomplished all that. She couldn't have been the killer, even with her family to cover for her.

Her family—the thought came to me with a gasp. A trumped-up alibi wasn't the only way family could help you. What if, after she'd decried William's behavior directly to her family and his, one of her two brothers decided to do more than just have a talk with William?

I flipped desperately to the few extended-family pictures. As far as I could tell from the black-and-white photos, both my great-uncles Gianni and Stefano had light eyes, probably blue, and certainly had dark hair. They were both within a couple of inches of my grandfather's height. Both of them could have been mistaken for him in low light—and they were both younger than my grandfather.

Either of them could easily have been Overkill Bill.

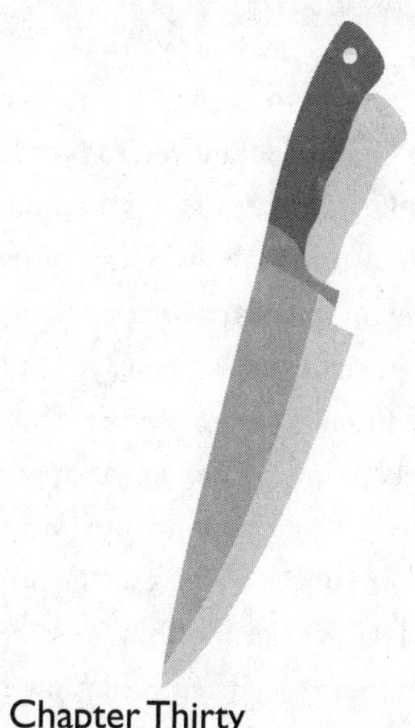

Chapter Thirty

I stood up and paced the dining room again, this time trying to get my heart to stop racing. Then I grabbed my notebook and started to jot down everything I'd just noticed in the diary and scrapbooks about the family, and tried to come up with a plan of attack.

What I really needed to know was where Great-Uncles Gianni and Stefano had both been on the nights in question, but since that wasn't possible, I'd have to settle for finding out more about them. They'd both passed, as had most of my other aunts and uncles. So I pulled up my contact list and jotted down the names and numbers of my five cousins from that side of the family—mine wasn't the only branch that had lost a son in Vietnam. None answered their phones, but that wasn't surprising given it was dinnertime. All I could do was hope someone would call back sooner rather than later.

In the meantime, I scoured the records available online for that generation of my family. The 1960s census wasn't yet available to the public, so I dove into local directories for that decade—back in the day, phone books contained a surprising amount of information besides phone numbers and addresses, including occupations and places of employment. An initial run-through informed me my great-uncle Gianni had moved to New York for his work as a stockbroker in 1963; while it was possible he'd come back to San Francisco to kill the women, the logistics of traveling, stalking, and killing three women in the course of a single year, all while keeping up with such high-intensity work in an age before cell phones, seemed highly unlikely to me. My great-uncle Stefano was listed as a head chef, and I tracked down some newspaper articles that showed he'd recently opened a restaurant in North Beach.

North Beach—where all the prostitutes had hailed from. How hard could it have been for him to stake them out? On the other hand, all the murders occurred on Friday night, an important business night for restaurants. Wouldn't the head-chef-slash-owner of a restaurant need to be present on Fridays? I wasn't sure how logistically likely it was for him to have ducked out for a little murder-stalking.

The phone rang, interrupting my research—my cousin Jennifer. As the amateur genealogist of our clan, the opportunity to vomit family history facts had motivated her to return my call before the last bite of dessert hit her stomach.

"Hey, cuz, great to hear from you," she said. "You said you want some history on Great-Uncle Gianni and Great-Uncle Stefano?"

"I do. I don't suppose you know much about them?" Neither was her father.

"You have a pen?"

I assured her I did, but what I really needed was a recording device, because she gave no sign of pausing for breath. I opened the recorder app on my phone and let it run while I scrawled down as much as I could.

"No, you're totally right," she said when I asked about Great-Uncle Gianni visiting California from New York. "He hated airplanes. Despised them. Told my mother it made no sense how they stayed in the air and that if God had wanted humans to fly, he'd've given them wings. The only way he'd travel was by train . . ."

As she continued on, I drew a thick black line over Gianni's name. If he didn't fly, it was logistically impossible for him to be the murderer. And it sparked a memory; while Jennifer switched into a description of his career accomplishments, I located an entry in my grandmother's diary about how annoyed the family was when Gianni refused to come visit even for Christmas.

When Jennifer finally paused for breath, I managed to shift her onto Great-Uncle Stefano.

"Oh, his restaurant was a *huge* deal. Apicius. *The* hotspot for Italian Americans in the 1960s and '70s, right up until he died of a heart attack."

When I gently pressed her about whether that was just family bias, she texted me pictures of several articles about Apicius from both the *Chronicle* and the *Examiner*, along with Stefano's obituary. I skimmed them as she talked; among other praises, the obituary claimed he hadn't missed a dinner shift in over forty years. While possibly influenced by a degree of hagiographic hyperbole, it put the kibosh on him missing *three* Friday dinner shifts in the same year.

Having come nowhere close to running out of steam, Jennifer launched into what she knew about Grandpa William's two brothers, too. I started to break in, but then figured I shouldn't rule them out—if they'd felt he was harming the family honor, it was possible they'd decided to send him a message.

"Uncle Frank was never the same after his dock accident in 1963. Limped so bad he walked with a cane, and could barely lift a pot of coffee. But he became a union rep once he was a desk donkey, and it turned out he liked that better, even though he'd never admit it . . ."

I drew a line through Great-Uncle Frank's name; no way someone with physical restrictions had been an effective murderer of young, healthy women.

I gently shifted Jennifer onto my great-uncle Tony, William's other brother.

"Everybody was afraid of him, like even his own father," she said. "Ma always said his temper was lightning quick and hurt just as bad."

My brain perked up, and my pulse sped. A bad temper didn't necessarily make him a killer, but it sure was compatible. Maybe my grandfather's behavior had triggered him, sending him on a revenge tour. I took notes as Jennifer loosed a litany of supposedly funny stories about things he'd said and done—and people he'd hit—while being "crazy Uncle Tony."

By the time she finished her recitation and we said our goodbyes, it was past ten at night. I considered my next steps. I needed to dive deeper into Great-Uncle Tony, but if that didn't yield anything, I'd need to launch into my last resort—a day-by-day search of the local papers during the time of the killings. Both would likely take considerable time, and I really needed to catch up on some quality sleep. So instead of starting something that would keep me up all night, I recorded another episode of the podcast to catch up on everything I'd learned, then slipped under the covers with visions of geeky archive-diving dancing in my head.

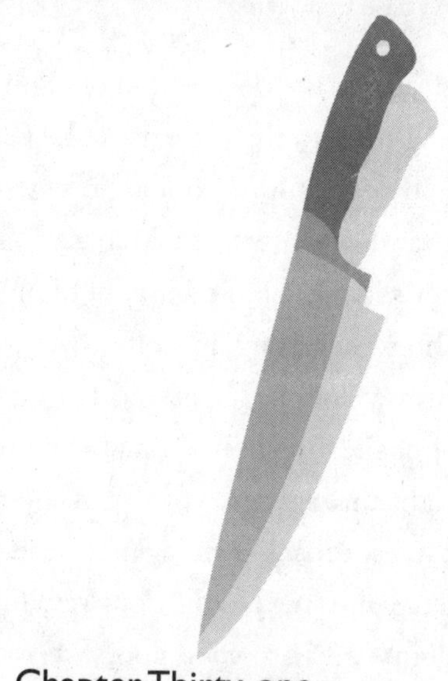

Chapter Thirty-one

For the first time in days I got a good night's sleep. Things were looking up—I'd uncovered important evidence in Sylvia's murder case that pointed away from me and Morgan, I had several episodes of the podcast in the can, and I was actually making progress in the Overkill Bill investigation. Admittedly, it was gonna be one hell of an uphill climb to get any evidence to support my theory about Great-Uncle Tony, but I felt excited and optimistic and couldn't wait to dive in. Luckily my tasks for the next two days consisted of researching several new tours we were considering adding to our roster, and I had a fair amount of flexibility with respect to the timing.

I showered quickly, humming Katy Perry's "Firework" in self-congratulation, grabbed a cup of coffee and some oatmeal, and trotted it all into my office to start work. I pulled up the *San Francisco Chronicle* database, plugged in my date, and started scouring two weeks before the first murder.

Research has always been my happy place, even back when I was a little girl. It's like some form of immersive meditation where my brain builds up a sort of virtual-reality image, hazy at first, but clearer and clearer as the details flesh out and build up a cocoon around me. Coming back to the present is like falling hard out of a magical tree house hidden in the woods. So when my shrilling doorbell yanked me away from Brezhnev, Mao Zedong, and the death of the Lone Ranger's horse, I bolted up out of my chair like I'd received an electric shock, knocking my coffee over in the process. As the liquid ran toward my laptop, I managed to intercept it by sweeping the flow in the opposite direction—straight into my midsection, where it scalded me right through my yoga pants. With a screech of pain I jumped back to escape my own leggings, catapulting my office chair into the golden pathos next to the doorway. The planter crashed, spraying wet soil across my hardwood floors.

I strode abruptly out of my office before I could somehow make the mess worse, and with stinging thighs and flowing profanity, flung open my front door.

Petito stood on my porch, not even trying to hide his laughter.

"You okay?" he asked when he was able to draw breath. "Should I call the paramedics?"

I narrowed my eyes at him. "I'm fine, thank you."

He stared at my wet pants. "Glad to hear it. Can I come in?"

I seriously considered telling him to go to hell, but as satisfying as that would have been in the short term, antagonizing the member of law enforcement who held my future in his hands was not wise. I stepped back and led him to my kitchen. "Would you like a cup of coffee?" I asked, expecting him to turn it down.

He settled into the furthermost kitchen chair, which gave him an excellent vantage point to watch me. "I'd love one, thanks. Do you want to go change your pants?"

"I'm all set, thanks." No way was I leaving him alone in my house. I yanked the pot out from the machine, filled a mug, then slid it over to him. "I'm assuming the contents of those memory cards were helpful?"

He nodded, the remainder of his laughter still tugging at his eyes. "Very interesting. Thank you."

I waited for him to say more as I filled myself a new mug, but he didn't. I dropped into a chair and a sarcastic attitude. "So how can I help you today?"

"A few ways. First, I'd like to hear your thoughts on the Overkill Bill murders. Have you uncovered anything interesting?"

"I have, actually." I took a deep mental breath. "It's odd that the Overkill Bill victims' clothing was undisturbed, since that's unusual for a sexually motivated serial killer. And Sylvia's clothing was disturbed, which is a change in MO from Overkill Bill, and suggests a very different motivation. But even more problematic is that the witness testimony used to identify William Sanzio actually claimed to see a man two decades younger than my grandfather, wearing a different style of clothing, who had no birthmark."

"The lighting was bad," Petito said, face professionally blank.

"Maybe. Or maybe whoever she saw just happened to look something like my grandfather. You and I both know eyewitness testimony is notoriously unreliable."

His professional demeanor dipped for the tiniest of seconds, and his gaze dropped—he agreed with me, even if he wouldn't admit it. "And you don't find her recognition of an initialed signet ring compelling?"

I threw him my best scornful look. "Come on, now. At least fifty percent of Italian men in that generation had rings like that. Would that hold up in court today?"

He didn't answer that. "Your grandfather spent time with all three victims."

"Are you telling me that it's unusual for a john to find multiple prostitutes in the same area? Because I know it's not unusual for prostitutes to find multiple men." I shared my two alternate-suspect theories, that a look-alike stranger may have used William Sanzio as a patsy, or one of my great-uncles had decided to take matters into their own hands.

He sipped his coffee as I spoke, then set it down. "Why would your great-uncles kill the women instead of your grandfather?"

"Because it's crazy hard to put food on the table and pay the mortgage when you're dead." I picked up my own coffee and widened my eyes pointedly at him over the mug.

"If it were some sort of warning to your grandfather, wouldn't one victim have been sufficient?"

I mentally winced—it was a good point, but I wasn't about to admit it. "Every single person on both sides of my family is as stubborn as a San Francisco stroll is steep. You should meet my father sometime."

His eyes briefly widened. "I did, earlier. You're not wrong."

I laughed out loud before I could stop myself, then hurried to cover. "The point is, I've been researching my great-uncles, and there's one who very well could have done it—my great-uncle Tony." I ran him through the logic of why I'd eliminated the others.

"Nice work." The glimmer of respect in his eyes sent prickles of pride down my neck. "Of course, it's pretty much impossible to prove one way or the other."

I shrugged. "Most people would've said it was impossible for me to narrow it down from three to one, but I did."

I caught a glimpse of a smile at the corner of his mouth before it disappeared behind his mug. "So what's your theory about how it relates to the copycats?"

"I think there are two possibilities. One is a killer who resonated with Overkill Bill's methodology, but has an issue with society ladies rather than prostitutes," I said.

"Fairly big coincidence to just happen to pick your mother-in-law."

"I'm not so sure. If the killer was someone who'd been slighted by people in that circle, they may be purposefully stalking them." I wrapped my hands around my mug to warm them. "And if they did any research whatsoever, it wouldn't be hard to find out Sylvia was related to the granddaughter of Overkill Bill. That would provide them with a method, because the psychology of going after a particular group of women would have been the same. But that's not the theory I'm leading toward, anyway."

"What's your other theory?"

"You saw what was on the memory cards. I think she blackmailed either Nancy or the CEO of My Kind of People and Rithmology, Brighton Keyes, and they didn't take kindly to it."

"And where does Katherine Harper fit in?" he asked, face professionally blank.

I grimaced, and took another sip before answering. "My best guess is that Katherine, because of her husband Steve's connections in the tech world, stumbled on something that showed My Kind of People and Rithmology weren't on the up-and-up. Since she was trying to break into Sylvia's circle, she tried to warn her. I think it got back to Keyes, either through whoever Katherine talked to or via Sylvia, and Keyes, or whoever owns the companies, killed them both."

"Just coincidentally using your grandfather's MO?"

"Like I said, it wasn't a secret her daughter-in-law was related to a famous psychopath. In fact, I have zero doubt that the day my divorce from Todd was finalized, she had some brand of cotillion blowout down at the headquarters of the Ligue Louis Quatorze to celebrate being free of my legacy."

He nodded. "And that would have the side benefit of throwing suspicion on you."

I shuddered. "And if you don't like that theory, I have others."

"Such as?"

"Blackmail for other reasons unknown. For example, Katherine may have been having an affair with Nancy McQuaid's husband Robert, and Sylvia found out. Then when Katherine turned up dead, she realized Nancy must have killed her, and blackmailed her for that. Hopefully you'll find something in her personal records that will help."

He nodded, and glanced down at his watch. "I have to run soon, so I need to switch gears to the other reasons I came by."

Something in his tone made me deeply wary. "Okay."

"I need to confirm your husband's location the day Sylvia died. You said he was in LA, correct?" he asked, watching me carefully.

Why was he asking *me* this and not Todd? "That's what he told me."

He slid out his phone and played a video for me. "Todd's SUV was at a gas station in San Jose the morning Sylvia was killed."

I gaped at the grainy video—San Jose was about forty-five minutes south of San Francisco, depending on traffic. It was hard to say for sure the man was Todd, but the vanity plates—LXRYTRP—were, and the vehicle matched his Suburban. "That's not possible. He didn't make it back until Tuesday evening."

"Do you know why he'd be in San Jose?"

I shook my head. "Whatever it is, it has nothing to do with this. He loved his mother very much."

He put the phone back in his pocket without answering. "Last issue. I've been as patient as I can be waiting for your daughter to return my calls. If I don't hear from her today, I'll have to bring her in."

Confusion scrambled my brain as that sentence jumped around looking for a place to land. "I know for a fact Morgan's been trying to call you. But—you saw what was on the memory cards. Why do you even still need to talk with her?"

His expression returned to professionally blank. "She's been trying to call me? I haven't received any messages."

"That can't be right. They must be sitting on your desk or something."

"I left her my direct number, the one you've been using. You haven't had any difficulty reaching me."

"Hang on." I strode out of the room, grabbed my phone, then strode back in. "I'm sure it's a misunderstanding. I'll call her now."

His posture remained taut. "I'd appreciate that."

I tried to calm the stabs of anxiety perforating my gut as I pulled up her contact by reminding myself that Morgan had no reason to kill Katherine. But then I remembered what that true-crime portion of my brain had whispered to me when I made the same objection about myself: a clever murderer would copycat a recent high-profile murder, in effect copycatting the copycat, in order to deflect suspicion away from themselves by making it look like Sylvia's murder was related to Katherine's. Petito wouldn't be willing to rule either of us out on those grounds.

Morgan picked up on the third ring. "Hey, Mom. Is everything okay?"

"I'm here with that homicide inspector I told you about, Dan Petito. He says he hasn't been able to reach you and I told him that was ridiculous because you've been calling him. I'm going to put you on speakerphone, okay?"

She was silent for a moment before answering. "Okay."

Her tone plunged the knives deeper in my gut. Too late it occurred to me that maybe I should have called Morgan privately first—but no, this was all ridiculous anyway, and we needed to get it straightened out. So I tapped to put the call on speaker, then slid myself into a chair and the phone across the table halfway between Petito and me.

"Miss Clement. I have a few questions I need to ask you," he said.

"Um, sure, I guess, but I'm pretty busy right now, so—um—I'll try." She'd clearly inherited my ability to remain cool and breezy under pressure. But what did she have to be nervous about?

"Where were you Sunday evening after six?" he asked, watching my face as he spoke to her.

"I was at home, studying." I detected a slight quiver in her voice I hoped he wouldn't notice.

"All night? Alone?" he asked.

"Yes."

"And you spoke to your grandmother that night?"

"Yes." Her response was clipped.

"When?"

"Just after six. I think around six fifteen?"

Petito paused, eyes still glued to mine. "And you only spoke to her once?"

What the actual hell? My eyes bounced frantically between his eyes and the phone.

Morgan cleared her throat. "No. But I'm guessing you know that already."

An arctic chill squeezed my chest. "Morgan, what are you talking about?"

"I'm sorry I didn't tell you, Mom," she pleaded with me. "It's just that things got so—it doesn't matter. I called her and left a message, and since Grandma only ever cleared out her voicemails like once a year, I'm guessing Detective Petito has heard it."

It was my turn to stare down Petito—but he gave nothing away. "Morgan. What did you say?"

"I was angry, Mom. She'd just completely blown up my life and didn't even give me an explanation. I tried to calm down after we talked like you said, and I put on some trash TV and poured myself a big glass of wine. But the thought of you having to do even more work than you already do just to keep me in school got me angrier and angrier, and one glass turned into two—"

I winced. She'd always been a lightweight, another trait she'd inherited from me.

"—and then three, and I called her. I told her what I thought of her, that she was being a bitch, and if this was how she wanted to treat you and me, then she was dead to me."

My gasp turned to a gurgle—I could barely breathe. "What else did you say?" I whispered.

"I don't completely remember. At that point I was pretty drunk. I remember throwing my phone after I hung up, and then I don't remember anything until I woke up Monday when my alarm went off with a headache and cottonmouth and I had to race to get to class on time."

My arm shot out toward the phone; Petito intercepted it and pinned it in place with his hand. "Why didn't you tell me this?" I croaked.

"Because I didn't want you to have to lie. I don't know what happened, Mom. Maybe I got in my car and went over there, and maybe—"

My voice came back, full force. "Stop talking, Morgan. Right now."

"Ms. Sanzio, please let her finish," Petito said, compassion and resignation fighting on his face.

But my daughter wasn't stupid. She stayed silent.

I stared into Petito's eyes. "None of this matters anyway. Inspector Petito has evidence in his possession that Sylvia's businesses were involved in some illegal activities, and Sylvia was blackmailing one of her friends. He knows neither you nor I had anything to do with this."

Petito shook his head. "Nancy McQuaid has a solid alibi for the night Sylvia was murdered—she was at a dinner party with a room full of witnesses who say she didn't leave until well past midnight. And Brighton Keyes works out of a property in Bakersfield, where we have him on several security cameras over the course of that evening. There's no way he could have made it to San Francisco in time to kill her."

I yanked my hand out from under Petito's and jumped up from my chair. "Of course Keyes wouldn't have done it himself, he's not stupid. There are other people who work at Rithmology who could have done it, or it was whoever owns both of the companies. You need to find out who that is, whoever owns the parent company, Anchor and Shields."

Petito stood up, his eyes holding mine, his tone firm, but compassionate. "Why would he want her dead, Capri? Sylvia made it clear in that video she needed money, and turning in her partner wouldn't have fixed that. He's smart enough to realize that, especially since the video incriminated her just as much as it did him. And killing her would just bring attention to what was going on in her finances."

"But—there must be—someone else—" I sputtered myself out.

Petito gave me a moment, then spoke. "I promise you, we're investigating every possibility. But I'll need to take an official statement from Miss Clement as soon as possible." He held my eyes again. "The best thing you can do right now is get your daughter a lawyer."

Chapter Thirty-two

I told Petito it was time for him to leave. As I watched to be sure he drove away, anger and betrayal washed over me. Despite my mental preparation, he'd done it again. Between those eyes and the charming smile and the camaraderie of discussing Overkill Bill like equals, he'd suckered me back into thinking he was a good guy.

As soon as his car rounded the corner, I snatched my phone up and called Morgan back.

"Mom?" She was crying now.

I tried to keep my tone calm. "I don't understand. Did you think you were just going to be able to dodge the police forever?"

"Not forever. But I figured if I *wasn't* really the one who did it and I delayed a few days, they'd get to the bottom of what really happened. You found all those documents and those cards, and I figured he wouldn't care anymore, so I just . . ."

Her voice took on a childish quality that both squeezed my mother's heart and annoyed the crap out of it. Because she was twenty-four, not fourteen, and she knew better than to hide from her mistakes. But pointing that out wasn't going to help in the current situation.

"You couldn't have gone anywhere when you were that intoxicated, Morgan. And now they think you're hiding something, because you were."

"Yes, I could have. People do all sorts of things when they black out. I had a friend who walked all the way across campus, woke up her ex-boyfriend, then walked back to her place when he kicked her out, and she didn't remember a thing the next day."

Hard to see why he'd broken up with her. "But you're not a heavy drinker. Have you ever blacked out before?"

"How do you know if you blacked out or not unless someone tells you something you don't remember doing?"

It was a valid, if frustrating, point. "It's just not possible to drive that far if you're drunk. And you hadn't even heard about Katherine Harper's death, so how could you have copycatted the copycat?"

She paused. "I *had* heard about it."

White spots hovered on my periphery. "You told me you hadn't."

"I never said I didn't. I just let you assume."

I pushed aside the deception. "It doesn't matter. You don't have it in you to hurt your grandmother, drunk or sober or any other way."

Her voice thickened. "How many people said that about Great-Grandpa Sanzio? That he didn't have it in him to be a murderer?"

I suddenly felt like all the blood had drained from my body. "Stop. Just stop right there. This isn't even a possibility. I'm going to call that lawyer Jacinda recommended right now. We'll go from there."

We said our goodbyes and our *I love you*s and we hung up. I paced the kitchen as I called the lawyer, then collapsed into the closest kitchen chair.

I'd started my morning feeling positive about all the evidence I'd found. Now I felt like a boa constrictor had wound its way around my chest and was squeezing the breath out of me. Petito had seemed so genuine, like he actually respected what I'd done. Like he was actually concerned about Morgan and me. How had I fallen for it *again*?

Because I'd *wanted* to fall for it. I wanted his respect. I wanted to believe he cared.

There was no point dwelling on it. We were the primary suspects again, and I needed a plan of action. First off, I needed to call Todd.

He didn't answer, of course. But when the voicemail picked up, I let loose. "Todd. Homicide Inspector Petito was just here, and he's looking to arrest our daughter. And he said something about you being in San Jose on Monday morning? Why did you lie to me? What are you hiding? Whatever it is, you need to tell them what's going on because they don't trust any of us and they're going to bring Morgan in. So you need to straighten this all out with him as soon as you get this, and you need to call me back and let me know what the hell is going on. Immediately." Then I hung up, feeling better having vented my anger on such a deserving subject.

But more than ever I needed to figure out what was going on. Petito was right that Keyes didn't have a direct motive, since Sylvia would never have taken herself down willingly. But would his boss—whoever owned Anchor & Shields—be as sure of that? Maybe, but maybe not, and I needed to figure out where that company existed and who owned it. Also, what about the blackmail angles? There was so much viper behavior going on in Sylvia's circle, who knew what could possibly be happening?

I rubbed my temples—everything was blurring together in my mind. I needed to step back and look at the basic facts with fresh eyes. I grabbed my coffee and strode into my office. I wrote out a new time line for the current victims on my whiteboard, then did that thing you always see on the true-crime documentaries where they tape up a picture of each victim along with a summary of the facts about them.

When I laid it all out like that, an important fact screamed out at the top of its lungs: this all started with *Katherine*. I'd been looking at everything through my own egocentric perspective, with my family and Sylvia at the center of it all. But what if this all revolved around Katherine?

I jotted down the implications. In murder mysteries, the second person to die often was killed because they'd seen something or knew something about who the actual killer was. From that perspective, the blackmail theory leaped to the top of my list, but in a new form: Maybe Sylvia had figured out who killed Katherine, and had then blackmailed the killer. It lined up with the few things I knew for sure: Sylvia needed money, and she had no compunction against blackmail.

So why would someone want to kill Katherine? Pretty much the only thing I knew about her was everybody—including her husband, Steve—agreed she was a social climber. And people had been known to do crazy things to climb the social ladder—

My phone shrilled, scaring me so completely that I actually let out a little scream. I snatched it up.

"Hey," Ryan said. "I got into Sylvia's email."

• • •

I told Ryan I'd be down to The Hub immediately, then flew out my front door and down the three blocks.

He was bent over his laptop when I pushed through the door, with Heather already watching over his shoulder. He slid away from his computer to make room for me.

"What's the password? Some combination of Todd's name and birthday this time?" I asked.

"No, actually, it's something really weird." His brow creased, and he pointed to a pad of Post-it notes next to the keyboard.

I looked down, and laughed. "Ligue563Ren."

"That means something to you?" he asked. "I figured it was a nonsense string."

"Oh, no, far from it." I rolled my eyes. "Ligue is a French word, it means 'league.' I'm pretty sure it refers to this stuffy old club she belongs to, for rich San Franciscans of French descent, Ligue Louis Quatorze. Renard is her maiden name, so I'd bet anything the rest of it is her membership number or ID or whatever. She's always been ridiculously proud of belonging to it, but I never realized she was so obsessed she'd make it her email password."

Heather grimaced and tapped her temple. "I knew it felt familiar. Didn't she want Morgan to join?"

"Morgan did join, as a consolation since she refused to do the whole coming-out thing. That was the only reason Sylvia didn't blow up like a tunnel filled with dynamite," I said.

Ryan looked comically confused. "Morgan's gay?"

I stared at him for a moment trying to figure out what the holy hand grenade he was talking about, then burst out laughing. "No, not *come out* like that. *Come out* as in be a society debutante. Have a coming-out ball, wear a white dress, officially put herself on the market to find a rich, society-appropriate spouse."

His confusion shifted to horror. "I thought that was something people only did in the south. In 1865. Or in Jane Austen books. At least not since the dawn of feminism."

I patted his shoulder. "That's because the real purpose of those traditions is to keep the money safely in the inner circle. It matters not whether the men or the women are the CEOs."

"But here? In counterculture San Francisco?" His eyes flicked around the room, trying to find that part of his idealistic innocence I'd just beheaded.

Heather laughed. "San Francisco just means the debutante dinner would've had vegan, gluten-free, and non-GMO options."

"True story." As I turned to enter the password into the waiting account, the train of thought I'd been pursuing before Ryan called came flooding back to me. "Ryan, you made it sound like you could hack into anybody's email. Can you get me into Katherine Harper's?"

His face screwed up and he jabbed a finger toward the monitor. "You haven't even looked at this one yet!"

"I know, and I will. But I think I need to get into Katherine's, too. But I don't want to ask too much of you and I know it's getting more morally ambiguous to ask you to crack into someone's account I don't even know."

His face softened, and a mocking half smile spread over his face. "Hey, if you go to jail, I'm out of a job. So give me her email address."

"I don't know it yet, but Sylvia should have it." I turned to the monitor again. The browser transitioned to a page cascading with emails.

"Wow," Heather said. "I thought you said she was organized?"

I glanced at the dates on the side column. "These are all recent, from the last few days." I cursored over to her folders and scrolled—and scrolled, and scrolled. "See? She's just as pathologically organized in the virtual world as the real one. But all I should have to do is search for Katherine Harper." I did, and a handful of emails popped up. I clicked the top one to open it, and jotted down the email address at the top.

"That's a HarperWare email address," Ryan said as I stood up and he took the chair again.

"Is that a problem?" Heather asked.

"Just a little harder to access than something like Gmail," he said. "Give me a minute."

As Heather watched his fingers fly furiously over his keyboard, I shifted to my computer and pulled up Sylvia's Gmail account.

"Got it," Ryan said, pointing to a login screen. As I crossed back over to him, he entered Katherine's email address.

A red error message popped up.

"Dammit," Ryan said. "The account's frozen."

"Frozen? Did the police do that?" I asked.

"Not directly, I don't think. I'm not sure they can, legally."

"And if they were going to do that, wouldn't they freeze Sylvia's, too?" Heather asked.

"Then what's going on?" I asked.

"Could be this system is set to lock up after X number of failed login attempts. But I think it's more likely Steve Harper froze it."

"Why would he do that?" Heather asked.

"To keep people from doing exactly what we're trying to do," Ryan said.

"Or, because there's something he wants to keep hidden." I hopped back over to my own computer and finished pulling Sylvia's account up. "But if it had to do with Sylvia, a copy of any correspondence would be in Sylvia's account, too." I scanned the results that popped up when I searched Katherine's name again. Most had "Damsels in Distress charity luncheon" in the subject line.

"'Damsels in Distress'?" Heather, now staring over my shoulder, gave me a death-ray glare. "Please tell me it's an organization dedicated to funding Disney drag queens and *not* an organization that helps abused women."

"Wish I could," I said. "And don't give *me* that look, I didn't name it."

She closed her eyes and shook her head, telegraphing her loss of faith in humanity.

I clicked through the first few, which had been sent to an entire mailing list. "Wait, this one's different—Sylvia's the only recipient." My pulse sped as we all leaned in to read it.

Subject: Time line

Dear Sylvia—

I'm so glad we had such a productive conversation the other day about our mutual interests. I've attached my application for the Ligue; you should be able to get whatever information about me that you need from it. Although I'm sure you already have it, I've also attached the recommendation form. Please confirm for me by the end of the week or I'll move forward.

Have a lovely time in Hawaii,

Katherine

Heather let out a low whistle. "I might not know the moneyed class well, but I do know bitchy when I see it, and the Bitch Force is strong in this one," Heather said.

"The kind of undertow that lulls you in with sun glinting off gentle waves, then sucks you under and crushes your lungs to oblivion," I agreed.

Ryan's gaze bounced between the two of us. "Are we reading the same email? It's rigidly professional, yes, but she says outright they had a good talk."

I'd already burst one of his bubbles that day, I wasn't sure I could bear to school him on the relational-aggression skills most women are forced to master before they're out of diapers. Luckily, Heather jumped right in and took over for me.

"Not good, *productive*. Also note the 'I'm sure you have it already.' That's a dig—you don't speak like that to someone you're asking for a recommendation. You'd say 'just in case you don't have it,' or 'so you don't have to search for it.' And then there's that last line. She'll act if she doesn't get confirmation—that's a threat."

He blinked down at the email, processing. "But—we're talking about entrance into a *social club*, right? Who'd blackmail someone over something like that?"

"The type of person who aspires to attend organic, vegan debutante balls." I hit the print-screen button and confirmed the preview. "The problem is, it's running the wrong way. Sylvia is the known blackmailer, but here Katherine is pressuring Sylvia."

Heather rolled her eyes. "Like I said yesterday. They're all a bunch of menacing puff adders."

"Except the more I follow it through, the more it doesn't fit. Let's say Katherine blackmailed Sylvia because she wanted into the Ligue so badly. But would Sylvia have been so against it that she'd kill Katherine rather than recommend her? And even if we're willing to go for all that, how does *Sylvia* then end up dead?"

"Maybe Katherine's husband Steve took his revenge," Heather said with a gasp.

I took a deep breath as I considered. "Katherine was killed in the early hours of Friday morning, and Sylvia's flight for Hawaii was also early Friday morning. It's possible, depending on exactly when both happened." I stared up at her. "Do you really think Steve Harper would kill Sylvia rather than go to the police?"

"Dollars to donuts," Heather said. "Rich people get used to getting whatever they want."

"After the last few days, I certainly can't argue with that," I said. "'Dollars to donuts.' That's such a strange expression. I wonder what it originates from?"

"No idea." Heather shrugged, then slipped into a sassy-street-slang voice. "Maybe because donuts are so *fire*, they're *money*?"

"Don't do that," Ryan said without taking his eyes off his laptop screen. "Nobody wins when you do that."

I shook my head and turned back to my own computer. Once I finished with the emails from Katherine without finding anything else, I searched for anything from Nancy or Robert. The few emails I found were brief and harmless, with no undertone and no business implications. I wasn't surprised by that; most of her communications with Nancy were likely by phone or text. I switched gears and looked for Rithmology, then My Kind of People, but in both cases again found nothing. When I searched for Brighton Keyes specifically, I again came up short. I said as much out loud.

"She must have a different business email," Heather said.

"Not on Gmail she doesn't," Ryan responded.

Frustrated, I tapped my nails on my keyboard, drawing an annoyed glare from Heather. "Don't you have a tour to prep for?" she asked.

I glanced down at the time—she was right, I had to be across town in less than an hour. I slammed my computer shut and grabbed my jacket. "Crap. Thanks, both of you."

I hurried out, mind filled with what non-charity-related mutual interests Sylvia and Katherine could possibly have had—and what Katherine had been holding over her.

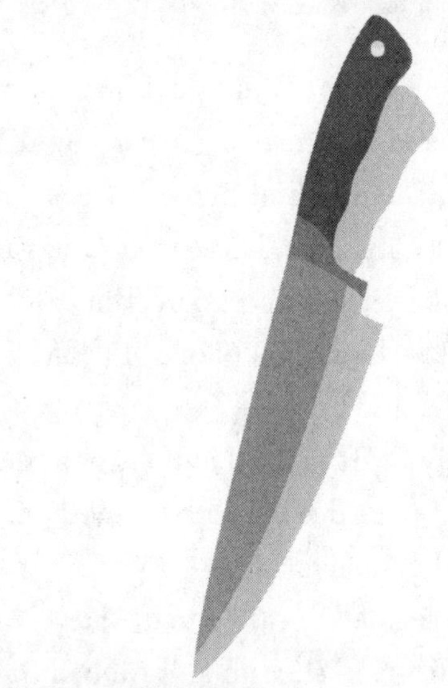

Chapter Thirty-three

I hoped the afternoon and evening tours would distract me from my problems, but with each passing day, more of the guests were asking more questions about Overkill Bill and the copycat killer. I didn't want to be rude, so I answered a few, but then drew a boundary, citing the very real need to focus on the tour.

But the questions were enough to keep me obsessing about it all. I was missing something, I knew it, and the whispers from the shadows of my mind wouldn't let me forget it. I couldn't get into Katherine's personal accounts, and Steve hadn't returned the call request I'd left with his assistant, or my follow-up after finding Katherine's email. Whatever address Sylvia used to discuss her businesses wasn't attached to the account Ryan found, and I had no idea how to track it down. The fact that she had hidden that account made me even more convinced she had a literal hiding place, too, where her Rolodex, documents, and God only knew what else were stashed away.

But I'd searched every inch of The Chateau, multiple times. There simply wasn't a hiding place. I was clearly losing my mind, unable to let go because I'd never been good at failing.

One thing I could do, however, was talk to Todd. He also hadn't bothered to return my call; a stupid, amateur move, since I knew exactly where to find him. And as soon as my tour was over I did just that, locating him in the main family room of The Chateau, talking on the phone, his expression grim.

He caught sight of me. "I'll have to call you back," he said into the phone, and hung up.

My heart panged at the sight of his expression. He had so much on his plate dealing with his mother's death, but I had to find out why he'd lied to me.

I decided to ease into it. "Hey. How are you?"

His hand shot up and rubbed the shadow on his chin. "Figuring it out as I go."

I cleared my throat. "Did you get the message I left? You never called me back."

He glared and waved the phone at me. "I've got a funeral to arrange, Capri. Calling you back really isn't my top priority right now."

His tone, possibly because of all the memories that rode in on its back, put my dander right up, and it took effort to keep my reaction compassionate. "I know you have a lot to deal with, and I want to help any way I can. But when you hide things, it makes it look like our family is up to something. Now Petito is bringing Morgan in, and no matter what, *your daughter* should be your top priority."

"Capri—" he snapped, then caught himself. He took a deep breath, and started again, mirroring my own words. "I know it's natural for you to be worried about Morgan. But first of all, I never 'hid' anything from the police. And second of all, Morgan's innocent, so she'll be fine. The police can't find her guilty of something she didn't do. So stop helicoptering."

Helicoptering? No he did *not*. "Tell that to my grandfather, who died in jail for crimes he didn't commit," I shot back.

"Just because you think your grandfather was innocent doesn't make it true. Old white men aren't the ones who get locked up without evidence."

His words knocked the breath out of me, for more reasons than I could count. "*Rich* white men, you mean. My grandfather wasn't rich, and he existed at a time when Italian wasn't a good thing to be."

"So now you're saying he was a victim because he was Italian?"

"Stop." I threw a hand up. Because this was what Todd always did, deflect and confuse the issue to deflect the heat off himself—and he was damned good at it. "The point is, Petito has evidence you were at a gas station in San Jose the morning Sylvia was murdered."

"And?" he said.

Was he kidding? "And you told me you were in LA."

He sent his eyes to the ceiling and shook his head, like he was dealing with someone two cards short of a full deck. "My personal life is my own business. I was with a woman, and you don't have a history of reacting well when it comes to me and women. So no, I didn't tell you."

My mouth dropped open. "The only time I've had a problem with you and women is when you were with them *while* we were married!"

"I'm not doing this with you, Capri." He flipped a dismissive hand at me, then turned and stalked out of the room, leaving me stunned and struggling to catch my breath.

• • •

"Well, that was a fun little trip into the way-back machine," I muttered to myself as I clambered off back to my car. "I was about due for a reminder why my marriage didn't work out."

Once I reached home, I started a pot of water boiling for pasta and some of my mother's homemade red sauce defrosting in the microwave. I put in another call to Steve's assistant, hoping that once I confronted him with the "mutual interests" in Katherine's email to Sylvia, he'd be more forthcoming. I did another dive into Anchor &

Shields, carefully researching how to research companies, but still couldn't find them anywhere. Which led me to an ominous conclusion: the company had been created somewhere overseas purposely to make it difficult for anybody to trace back. And the only reason you did that was because you wanted to hide something.

My phone shrilled, causing me to jump so hard I slammed my knees into the underside of my kitchen table. I scrambled for it, stunned to see Steve Harper's name on my screen. His assistant must be calling me to advise me of a pending restraining order.

I stabbed at the phone. "Hello?"

"Ms. Sanzio?" Steve's own voice came over the phone. "You've been trying to reach me?"

"I have." I snatched my notebook and pen over so I could take notes while mentally juggling which question I should ask first. Should I go with the element of surprise and throw out Katherine's veiled threats, or should I dance around and lull him into a false sense of security?

"You said something in your message about an email from Katherine to Sylvia?" he asked.

Right—so much for stealth. "I've been trying to figure out what Sylvia and Katherine may have had in common, and came across an email from Katherine." I pulled it up and read it to him. "She wanted Sylvia to get her into the Ligue Louis Quatorze, and mentioned they had mutual interests. Do you know what that's about?"

He paused for a moment. "How did you get access to that?"

I winced, then skirted around the truth. "You think her family doesn't have access to her email?"

"I'm not sure I understand your concern about the email," Steve said.

My eyes narrowed. Steve was smart, a bona fide genius, and he understood the concern as well as I did. "If she wanted to belong to the same club as Sylvia, that's a connection between them. Maybe somebody in the club is responsible for their deaths. Why did Katherine want to join so badly?"

Another pause. "She was trying to fit in to the circle."

"To the degree that she'd threaten Sylvia to get in?"

"I didn't hear a threat."

Yeah, no. I could believe younger, less-experienced Ryan didn't recognize the subtext, but for a mega-successful business czar to miss it? No way. "If there was no threat, what were the 'mutual interests' she was referring to?"

"I have no idea. But it sounds like *you* have a theory, and I'd like to hear what it is." Apparently he was tiring of the two-step, too.

I held my metaphorical breath and dove in. "Have you ever heard of an app called My Kind of People? Or a company called Rithmology?"

"Not that I'm aware of. What are they?" His voice shifted, taking on an edge.

"One is a sort of dating app, and the other deals with optimizing social media algorithms. What about Anchor and Shields?"

Still another pause. "Why are you asking about all these?"

"Because Sylvia was investing in them, and since they have to do with apps and software, that's another possible mutual interest. Maybe somebody was trying to get to you, and Katherine wouldn't cooperate."

"Why would they kill Sylvia if she was one of their investors?" His tone was guarded.

A strange shiver stabbed down my arms. There were hundreds of scenarios that explained why a business owner might kill one of their investors—and he'd been answering each one of my questions with his own question. Why?

I put on an apologetic tone, like I was exasperated with myself. "I don't know. My mind is working overtime and seeing things that aren't there. I think I need a good night's rest."

"Here's what I think, Ms. Sanzio. I looked you up." His voice was fully cold now. "Your grandfather was a serial killer, the one my wife's killer supposedly copycatted. I don't think that's a coincidence."

The stabs now shot down my legs, too. "I don't know what you mean."

"I also know you hated your ex-mother-in-law." His voice was now dangerously quiet. "I think you killed her. Further, I think you're desperately looking for someone to deflect the murders onto, and you've decided I'm that person."

"I don't—"

"I also think it's time I called the homicide detectives and let them know what I suspect. So I'm warning you right now—don't call me again." He hung up.

My lungs froze as the call disconnected. Not because he was going to call homicide—Petito had already decided Morgan or I was the killer. But because his accusation was the realization of my childhood nightmares. While other children had recurring dreams where they showed up in school hallways naked, my version was a crowd of angry people chasing me through hallways throwing stones at me and calling me a killer.

My kitchen timer blared a string of beeps, startling me and sending my knees again into the underside of the kitchen table. I jumped up and pulled the pasta off the stove, then drained it into the sink. By the time I rinsed it and threw some of the lukewarm red sauce over it, I'd stopped shaking, but my appetite was completely gone.

I slipped back into my chair and pushed the plate to the side of the table, then pulled over my laptop. I had to distract myself, but how? I'd researched everyone and everything, and come up with nothing solid. But I was desperate to give my mind something to do, so I began feeding names into Google one by one, scouring search results for every person and corporation I'd encountered since investigating Sylvia's affairs. I clicked and scrolled through page after page of news articles and company missives, then charity events and soigné evenings attended by Sylvia's circle. The pages of fancy gowns and black tuxedos and plates of gourmet food began to blur together, swimming with champagne flutes and jewels and practiced smiles, interrupted only by the sort of bizarre themed events only the rich could pull off, including one where the ladies wore excessive hats straight out of *My Fair Lady*, and another where all the men wore strange plaid dinner jackets with ostentatious family crests on the pockets. I leaned in to examine the crests in a picture where Sylvia and Nancy stood with Philip and Robert amid a slightly larger group of people I didn't know. Philip's red-and-gold crest sported a leaping fox under a coat of arms, the Renard family crest; had he worn that to please Sylvia, or had he just not known what the Clement family crest was? I certainly didn't know what the Sanzio crest looked like, if there was such a thing. I shook my head in sympathy with the strange position that must have put him in as my eyes slid across the other crested jackets.

And froze on the man standing next to Robert—whose crest consisted of an anchor on a shield.

My eyes jumped to the text beneath the picture identifying each of the people present. The man was identified as Shawn Malger.

Malger—where had I heard that name before?

I flipped back through my notes, skimming frantically for the name. At nearly the beginning of the notebook, I found it—Malger was Nancy's maiden name. The Malger family crest consisted of an anchor on a shield, the same symbols used to name the umbrella corporations for the shady companies Sylvia was involved in. That couldn't be a coincidence, could it?

I snatched my phone up again and put a call through to Petito. His voicemail picked up and I launched into an explanation of the dinner-jacket crest. But as I described the family crest and why I thought it meant Nancy's family owned Anchor & Shields, I heard it through Petito's ears, and a flush of embarrassment crawled up my neck and scalp. I sounded like a raving lunatic—there were probably a thousand family crests with anchors and shields on them, since both were common military symbols. I ended the call and turned back to Google, plugging in Shawn Malger. He turned out to be a much-lauded and high-powered attorney who specialized in medical malpractice suits, and despite an hour of digging, I could find no connection whatsoever between him and any sort of tech company.

Too bad I hadn't done that search *before* leaving Petito a rambling, rabid message.

Frustrated and disgusted with myself, I pushed aside my computer and called Morgan.

"Were you able to get a time set up with the attorney?" I asked after our initial greetings.

"No, but it's okay, because Grandpa suggested we just go together with his attorney because the police want a statement from him, too. We made an appointment down at the homicide department or division or whatever tomorrow morning at ten thirty." She was trying to sound breezy, but her voice held a slight tremor.

I pulled up my schedule in my mind. "What time? I'll shift around whatever I need to."

"Mom. I don't think they'll allow you to be present for the interview, so there's really no point."

Panic crept through me at the thought of not being with her—for all I knew, Petito planned to arrest her right then and there. "But I—"

"Mom, stop. I have two subject interviews I have to do on campus after and I'm not sure how much time I'll have in between. Grandpa and I are even driving separately so I can head straight to school. I'll call you when I'm driving and let you know how it went."

I hesitated, wanting badly to push back—until the word "helicoptering" echoed through my brain. She was right, she wasn't a child anymore, and they likely wouldn't allow me in anyway. "Okay. If you're sure."

"I'm sure, Mom. It's all good."

We said our goodbyes and ended the call, and I stared up at my ceiling trying to convince myself that was true.

With a sigh, I grabbed my cold, congealed plate of pasta and dumped it into a leftover dish and quickly cleaned up the kitchen. Then, without any intention of going there, I found myself pacing the length of Morgan's old bedroom with her childhood teddy bear clutched to my chest.

My little girl was in danger, and there was nothing I could do. I'd failed her.

I'd uncovered so much—Sylvia's financial difficulties and her potential blackmail, Katherine's blackmail of her, even illegal dealings in Sylvia's company. But, despite everything I'd dug up and everyone I'd harassed, none of it mattered. My little girl was staring down life in prison. And as much as I wished I had Todd's blind faith in the justice system, I just didn't. During our single meeting, my grandfather had told me how certain he'd been that the American system of justice wouldn't find an innocent man guilty, and how he'd put his trust in that right up until the jury read out the verdict. Was this sickening despair how he'd felt in that moment, when hope and faith drained away, leaving nothing but cold blackness?

Without warning, the emotions I'd managed to control so well over the last few days overwhelmed me. Wailing like an injured animal, I sank onto Morgan's bed and pulled her comforter over me, soaking in the smell of her, my sobs shaking her bed and my tears soaking her pillow.

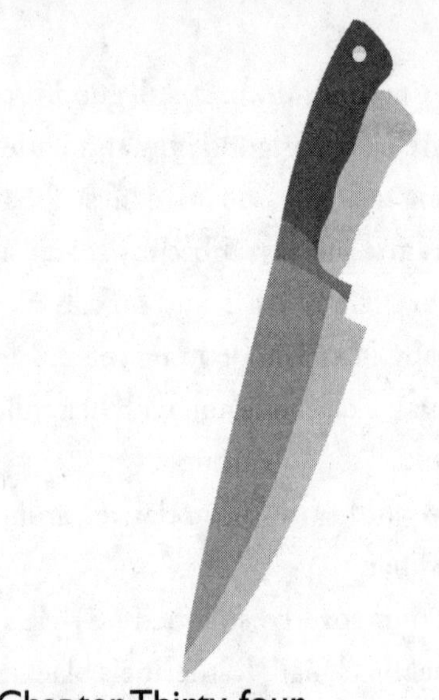

Chapter Thirty-four

I woke the next morning still frustrated and frightened, but now also exhausted thanks to a night of waking dehydrated and crying myself back to sleep. I dragged myself through my morning routine, forcing myself not to text Morgan every five minutes under the guise of reassuring her when what I really wanted was to reassure myself. I couldn't bear to be in the house where I'd raised her for a second longer, so I grabbed my laptop and bolted down to The Hub, where I'd hopefully be protected from my own worst instincts by a fortress of tour research and strong coffee.

"You okay? I've seen zombies that looked more alive," Heather said when she arrived an hour later to take care of her own administrative tasks.

"Gosh, thanks," I mumbled. "Being compared to the living dead is just what I needed today."

"Seriously, though." She peered over at me. "Are you okay?"

"If by 'okay' you mean tending to all my responsibilities despite the dire specter of impending imprisonment for my daughter, then I'm doing just dandy. I'd even go so far as to say I'm excelling."

A sympathetic ghost-smile flitted over her face. "What can I do to help? A long weeping sesh over a dozen donuts from World's Fare?"

"I've done enough crying, and there are some things even donuts can't cure."

"Ah." She nodded sagely. "Bloody Marys over at Lenny's, then."

"It's ten in the morning!"

She squinted at me. "Oh, please. Don't forget I've been to Cabo with you."

I laughed despite myself. "Vacations are one thing. Morning drinking on a work day is the beginning of a cycle that ends with my name on a liver-donor list."

She smiled a real smile, glad she'd made me laugh. "Seriously, though. How can I help?"

Ryan walked through the door as she said the last words and instantly went on alert. "Are you okay? Did something else happen?"

I shook my head. "Morgan will be talking to the cops sometime within the next hour. All I can do now is wait, and hope the police find something on Sylvia's devices or in her accounts that pulls their attention away from Morgan."

"Or that Sylvia's killer decides to confess," Heather said.

I sighed. "If you guys want to help, distract me. I'm putting together a list of sites to scope out for the Hitchcock and Hammett tours. I only have one tour today, so I figured some purposeful sightseeing will be a good way to keep busy. Any thoughts you have for either of those tours or any other would be great."

Heather sat and pulled out a notepad. "Sounds good. You want to go first, Ryan?"

He fought back a goofy-happy look—this was the first time we were fully bringing him into the fold. "I've been thinking about it, and I think we should run with the movie-slash-book theme crossing over from true crime to crime fiction. Hitchcock is a great start, but we could dive into the whole San Francisco noir subgenre. There are tons of books that have been set here, even a Charlie Chan novel—"

"Charlie Chan is very controversial—" I started.

Ryan interrupted me. "He is, and I think we should discuss *why* he's controversial. He was based on an actual Chinese detective who faced a tremendous amount of racism—"

"Chang Apana," Heather interrupted *him*. "On the Honolulu police force at the turn of the last century. It's an interesting possibility."

"And of course there's *The Last Good Kiss*, by James Crumley, which tackles a whole other era and area of San Francisco history. And Marcia Muller, and Joe Gores and Bill Pronzini, and—"

Heather waved her pen. "But everybody knows Sam Spade, even people who don't like to read. Do you think enough people would be pulled in by those other names?"

My jaw dropped. "We could probably do a Sharon McCone tour all her own, and same for Nameless."

Heather blinked at me. "I recognize each of those words independently, but have no idea what they mean together."

"Trust me," I said. "There's potential. We could give it a trial run, especially with Ryan to help with the background research."

Ryan's gaze dropped to his desk. "If you guys are worried about resources, I could trial-run something myself so it wouldn't take up your time . . ."

I forced myself not to smile—I wondered when he'd work up the courage to ask to lead his own tour. "Why don't you get started putting an outline together that shows the stops you'd want to include and what sort of information you'd use to frame them."

Little happy blotches of color crept into his cheeks. "Okay. Thanks."

"My turn," Heather said, a grin spreading over her face. "Okay, I know this is getting farther afield, but lately I've been obsessed with the jazz age in San Francisco. I'd love to do something that looks at Prohibition-era crime. And the other day I stumbled on an article about a Prohibition room at the Sir Francis Drake—I mean, the Beacon Grand—that they'll let you see if you ask nicely. Maybe we could even do something focused around speakeasies and Prohibition rooms."

"What's a Prohibition room?" Ryan asked.

"Little spaces where they hid alcohol during Prohibition so the cops wouldn't find it if they came and raided," Heather said.

Ryan's brow creased. "Isn't that the same as a speakeasy?"

"A speakeasy is a place where people gathered to *buy* alcohol, like a bar or club. Prohibition rooms were much smaller spaces inside people's homes or unrelated businesses for private use. They're designed mainly to store alcohol, although some are big enough for a couple of people to sit and drink. Basically like a hidden closet—" She stopped, staring at my face. "Are you okay?"

I must have looked like I was having a stroke, because I certainly felt like my brain had exploded. "Hidden spaces in private homes. I searched high and low for a *safe*, but of course an entire room or dedicated space would be very different—"

Heather's mind clicked into sync with mine, and her face transformed. "You think Sylvia had a Prohibition room?"

I jumped out and over to Heather's desk. "Do you have pictures of what these rooms looked like? And how people hid them?"

She brought up a couple of browser windows on her laptop. "There's all kinds. This one's basically a cubbyhole hidden under the floorboards. This one is a whole room hidden behind bookshelves."

My gaze flicked across the pictures. "If neither Philip nor Todd knew about it, it must be well hidden. Not something just under an area rug."

"You think she'd keep something like that from her *husband*?" Ryan said, scandalized.

"She didn't discuss her business investments with him, or tell him she had a nanny cam," Heather said. "And the whole time I was married to Ken, I kept all my finances separate from his."

Ryan's jaw dropped. "You were married to a man?"

Heather rolled her eyes. "I expect this from my mother, not from a millennial. Yes, I was married to a man before I met Rose. Don't label me."

I hurried to wrestle back control of the conversation. "I don't suppose you've stumbled on any tricks for locating the rooms?"

"The whole point was to make them hard to find. Like this one here?" She pointed to a video. "This woman owned her house for over thirty years and noticed a weird crack at the top of her linen closet while doing a deep clean. Her grandson pushed and prodded at it to see if it was something he needed to fix, and it came loose, leading up into a small portion of her attic that had been walled off. Check it out, they even found vintage moonshine bottles in it."

She clicked on the video, which followed a man as he climbed up, then inside the room. Several moonshine bottles that looked like they'd come from Saturday-morning cartoons sat next to a box filled with brown-glass pint jars.

"Can you go back to that Google search result you were on before?" I asked.

She did, and I scoured the pictures. Forgotten cubbies seemed to be a big part of the equation, especially those hidden amid architectural anomalies, a few feet of space you'd never realize were missing unless you were looking at blueprints. Decorative architectural elements often covered them, making it look like they served another purpose.

As I scrolled, a nebulous theory began to come together. "Is there any chance one of you could take over my Barbary Coast tour today? I need to pay another visit to The Chateau."

Chapter Thirty-five

As I drove, I worked on refining my theory about the location of the Renard family Prohibition room. The Chateau was covered in the right sort of architectural flair—paneled walls, moldings, built-in cabinets and shelves and mantels and bookcases. And while she and Philip kept the house up to date in terms of modern conveniences, she'd always been adamant about keeping the period details installed by her hallowed ancestors, so not much had been narrowed down over the years. So I asked myself: if I were a Prohibition room in Sylvia's house, where would I be?

Any such room would have predated Sylvia, so she wouldn't have had any control over its location. Where would a wealthy 1920s robber baron stash their illegal liquor? If it were me, I'd've put the room somewhere relatively easy to get to, but far away from obvious spots that would attract police suspicion.

A car swerving into my lane in an attempt to avoid a double-parked car jolted me momentarily out of my mental pigeon hole. Once I'd safely navigated around them, I returned to the psychology of it all.

Sylvia might now have had control over the location, but when she chose which rooms were used for what, she'd have kept its location in mind. She wouldn't have used that room as Todd's bedroom, for example—not only would that make it difficult for her to access when needed, who knew what damage a rambunctious, sports-loving teen would wreak to walls and fixtures? Maybe her bedroom, since she and Philip had separate suites—but since Philip spent a fair percentage of nights there, it would've only been a matter of time before he'd stumble on it, or on her using it. And based on what I'd learned about Sylvia over the past few days with her nanny cam and her locked desk, she'd want to be damned sure nobody stumbled on it.

In fact—she'd have pointed that nanny cam right at it so she knew the second anyone did.

Taking advantage of a red light, I squeezed my eyes shut and tried to dredge up the video in my head. The shot had been wide, and had captured most of the room. Certainly the desk, and the two women who'd been sitting across from it. Then past them, two twin built-in bookshelves with a small enclave in between.

A horn honked behind me. My eyes sprung open and I hit the gas, waving my apologies to the Ford Taurus behind me. He waved back, and I focused my attention on making sure I didn't crash my car on the rest of the drive.

Once I parked and made my way upstairs, I found Todd at the dining room table making phone calls, surrounded by stacks of paper. He looked up at me and grimaced. I pushed back the spurt of spiteful anger that rushed up my spine.

"You managing okay?" I asked.

He nodded, but his haunted, fatigued eyes told me different. "There's just—so much."

I nodded. Dealing with a loved one's death was a deluge of details and phone calls and managing other people's emotions at the exact moment when all you wanted to do was curl up into the fetal position and cry. I'd heard theories that dealing with all of those logistics is actually a help, that it gives you direction and purpose that keeps you from shutting down and propels you through those first few days of life without your loved one. Maybe that was true, but this was also the first time in Todd's life that he'd had to deal with losing someone he loved, and that made it twice as difficult. I pushed my lingering anger aside and reminded myself to be empathetic.

"Is there anything I can do to help?"

His gaze skipped across the piles on the table like he was trying to identify something he could hand off to me. "No—no. Morgan's helping where she can. I'm glad she went with Dad to see the detective together, he'll need an emotional support through that. He's just—I don't know. I've never seen him like this, quiet and defeated one moment, restless and angry the next."

"His wife of fifty years was just murdered. That would make anyone angry and defeated."

He rubbed both hands on his thighs. "I just wish—" He shook his head. "I don't know what I wish."

I put a hand on his shoulder and squeezed.

He put his hand over mine, then gave me a watery smile. "I haven't said how much I appreciate everything you're doing. I know my mother was never very nice to you, but still, here you are. Thank you."

"You and Philip and even Sylvia will always be my family. And I don't like it when people hurt my family. Speaking of which, I think I may have figured out where Sylvia's hiding place is."

Annoyance flashed over his face. "You're like a terrier hunting for a bone. It's one of your most frustrating traits. Don't you have other things you need to be doing?"

And there I'd been worried for a second he'd lost his sting. I straightened. "Do you mind if I go test out my theory?"

His eyes bounced around the room like he was searching for something to say; he clearly rathered I didn't. But they finally dropped back to the documents in front of him. "Do what you have to do. You're not going to find anything, anyway."

• • •

I hurried out of the room and through the house, up to Sylvia's office before he changed his mind. Once there, I beelined for the small indented enclave between the two gorgeous built-in bookcases. That space was actually my backup guess, but it was easier to test, so I figured I'd knock it out first. I tugged away the table sitting in front of the wall, wedging my leg in behind it and leveraging my lower-body strength to move the heavy wood. After a few hefty shoves, I had a clear view of the wall panels behind it and the floor underneath.

I pushed against the seams where the panels met molding, going inch by inch, but nothing gave. I knocked on the wall in several places like I'd seen people do in movies, hoping for some sort of hollow, echoey sound that would signal a secret chamber. I wasn't sure that method even worked, and as best I could tell there was no appreciable difference. I pushed the table back into place.

Then I turned to my actual prey: the bookshelves themselves. It was possible they'd been added to hide something behind them; from what I could tell visually, there was a small discrepancy of maybe six inches between how far the bookshelves went back and how far the enclave went back. Possibly due to a support beam or the like—but possibly due to a hidden space.

I stepped closer to examine the scrolled woodwork around the edges, trying to detect if it camouflaged a seam. I ran my fingers over it, pushing as I went, wishing I had any clue whatsoever what I was looking for. I worked my way fully around, but found nothing.

I removed everything from the shelves so I could get a closer look, examining each item for any oddities as I went, then went back over the entire bookcase inch by inch. On the second-from-the-bottom shelf, I found it. A very faint watermark in the bottom corner of the back panel, almost like a defect in the wood, just big enough to rest the tip of your finger on. In fact, it may have been made by decades of fingertip oils accumulating over time. My breathing sped as I pressed the spot.

Nothing happened.

I pressed again and simultaneously tried to slide the panel. It didn't move—but there was the teensiest bit of give, so tiny I almost wasn't sure I'd felt it. The room seemed to brighten as my sympathetic nervous system dilated my pupils and pounded my heart against my sternum. It couldn't be a coincidence—there had to be some sort of mechanism there.

I took a moment to reflect. Would a Prohibition room really be something you'd want someone to be able to stumble on while, say, polishing the wood? It would be smarter to require a combination of actions to trigger a mechanism—push on one thing while pulling on the other—so any no-good outsider like me would be stymied.

Plopping back onto my tush, I reached over to my purse and pulled out my phone. I'd been so taken in by all the cool hidden Prohibition room pictures I hadn't thought for one second to research how the mechanisms for opening them actually worked. As it turned out, I couldn't find much information about that, anyway, but what I did find was a smattering of hardware options designed to create invisible doors and cabinets. I clicked on that, figuring the basic principles behind modern solutions probably weren't too different from the ones used in days of yore.

Most of the options were easy to eliminate right off the bat. Anything smart-phone related was out instantly. Pressure sensitive springs couldn't be the answer—I'd pushed every inch of every surface on the bookcase. Obviously there was no keyhole, and there wasn't even a slot to insert a pin. It had to be something you could work completely invisibly.

I continued scrolling, tense and focused, heart still thudding and blood still rushing—and came to a screeching halt when I hit the word "magnet."

The perfect solution. An invisible technology, one you couldn't stumble on accidentally, and one that had likely been around since the iron age when newly organized farmers needed to protect their newly tamed chickens from homicidal hyenas.

I jumped up, already halfway out of the office in search of some sort of magnet when I realized Sylvia must have kept one somewhere close by. But I'd gone through everything in her office, and hadn't found anything like that. Maybe she kept it in her bedroom, and brought it in when she needed it? I frowned to myself—that didn't at all seem like the hyper-efficient and paranoid Sylvia.

But, I realized—how would I know if I'd found a magnet in here? Unless you put magnets in proximity with things they could attract, you'd never know they were magnets. And I *had* found a puzzling object in this very office I hadn't been able to identify.

I sprang over to Sylvia's desk drawer, which luckily was still unlocked. I pulled open the top drawer and found the random paperweight wood block with the carved Renard crest on it. I'd asked myself what sort of paper weight you stashed *inside the desk* rather than on top of it—apparently one that was actually a magnet you didn't want anyone to know about.

I hurried back over to the bookcase. I put my finger over the depression then placed the magnet just above my finger; I felt a slight click as the magnet's pull kicked in, and did a mental happy dance. But when I tried to slide the panel, nothing moved. I pushed, but still nothing.

Maybe the panel didn't need to move, maybe the latch inside the panel did; in that case, I'd need to move the magnet in order to move the latch. There weren't any scrapes that I could see in the wood to suggest which direction I should move the magnet; Sylvia must have been careful never to touch the wood directly and leave telltale signs. I didn't care about scratching the wood, so I slapped it right up against the panel and moved the magnet up. When nothing happened, I re-oriented it and moved the magnet to the left.

A tiny rumble told me something was shifting. When the rumbling stopped, I tried sliding the panel again.

The entire section of wood behind the three bottom shelves slid open.

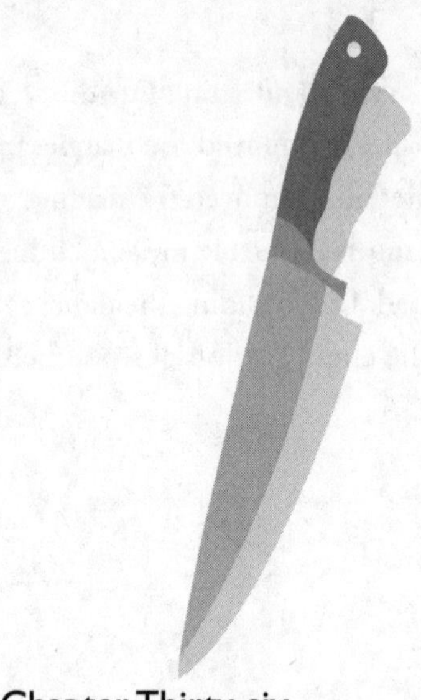

Chapter Thirty-six

I literally shouted "Yes!" and pumped my fist in the air—then remembered where I was and sighed with relief that the nanny cam was no longer present.

The space recessed up and back behind the panel, taking up the entire length and height of the bookshelf, extending back a little more than a foot. Recessed lighting intermittently dotted the sides, so I hunted for a switch. When I found it, the space illuminated like a museum exhibit.

Three small shelves lined the top. The first and second contained a scatter of jewelry cases, along with some cash in dollars and euros. The third contained a stack of file folders and the missing Rolodex. I grabbed them and stashed them in my messenger bag so I could look them over carefully later, then turned back to examine the large black safe that sat in the space below. Tingles ran down my arms—if Sylvia hadn't considered the jewelry and cash important enough to put inside the additional security of the safe, what the hell *was* in there? I reached for the handle under the combination dial, hoping Sylvia had left it unlocked.

Of course she hadn't.

I swore profusely into the cubby, venting days of frustration and desperation. Because seriously? After breaking into her desk to find her magic magnet and hunting down her top-secret Prohibition room, I now had to figure out how to open a safe? If she wasn't already dead, I'd be tempted to kill her myself.

"You kiss our daughter with that mouth?" Todd's mocking voice came from behind me. "I warned you that you weren't going to find anything."

I whirled around to find him leaning against the doorjamb, staring at what must have looked, from his angle, like me cussing out a bookshelf.

"Oh, but I did," I crowed. "Come check this out."

His brow knit and he pushed away from the doorjamb. "Holy shit," he said when he reached my side, his expression suddenly sober.

"You kiss our daughter with that mouth?"

He ignored me and reached for the cash. "What the hell? She was holding out on me. Why am I not surprised?"

"I don't suppose you have any idea what the combination to the safe is?" I asked.

"None whatsoever. I can't believe she'd . . ." He shook his head.

"I think she was trying to protect you and Philip." I pressed my palms against my eyes as I tried to think. Ryan had discovered two passwords now for Sylvia's accounts. Her email password was too long and contained letters, but he'd said the memory card password had been a mix of Philip's birthday and their anniversary. I reached for the dial.

"What are you trying?" Todd asked, his eyes flicking between me and the safe. "Maybe we should just wait and ask Dad—"

"I'm trying your birthday, month, date, year." I put them in left-right-left, then pulled on the handle. It didn't open. "And now, Philip's birthday."

Still nothing.

"Okay," I said, trying not to let my frustration panic me. "Last birthday. Her own."

Again, nothing.

Todd opened his mouth to speak, then closed it, then seemed to make some sort of decision. "You got that wrong," Todd said. "She was born in 1949, not 1951."

"Oh, I'm quite certain it was 1951. We had that conversation more than once."

He treated me to a withering stare. "You actually think she told you the truth about her age?"

I rubbed the bridge of my nose and tried not to feel like an idiot. Had anything Sylvia said been true, to anyone, ever? I reentered the date, switching out forty-nine for fifty-one.

The door swung open.

As it did, the shadowy interior revealed its contents: two strange wooden briefcases, several stacks of small cardboard boxes, and an envelope.

I reached for one of the cases. When it opened to reveal a revolver, I nearly dropped the case. "Your ultra-liberal anti-gun mother was *packing*?"

"Not that I ever knew." He frowned and pulled out the second one. "I'm no expert, but these don't look modern. My guess is they belonged to my grandfather."

"Why didn't she get rid of them?"

He shrugged as he lifted up the second revolver. "Probably couldn't bring herself to sell something that was his."

The conversation with Brighton Keyes flashed through my mind. "Or maybe she kept them in case she ever needed them."

"The boxes must be ammunition." He grabbed for the envelope.

My hand was closer, so I reached it first. I opened it and pulled out a stack of pictures.

I gasped—Philip was doing very inappropriate things to a woman in what looked like Santorini. A very *young* woman.

Todd's face transformed at the sight of the pictures. He rolled his eyes and shook his head. "Not cool, Mom. Not cool."

I gaped at him. "Not cool, *Mom*? How about not cool, *Dad*?"

He waved me off. "It worked for them, so who am I to judge? But it's one thing to have an arrangement where you pretend not to know about your husband's indiscretions, and another entirely to hire someone to take pictures of it and keep them hidden in your safe. That's just—*weird*."

Either I was having a stroke, or words had stopped making sense. "Wait, back that truck right up. You're telling me your father cheated and *your mother knew about it*?"

He blinked down at me. "Come on, Capri. You've been a member of this family for how long and never figured that out?"

"But she—she always reacted to any mention of cheating like she'd been stabbed in the eye with a burning needle."

He shook his head bemusedly. "And why do you think that was?"

I peered down at the brunette whose breast resided in Philip's hand. "So it wasn't just this one time?"

Todd's expression turned serious again. "No, that's why they took separate vacations. Far-off flings are meaningless and clean. That way he wouldn't be tempted by anything closer to home that would have gotten sticky."

I struggled to close my jaw. He was absolutely right—her condemnation of infidelity had the visceral ring of a very personal pain. How had I never seen that before? And really, what the actual hell? My grandfather, my father-in-law, my husband—if I thought about it too much, I'd never be able to trust another man.

I flipped through the pictures again. "These are all of the same girl, and the same trip. But if you're obsessed enough about your husband's philandering to keep pictures, wouldn't you keep pictures of *all* the girls? And if you wanted to bury your head in the sand, you wouldn't keep *any* of them. So why does she have only these?"

"Like I said, weird." He craned his neck to try to see around me. "Is there anything else in there?"

"Nope." I sighed.

His face morphed into his *I'm now bored by this* expression, and he stood up. "Well, I have to head out. That's actually what I came up to tell you. I have to run over to the funeral home to make some final decisions. You can let yourself out once you close all that back up, right?"

I nodded. "Sure thing."

He took off. I put the guns and pictures back into the safe and closed it securely. Then I checked my watch; I had several stops to make for planning the tours, but could afford to take a quick peek at the folders I'd found. I slipped them out of my messenger bag and dove in.

The quick peek turned into several hours of me going through everything word by word, despite knowing within minutes I'd found what I'd been looking for. The missing business plans, the missing financial records, and scads of research about exactly the sort of scams I'd suspected. Pages of notes in Sylvia's script that outlined the real purpose of the businesses, including examples of fraudulent ads and products and the sort of revenue she'd been told she could expect. And relevant contacts in her Rolodex—she'd kept everything she needed to maintain the relevant network in hard copy, safely tucked through multiple layers of security. No wonder I hadn't been able to find anything in her email.

I sat back on my heels and sorted through the mountain of emotions tugging at me. Sylvia must have been beyond desperate to resort to a scheme like this; the prospect of losing a generations-old fortune must have been ego annihilating for her. But that paled in comparison to the possible consequences of the fraud—how many lives like

Margie Francis's had already been ruined? The only redeeming aspect I could find was her desire to protect her family—through everything she was facing, destitution and jail, her top priority had been to make sure their lives weren't ruined by it all. It wasn't much, but at least it was a small redeeming thread in her carpet of heinous choices I could give Morgan and Todd to hold on to.

I stared down at the documents again, and an uneasy feeling settled over me. These documents were dangerous—extremely dangerous. I didn't know how exactly it had played out, but they were evidence that would put Brighton Keyes and his associates in jail; Sylvia most likely had been killed to keep this quiet. I was positive whoever was responsible wouldn't hesitate to do the same to me or the rest of my family to keep the information out of police hands.

I stood and grabbed my car keys. I needed to get it all to Petito immediately.

SF Killer Crime Tours

Fort Point

Gently tucked under the shadows of the Golden Gate Bridge, Fort Point silently and stealthily watches over the strait from the San Francisco Bay to the Pacific Ocean. While the fort was designed to protect San Francisco Bay first from pirates looking to steal all the 49ers' gold, then from Confederates trying to do the same, it never faced an attack—although during the Civil War, the CSS Shenandoah did try. She was on her way to attack when, several months after Lee surrendered, she received word that the war was over.

The Golden Gate was carefully constructed around the fort in the 1930s, financed by the Bank of Italy (now known as Bank of America) to make crossing into posh Marin County easier for people looking to escape the city's hustle and bustle. Just on the other side, right off the first exit, is San Quentin, filled with the state's most notorious criminals.

While no notable murders have taken place at Fort Point, more than a few movies have used the beauty of the surroundings and the eerie stillness of the structure itself to excellent effect. In Vertigo, Kim Novak tried to kill herself by jumping into the Bay; you can feel both her desolation and the icy cold of the waters during her plunge. In Dark Passage, Humphrey Bogart takes part in a hide-and-seek chase through the series of corridors and stairs that raise ever higher above the deep blue currents lurking perilously below.

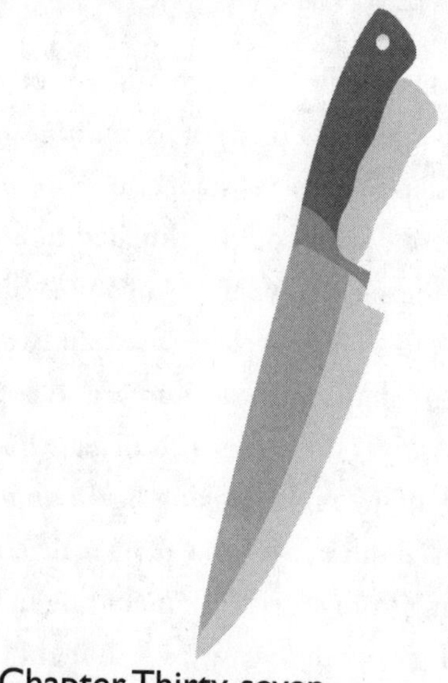

Chapter Thirty-seven

Petito didn't answer his phone. I tried Kumar and Garcia directly, again with no luck. But Morgan had promised to call when she was done and she hadn't yet, so maybe they were all still talking with her and Philip? I glanced at the time; just after three in the afternoon. I fought back the little daggers stabbing my stomach, because even if they'd started late, they'd been at it over four hours. But, I told myself, they were interviewing *both* Morgan and Philip, and it was very possible each interview could take two-plus hours. My finger hovered over Morgan's contact, and I had to force myself to swipe away—whether she was still in the homicide division or was rushing to get to school in time for her research appointments, she wouldn't appreciate me bugging her when I'd promised not to.

Nonetheless, I still had a satchel of incendiary documents burning a hole in my soul. So I drove myself down to homicide and dropped everything off for the detectives, then tried to put it all aside and focus on scoping out sites for our potential Hitchcock tour.

Tried, but failed. I should've felt better once I dropped off the paperwork, but Petito had shut down my discoveries before, and a thousand little uncertainties kept bouncing around my brain like gnats stalking a piece of rotten fruit.

Like Steve's resistance to help me. Shouldn't he want to talk to someone who could help shed light on his wife's death—unless he was the secret owner of Anchor & Shields?

And Nancy's claim that she was happy to give Sylvia money. Wasn't that a little too simple and convenient?

And Todd's presence in San Jose—it had been hovering in the back of my mind, making my brain itch. Todd had always been close to his mother, but none of us realized just how much Sylvia had been hiding from everybody, including him.

I gave a little gasp as a thought occurred to me—was it possible he was also involved in the direct-marketing fraud? He'd been oddly eager to see what was in the envelope in Sylvia's hidden safe, then lost interest when he saw it was pictures of Philip. But I'd slipped the relevant documents into my bag before he came into the room—he'd never known about them, and so might have thought he was in the clear. Was he the one who'd talked Sylvia into being part of the scheme? Is that why he'd signed the house over to me before he supposedly left for South Africa, so he didn't have to worry about losing it if they all got caught?

I scrabbled to pull my phone out of my bag while keeping my eyes on the road, then put through a call to Petito. When he again didn't answer, I left a message outlining my suspicions about Todd. Hopefully Petito was already tracking Todd's reason for being in San Jose, but just in case, I needed him to know.

By the time I finished my stops at 900 Lombard Street (the house where Jimmy Stewart's character lived in *Vertigo*) and 1000 Mason Street (where Kim Novak's character lived), the fog had crept farther over the edge of the bay faster than I'd hoped. If I didn't get out to Fort Point soon, the entire fort would be swallowed before I could get what I needed, so I stepped on the gas.

As I hurried, the gnat kept finding inconvenient places to land. First, on Katherine's role in everything: Was she the blackmailer, the blackmailee, or both? Or was Steve the one involved? It seemed ridiculous he'd be involved in such penny-ante crime given how rich and powerful he was, but at this point nothing would surprise me with these people.

Hush, I swatted at the gnat. *The police will find whatever connections exist, and they'll know what to do.*

I enjoyed about thirty seconds of mental peace before the gnat flitted onto the pictures of Philip cheating in Santorini. Their presence in the safe just didn't make sense. Was Todd wrong about Sylvia knowing about the affairs? Maybe Todd just wanted to believe they had an arrangement because it made him feel better about his own infidelities. Maybe Sylvia only just found out and confronted him with it. But what would that matter? It wasn't like Philip's lifestyle was at stake if she divorced him—they were broke.

Real life isn't neat and clean, I swatted again. *Everybody had secrets, and not every secret is related to murder.*

That was the trick, wasn't it? Sorting out which lies and secrets mattered, and which didn't. I'd probably never know the answers to most of these questions, and I needed to figure out how to accept that, so I could put my focus on creating my new tours and working on the Overkill Bill book that would pay Morgan's tuition.

Except I wasn't the sort of person who was okay with not knowing the answers, never had been and never would be. As long as my brain kept screaming something wasn't right, I'd keep digging until I knew everything.

• • •

As I turned off the highway onto the road that circled around and down to Fort Point, I eyed the wisps of fog sneaking over the tops of the trees, threatening to slip downward over the ivy fronds and nasturtiums growing up into them. The road ahead of me was still visually unobstructed, so if I hurried, I'd be fine. Besides, a few shots that artistically exploited the fog would add a lovely bit of atmosphere to pictures and video for the tour. After all, there was a reason Hitchcock chose to use the location, and a little bit of ambient menace would help that mood shine right through.

I smiled as the Golden Gate Bridge peeped through the veil; despite five decades as a native San Franciscan, the sight never ceased to please. Two cyclists passed on my right, going against traffic; I gently shifted toward the double-yellow line to give them room, then continued to the parking lot and slid into a spot just feet outside the fort.

And just feet away from the water. In *Vertigo*, Kim Novak's character jumps directly into the Bay from the promenade outside the fort, causing Jimmy Stewart to dive in and save her. I've heard more than one person express skepticism about that, objecting that there must be safety precautions in place to prevent it. So I snapped a few pictures and took a video of the promenade to show that, yes, even today you can walk right up to the edge of the cement and dive into the San Francisco Bay on the one side of the fort, and into the strait out to the Pacific Ocean on the other. And that walkway around the front half of the fort? It's only a few feet wide, making it pretty darn treacherous even on a clear day.

I snapped a few shots of the fort's facade and as much as I could of its unusual *hey you smashed your star into my rectangle* shape. Then I scuttled over to the sally port and through to the interior of the fort, staring up to plan out the most advantageous angles. If I'd wanted picturesque, I couldn't ask for more—the slinking fog had already partially obscured the orange beams that held up the Golden Gate, giving the illusion of a giant orange spider spinning a web around the redbrick building. I wouldn't be able to capture the expansive roof views to the north today, but hopefully would have time to get a few facing back to Alcatraz and downtown San Francisco.

Shooting strategic pics and video intermittently as I went, I made my way across the interior and up through the levels, purposefully tracing Bogie's path in *Dark Passage*. Even if the tour ended up focusing on Hitchcock, guests would certainly be interested in hearing about another movie shot here, and I was intrigued by Ryan's suggestion for doing a dedicated San Francisco Noir tour in the future. Two birds, careful planning, all that.

Back in the courtyard, I paused to double-check everything I'd shot. More than once I'd left a site thinking I had everything I needed only to realize I'd hit pause when I thought I'd hit record and my only footage was of trainer-clad feet tromping along, or that I'd inadvertently caught a child in the background furiously picking his nose. I also checked the upload status to make sure everything was being copied into the cloud; I'd once had a phone die before I'd backed up all my files and hadn't been able to recover them. Backing up your files is a lesson you only need to learn once.

A lesson you only need to learn once.

The thought careened off the sides of my skull, screeching bloody murder at me. Sylvia was far savvier than I'd given her credit for about technology, and as paranoid as she was with her cameras and secret Prohibition rooms and locked desks, wouldn't she have been sure to automatically back up her recordings to the cloud? If she had, her cloud might still have the full recordings from the night she died. My security cameras recorded directly to the cloud and saved a week's worth of footage—but then, my cams didn't have removable memory cards, and Sylvia's nanny cam did. Maybe the cameras only did one or the other. Either way, it was worth a shot to try to find out.

With my heart thumping around in my chest, I strode over to the wooden bench at the far end of the courtyard, dropped down onto it, then put a call through to Ryan.

"Hey. That nanny cam I found in Sylvia's office. We know she recorded onto memory cards with it, but would it have also automatically backed up to the cloud?" I asked.

His tone verbally shrugged. "It's possible. Some do one or the other, some do both."

"If it did have a cloud backup, how would the cam access that?"

"For someone who knows their way around tech, it can go a lot of ways. Sylvia would probably have taken an easy route, most likely loading to a cloud service provided by the manufacturer of the camera."

"So, for example, if it were a Sony device, the cloud service would probably be provided by Sony?" I asked.

"You got it."

"She'd have had to set up some sort of account, right? It wouldn't be free, she'd have to pay for it, and she'd have to have some sort of sign-in?"

"Possibly. For a bigger company like Ring she'd have an app on her phone. If not, or if she didn't want to use an app, there could be some sort of browser-based sign-up."

Since the police had her phone, I had to hope there were other options. "Either way there's probably some sort of account setup email she received, right?"

"Most likely. Let me know if you need me to figure out the password for you."

"Will do. Thanks."

Once I hung up, I pulled up Gmail and signed into Sylvia's account. I had no idea what company had made the device or where she would have stored the email in her complex system of folders, so I plugged *webcam* into the search bar and prayed for the best.

Three emails popped right up. The most recent two were yearly statements for the unlimited cloud account she'd signed up for. The oldest was a confirmation of the account, complete with links.

I clicked to a home page asking for her login and password. I plugged in the account login I'd seen in the email, then tried a few variations of the passwords we'd found so far for Sylvia, hoping for instant gratification and a way to avoid bothering Ryan again.

This time the birthday-slash-anniversary combo melted the sign-in page to a list of files recorded over the last two weeks, each with a date and time stamp as title, most recent on top. As far as I could tell, the system was set to divide files into one-hour chunks; I scanned the list and found the set of files for the day Sylvia died. I clicked the most recent and caught sight of myself crossing the room to search for the webcam; I simultaneously fist-pumped to celebrate successfully finding the backups while resolving to restart my abandoned yoga regimen ASAP. Then I searched for the video from the six p.m. hour of the night she died; her office was empty, so I clicked on the fastest speed until she appeared in the room.

A sense of déjà vu took me over as she sat and picked up the phone. I listened for a minute to make sure it was the conversation I'd already seen with Brighton Keyes, then fast-forwarded to the end. After she finished the call, she got up and removed the memory card—I couldn't tell if she inserted another one in its place—and pulled out her laptop. She opened the files on the card, deleted and trimmed, pulled a bunch of other files off her computer onto the card, then placed it in the top drawer of her desk. After that she crossed over to one of the windows and stared out of it; as she stood there, her posture shifted, changing from erect and purposeful to hunched and despondent. When she turned back and picked up her phone, she was crying.

My throat tightened. I'd never seen Sylvia cry before. Not when Todd and I got married, not in the midst of three extended-family deaths during our marriage—not even the day her granddaughter was born. And something about seeing someone so stoic lose even the smallest amount of emotional control was deeply unsettling.

She pulled a handkerchief from the pocket of her slacks and

cleaned up her face. Still facing the camera, she looked down at the phone and dialed.

Morgan's voice came over the line, bubbly and happy to talk to her grandmother. Sylvia's voice turned to steel, and she informed Morgan she was cutting off her tuition. When Morgan responded, hurt and surprised, Sylvia's profile screwed up in pain and her free hand gripped the edge of the armchair like she expected it to take flight.

I grimaced. I'd figured out early on that Sylvia's choice to cut off Morgan's tuition wasn't really a choice, but I hadn't realized just how much it had hurt her to do it. I saw now that her pauses, easy to mistake for detachment if you couldn't see her, were because she was trying to keep hold of her composure—her jaw clenched and her eyes squeezed shut and her face screwed up with emotion as she kept from crying audibly. When the call ended, she sat still, tears trailing down the visible side of her face.

Making that phone call to Morgan had destroyed her.

I fast-forwarded until she again picked up the phone, this time to answer my call. Her profile, posture, and shaking hands showed her emotion clearly; her cold pauses and the abrupt hang-up took on a new and very different meaning. Even as she told me off, tears welled in her eyes.

My own squeezed shut as I paused to process what I'd just seen, and Sylvia's pain washed over me. My father's face popped up unexpectedly in front of me—and I realized Sylvia's choice here would have made perfect sense to him. Maybe it was a generational thing or maybe they just had similar personalities, but they'd both taken on the bad-guy role in order to deal with harsh realities that were facing their family. But to my Gen-X perspective, it all looked like needless suffering—even selfishness—due to an insulting failure to trust your loved ones to stay with you during bad times. But then, judging them through my own sensibilities wasn't fair, either.

I shook my head at myself and clicked on the video again. For another few minutes after hanging up on me, Sylvia sat at the desk, pulling out papers and poring over folders, most likely trying to find any way out of the mess she'd gotten herself into.

Then someone knocked on the door, and she swiveled toward it.

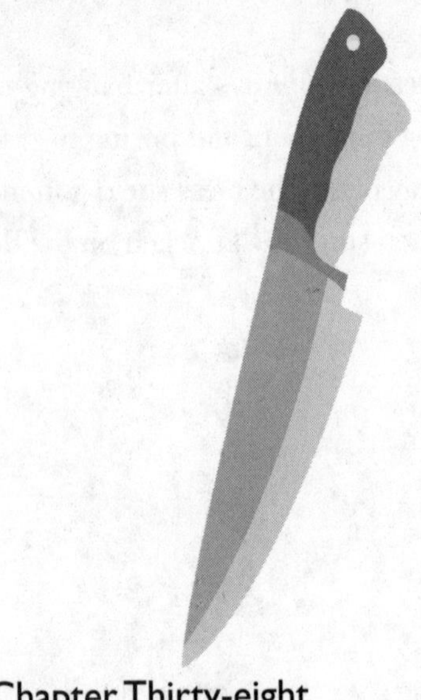

Chapter Thirty-eight

My pancreas dropped into my small intestines at the sound of the knock on the door, and I leaned closer to the screen as though that would allow me to see or hear better.

"Who is it?" Sylvia called out.

I heard the door open, and Philip stepped into the frame.

I sagged back against the bench again, disappointed. Just Philip, resplendent in his casual golf-resort wear, pompadour flip to his gray-blond hair, carrying two mugs of what I guessed was tea.

But hadn't he told me he didn't see Sylvia after her initial return home? That she'd gone directly into her office and hadn't come back out? But maybe he figured bringing her tea wasn't important enough to mention, or maybe it just slipped his mind. It was the sort of routine thing that was easy to forget.

Sylvia's expression, even in profile, was annoyed. "Philip. I told you I'm dealing with some unpleasant business. I really can't—"

"I've been waiting to talk the whole time you were in Hawaii. I know whatever business you're dealing with is important, but this issue is important, too, and I have good news. You can't just push me to the side."

Her jaw clenched as he spoke, and her reply was a cobra strike. "Push you to the side? I've just spent the last hour trying to make sure you don't end up in j—" She stopped short and waved dismissively at him. "That's fine. You're making this easier."

I winced—I knew from the previous videos that Sylvia had just trapped Brighton Keyes into admitting Philip knew nothing about the direct-marketing fraud. But Philip didn't, and she couldn't tell him, because that would defeat the whole plausible-deniability plan she was setting up for him. She must have felt like she was trapped in some sort of nightmare.

He stepped closer to her. "Spent the last hour trying to what?"

"It's nothing you need worry about." She pushed her shoulders back and gestured to the closest armchair. "But you're right, we need to talk. I was going to wait until tomorrow to do this, but it might as well be now."

Philip set the mugs on the desk, and sat.

"I won't cave to Katherine's blackmail. There's no way I can recommend her for membership in the Ligue. I'd become a laughingstock overnight, and my credibility would be destroyed. The Ligue runs on history and lineage, not money. Some people belong and some don't. If she chooses to show the Santorini pictures all over town, I can't stop her."

"Of course." He nodded eagerly. "But that doesn't matter anymore, because Katherine Harper's dead."

Sylvia's head jutted forward. "She's what?"

"I've been waiting to tell you all night. She was attacked Thursday night at the Legion of Honor. We don't have to worry about her showing the Santorini pictures to anybody."

I paused the video for a moment to process what was happening.

Katherine was the one who'd hired someone to take the pictures—that was the "mutual interest" in the blackmail email Katherine had sent Sylvia. But, fortunately for both Sylvia and Philip, she'd died before deploying the evidence.

When I started the video again, Sylvia's hands flew up to her face. I could picture them, one on each side of her nose, rubbing the bridge in the gesture I'd seen a million times—but one of annoyance, not relief. Why?

She sat that way for a good minute while Philip stared at her, his face changing from hopeful to afraid. "Sylvia—what—" he asked.

Her hands dropped back to the desk. "It doesn't make a difference, Philip. Because I've decided I want a divorce."

He shifted forward onto the very edge of his chair, and reached for her hands, his voice soft. "Sylvie, I don't understand. The pictures aren't a problem anymore. Why—"

I peered down closer to the screen, heart thumping, sharing Philip's confusion.

She pulled back her hands and turned slightly away. I could now see the same pain on her face I'd seen when she'd been talking to Morgan, and her hands clenched the arms of her office chair the same way she'd done then. "Whether anyone sees the pictures or not, I—I can't just forget about them."

Philip's brow creased like he was trying to solve a trigonometry problem. "I don't understand. We've had an understanding for years. You know these women mean nothing to me. They're a way to relax on vacation, no different from drinks or massages. Why would this time be different?"

Her hands clenched the chair even tighter and my déjà vu with the earlier conversations struck again, this time sliding all the pieces into place. To verify I was on the right track, I clicked out of the video and back to her conversation with Morgan: I watched her expression when I could and her body language when I couldn't. Then I switched back and compared them to the same moments of desperation and sadness in her expression when she was talking to Philip.

The expressions and motions were her tells, like in poker. Leaking emotion. She was *lying*.

Sylvia wasn't asking for a divorce because of Santorini, that was just an excuse—that's why it didn't matter if Katherine wasn't alive to blackmail them anymore. Sylvia was asking for a divorce because she knew the *direct-marketing fraud* could be uncovered at any minute—everything was hitting the fan. She'd spent the evening protecting the ones she loved—giving Morgan as much lead time as possible to find another way to pay her tuition, and getting evidence that would put Philip in the clear. Brighton Keyes's admission that Philip knew nothing would keep him out of jail—and a divorce would keep him from being liable for any restitution Sylvia would need to pay. Keeping him in the dark would allow him to pass a lie-detector test if he was called on to do so. She was handing Philip a literal get-out-of-jail-free card.

She wiped away the tear that slid down her cheek. "I suppose this affair was one time too many."

He stood and quickly skirted around the large desk, then dropped to his knees next to her. "I'll do whatever you want me to do, Sylvie. We can go to counseling. I won't go on another vacation without you. And I'll never touch another woman, I swear it on my mother's grave. I love you, Sylvia—I can't lose you."

Her hands had turned white again, and a battle of emotions played over her profile—I could see her struggling not to tell him the truth. Finally, she said, "I'm sorry, Philip. I won't change my mind. I'll start the proceedings tomorrow."

Philip stared at her, blinking. "No, Sylvia. There must be something I can do."

Sylvia pushed her chair back away from him, strode across the room, then pulled herself up to her full height. "Please don't beg, it's beneath both of us. Let's handle this situation with dignity, to preserve the mutual respect between us."

Philip, still on his knees, dropped his head in his hands. Every muscle in my body tightened as I watched to see what he'd do, muttering "no" repeatedly under my breath and praying he wouldn't do anything to harm her.

With a sweeping gesture, he raked his fingers back through his hair and stood back up. Then he walked out of the room, face a stunned blank.

• • •

I exhaled as the door clicked behind him—for a moment I'd actually been convinced he lashed out in a fit of temper and killed her. I laughed my relief out loud, never so happy to see someone leave a room in my life, or to see Sylvia safe and sound.

That's why he hadn't told me or the police that he'd talked to Sylvia after she shut herself in the office—telling us she'd asked for a divorce would only have given him a motive for murder. Since he didn't know the video existed, he must have figured there was no reason to bring it up, and I really couldn't say I blamed him. I returned eagerly to the tape—time was running out, and whatever happened next must be the critical event.

For the rest of the video file, Sylvia sat at her desk and cried again for several minutes, then returned to whatever paperwork she'd been doing before. I started the next on the fastest speed, waiting for any sort of phone call or other visitor. Nothing happened, but in the following file, Sylvia swiveled toward her office door again. I hurried to restore the speed to normal.

Philip reappeared in the frame, his face red and swollen and his hair mussed.

Sylvia stiffened, and the steel leaped back into her voice. "There's nothing more to be said, Philip."

He nodded. "After all these years, I know you well enough to know when your mind is made up. I came to tell you I won't fight it. And that you're right, we need to do this with dignity and kindness. We should end the marriage the way we started it—two people who love each other and want what's best for each other. So I thought we could start talking through the details the way we always used to talk about major decisions, over a stroll in the park. A fitting tribute to the life we've shared, don't you think?"

Chapter Thirty-nine

I sat frozen, staring down at the now-empty room that Sylvia and Philip had just vacated, running through the facts, a lump in my throat the size of a cantaloupe.

Most of it made sense. I understood that Katherine had blackmailed Sylvia, threatening to release pictures of Philip's infidelity to their social circle if Sylvia didn't recommend her to the Ligue. I also understood that Sylvia was using that as an excuse to ask for a divorce, and that the real reason she wanted a divorce was she'd gotten herself in deep trouble with a direct-marketing scheme; she was trying to make sure Philip didn't spend the rest of his life destitute and in jail because of that scheme. And I understood that, since Philip asked Sylvia to go for a walk she never came back from, Philip must have killed her, copycatting Katherine's death to make it look like Sylvia and Katherine's deaths were related. And that explained why Sylvia hadn't taken her purse or her phone or a flashlight; Philip would have had his keys, and with him by her side, Sylvia wouldn't have been scared to go into the park at night.

But that's where it *stopped* making sense. Because why would

Philip kill Sylvia to keep from getting divorced? I'd seen a prenuptial agreement in Sylvia's files, and if it was anything like mine, it had an infidelity clause that left Philip with nothing if he cheated. *But there were no assets left to divide up.* The only thing left was debt, and the divorce would *protect* him from debt. And a divorce wouldn't ruin *his* reputation; the thousand-dollar-cigar crowd would shake his hand in congratulations over the hot young woman he'd bagged. And if he was just deeply heartbroken, surely the best approach would have been to give Sylvia space and try to win her back? No matter how I looked at it, I simply couldn't find a motive for him to kill her.

And Philip had been so devastated by all of this—he'd been on Xanax almost nonstop since Sylvia had been found dead. And he was the one who insisted I take the memory card to Petito—why would a guilty man risk turning over memory cards that might have incriminating evidence on it to the police? I squeezed my eyes shut and shook my head. Maybe I was jumping to conclusions, and he hadn't killed her in the park. Maybe they'd fought over the divorce and Philip had come home without her, and someone killed her while she was alone. He wouldn't have wanted to admit he'd left her out there vulnerable.

But, that back corner of my mind whispered . . . *Maybe Philip did know what was on the memory card.* I only had his word that he didn't know about the nanny cam. Maybe he knew about it the whole time, and had destroyed whatever memory card contained his conversations with Sylvia. He wouldn't have had to worry about what was on the other memory card because he knew what *wasn't* on it. *And*, the back corner of my mind continued, *if you'd just murdered your wife, a little Xanax to calm your nerves might come in handy* . . . If nothing else, it gave him an excuse for being too out of it to talk to the police initially.

My eyes snapped back open. It didn't matter. Whatever had or hadn't happened, I had to tell Petito as soon as possible.

As I looked next to me to grab my bag, I noticed how completely the fog had snaked around the fort while I'd zeroed in on the recordings. The arches across the courtyard were no longer visible amid the gray; in fact, I could only see a few feet in front of me. A strange foreboding crept up my spine—this situation wasn't safe. The smartest thing to do was call Petito now, right here on this bench, before I moved an inch.

I unlocked my phone again with my fingerprint, and tapped the screen.

Something poked firmly into my upper back, accompanied by a cold, steely voice. "Hand the phone to me, now."

Chapter Forty

"I have a gun." Philip jabbed harder into my back to be sure I understood. "I can shoot you and be long gone in the fog before anyone even realizes what happened. Do as I say."

A burst of electricity shot up my spine and time seemed to stop as my nervous system tried frantically to decide between *fight* or *flight*. It settled on *freeze*, and I couldn't get my hand to move.

Philip solved the problem by plucking the phone from my grasp. "What's your password?"

I gave it to him. But the phone was currently unlocked, so why did he need it? A litany of intermittent clicks stretched on for what felt like hours. What was he doing?

"Now stand up, slowly."

Thankfully, my legs followed directions better than my hands, but while I managed to stand, they were so shaky I had no confidence in my ability to stay upright.

He grabbed my left arm firmly and nestled the gun in my lower back. "Forward."

My brain kicked back into gear with an almost audible whoosh as time started up again. Everything around me—the sound of the gulls flying overhead, the smell of the ocean brine, the chill of the air biting through my coat—became heightened, as if compensating for my inability to see through the fog. I stepped forward, willing my trembling knees not to fail, and tried to get my bearings. He was leading me away from the sally port, the only exit I knew of. "What's going on, Philip?" I asked, barely managing a whisper.

"Please don't play stupid, Capri. Neither of us is stupid, even if everyone has underestimated us our whole lives. I heard what you were watching, I was standing next to the column behind you." His whisper was brusque.

No, he wasn't stupid, and I wasn't going to convince him I didn't understand what was happening. But as things stood, he was hyperfocused on whatever he had planned, and the smartest thing I could think of was to get him talking, maybe even trigger some emotion that might allow me a precious moment to get away from him.

"And I know you found the pictures in Sylvia's safe," he added.

That surprised me enough to forget about my wobbly legs. "How?"

"Todd called me to check in and mentioned it. *He* thought it was funny, but I knew that meant it was only a matter of time before you put everything together."

"Put what together? It makes no sense to me. Why would you kill Sylvia because she asked for a divorce? Even if your prenuptial agreement covers cheating, there's no money left. You're so far in debt even her relatively piddly life insurance is spoken for."

The sarcastic laugh disappeared, replaced by an angry edge that chilled me to the bone. "So very true. Too bad I didn't realize that *before* I killed her."

"Before you—" I stopped, my brain too busy with the implications to form a complete sentence.

"I found out about the debt when I pulled the papers out of your hands. You think she kept me in the dark about her investments, but gave me detailed financial breakdowns of all our accounts?"

A cascade of realization filtered down through my neurons, facts and memories combining in ways they hadn't before, clashing into an almost-painful burst of clarity. Of course Sylvia had kept vise-grip control over the Renard money—Philip didn't work and hadn't brought any money into the marriage. And Philip's face when he caught me going through Sylvia's papers—it felt strange at the time, but I'd thought that was because I'd been caught doing something compromising. He'd been annoyed, yes, and he'd pulled the papers from my hands and from the floor next to me—but his face hadn't gone red until *after* he scanned them. *Then* he'd turned to the window and refused to speak to me for several minutes. At the time I'd assumed he was embarrassed and was trying to bring himself to face me. He was trying to get his emotions under control, all right, but not for that reason. If Philip hadn't known the money was gone, he would still have been under the impression his prenuptial agreement would have dire consequences in case of divorce, leaving him with nothing. He would have believed that if Sylvia were dead, he would continue to live his comfortable life until his own death, when the assets would pass down to Todd and Morgan.

In that moment, scanning the documents he'd snatched from me, he learned he was penniless and had killed his wife for nothing.

I forced myself to speak again. "So when Sylvia asked for a divorce, you figured you'd kill her the same way Katherine Harper was killed, hoping the cops would blame it on Katherine's killer?"

A derisive laugh puffed through his nose. "Maybe you're *not* as smart as I gave you credit for."

I gasped as the implication of his derision hit my brain like a Bouncing Betty.

He hadn't just killed Sylvia—he'd killed Katherine, too.

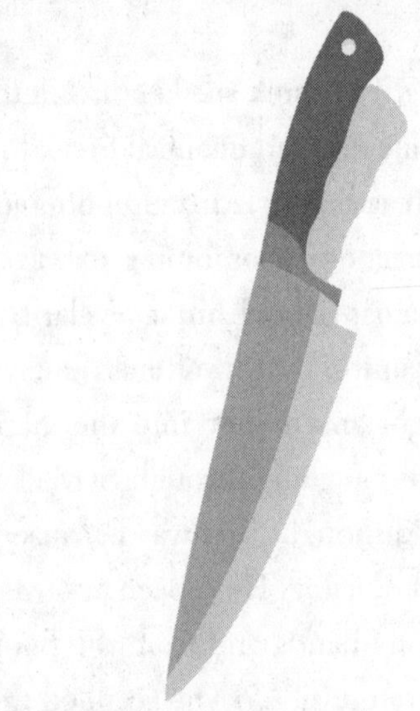

Chapter Forty-one

My mind reeled as I tried to make sense of the new revelation—Philip hadn't *copycatted* Katherine's killer, he *was* Katherine's killer.

"But you barely knew her," I asked, still trying to put the pieces together. "How did you know where she'd be that night?"

"I had to listen to Sylvia complain about how Katherine was screwing everything up for the last two months. I knew far more than I wanted to about the remaining steps Katherine had to finish before the luncheon planning was complete."

I'd recovered enough from the new information to pay attention again to where he was taking me. Unless my sense of direction was off, we were headed to Fort Point's spiral staircase. Which was potentially good news—made with uniform slabs of granite without safety strips or railings of any sort, the steps were treacherous, especially when wet due to rain or fog. If I could keep him talking and thinking about something else, maybe I could use them to my advantage to get away from him.

"So you knew she'd be at the Legion late that night, and you took the opportunity to end the blackmail. And you figured, hey, why not throw suspicion on my ex-daughter-in-law by imitating her grandfather's serial killer technique?"

"I never intended it to reflect back on you specifically. You'd never even met Katherine, so why would it? I didn't know I'd need to kill Sylvia then. But yes, it seemed to me that copying a famous area serial killer who attacked women would make it seem like there was a maniac on the loose, and the police would never bother to look into her life too closely. When I had to kill Sylvia, I had to stick to the same method so the police would think the same killer murdered them both."

"But you called me in to help you find Sylvia. You purposefully involved me," I said, eyes desperately scouring the fog, hoping for any visual break.

"You hated Sylvia! How was I to know you'd jump in trying to avenge her? I just needed someone to be there to witness my distress and to talk to the police after I took the Xanax." His voice took on an accusatory tone.

"And you took the Xanax and alcohol to knock yourself out so you'd be impaired and nobody would look too closely at your reactions."

"I never took the Xanax, I palmed it. But, yes, that was the general idea. Make everyone think I was incapacitated. You don't have to worry about your acting skills when everyone thinks you're medicated."

He was keeping his cool—he was proud of his cleverness. I needed to rouse some emotion if I was going to distract him. "And Sylvia? You bashed her and stabbed her and slashed her. How could you do all of those things to the woman you shared your life with all of those years? To the *mother of your son*?"

His fingers dug into my arm. "You think I *wanted* to do that? I didn't have any choice. The whole point of killing Katherine was to fix the problem. I had to keep Sylvia's death connected to Katherine's.

As it was, I had to fight to keep from vomiting the entire time." He snorted a frustrated puff of air. "I still don't understand it. There was no reason for her to ask for a divorce. With Katherine dead, that should have been an end to it. Sylvia never even had to know I was the one who killed Katherine—it should have all been behind us, with her none the wiser. I still can't understand why our status quo was suddenly unacceptable."

I mimicked his earlier scoff. "I guess we're both not at our brightest lately."

His grip tightened still further. "What do you mean?"

"She wasn't divorcing you because of the cheating. She was divorcing you to protect you."

"Protect me from what?"

"Those two tech companies she'd invested in? They were executing a big direct-marketing fraud scheme. She'd lost so much money in her investments over the last few years, she was desperate. But law enforcement are cracking down on schemes like that, and they were coming after My Kind of People and Rithmology."

His step faltered for a moment—but before I could take advantage of his divided attention, he caught himself. "There's a staircase in front of us. Take one step at a time, slowly. Any fast moves and I'll shoot you, understand?" He waited for my confirmation, and for me to take my first step up. "That makes no sense, Capri. What does any of that have to do with protecting *me*?"

"I told you the gist of Sylvia's conversation with Brighton Keyes. What I didn't tell you, because I didn't see the point, was that she took great pains in that conversation to get Keyes to admit you knew nothing about the fraud. She put the recording of the conversation on a memory card so that when the time came you couldn't be prosecuted. And she asked for the divorce so that if they came after her assets, you wouldn't have to lose everything—like that gold Rolex on your wrist and the Ferrari you drive—or spend the rest of your life paying off restitution for crimes you didn't commit." My anger was taking over now, and I was suddenly stifling in my jacket despite the chilled air around me. "She turned herself into a felon to provide for you because she loved you so much, then tried to protect you when it all went wrong. And as a thank-you, you murdered her."

"You're wrong," he tried to scoff, but it fell flat, caked in an undercurrent of doubt. "She told me she was considering divorce before she left for Hawaii, to avoid the embarrassment of Katherine handing around those pictures."

"That's apparently when Keyes called her the first time to tell her there was trouble brewing. He told her he'd have it under control by the time she got back from her trip, but she's not stupid, and she knew she might have to take action. When Katherine showed up with those pictures, she must have decided it was the perfect excuse to ask for a divorce if need be." My brain was clicking and whirring at top speed now. "That's why she didn't respond to Katherine right away—she was waiting to see what would happen with the direct-marketing scheme. And when she got off the plane there was a call waiting telling her things were worse, and Brighton was pulling the plug. She knew it was time to start protecting her loved ones."

He didn't respond—I could feel the wheels turning in his mind through his grip on my arm, but still he didn't pause. I continued up, step by step, my mind flying to the corridors of nooks and crannies we were approaching, pathways that led to rooms where soldiers slept and alcoves where cannons used to stand, now draped in fog so thick I couldn't see more than ten steps in front of us. He'd have his pick of plum locales to bash my head in, stab me, and slice my throat—most likely the park service wouldn't even find my body until the next day.

I tried to shift my step slightly, hoping to fall backward or make a run for it when we got to the next floor. But when we reached the doorway, he continued past it. He also matched my shift, keeping slightly behind me; if I tried the falling-backward move, I'd fall into him and he'd shoot me right in the back.

"She didn't become a felon to provide for *me*." His tone took on a wheedling quality, like he was trying to convince himself. "She did it for herself, to protect her reputation and the Renard name. And possibly to help Todd, because his business is in trouble again. But not for me."

"She did it for those reasons, too. But also because she loved you. If she didn't, why go to the trouble to keep you in the dark and get the admission from Brighton?" My own tone stiffened—no way was I going to let him off the hook for what he'd done. "She's always loved you more than anything in the world. Do you really think that after standing up to her parents to marry you rather than whatever robber baron they'd picked out at her debutante ball, *and* dealing with integrating you into her social circle all these years, that she'd actually divorce you rather than suffer the temporary embarrassment of people knowing you'd cheated? *Please.* Everybody in that circle cheats every other day. It just shows how out of step Katherine is with those people that she actually thought the Santorini pictures would cause anything more than a momentary sting."

He was silent as we climbed the next few steps. Finally he responded, his voice now thick. "Well. None of it matters now. If what Sylvia wanted was to keep me out of jail, there's only one way I can ensure that. Get rid of *you*."

My heart pounded so hard I could hear the blood rushing in my ears—I'd pushed my hand too far. "That won't help, Philip. It's only a matter of time before the police find her webcam cloud account."

"That's why I just deleted the files when I took your phone." His voice turned self-congratulatory again. "And changed your password, so I can take care of a few other pieces of business before I finish here. Thank you so much for finding the account—it never occurred to me she might have a backup other than the card I pulled from the webcam and destroyed." His voice strengthened again. "Yes, the webcam is one of the few things I *did* know about."

Another burst of ice shot through my spine and out to my limbs. On the recording I'd seen of Sylvia swapping out the card before leaving the office for the last time, that hadn't been what I'd seen at all. Thinking back, I hadn't *seen* anyone on that video—I'd only heard the door to her office closing. She wasn't the one who'd swapped out the memory card and left without showing herself on camera—Philip was.

My mind scrambled for something to grasp on to. "The police aren't stupid, either, Philip. When I show up dead the same way Katherine and Sylvia did, they're going to know this wasn't a copycat. And it won't take long to figure out it was you. They can track the pings on your cell phone—"

"*My* phone." He snorted his derisive laugh again. "Capri. How do you think I knew you were here?"

My brain stopped short—why was that relevant? "I—I don't know. You must have followed me."

"So just followed you around, hoping my son wouldn't notice I never came back from my police interview?"

My stomach flipped. "How, then?"

"Location tracking."

"Location tracking? You can't track my location without my knowledge. Morgan's the only one who—" I cut myself off as the horrible truth slammed into place. "You stole Morgan's phone."

He didn't reply.

Despite grappling with that information, some section of my brain registered the entrance to the fort's next level as we passed. The next stop was the roof, and nothing good ever happened on roofs. Especially roofs like this one, with very few safety features in place.

My voice raised an octave without my permission. "But how did you get *into* her phone?"

"I've known her password for years. She loves her grandfather."

I barked a laugh which rang hysterical even to my own ears. "They'll check *her* GPS, too, Philip. They'll know the phone was out here, without her."

"But Morgan is about to arrive. In response to the suicidal email you just sent her, saying you couldn't stand the guilt of killing Sylvia and Katherine any longer, and how you can't let her go to jail for something you did. Or, rather, the one I sent from your phone while we were downstairs. She's speeding here as we speak."

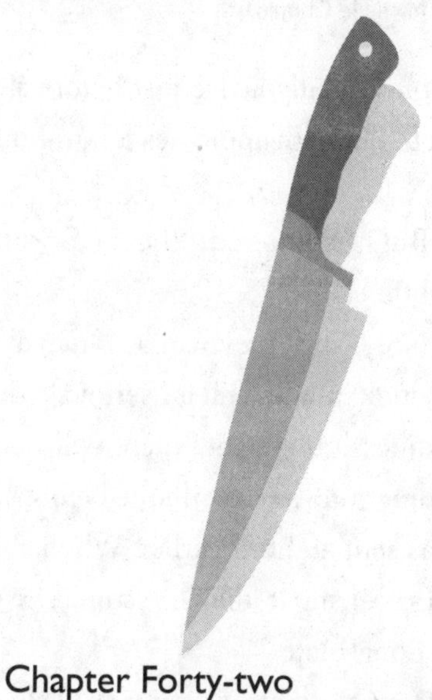

Chapter Forty-two

I found myself struggling to pull air into my lungs, and to keep my legs moving forward. Morgan was on the way, in response to a suicidal email she believed was from me? I couldn't let her be the one to find me dead—and I had to warn her about Philip. But he'd shoot me the instant I tried to break away—maybe I could stall long enough for her to arrive? But no, Philip wouldn't risk that, and it would take forever for her to search the fort in the fog anyway. My only hope was to get him to see one of the hundred flaws in his plan that were springing through my mind like starving fleas.

"She's not going to get the email if she doesn't have her phone—" I cut myself off because she always had her laptop when she was working, and would get it that way. "But"—my hope surged again—"she must have realized by now she doesn't have her phone. As soon as she got an email like that, she would've tried to call me. She'll tell the police she didn't have her phone with her."

"Of course she will. But by now she's called both her father and me from someone else's phone or a landline. And, alerted by her call,

I'll conveniently arrive just before she does, and will give the phone back to her with apologies for grabbing it accidentally after our interview."

"But," I sputtered, "the times won't line up. The police will notice the difference."

"No, Capri, they won't." His voice was level, controlled. "If they even look into it, which I seriously doubt they'll do in a clear-cut case of confession suicide, there will be no time discrepancy. I changed the time zone in your phone before sending the email, so it'll look like it was sent an hour earlier. When she tells them she left immediately after receiving it, they'll assume she got the times muddled given her emotional state."

He was right—they most likely wouldn't bother to pull the records. But we were nearing the roof now and time was running out, so I had to try everything I could. "But Petito's not stupid, and if there are any strange questions, they'll check your records, too, and *your* phone will show you were out here before Morgan."

He chuckled—he was enjoying this now, again reveling in his cleverness. "You think I was stupid enough to bring my own phone out here? It's safe at home on my bureau, where I forgot it in my rush to get here and help Morgan."

My heart sank. My supposed suicide note would be all the confession the police needed, since Petito had suspected me from day one—it would tie up everything nicely, and the press would have a field day with the granddaughter of Overkill Bill turning out to be a psychopathic killer.

"No," I said. "Morgan won't let that happen. She knows I'd never do any of this."

"Does she?" He leaned close to my ear. "You should have heard what she told the police today. She's already convinced herself *she* could be a killer because of who her great-grandfather was—if she believes that about herself, why wouldn't she believe the same of you?

Would it be so impossible for her to believe 'mama bear' killed the woman who just cut off her cub's tuition?"

Oh God—he was right.

I couldn't let that be my legacy. I couldn't let my daughter live with the trauma of finding me and living with the belief I was responsible for Sylvia's death. I had to find some way to stop this.

The final opening to the staircase suddenly loomed up in front of us, and he prodded me through it. Then he stopped and looked around, orienting himself as much as he could in the fog.

"This way." He firmly tugged my arm to the left.

Adrenaline xylophoned up my spine—I knew where he was taking me. My mind flew back to the small, treacherous catwalk edging the waters of the strait. No wonder he was taking me to the roof—if he wanted a way to make my death look like a suicide, throwing me over would be the perfect way to do it. Whether I hit the water or the pavement, there was no way I'd survive. And there was a raised platform with an octagonal cannon mount that edged right up to the roof, with only a short wall next to it—the perfect place to push me over.

I wracked my brain trying to pull up a complete visual of the video and pictures I'd taken just an hour before. My only chance now was to figure out some architectural element I could use to my advantage.

"I have friends, Philip," I gasped as I struggled to think. "Friends who know me and know I'd never kill myself. They'll dig, and eventually they'll find something that will convict you."

There was a shrug in his voice now. "Probably. That's why I won't be sticking around. I've been tucking away a little money here and there for years in a Swiss account. It's not much, but I'm not young and it will stretch for the years I have left. There are plenty of places to hide cheaply if you're forced to it. Todd has shown me so many corners of the world."

I begged my brain to kick in as I tried to resurrect my mental images of the area. There were a couple of steps before the platform—was it two, or three?—then a large, even, rectangular plateau. And at the far end of that, an octagonal mount raised up about a foot off the ground, just before the wall that ringed the roof.

My silence must have clued him in. "Before you get any ideas about putting up a fight, I'm just as happy to shoot you rather than throw you over. I'm wearing gloves, so all I'll have to do is put the gun into your hand after the fact." He lifted the gun to the side of my head to punctuate his point.

I squeezed my eyes shut against the visual of the bullet shearing through my brain and kept my focus on the octagonal. With me in front of him, there was no way I was going to get away with a fake stumble either on the steps or when we reached the octagonal cannon mount. But, if I was remembering correctly, the octagon didn't actually meet up flush with the wall—there was a gap in front of it that I'd almost slipped into earlier.

"By the time anyone gets up here to see what happened," he continued as he guided me up the stairs, "I'll have slipped away into the fog."

"There are security cameras, Philip—"

His laugh cut me off. "Now you really are getting desperate. How much do you think they pick up in this fog? And even if they do, I've been careful to keep my face covered." He shoved my arm as the octagon appeared out of the fog. "Up."

I stepped forward, a little faster than I had been, hoping he was looking up toward the wall and not down toward the ground. That gap was the only chance I had left.

"When we get to the wall, you're going to pull yourself up onto it."

My eyes strained against the fog to find the edge of the octagon. Suddenly, it was in front of me.

As I took the step down into the gap, I bent my knees completely and ducked my head, collapsing down between the octagon and the wall.

As soon as he felt me pull, he fired the gun—but the bullet whizzed over my now-ducked head. He fell with me but landed on the higher edge of the octagon, and his hold on me broke. I swung my now-free arm at him—the gun flew out of his hand and skidded across the pavement.

He scrambled to get back up. As he got his feet under him, I grabbed his ankle. He tried to shake me off, but I held tight and yanked as hard as I could. He resisted, so I grabbed with my other hand, too, then yanked and twisted with every desperate ounce of strength I had.

It was enough. His other leg swept out from under him, and he landed on the cement with a sickening crunch.

I shifted past him, trying to spot the gun.

"You fucking bitch! You broke my arm!"

I don't know if it was the name he called me or one adrenaline rush too many, but for whatever the reason, I lost it. I rounded on him, gun forgotten. "*I'm* the bitch? You bring me up here to kill me and *I'm the bitch*?"

His snarling face appeared out of the fog, and his good hand shot toward my neck. I just managed to dodge it, and the years-ago self-defense class my mother'd insisted I take kicked in without warning. "No!" I screamed at the top of my voice as I kneed him in the groin with all my might. When he hunched over, I punched him square in the face—then punched him again. And again, until a voice interrupted me.

"Freeze! Hands in the air!"

I looked up to see two vague police shapes standing in the fog, weapons pointed directly at us.

Philip cried out. "Officers, help! She's trying to kill me!"

My jaw dropped. "*He* tried to kill *me*! He just shot at me! I'm trying to get away! The gun is over there somewhere." I pointed with my chin.

"*She* just tried to shoot *me*!"

"I said hands in the air!" one of the cops said.

I followed his instructions—but as I raised my hands, I punched Philip in the face one last time.

Not surprisingly, one of the cops tased me. It hurt like hell.

But it was totally, completely worth it.

Chapter Forty-three

When I woke the next morning, I was greeted pointedly by an enormous bruise on my left hip, one on each of my knees, and what I could only generously call a serious crick in my back.

The officers had taken both Philip and me into custody. After they contacted Petito, however, Philip's claims of victimhood quickly fell apart and they released me. By the time Morgan drove me out to retrieve my car from Fort Point and I made it back home, it was nearly midnight. Morgan tried to spend the night at home with me, but I insisted she go be with her father. On top of everything else, he now had to come to terms with the fact that his father had killed his mother.

I hobbled gingerly into the kitchen to make the two or three pots of coffee I'd need to wash down all the Advil I'd be taking that day. As I stood trying to decide if it was worth the pain of standing long enough to make myself breakfast, my doorbell rang.

Petito stood on my porch with a pink bakery box, two large Java Jive coffees, and a look of urgent concern on his face. "I hope it's not too early, but I wanted to check in on you after yesterday."

A tingly warmth washed over me, taking me by surprise. Sure, when someone switched from trying to put you and your daughter in prison to bringing you baked goods, a shift in dynamic was to be expected, but this was downright dramatic. As I tried to cover my reaction, heat bloomed on my cheeks—I, a grown woman with a grown daughter, was actually blushing.

Since my long-standing rule is there's no version of awkward that can't be covered with a joke, I pointed to the pink box as I stepped back to let him in. "Not fair. You can't show up at my door with that and expect me not to make a crack about police and donuts."

A relieved half smile crossed his lips. "Be nice, or no donuts for you."

I laughed and led him into the kitchen. I pulled out plates and paper towels and slid gingerly into the chair opposite the one he'd selected.

He noticed my cautious movement, and the concerned expression returned. "How are you feeling?"

"Worse than an intense trip to the gym, not as bad as childbirth. Ultimately nothing a few Advil won't fix."

He glanced at the laptop on the table. "You're not working today, I hope?"

"Ryan, one of my employees, insisted on taking my tours today. I didn't have the energy to argue with him."

"Good choice." He flipped open the pink box and pushed it slightly toward me.

I glanced down, barked a laugh, and looked back up at him. "It really *is* a box of donuts."

He pointed his single-dimple grin at me. "Some clichés are clichés for a reason. Donuts are highly portable and go well with coffee. Sugar and caffeine form the backbone of all good police work." He lifted his cup in a cheers motion.

"A man after my own heart," I said without thinking—then blushed furiously at the implication. *Smooth, Capri*, I berated myself. *Smooth like a dirt road after a hurricane.*

I thought I saw his dimple deepen ever so slightly. "I wasn't sure what you liked, so I got an assortment, and a plain latte."

"I'm nondenominational when it comes to my coffee and my donuts. But I will admit to favoring mochas and any pastry filled with custard." I grabbed the latte and took a big gulp.

"I'll remember that the next time someone attempts to murder you," he deadpanned, then slipped out a jelly donut.

Wait—did Petito have a sense of humor? But I hid my response, because as charming as his patter and smile were, I'd been burned by that dynamic duo before. "Well. While I always appreciate a random bestowal of baked goods and caffeine, I'm guessing you're here to chastise me and to tell me I'm lucky to be alive."

"Eyes on your own paper." He lifted his coffee again. "You're also lucky we didn't arrest you for obstruction."

I sat up ramrod straight despite the pain. "I didn't obstruct anything. I told you immediately whenever I discovered something. But if you think I was just going to sit back and let you send me or my daughter to jail, you've got another think coming. And if I hadn't kept digging—"

"Stop right there." He raised his hand. "We're not amateurs. We investigate carefully, *and* in a way that preserves evidence and our ability to prosecute effectively."

I glared at him. "So let me guess. You were mere moments away from discovering Sylvia's Prohibition room."

He tilted his head. "We were not. But we were well on our way to tracking down all of the leads you discovered inside."

"And without those photos from the Prohibition room, how long would it have taken you to put together the connection with Katherine? And how long after *that* would it have taken you to figure out Sylvia used Katherine's blackmail as a smoke screen to ask for a divorce from

Philip, because she was trying to protect him from her direct-marketing fraud scheme? And that Philip killed her as a result, because he didn't realize they were broke?" I snapped.

He shifted slightly in his chair. "As I say. We have to proceed in a way that preserves evidence, doesn't break the law, and allows us to prosecute effectively. That doesn't always happen quickly, but it's better than a killer going free on a technicality."

As much as I wanted to, I couldn't argue with that. I dropped my gaze to the box and slid out a glazed old-fashioned.

"But that's only one of the reasons I'm here. I also want to keep you apprised. We were able to recover the video files Mr. Clement tried to erase from Sylvia's cloud account."

I was impressed. "So fast?"

"Not at all hard to do when the account automatically holds deleted files for thirty days." He bit into his donut.

I barked another laugh. "You're kidding me. That's perfect."

"We presented him and his attorney with a few inconvenient facts, including the video and the lack of gunshot residue on your hands." He licked a dollop of raspberry jelly that had dropped onto his wrist. "He turned a shade of puce I've never seen before."

A mix of emotions panged at me. "Those must be the moments you live for."

He eyed me suspiciously. "Catching a man who murdered two women and tried to frame his own family? One hundred percent."

"Sorry, I didn't mean anything by it. It's just that I've always liked Philip." I sighed, and set my donut back onto my plate. "I'm usually a decent judge of character. I think up until the minute he pulled the trigger, some part of me still believed there was an explanation for it all."

His face softened again. "That's the difficulty with psychopaths. High up on their list of skills is the ability to make you believe they are who you want them to be."

I nodded. "Still."

He continued. "And I used what you told us in the interrogation. Like you said, he tried to claim he knew about the dire financial straits they were in, and thus had no motive. So I questioned him about when he found out, and it was pretty clear he hadn't thought through his answers. I pressed, and he started contradicting himself, then broke down and confessed it all. He's been arrested now, and you don't have to worry about your or your daughter's safety."

"Thank you." I took another gulp of coffee as I processed my battling emotions. "I guess it doesn't really matter now, but did you ever find out who owns Anchor and Shields? Is it Nancy's brother Shawn Malger?"

"I wasn't able to find a connection. But I turned the information over to the team that investigates those crimes. Hopefully they'll be able to track it down."

My mind slipped back to what Margie Francis had told me, about how difficult that type of fraud was to prosecute unless huge sums of money had been stolen. I wasn't optimistic about the outcome.

Petito tapped the side of his coffee with his index finger. "The next part is sensitive, but it's something I think you should know."

My eyes widened—what more could there possibly be to this nightmare? "Okay."

"You know your ex-husband was in San Jose the day your mother-in-law was murdered."

"Yes."

"We looked into why that is, tracked his phone calls and movements that day. He's had a string of business failures recently, and he's gotten himself involved with some unfortunate people. He called Sylvia the day she died asking for a loan to repay them."

I frowned. "I watched all the footage from her nanny cam, and I didn't see a call with him."

Petito shook his head. "He called her when she was driving back from the airport. She refused to give him any money. After he got your call, he waited in San Jose until he would have legitimately been in the area if he'd driven back from Los Angeles. He didn't want his plate to show up anywhere, and was rightfully afraid we'd consider him a suspect if we knew about the call."

I shook my head. "Wow. Like mother, like son, apparently." I looked up at him. "But why are you telling *me*?"

He cleared his throat. "After Sylvia refused to give him any money, he called you. He hung up right away so it didn't register on your end, but still. His inheritance may be enough to get him out of trouble, but it's possible he'll be right back in it again. You should protect yourself and your daughter."

"Got it. Thanks." I said a silent prayer of gratitude that Todd had signed the house over to me.

Petito's index finger started tapping again. "The good news is, all of this means the copycat aspect of Katherine's and Sylvia's murders is coincidental to the Overkill Bill murders, just inspired by his knowledge of your grandfather's methodology. So the interest in that case will likely die down again." He watched my face carefully.

Now we were getting down to it. "Not fully coincidental. Philip chose it because it was a local killer who'd targeted women in parks. He knew Katherine was going to be at the Legion of Honor, so he thought invoking it would keep you from looking too closely into her personal life. But regardless, I didn't start in on the Overkill Bill case because of the current murders. I've always wanted to find out the truth. And once I start something, I don't leave it unfinished."

He nodded, face blank. "So I see."

I waited, but he didn't say anything more. "Is that a problem?"

A laugh exploded out of him, startling me. "You think I'm trying to talk you *out* of it?"

I blinked at him. "Aren't you?"

His eyes glimmered. "Just the opposite."

"Wait." I waved a hand at him. "Didn't you just get finished telling me I should stay out of homicide investigations?"

"The Overkill Bill case isn't an active investigation. It's not even an open case, since the purported killer was identified, sentenced, and is now dead. As it stands, we have more active homicides to work than hours in the day to work them, and there's no justification I can produce for spending even a minute of my time on Overkill Bill."

Light began to dawn, and little jabs of excitement tickled my stomach. "You think William Sanzio was innocent. You want me to work it since you can't."

"I never said any of that." He held my gaze, his dimple reappearing. "But nobody can say you haven't raised some interesting questions and alternatives. If you do continue, I'd be interested to hear what you dig up."

My heart raced—if he was making a point of telling me this, I must be on to something. "To the point where you'd help me?"

"To the same extent that I'd help any civilian who's researching a case now open to the public." He watched my reaction.

I nodded—he was saying he couldn't do anything officially, but he'd do what he could, where he could.

"I have an appointment I have to get to." He glanced at his watch and stood, and his voice softened. "I'm glad you weren't seriously injured. I'll check in on you again as soon as I can."

For a moment, there was an intensity in his eyes that made something in my chest do a little flip-flop—but as soon as I thought I saw it, it was gone.

"Thank you." I stood and saw him out. He said an abrupt goodbye, then strode quickly to his car and drove off.

As soon as I closed the door, a hundred somethings burst through my chest and my mind, erasing the pain in my legs and back, and I flew into the house to jump back into the case.

Chapter Forty-four

I slammed the rest of the coffee that Petito had brought and refilled the cardboard cup from my pot. Then I grabbed my computer and brought it into my dining room so I could dive back into the *Chronicle*'s digital news archives while my grandmother's boxes were close at hand. I was searching for a needle in a haystack among screen after screen of newspaper articles, I knew that—but what other choice did I have?

I picked up where I left off, skimming headlines and pictures day by day, stopping only to pour coffee and donuts down my gob. Early news about Vietnam sprinkled the headlines and, thanks to my abundance of hindsight on the topic, filled me with a low-level ominous dread. I tried to divert myself from that by relishing the happy flashes of the past; although I wasn't even yet a twinkle in my father's eye in 1965, plenty in the pages took me back to my childhood. Like the ads for Woolworth's and Capwell's, stores now long defunct, where I'd gone on fondly remembered shopping trips. Especially at Christmastime, when Woolworth's had inexpensive—but not cheap—Christmas decorations that allowed my mother to spread her budget much further than she could have otherwise, and I'd walk up and down the aisles with her carefully weighing every possibility on offer. Then I spent far too long poring over the vintage ads, like the horrendously tortured torpedo bras captioned *Lovely bras for a shapelier you!* I gasped with delight when I came across a half-page Chevy ad that featured not only a 1965 Corvair Monza, but a used 1962 version that looked exactly like my uncle's. I printed it out to give to my father; whether or not he ever spoke to me again, he'd enjoy having it.

I sorted through pages and pages of San Francisco summer activities, and as I neared the date of each murder, I slowed my skimming several days before and doubled up on my attention. I found nothing even vaguely relevant to my father's alibi or to any of my uncles, and as I neared the third and final murder, I began to worry.

Sally Reyes was killed on Friday, August 20. I scoured each line of that day's paper twice, but found nothing.

Out of sheer desperation because I had no other avenues left to follow up, I continued to read past the night of the murder. But by the time I got to the about-town section of the Sunday paper that reported happenings from the Friday and Saturday nights before, my eyes stung with disappointment.

So much so, I almost missed it.

A piece about the grand opening of Damiano's, an exciting new restaurant in North Beach. The very restaurant my grandfather had supposedly taken his "date" to at the time Sally Reyes was killed.

I zoomed in on the article and skimmed the summary. I read about the menu, and the reviewer's opinions of the food. I read about the notable people who'd showed up throughout the evening. I read about the huge, wedding-style cake the restaurant made to mark the occasion, and how excited the guests at the late seating were to be given complimentary slices and flutes of champagne. I studied the accompanying picture of said cake, and of said guests looking on excitedly as it was sliced.

There, in the back-left corner of the picture, sat a dark-haired, light-eyed man with a diamond-shaped birthmark on the left side of his forehead and a signet ring with the initials WS on the hand holding up his flute of champagne.

• • •

As I stared at the picture, the world spun around me, so much I clenched the edge of the table to steady myself. I leaned in, peering closely to be sure of what I was seeing. There was zero doubt—the man in the picture was my grandfather. I grabbed the police files and found a picture of the woman who'd provided his alibi for that evening—sure enough, she was the woman sitting with him at the table. The large clock on the wall showed nine fifteen, and he was sitting at the table with a half-eaten plate of pasta in front of him. Even if he left immediately after the picture was taken, there was no possible way he could have made it all the way over to the far end of Golden Gate Park in time to kill Sally Reyes by nine twenty.

William Sanzio was innocent.

Tears overflowed my eyes, and I suddenly felt like I was floating, like a psychological lead blanket had been lifted off me. I sprung up and strode alongside my kitchen table, arms wrapped around my abdomen, unable to stay still. I hadn't realized how very heavy the weight I'd been carrying was until it was stripped away.

Just as I thought the tears were subsiding, they shook me again—but this time they were sobs of despair, for everything that had been wasted. My grandfather's life. My grandmother's heartbreak. My father's happy, positive nature. My relationship, and my brother's and daughter's relationships, with my father.

I sank down into the nearest chair and dropped my head into my hands, no longer even trying to maintain control. The evidence to exculpate him had been there the whole time, in black and white in the Sunday paper. But my grandfather only read the front section of the paper, and by the time he'd been arrested and thrown in jail, that Sunday's paper would have long been thrown out, in a time without instant internet recall. And why would he, or anybody for that matter, think to check the about-town sections of local papers on the off chance they'd find something to support his alibi?

But something about the picture tugged at me—I was still missing something important. I ducked back into the other room and went over it millimeter by millimeter like I'd done with the "Find the Differences" puzzles I'd adored as a little girl, looking at each and every detail hoping to feel a telltale tingle. Was it something about the clock, or the cake? Or the woman next to him?

No. But when my eyes landed on the signet ring shining up from my grandfather's finger, a bell rang in a far-off corner of my mind.

But why? Vera had claimed to remember seeing it when she spotted it in the courtroom, and that was part of what convinced the jury to convict. I hadn't believed her, partly because male signet rings were popular then, particularly among Italian men. They were a declaration of family, and to a degree, of adult manhood. *If* she hadn't been flat-out making it up, she'd seen *a* ring but not *his* ring, despite her claim to have noticed the WS engraved on it.

Then I remembered. And I knew Vera hadn't been lying.

I dove into my grandmother's boxes and flipped through the family photos until I found the confirmation I was looking for. As I stared down at the photo, everything came together in a rush of crystal clarity.

I knew beyond a shadow of a doubt who had committed the Overkill Bill murders.

And I might even be able to prove it.

Chapter Forty-five

My mother's expression was wary and uncomfortable when she opened the front door.

"Capri. Is everything okay?"

"No." I pushed past her. "But it's going to be. Where's Dad?"

Her eyes flitted over my face as I watched her make some sort of decision. She sighed, but nodded. "In the backyard."

"Thank you." I kissed her cheek as I strode past her, out onto the patio.

My father looked up from where he stood watering his rhododendrons. His face instantly hardened. He set down the watering can and moved to leave.

I held his eye, and spoke firmly but gently, inserting myself in his path. "I know the truth, Dad."

Several emotions flashed across his face as he processed that. Fear, anger, skepticism, desperation—then defiance. He drew himself up to his full height, and squared his body toward me. "You don't know anything, little girl."

I pulled the photocopy I'd brought of the Damiano's picture and thrust it out to him without a word.

For a long moment, he refused to take it. Then, when he realized I wasn't going to back down, he snatched it from my hand and examined it.

"Where did you find this?"

"*Chronicle* archives. Printed the Sunday after Sally Reyes's murder. He was exactly where he said he was, but probably never considered he might have made it into one of the pictures, or that the pictures would show up in the paper. The point is, he couldn't have killed Sally Reyes, and if he didn't kill Sally, he didn't kill the other two."

My father dropped into one of the patio chairs and stared across to his flowers. "You just couldn't leave it alone. I begged, threatened, everything I could think of, and you just wouldn't leave it alone."

"And now I finally know why."

"But you don't understand."

"Then explain it to me."

He continued to stare at his flowers in silence.

"Okay, then, I'll tell you what I believe. Grandma knew about Grandpa's infidelity, and she didn't keep it to herself. She wrote in her diary that she told the whole family about it all."

He started to speak when I mentioned the diary, glanced toward the house where my mother was inside, then clamped his jaw shut. She'd have hell to pay later.

"The witness saw Sally Reyes with someone who looked enough like Grandpa to be mistaken for him, who had the same hair, eyes, and a similar build, but who didn't have the birthmark on his head. There's no way Grandma could have ever been mistaken for him, even if she put on a disguise. And not only were you too young and slight at twelve to be mistaken for him, you also weren't old enough to drive.

Grandma also mentioned in her diary that you and Vincent were home with her and your aunts on the evening of the murders. But Grandma and Grandpa both had brothers who fit the same descriptions, so I narrowed down which of them might have done it."

Still nothing.

I pulled out the picture from Grandma's album, and held it out to him.

"But it wasn't one of *your* uncles, was it? It was your brother, *my* uncle Vincent. Grandma mentioned the kids were in the other room playing games and watching TV on her bridge nights. But Uncle Vincent was sixteen, and every teenager knows how to sneak out without being seen. He'd saved up for a car, and fixed it so it ran well. And he was the spitting image of William Sanzio, in a still-growing, younger version."

My father glanced at the picture of Uncle Vincent standing next to William Sanzio, then glanced away.

"I think Uncle Vincent saw how hurt Nonni was by Grandpa's infidelity. I think he hated Grandpa for it, but he didn't know how to process those feelings—feelings like that were disloyal because they went against the family. But the prostitutes—*them* he could hate, and if *they* were evil home-wreckers, well, he could solve the problem by getting rid of them."

My father finally met my eyes. "You don't know what you're talking about. Your uncle Vincent would never do anything like that. If it wasn't your grandfather, then it must have been one of Grandma's brothers."

His sudden willingness to claim something other than my grandfather's guilt told me he knew I was right. "Except the witness reported seeing a signet ring on the killer's left hand, an onyx one with a gold WS on it." I pointed to the ring on Grandpa's hand, and the matching ring on Uncle Vincent's, which he was showing off in the picture taken on his sixteenth birthday. "I'm guessing he gave a matching ring to Uncle Vincent for his birthday, a marker of his approach into manhood. And the engraving VS would have been easily mistaken for WS, especially by a witness whose memory was triggered only months later during the trial."

A tear rolled down my father's cheek, and he angrily swiped it away.

I continued. "I think you all knew Uncle Vincent was the one who killed the women, including Grandpa. I think Grandpa was determined to protect Vincent—maybe he even thought it really was his own fault since his infidelity was what triggered Vincent. But what I don't understand is why, if Grandpa decided to take the fall for the murders, he didn't just plead guilty."

"My mother hated him for refusing to plead guilty." He shook his head and wiped away another tear. "Your grandfather was old enough when his parents brought him to this country to remember what life was like in Italy, and to see how different America was. He watched his family's hard work be rewarded with a decent life, without interference from the Mafia or corrupt police who overran their village back home. He was in awe of the American justice system and believed it was impossible for an innocent man to be found guilty here. Since he was innocent, he was certain the jury would acquit him, and he'd be able to come home to take care of his family."

"But surely if the jury had found him innocent, there was a risk the police would keep investigating and would have figured out Uncle Vincent was guilty."

"That's why my mother hated him. But he told us very clearly that the moment the police came after Vincent, he'd confess to the crimes and that would be that. So much the better if he'd already been found innocent, because with double jeopardy, they wouldn't be able to retry him, and they'd never be able to convict Vinnie if someone else was on record confessing to the crimes." He rubbed his face then looked back up, his eyes pleading with me. "Vinnie had his whole life ahead of him. He was young and he was a gifted auto mechanic. So my father took a calculated gamble that they could both walk away free."

"But he must have realized that Uncle Vincent needed help? That it wasn't normal for a young man to viciously kill three women?"

My father shook his head. "It was a different time, people didn't think like that. Psychologists, all that—it wasn't done. But mostly, my father, my mother, and I, too, believed Vincent never would have committed the murders if it hadn't been for my father's infidelity. If he wasn't unfaithful again, Vincent would never be tempted again."

"You couldn't know that. And what about the women whose killer walked away scot-free?" I asked.

My father's eyes flashed, and pink spots bloomed on his cheeks. "Taking away my brother's life wasn't going to bring back theirs."

I knew from long experience that I wouldn't be able to get him to see that wasn't really the point. "So why continue with the charade after Uncle Vincent was killed in Vietnam?"

My father's harsh, ironic burst of laughter made me jump. "You talk about justice and you talk about healing. Can't you see that justice was done? My brother lost his life, my father rotted in prison, and my mother died of a broken heart." He lifted his chin. "She didn't die of pneumonia, you know. She killed herself. Took an overdose of sleeping pills."

My stomach dropped, and I fought back a wave of nausea.

"I don't know how much more justice you want, Capri. My brother, my father, my mother—they all paid a heavy price for those murders."

I shook my head. "And so did *you*. But that doesn't answer the question. Why not tell the truth at that point?"

He threw up his hands like I was being thickheaded. "To what purpose? Nobody would have believed us, and even if they did, it wouldn't have gotten him out of prison. You can't appeal unless you have *evidence* that would have changed the outcome of the trial. Without hard proof, his claim alone would have been useless. All pointing the finger at Vincent would have done was make my father look like a desperate man willing to destroy his veteran son's reputation to escape the consequences of what he'd done."

I tried to keep my voice steady. "You could've at least told Leo and me. We're your children. His grandchildren."

"I made a promise to my mother, on her deathbed. The best thing for you and your brother, and everyone else in the family, was to move on. Why would I put anyone through an ounce more pain for his benefit? He'd subjected the family to insurmountable heartache through his actions and his failures to act. He was the one who deserved to bear the brunt."

With that, I finally understood. "You believe Grandpa Sanzio really did kill those women, even if he wasn't the one to physically harm them."

His neck turned red and he leaned forward toward me. "Vincent never would have hurt anyone if my father had been faithful to my mother. And if you put any of this in your *book*"—he spat the word—"you'll only be destroying two people instead of one."

"What if someone murdered *me*? Or Ma?"

His stared at me, confused. "What do you mean?"

"If Ma or I were murdered, would you be okay with the perpetrator not being held accountable? Would it be enough that *someone* served the time in jail, even if it wasn't the actual killer?" I asked.

"That's not what I'm saying."

I struggled to keep my voice level. "That's exactly what you're saying. That you have the right to decide who gets punished for those women's deaths. That you have the right to let their killer walk free just because it was somebody you loved. And to this day you believe you have the right to decide the victim's truth doesn't matter, that they and their families don't have the right to know what happened to them."

The flush crept up to his ears. "They're dead, Capri. They're dead and their families are all dead, and Vincent's dead, too. It doesn't matter to any of them anymore."

"I disagree. Grandpa was unfaithful to Nonni and he deserved to be held responsible for that. If she wanted to end their marriage, she had the right. But he didn't kill those women, Uncle Vincent did, and *Vincent* deserved to be held responsible for *that*." I replaced the picture into my bag. "I also disagree that the truth doesn't matter here. I know you turned your back on the Church long ago and call yourself an agnostic. Not an atheist like Mom, but an agnostic—open to the possibility that there may be a God and there may not. If there is a God and an afterlife, those women are looking down, watching us, screaming for justice every moment of every day. Either way, you always taught me it's my responsibility to stand up for what's right."

"It's not your decision to make, Capri. It doesn't have anything to do with you."

Tears I hadn't anticipated pricked the back of my eyes. "It breaks my heart that you believe that. As a result of your decision to determine what the rest of us got to believe and feel about it all, we haven't had a decent relationship since I was eight. Leo lives in a different state because he could never connect with you. Your choices have kept Morgan at arm's length too, because while she loves you, on a gut level she knows not to trust you. She doesn't talk to you about anything deeper than the weather, she doesn't spend time with you unless I'm there, and I can't remember the last time she gave you anything other than a stilted hug. You don't know her, and that's a tragedy, because she's an amazing young woman. So I have to ask—was nursing your anger against your father's infidelities worth losing your daughter, your son, and your grandchildren?"

I'm not too proud to admit I got satisfaction from the range of emotions and self-doubt that paraded over his face while he chose a response.

He settled on bullying. "You can't put this in your book without proof. You'll sound crazy."

And with that, the last bit of my hope died. My chest went cold, and I fought back my tears. How stupid was I that I'd actually believed I might get through to him?

I shook my head. "I have the picture proving Grandpa Sanzio didn't kill Sally Reyes, and I have the picture of the matching signet rings."

"That ring doesn't prove anything," he said. "I'll tell anyone who asks that Vincent lost his ring well before the murders took place. He was buried with it, so you'll never get your hands on it."

I sighed, pulled out my phone, and put through a call. I watched my father's confused glare as I did.

"Capri," Petito answered without preamble, sounding alarmed. "Is everything okay?"

"I'm sorry to bother you again," I said. "But I have reason to believe my uncle Vincent is the person responsible for the Overkill Bill murders. His 1962 Chevy Corvair Monza is in my father's garage, and if he was the killer, he would have used it to get himself and the women to and from the crime scenes, likely tracking blood into it in the process. My understanding is you can still detect blood even decades later, correct?"

Petito didn't even pause. "Correct. I'm on my way."

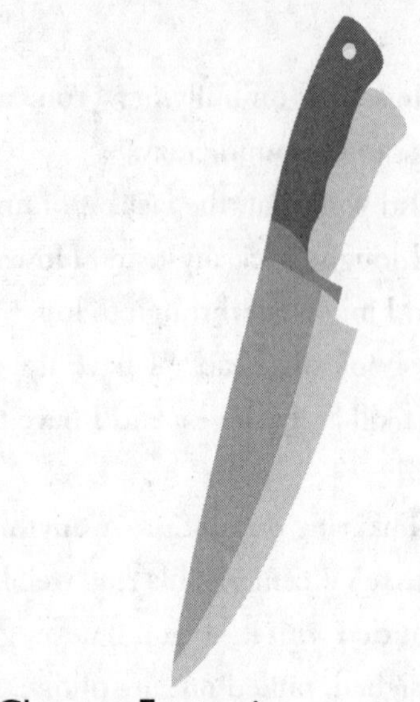

Chapter Forty-six

I don't know if my father will ever speak to me again. Most likely he won't. I hope I'm wrong.

The police carted off my uncle's Chevy that same afternoon, but Petito warned me it could take months for any test results to come back. A closed case from the sixties just wasn't a very big priority, so the processing would go to the back of the line behind active cases. And that was fine with me. I didn't want to delay any current investigations. I was just thankful they were willing to do it at all.

While I waited, I organized everything I'd learned into two remaining episodes for the podcast, then started writing the book. Heather razzed me, claiming I could easily turn the five episodes into a ten-episode run if I spun in the story of my family's history and profiled each of my great-uncle suspects. I agreed that some background context was necessary, but I couldn't bear the thought of people suspecting anyone I knew for a fact was innocent by the end of a given episode, so that limited how much I was willing to stretch things out. It was one thing to be truthful about who I'd investigated, but another to have Reddit groups actively researching people I knew hadn't done anything wrong.

I also had to have a lot of conversations with my family, and each and every one terrified me. My mother was somber but supportive, and said I'd done the right thing—but I noticed she stopped short of saying my father would get over it. Leo's reaction was quiet and careful, checking the facts and asking about repercussions with the precision I'd come to expect from my accountant brother. No, I told him, Dad wouldn't face charges for withholding information; they only had my word for it that he knew my uncle Vincent was responsible, and it would have been impossible to get a conviction. No, ultimately, it wouldn't make much difference with respect to our family's reputation, since we were still related to a serial killer. But yes, Grandpa's name would be officially cleared.

Morgan's reaction was eerily parallel to mine. She cried, first with relief for her grandfather's legacy, then with infinite sadness for everything our family had lost. We spent an evening going through all my grandmother's scrapbooks and diaries together, processing who William Sanzio and our family truly was from the perspective of the full—if still ugly—truth.

Everything kept me so busy, I was almost able to ignore the visions of Petito's crystal-blue eyes when they popped into my head. When I couldn't, I chastised myself soundly for being pathetic. I was far too old to waste time on a ridiculous schoolgirl crush; even when I was a schoolgirl I'd never fallen for guys I knew I could never have. Petito had seen me and my family at our worst, all while I subverted his authority at every turn. And sure, it turned out I wasn't the granddaughter of a serial killer, but I was the niece of one and the ex-daughter-in-law of another. Either way, not the sort of person a homicide detective would want to associate with.

In November, nearly two months after they'd towed the Chevy out of my father's garage, Petito showed up at my door with another pink box of donuts (all custard-filled), two large coffees (one a mocha), and an update.

"After Philip confessed to everything, we found the weapons where he told us he'd dumped them on the other side of the Presidio," Petito told me over his cup of coffee. "That meant there was no way he could retract the confession, and his attorney advised him to take a plea. He'll be in jail for the rest of his life."

I shook my head over my own coffee. "I still can't believe it's real. I just can't conceive of killing your partner because you might not be able to golf at the club anymore."

"I've seen people murder for a lot less," Petito said. "People have been killed for a few dollars in their pocket."

I almost objected that people who do those things are in desperate circumstances, but my mind flashed back to Philip's voice at Fort Point. "Desperate" is relative—money was a synonym for security, and he thought his security was about to be ripped away. I myself had been frantic when I didn't know how I was going to pay for Morgan's tuition—sure, nowhere near desperate enough to commit a criminal act, but what if she'd needed that money for a lifesaving surgery? Would I have been willing to steal or even hurt someone if I had to? As much as I wanted to believe the answer would be no, if Morgan's survival had been in question, I couldn't be sure. Philip hadn't worked a day since he'd married Sylvia, and he was now in his late sixties. He had no career to fall back on, and the thought of starting over must have been terrifying. Would he have felt any less desperate than an addict who needed money for his next fix?

"But no," I blurted without context. "That still doesn't excuse *killing* someone. I had no career when my husband and I divorced. No way to support myself, and a daughter to care for. If I was able to reinvent myself and build a new life, Philip could have, too."

"You did indeed." Petito held my eye. "But not everyone is as strong as you are."

Heat rose up my cheeks, and I hurried to cover by rolling my eyes and flexing my biceps. "Strong like bull."

He smiled. "I also came to tell you that we matched the blood of two out of the three Overkill Bill murders to traces of blood we found in your uncle Vincent's Chevy. Because your grandfather maintained his innocence until he died, his defense attorney asked that the evidence not be destroyed in case of appeal. He must have really believed in your grandfather and had friends in homicide because even after your grandfather passed, the evidence wasn't destroyed."

"Maybe it just slipped through the cracks."

He glared at me. "The point is, whoever killed those women was in contact with that car. Given the picture you found in the *Chronicle* and the fact that your uncle fits the witness testimony better than your father, the DA will be releasing a press statement later today to disseminate the findings and make clear they now believe William Sanzio was not responsible for the Overkill Bill murders, and that Vincent Sanzio was."

When you're caught up in the middle of something horrible, your body and brain go into self-protection mode and throw up walls so you're able to function. I told myself it didn't matter if the findings were official, it was enough to know the truth. But once I heard the tests confirmed my theory, those walls crumbled and my emotions roared out from behind the dam. Satisfaction that the victims' truth would be known, and my grandfather's name would be restored. Pride that I managed to clear my grandfather's name. Sadness at the pain I knew it all would bring to my father. I dropped my head into my hands and wept.

Petito silently shifted into the chair next to me, and put a hand on my back. When I leaned toward him, he gently guided me into the crook of his shoulder, one arm around me, and waited as the wave of my emotion washed itself out.

When it did, he handed me a bakery napkin. I wiped my face and ungracefully blew my nose. "I'm sorry about that. It sort of hit me out of nowhere. I think I got mascara on your shirt."

He didn't even look down at it. "Not a problem. If none of this moved you, you wouldn't be human."

I waved him off. "Well. You didn't come here to play the role of therapist. Thank you so much for the donuts and coffee, and for bringing me all the news. I know how busy you are, and I appreciate it."

He cleared his throat. "I did have one other reason for stopping by, but now I'm thinking it can wait."

I shook my head, embarrassed that I'd left him with the impression I was emotionally fragile. "No, please don't do that. Tell me what you came to tell me. I'd rather have the ax drop now than later."

He shifted uncomfortably and looked at his watch. "It's nothing that can't wait."

I glared at him, my embarrassment morphing into annoyance. "I realize it may not look like it"—I gestured to his shoulder—"but I'm not a child, and I don't appreciate being treated like one. Out with it."

His head jutted back and he crossed his arms over his chest. "Well, then. I *was* going to ask you if you were free for dinner sometime."

My neck and cheeks felt like they'd been set on fire, and my tongue refused to work. "Oh."

"That wasn't exactly the response I was hoping for," he said. "But it *is* fun to see you at a loss for words for a change."

"Oh," I said again, my mind still trying to wrap itself around what was happening. "Is that allowed? I mean, can you go out with someone who—" I stopped, not sure how to say what I needed to say.

"Someone who what?" An amused grin slid over his face. "You're not a suspect anymore, Philip confessed. So you're just a person who lives in San Francisco, and yes, San Francisco homicide inspectors are allowed to date people who live in San Francisco. In fact, most of us do."

"Right, of course, stupid of me," I stumbled. "But—you investigated me. You know some really unfortunate things about me and my family."

"I also know that you're smart, brave, persistent, and a firm advocate for justice." He tilted his head to the side with a smile that sent jolts of electricity shooting up my spine.

I slammed the rest of the coffee in an attempt to kick my brain into gear. "But wouldn't it be—"

He cut me off, and stood. "Like I said, this wasn't the right time to bring it up, with everything you're dealing with. And I have an appointment across the city I need to get to. So why don't you think about it, and get back to me. I know you know how to find me."

He headed out of the room with me scrambling after.

"Thank you again for the news, and the food," I said when we reached the door. "And, yes." I cleared my throat. "I'll think about it."

He smiled the electric smile again, then left.

And for the rest of the day, I couldn't think about anything else.

Acknowledgments

My first and most important thank-you goes to anyone reading this book. Neither time nor money is easy to come by in this life and I'm honored that you chose to spend yours here. Thank you!

This book would never have seen the light of day had it not been for Lynnette Novak, my agent, and Madeline Houpt, my editor. They both believed in the book, in my voice, and in me. They both helped shape it at crucial points, and Lynnette took it out into the world and found it a home and family—without her, it would be languishing still in the back of my brain (or, at least, my hard drive). Madeline nurtured every aspect of it to make sure it blossomed into the best version it could be. She pulled improvements out of me like a magician pulls coins out of a child's ear—skillfully, painlessly, and while ensuring I had fun along the way.

The rest of the team at Minotaur was also absolutely crucial to making this book what it is. My copy editor, Janine Barlow, is amazing, and without her, I'd have made a complete fool of myself with a slew of the most embarrassing mistakes imaginable. "Rock star" doesn't begin to cover it.

I'm so lucky to have San Francisco as my muse! I've loved her since the day I first set foot in her as a preschooler, and decades later she never ceases to inspire and amaze me. There's always a quirky surprise around every corner and I learn something new every time I walk down one of her streets. She's absolutely unique, and she's a part of my soul.

I'd be nothing and nowhere without my writing tribe. The most egregious offenders are D. K. Dailey, Laurie Sheehan, Erika Anderson-Bolden, Christina Flores, Dianna Fernandez-Nichols, Daisy Bateman, and Katy Corbeil. There are many more, too plentiful to name, especially among my SinC NorCal and MWA NorCal siblings. Thank you for everything you do and say and are.

My husband deserves a special thanks. . . . When I said to him, "You know, I think I'd like to write a book," he very easily could have laughed until he choked or patted me on the head and asked if I'd like to be a fairy princess, too. Instead, he does everything he can to help me, including listening to me drone on endlessly about plot points and character issues and red herrings. I suspect most of the time he doesn't actually listen, just nods his head and says "sure" at regular intervals, but either way it does the job and allows me to work through everything. He also doesn't complain when every November gets sucked into the void of NaNoWriMo and he's stuck eating leftovers and takeout and checking our marriage certificate for proof he has a wife. He's the best, hands down.

I had four fur babies who were my partners in crime writing: three cats who kept my lap warm and comfy so I had no desire to get up and stop writing, and a dog who forced me to get up anyway, accidentally providing long walks that allowed me to ponder many a plot hole. Lyssa has done that for all my books, but her role with this book went further, and farther—I went on tons of walking tours of

San Francisco to work out details, all with my sweet girl strolling next to me. Because of that, I see her smiling face as I imagine the place descriptions included in this book: she trotted around the Presidio with me as I searched for the ideal place for Sylvia's corpse, sniffed houses during the Pacific Heights architecture tour as I learned about the upper echelons of San Francisco society, and braved the fog at Fort Point as I researched my finale. The day she was diagnosed with terminal hemangiosarcoma part of my heart and soul died, and my world is so much darker without her pressed against me as I write. But, I also know I was incredibly blessed to have her in my life for eleven years—so thank you, Lyssa, for every smile and every Kermie face and every time you rested your chin on my shoulder and for always sharing your skinny nuggets with me. Thank you for filling my life with the joy that allowed me to fill this manuscript with words. I miss you more than those words could ever possibly express.

About the Author

Michelle Chouinard

Michelle Chouinard is the author of *The Serial Killer Guide to San Francisco*, and, under another name, the *USA Today* and *Publishers Weekly* bestselling author of eight previous mysteries. Michelle has a Ph.D. in developmental psychology from Stanford University and was one of UC Merced's founding faculty members. She lives in the Bay Area and enjoys caffeine in all forms, amateur genealogy, baking, and anything to do with Halloween or the zombie apocalypse.